W9-BKB-078

Praise for the novels of

KATE WILHELM

"Sure to delight any legal-thriller fan."
—*Publishers Weekly* on *Sleight of Hand*

"Wilhelm claims a leading place
in the ranks of trial suspense writers."
—*Publishers Weekly*

"Wilhelm creates a genuinely eerie atmosphere that
pulls readers in and keeps them turning the pages."
—*Booklist* on *The Price of Silence*

"The smoothest mystery novel
to come along in quite a while."
—*Associated Press* on *Clear and Convincing Proof*

"As always, genre veteran Wilhelm
creates a thought-provoking, complex plot
that will keep readers interested."
—*Booklist* on *The Unbidden Truth*

"Her carefully crafted approach to the legal thriller
continues to separate Wilhelm from the competition."
—*Publishers Weekly* on *No Defense*

"Sensitive, thought-provoking, and involving,
Death Qualified is an unqualified success."
—*Los Angeles Times Book Review*

"Wilhelm is a masterful storyteller whose novels have
just the right blend of solid plot, compelling mystery,
and great courtroom drama."
—*Library Journal*

KATE WILHELM
Sleight *of* Hand

MIRA®

MIRA

ISBN-13: 978-0-7783-2488-1
ISBN-10:   0-7783-2488-5

SLEIGHT OF HAND

www.MIRABooks.com

Printed in U.S.A.

First printing: September 2006

Sleight
of Hand

ONE

Frank Holloway liked the extensive library in the offices, and he liked being left alone in it. Now and then one of the junior partners of the law firm started to enter, saw him at the long table with stacks of books and discreetly withdrew. Once, one of them had been at the table already when Frank entered and claimed his preferred chair, dead center, where he had room to spread books on both sides. The younger man had wrapped up his own research quickly and fled. As well he should have, Frank had thought with satisfaction. He had been stocking the library when that fellow was still a suckling; he had certain privileges.

That morning he had already put aside a few volumes with yellow notes sticking out indicating page numbers. After he left, around noon, Patsy, his secretary, would photocopy the cases he had marked, add her own note about volume and page, and have the copies on his desk the following morning. Like clockwork, a well-oiled machine working efficiently, he also thought with satisfaction.

Thus it was that he looked up in annoyance when Patsy entered the library at ten minutes past eleven. Pointedly, he glanced at the wall clock above the door, then at his own watch, and scowled at her. She frowned back. She had certain privileges, too. She had been with him for forty years and was determined not to retire a day before he did, but now that he was a published author, and on his way to writing a second book, she was no longer hinting broadly at every opportunity for him to speed that day along.

"A Mr. and Mrs. Wallis Lederer want to see you," she said. "Walk-ins," she added disdainfully.

"Send them away. Or sic them on one of the loafers hanging out at the watercooler." She nodded and had turned back toward the door when he said, "Hang on a sec. Wallis Lederer? How old's the fellow?"

"About sixty."

"Well, I'll be damned. Wally Lederer. After all these years. Tell them to wait a few minutes. These are ready to go." He motioned toward the marked books, closed the one he had been reading and put it in the other stack. Patsy would put them all back on the shelves. The one time he had started to return them, she had been indignant.

In his own office Frank placed the folder of copies in his briefcase, washed his hands and then went to greet his visitors.

"Wally Lederer!" he said when he saw them. "It really is you. It's been a while."

"Forty-some years," Wally said, shaking hands, patting Frank's back, grinning. He turned to the woman at his side and said, "I told you he'd remember me. Meg, meet Frank Holloway, the guy who saved me back when I was a smart-assed kid. My wife, Meg."

Wally was five foot ten and stocky with wavy white hair and white eyebrows, a nice suntan and very white teeth. He was showing many of them in his broad smile. Meg was no more than five foot two or three, slender, with a round pretty face and curly brown hair showing streaks of gray. When she smiled, a dimple came and went quickly in her right cheek. They were both well dressed, he in a sport jacket and slacks, shirt open at the throat, and she in a nice blue pantsuit exactly the color of her eyes.

"Well, come on back. Lots of history to catch up with. This way." Frank led them through the hallway to his office, paused at the library door and looked in at Patsy who was shelving his books. "When you have a minute, maybe you could bring my guests some coffee." He didn't miss the glint of approval in her eyes when she nodded. He had said "guests" not clients. They could read each other so clearly, they were like a long-married couple. He knew none of the young attorneys would dare ask a secretary to bring coffee these days, but he also knew that Patsy would be outraged if Frank waited on guests or clients.

In his office he motioned toward the comfortable chairs at the coffee table.

Wally gave an appraising look at the immaculate desk, the glass-door bookshelves, the leather-covered furnishings. "You've come way up in the world," he said. "Folding chairs and a Goodwill desk in the early days," he said to Meg. "I knew him when. One of his first clients, in fact."

Frank laughed. "You look as if you've done all right for yourself, as well. What have you been up to?"

"This and that. I have an act, down in Vegas, sometimes in Atlantic City, casinos, things of that sort. Eight or nine shows a year, a week at a time. Not a headliner, just an act between the big draws. I brought a video to show you."

Patsy tapped on the door and entered with the coffee service on a tray. She poured for them all and left.

"A performer? Song and dance?" Frank asked.

"Not exactly. I'll show you. See, Meg and I, we were dating when I was on probation back in the early days, and we decided the day I was done with community service, all that, we'd take off and make a fresh start somewhere else. Then, down in San Francisco I got in trouble again. Our first anniversary. Broke, waiting for Meg at her work-place in an uppity department store, and this rich bitch left her purse on the counter while she was wandering back and forth trying to pick out earrings or something. There was a fat wallet in plain sight and my hands did their thing. I was nabbed. Five years. State pen."

Wally sipped coffee, added sugar and sipped again, then put the cup down. "So there I was, with an old black guy as my cell mate, in for twenty, four behind him. And he wasn't going to last the next sixteen, that was for sure. Old and sick. And mean. He cursed me out, swatted me a time or two and called me a goddamn idiot. Told me a gift like mine should make me a fine living, but I was too dumb to take advantage, and I'd be back looking just like him if I didn't shape up. And Meg, well, she said she'd wait this time, but if I crossed the line again, she'd be gone. Between them, they got through to me."

When he paused again, Frank asked, "Your gift?"

"Ambidexterity. I could do brain surgery with either hand." He reached into his jacket pocket and brought out a wallet, tossed it down on the table. "I think that's yours."

Frank felt his own pocket, then burst out laughing. "Son of a bitch! You're still doing it!"

"But legitimately. My act is putting on demonstrations for the credulous. A few pretty well-paying gigs a year, benefits for bunco squads, convention managers, things like that. A good living. And old Joey taught me how to play cards."

"Professional gambler?"

Wally shook his head. "I never gamble, and I'm not into card tricks. You don't have to cheat, just pay attention and learn how to count. That's the clue, paying attention. Same as with picking pockets. Joey taught me that, too. It's been a pretty good living, all in all."

Meg had been silent, but now she said, "As soon as Wally began to make money with his act, he sent ten percent to Joey. Every performance, ten percent."

Wally looked sheepish. "I owed him a lot," he said. "Least I could do. A few bucks in the pen makes a difference."

Frank nodded. "What brings you to Eugene?"

Meg answered. "Christmas Eve. We were in a hotel in Las Vegas, and I said, 'Let's go home, get our own house in the country.' We had moved around so much, apartments, motels, hotels, never our own house. I don't even know if I was serious when I said it, but it took, and we both knew that was what we wanted to do. We came home in February and bought a house in the country with two acres of blackberry brambles and a barn. We're fixing it up, restoring it." Her words were lightly spoken, but she was tense. She smiled and the dimple came, then vanished again.

Where did dimples go when they weren't visible? Frank wondered, drawn to this woman with her blue eyes and dimpled cheek, and carefully managed anxiety. While Wally was voluble and engaging, she appeared to be reserved and almost shy.

There was no trace of her dimple when Meg said, "Wally's been accused of stealing a little gold boat that's said to be worth about thirty thousand dollars."

"I haven't been accused," Wally said quickly.

She gave him a scornful look. "You have, or will be in the next day or two."

Frank held up his hand. "Hold it, you two. I should have made this clear at the start. I'm sorry I didn't. This office no longer takes on criminal cases, I'm afraid."

Meg didn't try to hide her dismay, and Wally took her hand. "Honey, this will blow over. Jay isn't going to press any charges. He's just having us on for kicks or something."

Meg kept her gaze on Frank. "Can you recommend someone else?"

"Indeed I can," he said, getting to his feet. He went to his desk and placed a call.

TWO

Barbara Holloway cradled the phone and sat regarding an open folder on her desk for several minutes, a case from a walk-in client at Martin's restaurant. More of the same, she thought, and closed the folder. She did not underestimate the importance to her clients of the problems they brought to her twice a week, doing double duty as she was while Shelley was away, but on the other hand, for her they were routine and, she had to admit, boring.

She considered the word boring with surprise and decided it wasn't exactly what she was feeling. Restlessness? Waiting for something to happen? It was the April blahs, she told herself firmly and stood up. A beautiful day outside after a few weeks of heavy rain had left her wanting to be out there playing, walking, doing something. Her father had warned her that after years of one difficult case after another, she might feel restless. But, he had added, she should relax and enjoy the respite.

She nodded. Right. She walked to the outer office and said to Maria, "Dad's bringing over a couple of people, and since it's getting on to noon, take off when you are ready. After I see them, Dad and I will go out for lunch and I don't think I'll come back afterward. Nothing for you to do. Go fly a kite with your kids or something."

"Want me to put on coffee?" Maria asked.

"Sure. Just measure stuff and if they want it I'll turn it on."

Ten minutes later Maria tapped on the door and Barbara opened it to receive her visitors. Frank made the introductions, then retrieved a third client chair from against the wall and positioned it in front of her desk. He angled it in such a way that he would have a good line of sight to watch Wally and Meg as they talked. Taking her cue from him, Barbara seated herself behind her desk and pulled her yellow legal pad within range.

Wally adjusted his position in his chair. "Your dad told us a little about you on our way over."

"I also told them that I'd fill you in on some background over lunch. So they can get right to their problem," Frank said.

"Yes, our problem," Wally said. "Not that it is a problem exactly, but Meg's afraid it could become one and we should be prepared, just in case. See, a fellow we know is missing a little gold boat and he told his insurer and the police that I must have taken it."

Meg interrupted before he could continue. "Ms. Holloway, let me tell it with a few more details. We ran into Jay Wilkins over at the casino in Florence on Saturday night. I recognized him right away because we had seen his picture in the newspaper a month or so ago."

"The Buick dealership Wilkins?" Frank asked.

"Yes. We all went to high school together. Anyway, when I saw Jay, I spoke to him, and he invited us to his house here in Eugene for a drink on Monday, when we'd all be back in town. He said to talk about old times. We went, but as it turned out, it was not a comfortable visit and we didn't stay very long. He wanted to show off his collections, for one thing. A wall filled with cases that held dozens of model cars, and another with Egyptian and Etruscan artifacts. He opened that case and we all handled a little gold boat. He said it was a model of Cleopatra's famous gold barge. It's very beautiful, about five inches long. Then we went into another room with a bar and we had our drink. He didn't really want to talk about the old days, but rather about his wife. Apparently she's away on a trip back east, and he seemed very preoccupied about it. He mentioned her on Saturday, and then talked about her on Monday. He's concerned because she hasn't called. As I said, it was not a comfortable visit and we stayed only long enough to have a drink, then left."

"That boat's of no interest to anyone on earth except a collector," Wally said then. "Not something you could take to a pawnshop and unload. He said it's worth thirty grand, definitely not the sort of thing to grab for a quick buck."

Meg put her hand on his arm. "Your turn's coming." She faced Barbara again. "That was Monday. Yesterday, I had just left the house to go get our mail. I was still in the driveway when a car pulled in and two men got out. A detective and an insurance agent. They said they wanted to ask us a few questions." She patted Wally's arm. "Your turn."

"About time," he said in a good-natured way. "Right away the detective said I might as well hand it over. Practical jokes didn't make it. Give it back and Jay would forget the whole thing. I didn't know what the hell he was talking about. They told me the boat was gone and we were the only two who had been in the house. They didn't tell me more than that, no details, except that it was gone and no one else could have taken it. I told Meg not to worry, it'll turn up. But here we are."

"Oh, Wally," Meg said despairingly. "What if it doesn't? Your word against Jay Wilkins's, and your word wouldn't be worth much if it comes to an arrest." She looked at Barbara, then Frank beseechingly. "Tell him how dangerous his position is."

"Why is it?" Barbara asked. "Is there a housekeeper? Who can say for sure no one else was in the house? When did they find out it was missing? Did Wilkins lock the case after you looked at things?"

Wally shook his head. "He didn't lock it. He took Meg by the arm and practically dragged her out to the bar. I trailed behind them and the case not only wasn't locked, it was wide open." He shrugged. "And as I said, they didn't give me any real details."

"I don't understand why your word isn't as good as Jay Wilkins's," Barbara said.

"I'm an ex-con," Wally said. "Your dad got me out of trouble when I was a kid, and a few years later I did time for lifting a wallet. They knew about the first one, Jay must have told them, and by now they probably know about the second one."

"Was he your drop man back when you were kids?" Frank asked. "You had to have had an accomplice."

Meg looked startled when Wally nodded.

Wally regarded Frank for a moment. "You never even asked. The ways of lawyers are mysterious. He was. We both worked at the car lot, the only time we were really together, and his dad kept him on a very short leash. Jay's old man was tight as a closed clam, and about as mean as a crab. Jay never had a cent." He paused a moment.

"It was a shock to see Jay in his father's skin, same expressions, same sort of grasping I've-got-mine-and-I-intend-to-keep-it attitude. Same everything. A real shock. I worked for the old man and hated him and here he was facing me again, reincarnated. I didn't want to have anything more to do with Jay. And as far as practical jokes go, forget it. He isn't the kind to take a joke."

Barbara glanced at Frank, dismayed. Meg was right; Wally was in a tough spot.

Wally was looking about the office. "Is there a television available, a video cassette player? I know what you're thinking, and you're wrong. I'm absolutely legitimate, clean."

"I'll haul it out," Frank said, rising. He went to the closet, rolled out a small television on a stand and plugged it in. Meg handed him a video she had taken from her bag.

"It's a demo, edited way down," Wally said. "My act is about thirty minutes from start to finish, this is under five minutes. No sound, but there's a running patter that goes with it, a few jokes. You'll get the idea."

The video opened with a camera panning a large dinner-show room, filled tables crowded as close together as they could be and still allow waiters to move among them. A spotlight came on and landed on Wally and Meg sitting with an older man at one of the most distant tables from the stage. Wally's hair glowed in the bright light. He stood up and began to make his way toward the stage, stopping here and there to shake a hand, to greet someone, with a good deal of backslapping, leaning across tables to shake hands. On the stage the master of ceremonies apparently had asked for volunteers to come up, and they were making their own way to the stage. Behind them a few scantily dressed women were setting up a table with a white cloth, arranging four chairs behind it, one at the head.

Wally reached the stage and evidently was enticing a woman to come up also. She was middle-aged and embarrassed, giggling. In a courtly manner he met her at the stage apron and escorted her to the head of the table where he seated her. Then one by one he spoke to the male volunteers and again there were vigorous handshakes, back patting and, taking them one at a time by the arm, he positioned them in the remaining four chairs. Wally apparently had a monologue then, and while at it, he reached into an interior pocket and looked astonished when he pulled out a man's belt. One of the men at the table clutched at his slacks and half rose from his chair. Wally tossed the belt to him. Quickly then, expressing surprise at each item, he pulled from various pockets a watch, a necktie, wallets, a flashy necklace…

People in the audience were rising, making their way to the stage and the role the woman played became clear. Wally placed all the wallets before her, and as each owner claimed one, she verified names.

"A couple of casino security guys come over to pat me down," Wally said. "They make sure nothing's left, and the act's pretty much over."

On the screen Wally was bowing and blowing kisses to the audience. He gave the M.C. a bear hug and started to leave the stage, stopped, returned to the M.C. and handed him his wallet. He left quickly then, and the camera panned the enthusiastic audience.

"My God!" Barbara said in awe when the screen went dark. "You're a human vacuum cleaner."

"I'm good at my job," Wally said modestly and flashed his big grin. "That's why it will blow over about Jay's little boat. You think I'd risk my reputation for something as crude as common theft? And never in my lurid criminal past did I ever steal from anyone's house."

"Okay," Barbara said, "you're on. Do you have the insurance agent's name? I'll ask the right people some of the same questions I asked you."

Meg looked in her purse. "He gave me his card. He said if the boat turned up, as if by accident, I suppose, give him a call. I also brought a list of the performances Wally's given over the past few years. I thought it might be useful."

Barbara took the list and, after a glance, she said, "I imagine it will be if we need it. That's pretty impressive." The list included some of the biggest, best-known casinos in Las Vegas as well as Atlantic City. "For now, just sit tight. The boat might turn up at Jay Wilkins's house, or he might remember moving it. If they come back to your place asking questions, give me a call, and certainly if anyone turns up with a search warrant call me and stall them until I get there. Don't make a formal statement or sign anything. I'd want to be on hand for anything like that."

There were a few other details and then they were finished. Both Barbara and Frank went to the outer office with them. Maria was still at her desk working at her computer. After seeing Wally and Meg out, Barbara told Maria to take off, pronto, which was what she intended to do as soon as she cleaned off her desk.

"Lunch," Frank said, following her back to her office. "Fast. I want to get home and get those tomatoes in the ground before the rain comes back. I'll fill in the blanks over food." He chuckled. "He pinched my wallet back in the office. Slick as a whistle. I didn't feel a thing and didn't even miss it until he handed it back."

THREE

Sitting on Frank's back porch Sunday afternoon, watching him puttering around from his little greenhouse to the garden he was planting, Barbara began to trace the strange restlessness that now seemed to possess her.

She realized it had begun when she stood on a dock in Newport watching the McGinnis yacht leave. On board with a crew of six, her colleague Shelley and new husband Alex had set off on their honeymoon, a cruise around the Hawaiian Islands. It had been a small wedding with only the two families, Barbara and Frank, and of course Dr. Minnick, Alex's mentor and doctor since his boyhood. Barbara had been Shelley's maid of honor. Mr. and Mrs. McGinnis had accepted Alex as their son without reservation, despite his grotesque disfigurement caused by a congenital birth defect. Since he didn't have to foot the bill for a lavish wedding, Mr. McGinnis had said, the least he could do was provide their honeymoon accommodations, thus the yacht at their disposal.

The two gold cats were sniffing around the newly planted garden rows, oblivious of mud. Barbara had always thought cats avoided anything wet, and especially anything muddy. They were an unholy mess, as if they had been rolling around. She got up and went inside for a glass of water that she really didn't want.

At the sink she mused that this was the first weekend since early March that she hadn't done something with Darren Halvord, or more likely with him and his son Todd. A bicycle ride, a bird-watching trip to the Finley Refuge, dinner and board games, something.

Too much, she thought suddenly. The guy was trying to domesticate her!

Frank came in with a colander filled with baby salad greens. He had left his muddy shoes outside the door. "Want to give these a quick wash while I go change clothes? I overplanted. Lots of salad greens coming along. And don't let those fool cats in until they clean themselves up. I have the cat door locked."

More domestication, she thought savagely, and rinsed the greens. She returned them to the colander to drain and crossed the room to stand at the back door gazing out. Both of them, trying to turn her into someone else. She cursed under her breath.

Later, as Frank prepared dinner, she told him about her visit with the insurance agent. "He's a reasonable enough guy," she said. "He'd already looked up Wally and knew about his past, of course. But they aren't going to do a thing until Mrs. Wilkins checks in. Looks like she took a powder, packed her bags, pretended a visit to an ailing sister and headed for parts unknown. Could be she swiped the boat. Could be something else. So there it's going to remain for the time being. The police aren't going to do a thing either unless Wilkins flexes muscles or something. They're not interested in gold boats or wives who pack bags and take off."

"Did you call Meg and Wally and tell them?"

"Yes. At least I told Meg. She's the deep one of the two, isn't she?"

"I think so. She's a good-looking woman and must have been a knockout when she was young," Frank said.

Barbara nodded. "I know where you're going with that. One of the what-ifs—Jay was hot for her and Wally got her. Payback time forty-some years later. Doesn't seem likely, but still…"

Frank laughed. "The evil mind of the criminal attorney at work."

"You know the saying—it takes one to know one. Want me to set the table yet?"

On Monday, Barbara was considering the rest of her day. It was going on one and she was in her court clothes and wanted out of them. Home, she decided. Have a sandwich, change clothes, then back to the office to clean up a few details. She was grumpy from the morning's proceedings, a plea bargain with a tough prosecutor who had wanted more than the book thrown at her nineteen-year-old idiot client who had had pot not only in his pocket, but in his jalopy and his apartment. He wasn't going to sell it, he had whined, just wanted it handy when he needed it. He had a bad backache, he had said unconvincingly.

She sighed. She had argued that he shouldn't be sent up for ten or fifteen years for being stupid. So it went. She was leaving, her car keys in her hand, when Meg Lederer appeared on the outside steps. Meg was pale and looked terrified.

Barbara waited at the landing. "What happened?" she asked when Meg drew near.

"I have to talk to you. Jay's dead. Someone killed him Saturday night."

FOUR

Barbara wheeled about and hurried back to the office door, unlocked it and practically shoved Meg inside. She locked the door behind them and motioned toward her own office. Inside, she took Meg's arm and seated her on one of the chairs by the ornate coffee table, sat on the sofa within reach and said, "Tell me."

Meg's hands were shaking and her voice was faint. "I saw it on the noon news. Just that he was dead, probably killed Saturday night. I don't know more than that. Barbara, first the boat, now this. They'll think Wally did it!"

"Pull yourself together," Barbara said brusquely. "Don't jump to conclusions. Where's Wally now?"

"Home. He was clearing brambles all morning and a man came to see about the barn roof. It leaks. Cedar shingles, but we want to repair it, not get a new roof. We want it all the way it was…" She jumped up and crossed the room to the window, pulled the drape aside and stood there.

"For God's sake, what difference does that make! Jay's dead. He could have sent Wally to prison for the rest of his life! Going back would kill him!"

Barbara stood up, went to the bathroom and returned with a glass of water. She put it on the table, approached Meg and took her arm. It was rigid, and her eyes were closed, her head bowed. "Come sit down, Meg. Calm down."

When Meg was seated again, Barbara put the glass in her hand and watched her take a sip. "Is there anything else you can tell me? You said Wally's at the house. Does he know about Jay?"

Meg shook her head. "I just left. I put a note on the table for him. I wrote 'shopping' on it. Shopping!" She drew in a breath. "Then I came here." Suddenly she looked down at herself, tan work pants, a paint-spattered T-shirt with a big sunflower on the front, old shoes covered with paint. "I never even thought about how I was dressed. I had to get out, talk to you. I never even thought…"

"You're fine, Meg." Barbara studied her a moment, then said, "What made you panic if that's all they said, that he's dead, murdered? For all you know they already have the killer, or know who it was."

The glass Meg was still holding began to shake and she bowed her head. Barbara took the glass from her and put it on the table. "What else, Meg?" she asked softly. "There's more, isn't there?"

Without looking up, Meg shook her head.

"You and Wally came in here together," Barbara said. "Whatever either of you says in this office is sacred and will never leave this office. You have to trust me, Meg. No power on earth could make you testify against your husband, and no power on earth could make me divulge anything you tell me."

Meg lifted her head, and gave Barbara a long searching look. Finally she nodded, but when she spoke her voice was no more than a whisper. "I was there Saturday night."

"Tell me about it," Barbara said, struggling to hide her surprise.

"Something you said when we were here, that maybe the boat would turn up at Jay's house. The day the detective and insurance man came, I was on my way to get the mail. We have a locked box down the street a way. I had put on Wally's raincoat. His is so long on me, nearly to my ankles, it keeps my legs dry all the way down. The rain had started again, and I put on his coat and dropped the key to our box in the pocket. I had an umbrella in one hand and a letter to mail in the other. I told them to go to the door and I crossed the street and walked to the mailbox and when I put my hand in the pocket to get the key out, I felt the boat. In his pocket. I knew that was what they had come about. I was terrified. What if they had a search warrant or something? I...I put it in the mailbox with my letter."

Meg's eyes were almost perfectly round as she searched Barbara's face. Although her voice and words had been disjointed and hesitating, she was very clear when she spoke again. "We've been married forty-two years. I know him as well as I know myself. He didn't take that boat. He didn't. Jay put it in his pocket."

"Saturday night," Barbara said, ignoring the questions piling up in her head. They would get to them, but first things first, she thought grimly.

Meg nodded. "What you said, that it might turn up in

Jay's house. I kept thinking of that, and decided to take it back and put it somewhere, behind a sofa cushion, or anywhere not too obvious, but where it would be found by the housekeeper. End it. Jay would know we were on to him and keep his distance. That afternoon, as soon as they were gone I got it out of the mailbox. I was scared to death every minute that they would come back and want to search."

Abruptly she stood up. "I'd like to use your restroom," she said weakly.

"Sure. This way." Barbara showed her the door. Anything to avoid getting to Saturday night, she thought, but that was coming, however long it took.

She glanced at the coffeemaker, shrugged and didn't go near it. Later. She suspected they would have plenty of time for more intermissions a little later.

Meg did not hurry, but when she returned, she walked swiftly to her chair and sat upright, composed. "On Saturday I knew I couldn't bear it any longer. We have been so busy working on the house. Early on we decided we didn't want to bring in decorators, let others do it. Our first real home, we wanted to make it ours from the start. Anyway, Wally was beat Saturday night, clearing brambles when it wasn't raining, painting, scraping woodwork. We're not used to such hard physical labor. That night after dinner we were watching a movie and he fell asleep. I knew he would sleep on the sofa until I roused him enough to go to bed and I decided that was my chance. It was raining again so I wore his coat, and put on gloves. I wiped the boat clean. I didn't want my fingerprints on it. Something like that was on my mind."

She leaned forward and lowered her voice. "When I got to his house I drove up and passed another car or van or something. I think it was a van, black, or very dark. I wasn't paying a lot of attention, and it was raining pretty hard. I thought Jay probably had company, and started to drive on out, but I stopped. It wouldn't matter, I decided. I'd make an excuse for being there, put the boat somewhere and leave. It seemed so simple as I thought of it. I went to the door and saw that it wasn't closed all the way."

She swallowed hard and grew more tense. "The door had been stopped by a sneaker, it looked like a kid's sneaker, little and muddy. I just pushed the door open and walked in and let the sneaker stop it again. That was even better. I could just walk in and maybe no one would see me. I thought whoever was there was in the bar, or some other room, because I couldn't hear anyone. The study door was open and that's where I went. That's where the cases are. I put the boat in the bottom drawer of his desk and walked out and I let the door catch on the sneaker again. I hurried back to my car and left."

"Have you told anyone?"

Meg shook her head, then leaned back in her chair, evidently relieved.

Barbara stood up and regarded her for a moment. "Relax a minute or two. I'm going to put on some coffee, and then I have some questions."

In the outer office she had gotten no further than putting water into the pot when Maria came back from lunch and quickly took over, making it clear that she was mistress of the coffee machine. "I'll bring it in when it's ready," she said.

For an hour Barbara asked questions and Meg answered, or sometimes futilely tried to answer. Maria brought in coffee, and when Barbara finally stood up and said that was enough for now, Meg looked exhausted.

"I'll turn my bloodhound loose and see what we can find out," Barbara said. "I'll want to talk to you and Wally tomorrow. I'll call first. Meanwhile, try to take it easy."

"I should tell the police, shouldn't I?" Meg asked in a low voice.

"Did you witness anything? See anyone?"

"No. Nothing."

"So mum's the word, at least for now. We need some information. Are you going to tell Wally?"

"I don't know."

"Okay. Your decision. Just let me know how you decide. I'll call tomorrow."

They went to the door, where Meg paused. "I didn't see anyone, but someone could have seen me."

"We'll keep that in mind," Barbara said, opening the door.

After Meg left, Barbara said to Maria, "See if you can reach Bailey."

Maria nodded. "Have you had any lunch?"

"No time. I'll get to it later." She entered her office and sat at her desk to make notes and to study a crude map of the drive and the only rooms of Jay Wilkins's house that Meg had seen. A semicircular drive from the street, the other car or van roughed in a dozen feet from the entrance, on to where Meg had parked, about the same distance past the van. A very large foyer with the study off to the left, the room with the bar on the right. Broad carpeted stairs in the center rear, and narrower halls on both sides of the stairs. Both back halls and the head of the stairs were dark, Meg had said. She was right, someone could have seen her while remaining unseen.

Maria buzzed, Bailey was on the line. Barbara was still talking to Bailey a few minutes later when Maria brought in a sandwich from the shop across the street.

At fifteen minutes before six Barbara called Frank to say that if he was free she would drop in, and ten minutes later she was in his kitchen where he was pouring her a glass of wine. He already had a plate of cheese set out.

"What's up?" he asked, handing her the wine.

"I want to watch the six-o'clock news, local news," she said. "It seems that on Saturday night Jay Wilkins was killed. Let's catch the broadcast, and I'll spring for dinner somewhere quiet and tell you about my interesting day."

"Christ on a mountain," Frank said softly. "I hope to God it's just a coincidence."

She made a rude sound and headed for his study to turn on the television.

When the news item came on details were almost as scant as what Meg had reported. Wilkins was killed sometime Saturday night, his body discovered Monday morning by his housekeeper. He had died of a blow to the head. Apparently robbery was not a motive. The police asked for anyone who knew the whereabouts of Mrs. Wilkins to please call in. She was traveling, they said. There was a number and her photograph, with a brief description: five feet five inches, one hundred thirty pounds, shoulder-length blond hair, brown eyes, forty years old. She was very attractive with clearly defined cheek bones and a wide, generous mouth, smiling in the photograph.

"How do you figure in?" Frank demanded.

Barbara was reaching for his phone. "I'll give Martin a call and get him to hold a back booth for us. I don't want you futzing around in the kitchen while I tell you about it." She believed cooking took superhuman concentration, and she wanted his full attention when she told him the predicament Meg presented.

Later, waiting for shrimp gumbo in a back booth at Martin's Restaurant, Barbara told Frank about Meg's visit. He did not say a word until she finished, then he cursed in a low undertone. Martin came with a tray and they were both silent while he chatted, placing the food on the table. He had beamed when they appeared. As big as a grizzly bear, black as a human being could be, he could have served as a bouncer if the need had ever arisen. He was an ex-NFL linebacker and looked it. And that night he had a bottle of Italian Soave. "I've been saving it for a special guest," he said pouring it. "My treat, this one time only," he added quickly when Frank started to protest.

"That's why we don't come here more often," Barbara said. "There go your profits for the week. We can't bear so much responsibility."

Martin laughed. "Let me know how you like it," he said, moving away.

As he had done so often in the past, Frank wondered what on earth Barbara had done for Martin that had earned his undying devotion to her. He suspected that he would never find out.

Barbara sipped the wine and closed her eyes, then

sipped again. "I knew it would be good, but I never knew how good it could be," she murmured. Then, between bites of gumbo she told him what she had been doing the rest of the day. "Bailey, for starters," she said. Frank nodded. They both knew Bailey Novell was one of the best private investigators to be had.

When she finished, he asked, "Did you believe Meg?"

Barbara stopped the bite she had been about to take and put her fork down. "I want to believe her. We both said she's deep, and she's also sharp. She knows exactly what Wally was facing if Wilkins had pressed charges. At best the ruination of Wally's career, at worst a long prison sentence, which she likens to a death sentence. And now she knows that when the boat is found, the decision could go either way. A bit of a mistake on Wally's part, a practical joke gone bad, all forgiven, or a malicious, mean-spirited frame-up, initiated by Wilkins and intended to destroy Wally. Justification for murder possibly. Or," she continued more slowly, "she suspects or knows that Wally took it and she, in trying to save his skin, might have made the problem worse. Or she might have knocked off Jay herself thinking no one would see her coming or going, only to come to believe a witness had been lurking about." She finished off the wine in her glass and refilled it. "In other words, I haven't got a clue about Meg yet."

"Fair enough," Frank said. Then, soberly, he went on, "But I hope we agree that Meg is in possession of evidence that could be vital in finding a murderer. And you're aware of the fact. Obstruction of justice can be a serious charge."

She nodded. She knew.

FIVE

Stephanie Breaux stood over her daughter, stroked her hair softly, and murmured, "Eve, wake up, darling. Please, wake up."

Eve did not stir. She was curled in a tight fetal position, her eyes squeezed shut in such a way it was impossible to tell if she was awake or sleeping. A light coverlet over her trembled now and then, the only sign of life she exhibited.

She was twenty-three, her hair was as gossamer fine as the purest wheat-colored silk. It was hard to believe any adult human being could be rolled as tightly as the mound on the bed indicated. Stephanie spoke to her again, then turned and walked from the bedroom, every step leaden. She realized how tired she was when she caught the wall in the hallway to steady herself.

More coffee wasn't the answer; she was already jittery from two nights of too much coffee. She walked down the few steps to the lower level and on to the kitchen where she checked the wall clock against her watch. Eleven-thirty. Why didn't Eric return her call? She had called her son at eleven and left a message on his voice mail at work. She kept moving, out to the patio to breathe deeply of the fresh air, trying to clear her head, to quell her rising tension.

Ten minutes later her son arrived. She hurried to the door to admit him. "Mother, something— What's wrong?"

"It's Eve," she said. "She's had a relapse."

"Evie? Where is she?" What he had come to tell his mother was forgotten.

"In bed."

He ran past her, up the steps and down the hall. At Eve's room he approached his sister and touched her hair gently, exactly as Stephanie had done. "Evie, it's me, Eric. Want to go for a walk?" After a moment he stepped back and took in the scene with a swift glance. His mother had dragged in the rocking chair from her room, arranged pillows and a throw, and no doubt had tried to rest there while she maintained a vigil. She was gray with fatigue and worry. He decided his own news could bloody well wait.

"When did it happen?" he asked, once they were downstairs again.

"Saturday evening. I was working at my desk and she was on the exercise bike. When I came down I found her huddled on the patio floor."

He didn't ask what had brought it about. They rarely found out. Eve could never tell them. She would have complete amnesia of the episode from before, during and for a day or two after; she always did. "Why didn't you call me? Where's Reggie?"

"She took a long weekend. She'll be back tonight sometime. And I thought maybe it was like the last time it happened. Eve slept sixteen hours and came out of it. I thought… It's been two years! We thought it was over. She's been so well."

Stephanie turned away. When she spoke again her voice was strained with the effort it was taking not to cry. "I called Dr. Mohrbeck this morning. He'll get in touch with Cedar View and they'll be expecting us. You'll have to drive. I have her overnight bag in the car."

Eric nodded. "I'll bring her down." He hesitated. "Is she dressed?"

"Just her gown. I changed her. She should be dry." Her voice quavered and she stopped.

Eric had seen the corner of the rubber sheet they used when Eve had a relapse. "Okay. I'll put her slippers on her, and wrap her in the cover. Wait here."

Eric knew Eve would be easy enough to manage, but she would not move of her own volition, and she would not open her eyes, not until it was over. Looking at her, drawn up like a baby, he felt only tenderness toward his sick little sister. Six feet tall, finally after years of being lanky, all legs and arms, he was starting to fill out the long framework of his body. He felt massive next to Eve. His hair was thick, dark, like his mother's, Eve's was golden. A changeling in their midst, he sometimes thought, unlike mother, unlike father, altogether her own self.

"Evie," he said softly, "it's time to go see Dr. Mohrbeck." He put her slippers on her, drew her to her feet and wrapped a thin blanket around her. He didn't try to pick her up, although he could have easily. She struggled if anyone tried to pick her up. Supporting her firmly around her waist, he led her down the stairs and out to the car where Stephanie was waiting.

Stephanie sat in the backseat holding her daughter, and Eric drove the twenty miles to Cedar View. They did not talk on the way. They never spoke in front of Eve when she was having an episode. They didn't know how much she heard or what it meant to her. And at the hospital, it would be routine, Stephanie thought dully. They would wheel Eve away and she would watch her out of sight. Paperwork, the comforting words, a nurse who would manage to be both cheerful and sympathetic. They would not want Stephanie to linger, they never did on the first day. Blood tests, an intravenous drip installed… She closed her own eyes and stroked Eve's fine hair.

Later, returning to Eugene, Stephanie sat in the passenger seat and leaned back with her eyes closed. Eric glanced at her, starting to say something, changed his mind. It could wait.

Back in the house, he went to the kitchen with his mother. "Sit down. I'm going to scramble some eggs. Did you eat anything yesterday or this morning?"

"A sandwich? Probably a sandwich. I don't remember. I don't think I was hungry." Stephanie smiled faintly; she had a crooked little twist of her lip when she smiled.

She sat at the table while he prepared scrambled eggs and made toast. When the food was ready, she found, to her surprise, that she was hungry. Eric poured orange juice for himself and sat opposite her.

He waited until she had finished, then said, "Mother, I have to tell you something, the reason I came over. I didn't

get your message, that wasn't it. This morning a police officer came to the office to tell me that Dad was dead. She
intended to come over here to notify you and Eve and I told
her I'd do it."

Stephanie had raised a glass of milk to her lips. She put
it down. "What did she say?" She stared at him, her voice
little more than a whisper.

"Not much more than that. He was killed, murdered,
Saturday night, they think. They didn't want his immediate family to learn about it from television or the radio."

She stood up and went to the glass patio door where she
stood with her back to him. "Do they know who did it?"

"No, and I hope to God they never find out. The guy de-
serves a medal."

She wheeled about. "Eric! Don't say such a thing."

"I'm glad he's dead, Mother. I'm glad." He waved his
hand in a curious gesture he used. "Anyway, there will be
reporters and people asking questions, wanting to talk to
you and Eve. I've taken the week off. I'll come over here
and stay. The cop wanted to know if I know where Connie
is. I don't. Apparently they can't locate her. Have you
talked to her in the past few days?"

She shook her head. "We were expecting her last Saturday, but she didn't come, and she never called."

There were possibly half a dozen people Eve cared
about. She loved her mother, and adored her big brother.
She had become especially fond of Reggie, their tenant
who was a companion for Eve on the days that Stephanie
worked. And she had formed an attachment to, or even had
come to love, her stepmother Connie. Her doctor and one
of the therapists along the way made up the group.

"Mother, you're ready to drop. Go take a warm bath and pile up in bed for a few hours. I'll be down here and you need some rest. The next few days are going to be hell."

SIX

Frank rarely brooded about past mistakes. His philosophy was to admit them, fix them if possible and, if not, live with whatever consequences there were. But he now thought it had been a mistake to bring Barbara into the Wally Lederer case. His intentions had been good, his instincts okay, but it had been a mistake. He had seen her growing restlessness and believed, even if she was dodging it, that part of the problem, a big part, was Darren Halvord. He was in love with her and wanted to get married. That much was obvious to anyone who had seen them together.

Frank knew that Barbara would never discuss her personal life, especially her love life, and that neither she nor Darren would ever mention it if he proposed and she turned him down, but, by God, if she said yes, she'd have to let him know. No one would be happier about it than Frank.

He thought Wally's case would be a distraction, not a major all-involving one, but interesting enough to make her accept that her restlessness was not caused by any work burnout. What he had thought would be a little distraction had turned into a goddamn mess.

Well, be damned careful what you wish for, Mr. Buttinsky, he told himself Tuesday morning on his way to her office to be on hand when Bailey reported.

Frank arrived at Barbara's office minutes before Bailey, who looked like someone he'd slip a dollar to if he passed him standing on a street corner. Bailey appeared more disreputable than usual that morning, with Band-Aids and red streaks on both hands, as if he had been brawling.

"That Austin rambler," he said, holding up his hands. "Hannah said it had to go or else I did. I took it out over the weekend." Bailey tended prize-winning roses, but some of the shrub roses had overgrown their boundaries and it appeared that he had fought one to the secret rosebush graveyard.

"Consider sympathy given and let's get on with it," Barbara said, showing no evidence of any sympathy whatsoever. They sat in the comfortable chairs around her table, and she did not bother with notes. As if to belie his appearance, Bailey produced meticulous written reports.

"Right. Not much yet. Wilkins was hit in the head with a cut-glass pitcher. That, or a brass piece on a bar stool did him in. He hit it when he fell. Saturday night, no definite time yet. Housekeeper found him yesterday morning around ten. No sign of a break-in, security system up and running, television on but muted, nothing missing apparently. Wife still gone. She packed a suitcase, had an e-ticket on order to Roanoke, Virginia, and was a no-show on the Saturday morning of the previous week. No sign that she took a different flight. Wilkins drove her to the Portland airport, left her at the departure gate and took off. He reported her missing Sunday evening, but the cops didn't take it seriously. They decided the lady wanted to get away for a while." He spread his hands. "I don't have much because they're playing it close until they locate the widow Wilkins. At the moment it looks like she might have beaned him herself. Then, there's the missing boat. But you know about that."

Barbara scowled at him. He scowled back. "I do what I can," he said. It was not an apology. "When they clam up, that's it. Two Wilkins kids. A son, Eric, twenty-six, a computer designer, Web designer, some kind of computer geek at the U of O. Gay, shares an apartment with a boyfriend. Daughter, Eve, twenty-three, a nut case, in and out of a private hospital down near Cottage Grove since she was about twelve. Schizophrenia. When she's out she lives with her mother, the ex-wife, Stephanie Breaux. Partner in the women's wear shop Gormandi and Breaux."

Barbara knew the shop. It had pricey clothes for, as their ads said, "Women on the go."

"No other kids in sight," Bailey said.

"What about the missing wife?" Barbara asked when Bailey helped himself to more coffee.

"Interesting," he said adding far too much sugar to his cup. "Connie Wilkins. She was widowed about three years ago. Married to David Laramie, the radio and television guy. He and their twelve-year-old son were killed by a Safeway truck on a trip to go skiing. She's loaded. Laramie had money, and there was a big settlement, plus insurance, plus a big expensive house. Married Wilkins seventeen

months ago, skipped out last week." He consulted a notebook that he had not glanced at before. "He drove a pow-
der-blue Buick, and she has a red Corvette, still in their
garage. And that's just about all I have so far."

"It may be more than we'll need if Connie Wilkins turns
out to be it," Barbara said. "Not much more we can do until
we see what develops." She glanced at Frank, who nodded
in agreement. Bailey was good at his work and he charged
accordingly. There was no point in having him dig unless
and until they had a specific charge and a real case.

"I did scope out a little about Wilkins last night," Bailey said. "His name struck a chord and I looked it up on the
Web. About the time you were gone," he said to Barbara,
"and your dad was out at the McKenzie place, not paying
much attention, I guess. Wilkins got involved in a lawsuit
with a few customers who charged him with violation of
truth in lending practices. They won. Shady credit deals,
padding expenses, add-on costs that drove the prices up,
things like that. I didn't dig much, just the highlights."

Bailey's sense of propriety had stepped in, Barbara realized. He had not been able to bring himself to say it was
during the tumultuous year following her mother's death.
Neither she nor Frank had dealt with it very well; she had
left the law practice, left the state, swearing never to return,
and he had moved all the way out of town.

Frank topped his own coffee. "I'll get the details if we
decide we need them," he said, keeping his gaze on the coffee carafe. He looked stricken. It hit like this, with incredible stabbing intensity, he was thinking, the overwhelming
sense of loss, the pain and grief. There had seemed nothing left to keep living for at the time. Life had become a

burden he no longer wanted to bear until he had managed to get Barbara back home.

"Well," Barbara said, rising, forcing a briskness in her voice that she did not feel, "I guess that's it for now. Tell your contact you really want the time of death as soon as the medical examiner makes his report, and then we'll sit tight and see what happens."

Bailey drained his cup and stood up. "Hannah's been complaining about the big bare spot in the shrubs, so I'll be around the house for a day or so if you want me." He saluted and ambled out.

"I'll give Meg a call and run out there," Barbara said, going to her desk, keeping her voice as even as she could. "I think for now she should just sit tight and not utter a peep. Are you coming with me?"

"What?" Frank shook himself slightly. "No. No. I'll go on home. Plant those beans maybe and a hill of zucchini." He looked uncertain as he spoke, then shook himself again. "Plant beans," he said more firmly. "It's going to be hot for a few days."

At the door he paused and glanced back at her. "Maybe you'd like a bite of dinner later?" He sounded almost shy.

"I'd love it. Thanks."

Barbara could have told Meg what little she had learned over the phone, instead of making the trek out, but she wanted to see for herself how long the drive took, and how isolated their house was. A real problem, or at least something to consider, was whether a neighbor had seen Meg leaving or arriving home again Saturday night. And that could go either way. It might turn out to be a blessing if someone had seen her, or it could be a serious problem. It would depend on the time of Jay Wilkins's death.

She passed the commercial sprawl on Eleventh, big box stores, the industrial park and a few more miles of not much, then turned onto Hunter's Lane. One mile to a second turn, to Owl Creek Road, a narrow road in need of repair, with a leaning sign that warned, No Outlet.

There was a ranch house near the corner, a stretch of unkempt trees and brambles and a green field of grass or wheat on the other side. Meg had said there were only five houses on Owl Creek Road and theirs was the first on the left. The nearest house in sight from it was at least a quarter mile away.

Most likely no one could have seen Meg. Barbara stopped her car thirty minutes after starting. Add another ten minutes to reach that point from Jay Wilkins's home. Now pray that Wilkins was killed at midnight or later, she added to herself after doing the numbers.

The house was tall and a little too narrow for its height, in need of paint. It had a deep porch with white pillars to the upper floor, a mixture of American late-twenties and pseudo-Colonial, not a good mix on such a tall house. Wally opened the door before she had a chance to ring the bell.

"Come in. Come in. Our first real visitor and even if we're not formally receiving yet, you are welcome."

The door opened into a living room where furniture was grouped in the center and boxes stacked about. The walls were dingy, like a peach that had grown moldy.

"We're doing one room at a time," Wally said with his big winning grin showing what appeared to be too many teeth. "And this one was low on the list. This way."

Meg joined them and smiled at Barbara as Wally led the way to a kitchen the width of the house, brightly painted in yellow and robin-egg blue. A big, much-scarred oak table and mismatched chairs were by a cluster of windows. "This was first," Wally said gesturing. "Needed new appliances, stove, fridge, microwave and such, but the cabinets were here. Pretty, aren't they? The table's from Meg's childhood, in storage for twenty years."

"Wally," Meg said, "I'm sure Barbara didn't come here to admire our house. Come this way," she said gesturing to Barbara. They ended up in a room with comfortable furnishings, a television, fresh pale green paint on the walls and sparkling white café curtains. The view out back was of a brick-red barn with a cedar shake roof covered with moss.

"I like your house," Barbara said. "It's going to be great when you're done."

"We had priorities," Wally said, beaming. "Kitchen first for food and drink. Bedroom next, rest and…rest. This was next, and that's when we decided to get away from the paint smells and breathe some ocean air. Wish we had stayed home, but there it is." He motioned toward a wing chair. "You'll find that comfortable," he said. Then he put his arm about Meg's shoulders and gave her a squeeze. They sat down on a sofa. "She told me," he said. "Too bad, but water under the dam, water over the bridge, water spilled, or something. It's done and what do we do about it now?"

"Not a thing yet," Barbara said. "Until we know when Wilkins was killed, we sit tight. Wally, are you certain you didn't accidentally pick up the boat and slip it into your pocket?"

His grin broadened. "Barbara, my coat was in the foyer. If I'd done that it wouldn't have been by accident. Nope. Jay did it."

"Why?" Barbara asked. "Was there an old score to settle? Was he jealous over Meg? Why would he have done such a thing?"

"I don't know. I can't figure it out, no way. We weren't really friends in the long gone days, just collaborators and coworkers. I never did a thing to him, and after they got me I told him he was out of it. And he was."

Meg shook her head. "It was pretty well-known that Wally and I were a thing. Jay never paid any attention to me."

"Okay," Barbara said. "What did he say about his wife when you saw him at the casino?"

"I saw him first," Meg said, "and he was not very interested. I didn't mean a thing popping up from the past. In fact, he didn't ask a single question about us, where we'd been, what we'd done. I don't think he was interested then or later. I said for him to come say a quick hello to Wally, that we were getting ready to leave, and he went with me to the blackjack table. He didn't mention his wife until Wally left the table and said hello. I don't think he liked the way Wally looked him over or something and he sort of moved back a step," Meg said. "It was as if to make up for that little bit of awkwardness that he began to talk about her, that she was away on a trip, and he was lonely. He could be quite charming, a salesman at heart. He asked when we would be back in town and invited us to come out to his house on Monday. We weren't together more than ten minutes. On Monday, we were with him a little longer, maybe half an hour."

"What did she mean, the way you looked at him?" Barbara asked.

"It was spooky that he was so much like his father. I might have looked him over pretty hard," Wally said.

"On Monday night, what did he say about his wife?" Barbara was feeling dissatisfied and frustrated and told herself there was nothing more to pursue in this line, but she asked and waited for their answer.

Meg supplied it. "He said he had called her sister and his wife had not gone there to visit. He didn't know where she was, and he was worried. He had called the police to report her missing, but they said to wait a few days. He said she'd had a nervous breakdown a couple of years ago, and he was afraid she was suffering major depression, that she might not be responsible, that she might even harm herself, commit suicide. He was not leaving the house, for fear she would finally call and he wouldn't be there." She glanced at Wally. "That's about it, I think."

He nodded. "We never met her but even so I guess my sympathy was for her, not him," Wally continued. "If he was as much like his old man as he looked like him, she had cause to hightail it out. He left to get her picture to show us. That has to be when he put the boat in my coat pocket."

"Full circle back to the boat," Barbara said. "Okay. But there could be a reason for his asking you to the house. Try to think of what it might have been." She started to get up.

"There's another thing or two," Wally said. He had his arm around Meg's shoulders again and drew her closer. "We know it was a mistake to take the damned boat back, and that someone could have seen Meg. I'll take the rap before I let them hang it on Meg. Keep that in mind."

No trace of her dimple or his affable grin was in sight. Her lips tightened slightly and she shook her head a little. Wally evidently tightened his grip on her shoulder.

"If Jay was killed hours before she got there, or hours after she left, Meg has little to be afraid of," Barbara said slowly, "even if someone saw her there. And that's still an unknown."

"There's another issue," Wally said, holding Meg close. "When I was in the stir years ago, Meg worked in a restaurant and she wrote some children's books and got them published. There was a television special once, with reruns now and then. Not a fortune, but a little coming in now and then. We lived on it a couple of years. And last November an editor who was having a fit of nostalgia recalled the books. He had loved them, apparently, and he's in a position where he can do something about it. They've been out of print for years, but he got in touch with the agent who handles the residuals, and now there's a new contract in the works to reissue them with new illustrations, and he wants more to go along with them. That's why we decided it was time to settle down, give her space and a real study, put the old girl back to work."

Meg smiled. "There was never much time when we were moving around a lot. I just put them out of mind after Wally came home, but I want to do more. Over the years I seem to have accumulated a lot of ideas."

"She can't afford to have her name mixed up in a theft rap, or a murder case," Wally said. "I think certain people would say she's not fit to speak to children."

Barbara sank back against the chair. "Did you use your name?"

"No. Margaret Waite. I thought it was appropriate, since I was waiting for Wally. But in this day and age I don't think that would be a secret for long."

Barbara felt a faint memory stir. "What were the books?"

"They're about a baby dragon," Meg said. "For four- to seven-year-olds, that age group."

"Good God! I loved those books! I think I memorized them all!" A vivid memory surfaced of sitting in her mother's lap, watching her slender finger trace the words as she read about the baby dragon.

Meg dimpled and Wally flashed his big grin. "That's my girl," he said. "And, Barbara, remember, she's to be kept all the way out of whatever comes next. I won't even have her name breathed by the cops."

SEVEN

Barbara sat on Frank's porch on Sunday afternoon, waiting for him to finish in the garden. She had brought out a glass of ice water for him. He would be as hot as she had become walking over.

Both cats came to her looking for a handout. She showed them the water glass and they walked away with disdain. Frank joined her. He took off his gardening shoes and put on house slippers, then sat in another rattan chair.

"Ah," he said, picking up his water. "Thank you."

"You work too hard."

"Noted. What's new?"

"Jay Wilkins died between two and four hours after his last meal, and take-out food was delivered at seven."

"Ah," he said again, and drank some of the water.

"Meg was there at about nine forty-five," she added.

"Ah," he said again. "I've been thinking about that." He took another drink. "You realize that the day's coming when you'll have to fess up. Material evidence in a murder case can't be concealed by an attorney, not if she expects to keep her license."

"I can't," she said. "Wally's prepared to lie to hell and gone to keep Meg out of it. If she contradicts him, he'll make it look like she's trying to save his neck. And his word would carry more weight than mine. They much prefer a confession to anything a lawyer might have to say."

"You think he'd lie under oath?"

"Dad, would you lie under oath to save my life?"

Gruffly he said, "That's a different question." He finished the water.

"And you have your answer. Also," she continued, "the insurance investigator called to let me know they found the boat. Just a little mistake, a bit of absentmindedness. He's happy to be out of it, he said. It can be messy when someone accuses a guest of theft. Messy! He doesn't know the half of it."

"Well, keep in mind two things—the widow is still out of sight, and someone else was present that night, and that person hasn't made a peep yet. When and if they come forward will be time enough to put on your worry hat." He stood up. "I'm going to rustle up a quick dinner." He went inside and she followed him.

They ate on the back porch with the two lion-sized cats watching every bite the way they would watch a mouse, ever ready to pounce.

"Funny how it works out that there's always enough left over for me to have at least one more meal," she commented later as he spooned peas into a plastic container and she washed the pots and pans.

"Like to make enough," he said. "Don't reheat the salmon. It's better cold on a salad once it's cooked."

It had been grilled to perfection.

"Were you busy this weekend?" he asked casually.

"We went to the Hult Center last night," Barbara said. "That Irish dancing group. I don't see the point of standing like a statue and moving your feet."

She didn't add another word, but Frank was satisfied. He cursed himself for clinging to whatever shred of her private life she cast his way. But, at least, Barbara and Darren were still on track, however slowly the train was moving.

The phone rang and Frank went to his study to listen to the answering machine. When Bailey's voice came on, he picked up the phone. "I'm here."

"Is Barbara there?" She was always there on Sunday nights. He didn't wait for an answer. "My contact got in touch a little while ago. Did you read about that woman's body they fished out of the drink a few days ago? Thursday, I think it was."

"I saw the item," Frank said. He had paid scant attention. Every year half a dozen or more poor souls ended up in the ocean.

"They've made a positive ID," Bailey said. "Connie Wilkins, the missing widow. They shipped the remains off to the state pathology forensics lab in Salem to determine when and how she died. They won't make an official statement until they notify next of kin."

For a time after hanging up, Frank considered this new development, and finally decided there was no point in speculating.

When her father left the kitchen, Barbara had started thinking about the previous night, and how frustrated she felt about things in general, and Darren in particular. They had gone to the Electric Station for a snack after the show, but it had been crowded, noisy, with live music, making talk almost impossible. Then, driving back to her apartment, Darren had asked her to go with him and Todd to explore ghost towns in late June.

"A week or ten days roughing it, with my cooking, yet. I guess it doesn't sound too enticing, but will you?"

"I can't. There's too much piling up with Shelley gone, and I have a case that could turn serious."

He had put his hand on her arm. "You don't have to explain."

At her door she had hesitated, then thanked him for a good evening and he had kissed her lightly on the lips and left.

Her answer had been too swift, she thought, drying her hands, done with the dishwashing. She should have given it at least a little thought first. She had not yet invited him into her apartment, and she couldn't think why. They both wanted to go to bed; it was in the air between them. He wouldn't make the first move at his house when Todd was around, and she had not gone there during Todd's weekends with his mother, and she had not once asked him in. She bit her lip and shook her head impatiently. Around and around.

"Bobby, a new wrinkle in the Wilkins business," Frank said, returning to the kitchen. He told her about Bailey's call. "Just don't start playing the various possible scenarios until we know more," he cautioned, as if aware that she was doing just that, all thoughts of Darren eclipsed instantly with his words.

She met a secret lover for a rendezvous and he killed her? One killer, two victims? She killed herself?

"Suddenly there are new players," Frank said thoughtfully. "There's a big estate to consider and someone's going to inherit it. Depends on who died first, doesn't it?"

Barbara switched her line of thought. If they had to send the body to a forensics lab to determine when she died, it meant she had been in the water more than just a day or two.

"I don't know a thing about her family, but on his side there's his ex," she said. "Probably she won't get a cent. But there are two kids, young adults, and one of them is mentally ill. It's like a Chinese puzzle box," she said. "Every time you think you have all the pieces, you find another one."

EIGHT

On late Monday afternoon Stephanie Breaux sat at her desk regarding the bill Cedar View had prepared for her. It would wipe out the savings account again, and if it weren't for Connie's monthly checks, she would have dipped into her credit line. She had just finished paying it off from the last hospitalization. The new prescription Dr. Mohrbeck had given her that day had come to two hundred forty dollars for a month's supply. Added to the others it ran the monthly total to over a thousand dollars.

She should have stuck it out with Jay, she thought bleakly. Now she would be the widow with assets, a house to sell, art objects, antiques. Whatever she could get for the dealership. No more money worries. She drew in her breath angrily; it was pointless to pretend she had had a choice when she was as glad as Eric that Jay was dead. The ultimate scene with Jay played in her head, the one that had made divorce her only option.

Eric had come to her home office and stood in the doorway looking awkward and very young. He had been almost sixteen.

"I came up to say goodbye," he said in a low voice, keeping his gaze averted.

She looked up from the ledger she had been working on. Then, as now, she had done the books for the shop, and her partner, Diane Gormandi, the traveling and buying. "What do you mean? Goodbye?"

"Dad kicked me out. I'm going to hang out at Woody's house. His mom and dad said it's okay."

She stood up. "What are you talking about?"

"He said I have to clear out."

She went to him and hugged him fiercely. "You'll never be told to leave my home," she said. "We'll see about this."

He was unresponsive and she realized how near tears he was. "I'll go pack some stuff," he said.

She found Jay in front of the wall-sized television screen.

"What did you say to Eric?" She walked to the television and turned it off.

"I told him to get out. I don't intend to have a pervert living in my house, in my father's house. Let him go down to San Francisco and be with others like him. No doubt some big-hearted six-footer will welcome a cute toy boy like Eric. I was watching a game," he said. "Do you mind?" Using the remote, he turned the TV on again.

She snatched the remote from his hand and threw it across the room. "This is my home, too, and by God you can't drive our son out of it!"

He stood up, brushed past her and went to the bar. Behind it, he finally looked at her. "Get this through your head. This was my father's house and he willed it to me. To me. Not us. And I don't have a son. I'm not even sure he's a boy. He can't bring his filth here and stay."

"If he goes, so do I."

"Your choice. Take your twisted kids and beat it. Suits me. She's a dummy, a mental case who should be in an institution. That deer-in-the-headlights act of hers turns my stomach, and he's just as sick. They both turn my stomach. *Your* twisted kids. Have fun with them."

She knew she could not have stayed with him, that she had stayed years longer than she should have, but she had been afraid for their sick daughter.

The day the divorce was finalized, he had dropped them from his medical insurance, and the day they reached eighteen, their monthly support checks had stopped. Stephanie had been denied insurance for Eve.

She pushed the new hospital bill away tiredly. Tomorrow she would bring her daughter home. Eve had been at Cedar View for eight days this time, one of her shorter stays.

Dr. Mohrbeck had found that hopeful. After two years of good progress, a little setback was not unexpected, he had told her. "There may be another one or two, but perhaps not. We wait and see. Call the downtown office for an appointment in a week or ten days. And get some sleep. You look exhausted."

That day when she told Eve that she had to stay only one more night, Eve had hugged her hard and whispered, "Mother, I'm sorry."

"Tell you what," Stephanie had said. "I'll make fried chicken and mashed potatoes with gravy. Plus strawberry shortcake with lots and lots of whipped cream. We'll celebrate your homecoming."

"Poor Reggie," Eve said. "There goes her diet again. Unless I eat it all." She smiled weakly, a crooked little smile that came and went fast.

Both Eve and Eric had that crooked smile, just like me, Stephanie thought.

Stephanie pushed her chair back from the desk and regarded her bed on the other side of the room. Her home office was a corner of her bedroom, a desk with her computer, a file cabinet, a wastebasket. The settlement her attorney had wrangled from Jay's attorney had made it possible to buy a small house, this split level, big enough for her and the two children. Now that Eric was gone, Reggie lived with them and used the topmost two bedrooms.

What Eve needed, an early doctor had said, was a stable home where she felt secure. Stephanie had provided it. She eyed the bed, then shook herself. If she took a nap, doubtful that she could sleep, but if she did, then she would be up again most of the night. She could not think of the last night she had had a long restful sleep. Tomorrow night, she told herself. When Eve was home and safely tucked into bed, then she would sleep through the night.

She closed her eyes, and let herself fall into a near reverie state, too tired to think clearly, too fatigued to stir. The doorbell roused her.

Eric was letting himself in when she went down the stairs. He had moved back into his own apartment the previous day.

"Mother, we have to talk," he said at the door. "Is Reggie around?"

"No. She'll be back later. What's wrong?"

"Come over and sit down," he said, motioning toward the sofa. He sat in an upholstered chair near it. "Late this afternoon, Mr. Berman called me at work and asked if I could meet at his office before four."

Stephanie stiffened. She loathed Berman, who had been Jay's attorney and had fought for his client all the way through the divorce proceedings as if protecting Samson from Delilah.

Eric was plunging onward as if unaware of the effect of his words. "Connie's dead. They won't make any announcement until they notify her family. Berman said they needed to know who to release Dad's body to since she's out of the picture, and Berman told them I'm next of kin. I have to make arrangements." He stood up and began to pace. "God, I don't care what they do with him! Berman said he'd take care of things. In a week or two there should be a memorial service or something. And we had to go to the bank to open Dad's safe deposit box with a detective. They were waiting for Connie to show up, but—"

"Stop moving around," Stephanie cried. "What about Connie? What do you mean, she's dead? When did she die? How? For God's sake, settle down and tell me!"

He sank down into the chair again and leaned forward. "Sorry. They don't know when or how. Her body was in the ocean and they don't know for how long. It might take a couple of weeks to find out." He jumped up again. "I left some beers here. Be right back." He hurried from the room.

Stephanie leaned back against the couch. Connie! She had met her for the first time in September when Connie had asked permission to meet her stepchildren. In October the monthly checks had started, twelve hundred dollars, to help with Eve, the memo had said. And now she was dead. Stephanie had liked Connie, and Eve had formed an attachment that was rare for her. Slowly, with tentative, hesitant steps, Connie and Eve had drawn together, formed a friendship that had become a strong bond by spring.

Eric returned with a bottle of beer. He drank, then set the bottle down on the end table by his chair. "I guess I'm reeling from too much, too fast," he said. "There's more. We went to the bank with the detective and opened the box. It had Connie's things along with Dad's. The deed to the house, papers, some of her jewelry, Dad's will and a copy of hers. The detective took charge of it all until they straighten out who gets what. Then I went back to Berman's office with him and he told me about the wills. He said she left half of everything to Dad, and the other half to be divided between her family in Virginia and Eve and me. He said it could be over a million dollars!"

He took another drink, longer this time. "Dad's will makes the same kind of distribution, but names somebody in New Hampshire to split half with us."

Stephanie, speechless, stared at him. Finally she said. "Are you sure?" It was a whisper.

"That's what he told me. The detective wanted to know if any of us knew about it before. They probably will ask you, too. I told him I haven't spoken to Dad or seen him in nearly ten years, and Connie never mentioned anything like that to me. I never even knew there was any family in New Hampshire."

"He told me he would leave you and Eve exactly one thousand dollars each, and a distant cousin in New England would get the rest." As far as Stephanie knew Jay had never met his cousin. "But he will carry on the Wilkins name," Jay had said meanly, "which is more than I expect from your fairy kid."

"Right now it's a real mess," Eric said. "A lot depends on who died first. If it was Connie, and they seemed to imply it was, then her half goes to him, and that plus whatever he had could add up to quite a bundle when they start dividing it up." His eyes gleamed. "Berman said not to start spending it yet because it could take months to work out. But I can't help thinking about it. I'll go to graduate school if it's true."

And Stephanie couldn't stop thinking about it, either, after Eric left. She was Eve's legal guardian. It would mean an end to money worries, real security for her daughter, the art lessons she needed, helping her toward the goal she had to achieve ultimately: a self-directed, independent existence, free of the threat of being institutionalized and started on the downward spiral to oblivion. The threat was real, sometimes looming near enough to destroy sleep, sometimes receding, but always there. The day Stephanie could no longer pay for Eve's medication, for her hospital care when necessary, the threat would be realized.

Jay had wanted to place her in an institution at a young age. Stephanie knew that would have been fatal. Two doctors had said what she needed was a stable homelife when she was between her episodes. They always referred to them that way, episodes; lapses into insanity was what they meant. In the beginning, the episodes had been frequent with long periods of hospitalization, six weeks at a time, seven. There were weekly sessions with a therapist between episodes.

Stephanie had homeschooled Eve after two unsuccessful tries in regular classes. Eve could not bear to be with other children rushing about, unpredictable, loud, threatening. She had been a slow reader, and still never read for pleasure.

Eve's mind struggled to keep things within their own boundaries, but if she lost control for a second, everything she saw merged into shapeless swirling colors rushing at her. Out of control. When she was eight, she froze one day when luncheon guests, strangers, rushed toward her to admire the lovely child. That was the day Jay had turned his back on his daughter. Later, from eleven onward, she collapsed into a fetal heap and refused, or was unable, to move or open her eyes. Catatonia. The first time that happened, a neighbor's little black-and-white cocker spaniel, wanting only to play, had run at her in the backyard, and she had fallen to the ground and drawn herself into a ball. That had been her pattern ever since. If she could not control it, she could only try to deny it through complete withdrawal from the world.

NINE

Meg Lederer stood at her office door and surveyed the small room with satisfaction. That morning she had installed the new blinds and the room was ready to use. It held a regular desk and at right angles to it a computer desk set up with her computer and printer, a two-drawer file cabinet, a reading chair with its own lamp, bookshelves on one wall and a closet with deeper shelves for office supplies. Perfect, she thought. Absolutely perfect. Her first office.

A sharp memory surfaced of the card table and second-hand typewriter on which she had written seven children's books. Typewriter on one side of the table, room for her meals on the other, none left over. It had been enough. Twenty-two years old, passionately in love with her husband, who would be imprisoned for five years, she had set out to learn to type, and then to write stories.

She closed her eyes as another sharp memory rose. Huskily Wally had said, "Honey, you're so beautiful, so young.

I know guys will be at your heels day and night. If you…
I mean if you can't resist or something… You know what
I'm trying to say?"

She had been crying. He wiped her cheeks. "Honey,
when I get out, just promise me one thing. That's all I'm
asking, just one thing. Give me a chance again. Can you
do that? Whatever else happens, I mean… No questions or
anything. Just give me another chance."

She brushed away the past and walked through the
house to the back porch to see what Wally was up to. Pes-
tering the roofing man, probably. The phone rang and she
went back to pick up the wireless handset in the kitchen,
then took it with her to the porch. She could see Wally looking up at the man on the roof. Barbara was on the line.

Meg listened with near incomprehension, then asked,
"What difference will that make to us? We never even met
Connie Wilkins."

"I think they'll put everything on hold until they know
more about how and when she died. What it means to you
is that nothing's likely to happen for a quite a while. So you
just sit tight and we'll see what happens. If they start asking you questions again, let me know, and I'll give you a
call if I learn anything. Okay?"

Meg said it suited her fine to be left alone forever as far
as she was concerned. She broke the connection and regarded Wally at the barn. It was hard to get used to him
wearing a John Deere cap, old blue jeans and work boots.

Was he content? Was he likely to remain content out
here in the country after the kind of life they had led so
long? The question kept recurring.

Casino shows, blackjack, and several times a year a

convention here or there, a weekend stay in a convention hotel. Wally picked the conventions with great care. No starving poets' convention or hungry artists'. No firefighters' convention—he had his own set of scruples and he refused to take money from a firefighter. The attendees had to be affluent enough to afford him, he had said.

After finding a suitable convention through the Internet he did a little research, then made a reservation at the same hotel, always to arrive a day before the convention was to start, and by the time the conventioneers were in place Wally would have struck up a bantering relationship with the bartender. It was never hard for him to get in on the attendees' bar talk and he always located a floating poker game and was invited to participate. The players for the most part were strangers to one another, and he was just another stranger. There was always a poker game somewhere, he had said in the beginning, and he had been right. He sometimes lost a little at the casino blackjack tables, but he had never lost a cent at the convention games.

Once Meg had protested that it didn't seem fair, and Wally had said earnestly, "Honey, look at it this way. Those guys are going to play, no matter what, and the losers are going to lose. I'm not changing a thing in the grand scheme of the universe. That's what some of them came for, to kick up their heels a little, to see shows their wives won't let them watch at home, to drink too much, maybe play around a little and to gamble. I'm there to work. They get what they came for and so do I."

There was a flaw in his argument. He was a professional taking advantage of amateurs, even if he didn't cheat. But, she had argued with herself, didn't those bankers take advantage of loan applicants with the fine print that they knew would not be read or understood if it was? Didn't too many doctors vacationing on pharmaceutical largesse take advantage of patients by prescribing high-cost medicines that their sponsors wanted to sell when generics or lower cost drugs would be equally beneficial? She had given up the argument and never raised an objection again. It was too difficult to determine, much less navigate, that elusive line that defined ethical behavior. All parties were getting what they wanted when they played poker with Wally, that was enough.

Wally had started to walk toward her and when he drew near he began talking, the way he always did. "I asked Andy what to do about all that moss on the roof. You know what he told me? You'd never guess. He said don't touch it. Leave it alone. It's all that's holding those shakes together. Exactly what I wanted to hear." He grinned and put his arm around her shoulders. "Gave me some advice about the fireplace, too. Let's go have a look and I'll tell you."

In the living room, which they had not yet touched, as he talked about the difference between open fireplaces and inserts, she leaned into him slightly. He stopped talking and looked down at her.

"Feel a little nap coming on?"

She nodded and he laughed and squeezed her shoulder. "Old folks like us need our naps," he said.

Even that, she thought happily. Even that. No matter what lay in the future, coming home had rejuvenated him, and her, too. She had never been happier, in spite of the fear Jay Wilkins had inserted into their lives. They left the living room and headed toward the bedroom, not really running, but not dawdling either.

After talking with Meg, Barbara regarded the slim folder with the Lederer material in it. She started to put it in the tray of "To File" folders, then changed her mind and put it with the active folders on her desk. She had a strong hunch that the Lederer case would not end just yet.

The evening newscast had a brief mention concerning the identification of Connie Wilkins's body and the ongoing investigation, but the following morning's newspapers had a longer account.

Barbara read it carefully while eating breakfast, then stopped at a name she knew: Adele Wykoph. Connie Wilkins had done a lot of volunteer work in the past, and one of the organizations she had helped had been the Women's Support Center. Its director was Adele Wykoph. Barbara had referred many women to the center over the years, and she and Adele were friends, comfortable with each other, trusting each other. She waited until she got to the office, then called Adele.

Adele's voice sounded strained and husky when she answered her phone, hesitant when Barbara asked if they could get together later that day.

"Maybe another time, after a day or two? I don't think I'm up to much right now. I just found out I've lost a dear friend. I think I'll knock off early and go home to the consolation of a stiff drink or two."

"I'm sorry," Barbara said. "I saw the center mentioned in the article about Connie Wilkins. That's what I wanted to ask about."

"She's the friend," Adele said. She sounded as if she were choking. "God, why her?"

"Let me pick you up and we'll go somewhere quiet and talk. It might do you some good, and I'll ply you with the drink or two and see that you get home safely. Think how many others you've advised to talk about it, whatever it is."

"I can't leave. The staff is ready to melt down. What would that do for our clients, to see the support team in worse shape than they're in?"

"Later," Barbara said. "Put on a brave face for them, buck them up, do whatever you have to. I'll pick you up at four-thirty and you can let go then. Okay?"

Adele Wykoph had a perennial New Year's resolution: this year she would lose ten to fifteen pounds. Her doctor had advised twenty, but she had decided that was being fanatical. She was a large woman, comfortable, comforting and, at the same time, decisive and very capable at keeping the center operating efficiently and seeing to it that her clients were well served. She usually wore long skirts and over blouses that reached her hips. Hers was an impressive figure.

That late afternoon she looked tired and despondent. "It's the pits," she said by way of greeting when she got into Barbara's car, and then not another word until they were seated in Sweet Waters Restaurant, by a broad window overlooking the Willamette River. No river sound reached them through the glass.

"Gin and tonic," Adele said to the waiter who had appeared instantly. Barbara ordered coffee. She would have wine with dinner, she added.

They both gazed at the silently rushing river until the drinks were served and the waiter departed. Then Barbara said softly, "Tell me about Connie." She understood that this was the long path to what she really wanted to talk about—Jay Wilkins—but it was a path that had to be taken. They would get to him.

Adele began slowly but soon her words were tumbling out haphazardly in a discursive ramble. Later Barbara would sort it out and form a narrative with a beginning, middle and end; at the moment she simply listened attentively.

Adele had met Connie and David Laramie soon after they arrived in Eugene with their infant son. David had assumed his uncle's duties at the radio station when his uncle retired. As soon as the child, Steven, was in day care Connie started doing volunteer work that included time spent at Adele's women's center. Her gentle smile, a vivacious personality and a charming Southern accent captivated everyone she worked with.

Now and then Adele's voice broke. She paused to gaze at the river. Tears filled her eyes, overflowed, and she talked on. She finished her drink and Barbara held up the glass for another. Adele was oblivious.

They had a fairy-tale marriage, Adele said. Inseparable. They adored each other, and they both worshiped their son.

Then the accident happened.

She turned to gaze at the river, longer this time, and when she spoke again, her voice was lower, duller. "She had a cold and they decided it would be best if she didn't go skiing that weekend. David wanted to postpone the trip altogether, but she insisted that he and Steve had been looking forward to it too much, they should go on without her.

"They were hit by a truck and David and Steve were both killed." Adele stopped and drank deeply. "She died, too," she said after a moment. "A living death. She was stunned and disbelieving, then paralyzed by shock, grief and guilt. She blamed herself for urging them to go. She became a zombie."

Her sister came to help her, but after a month she had to go home to her own family. Friends had tried to help. They took turns visiting her, taking meals, sitting with her, but she didn't respond to anything they said, and sometimes didn't seem to notice them at all.

"She wanted to die," Adele said. "Then the housekeeper got in touch with her lawyer and told him bills were piling up, she had not been paid for three months, and something had to be done. He got in touch with her family and her brother came to stay for a few weeks. He got her accounts straightened out, made arrangements for automatic payments and he tried hard to get her to go back to Virginia with him. She refused to leave her house.

"I talked to him," Adele said. "He said there were papers she had to sign, and she never even glanced at them, never read them. He said sign here, and she signed. That alarmed him. Then Jay entered the picture."

Barbara signaled to the waiter. Now she would have a glass of wine. This was, finally, what she had been waiting for. She pointed to Adele's glass and ordered antipasto for two. "We'll order dinner after that comes," she said and picked up her menu.

"Whatever you're having," Adele said indifferently without glancing at the menu. Several egrets were skimming the river, inches away from the flashing ripples. She appeared to be hypnotized by them.

After the platter of antipasto, wine and another gin and tonic were in place and the dinner order given, knowing they would be left alone for a time, Barbara said, "What about Jay?"

Adele looked at her new drink, then moved it aside. She picked up a piece of salami. "Connie's brother asked me about him. Jay had known Connie and David for years. They moved in the same circles or something. Anyway, he had dropped in on her a few times. I don't know how this came about, but apparently Jay said he'd help Connie sell the sailboat and the place on the coast, and eventually, when she was ready, help sell her house. He offered to look after her, and her brother was relieved. He just wanted to know if Jay was okay, not a child molester or something." She smiled bitterly.

"God knows she needed someone to look out for her. Most of her friends had given up. If they don't want to be helped, there isn't much you can do. You must find that in your practice as often as I do at the center."

Barbara nodded. "Unreachable, untouchable, unteachable."

"That's it. I never dreamed that a man like Jay would get through to her," Adele said.

"You knew him?"

"I grew up with his first wife, kindergarten through high school, all the way. She's a good friend. I knew Jay."

Pay dirt, Barbara thought, prepared to ask some questions. But before she could voice even one, Adele was off on another ramble.

Five months after Connie's brother left, satisfied that she was being looked out for by a respectable businessman,

Connie and Jay were married. Everyone who knew her was stunned by the news, no one more so than Adele.

"I waited for several weeks, hoping Connie would give me a call. She didn't."

Adele had gone to Jay's house to see Connie, but he had met her at the door and said that Connie was resting. She tried again a week later and was turned away. Then Jay had arrived at her office at the center to talk to her.

"He said he had talked to her doctor and they both agreed that she was making good progress, but every time someone from her past life appeared, it sent her back to her previous state of despair and depression. He asked me to leave her alone until she was really well."

Now when she lapsed into her silences, it was to pick up another tidbit from the platter and attack it almost savagely.

She had been a fool to believe Jay, but she had wanted to believe him. And the weeks passed, with her growing more uneasy until she decided she had to see for herself how Connie was faring.

She picked a time when Jay would be at the dealership and she had been aghast at Connie's condition.

"I've been running the center a long time," Adele said, "and I know an addict when I see one. She was addicted to something. Tranquilizers? Sedatives? I went to her medicine cabinet and had a look. My God, it was a pharmacy! I tossed everything in a bag and called Joan Sugarman. I told her I was bringing in an emergency case and I stiff-armed Connie out of the house and to her office."

Barbara knew Joan Sugarman, the volunteer doctor on call for the center. She was available for emergencies at all times.

Joan had wanted to sign Connie into a detox center im-

mediately, but Connie had refused. Jay was taking care of
her. They were taking care of each other. In the end, Joan
simply rewrote the prescriptions, reducing the dosage. It
would have been too dangerous to stop abruptly. Adele had
taken Connie home, and replaced the old medications with
the newly filled prescriptions. She told Connie not to mention the matter to Jay, but she knew that was unnecessary.
Connie was not up to initiating anything.

For weeks that was the routine she followed. Joan kept
a close watch on Connie and kept reducing the medications
carefully.

"It was like watching someone emerge from a coma,"
Adele said. "First a finger twitches, or a toe. The flutter of
an eyelid. It took months before she was clean."

The platter was empty and their dinners arrived, grilled
halibut steaks, pesto mashed potatoes, salads.

In spite of herself, Barbara had been drawn into the
drama of Connie's grief, marriage, addiction. "Didn't you
talk to her? You could see the pattern, the isolation, sepa-
ration from her friends, the whole works."

"Early on it wouldn't have done any good. She was an
addict," Adele said dryly. "You ever try to reason with an
addict?" She didn't wait for an answer. "Later, I tried, but
she wouldn't have it. As the drugs left her system, the grief
flooded back. She was not yet done with grieving. It had
been put on chemical hold. She was passive, silent, unques-
tioning, just accepted pain and guilt as her due. And she
would not hear a word about Jay. He had been trying to
help, she insisted. She had needed him, and he needed her."

She snorted. "She said he understood what she was
going through because his first wife had abandoned him

and deprived him of all visitation rights to his two children. They were dead to him, just as much as her child was dead to her. She had the impression that the daughter was a hopeless psychotic locked up in a state institution, and the son had turned to a gay lifestyle and had cut all ties to both parents. I asked if Jay had told her that and she didn't know. It was what she believed. I asked if she'd like to meet her stepchildren."

TEN

Adele had to persuade Connie. Although at first she shrank from the idea of meeting anyone at all, much less someone who might be ill, she was too apathetic to offer strenuous resistance to Adele's determination to make the meeting happen. Stephanie and Reggie were harder to convince, she said.

Barbara stopped her. "Who's Reggie?"

Adele laughed, a short almost barking kind of laughter as much in derision as mirth. "She's an unpublished writer with a folder full of rejection slips to prove it. She's about thirty-one, thirty-two, and she's been with Eve and Stephanie for nearly six years. The first companion for Eve who would stay. At first it was a job, no more than that. Kept a close eye on Eve when Stephanie was at the shop. Anyway, Reggie had written a short story in a writing class at the U of O, and the teacher thought it was a mess. I read it. A mess. She graduated, got a job, but kept thinking of the story and came around to agreeing with the teacher. She had tried to cram too much into too small a space. It was novel material. A fantasy novel full of weird creatures and other worlds. Lots of magic. She's been working on it for four years now, and it's grown again. She's thinking trilogy. So, even if the pay is very low, she has a room of her own, two now that Eric's gone, a lot of time off, nothing much to do except think and plot when she's earning her pay. Ideal situation for her."

Adele smiled, then said, "But a funny thing happened over the years. Reggie has become a big sister. She's a big girl, good-natured and a great sister. She's as protective of Eve as Stephanie and Eric. They go bike riding, walk to the university library, bike to the public library and through their neighborhood. They made a garden together and tend it. Cook together. They even bicker a little. A wonderful big sister. And she was really opposed to having Connie butt in."

She looked out the window, remembering that scene. "What on earth made you think I'd agree to having Jay's new wife come here?" Stephanie had demanded.

"What does she want from us?" Reggie had said.

"She should meet her stepchildren."

"She didn't set any speed records getting around to it," Reggie muttered.

Adele told them a little about Connie, then said, "She thought Eve was in a mental hospital. She doesn't know how she got the idea, but that's what she believed."

"Jay can do that," Stephanie said in a scathing tone. "He can twist words until you not only believe the earth is flat, but you think you originated the idea yourself."

"Whatever. I'm going to bring her over on Friday afternoon."

That hadn't ended it immediately, but that was what happened. Adele had been determined.

"On Friday," Adele said to Barbara, "Stephanie was like a cat on full alert, poised, ready to bristle and lash out, and Connie was ready to bolt and run. Eve and Reggie were on the patio when we arrived, and I took Connie by the arm and made her walk out with me. There's a lattice cover with a clematis vine that was just starting to bloom, casting deep shade on half of the patio. Eve and Reggie were sitting under it. Reggie had been reading to her. She does that, reads parts of her manuscript and Eve sketches while she listens.

"Seeing Eve and Connie eye each other was like watching two timid fawns, too shy and fearful to say a word, but curious. Then Connie looked at the garden, and said something like how lovely it was. That was the start."

Their food was gone and they were waiting for coffee. "When we left, about half an hour later, Connie asked Stephanie if she could come back the next week. It was the first initiative she had shown since the accident, just asking permission to return. The next week I went back with her and I knew she was on her way. She and Eve had not said more than half a dozen words on her first visit, but this time they talked about flowers a little. And Connie said she used to have a flower garden. They did—she, David and Steve had planted a flower garden and called it their secret garden. It was the first time she had been able to refer to the past even obliquely.

"It was all a matter of climbing out of the pit from there on," Adele said.

The light on the river was changing with the lowering sun. Ripples that had flashed silver were taking on golden hues and the ambient light was softening subtly.

"Let's walk by the river while the sun sets," Adele said.

Barbara waved her credit card and a few minutes later they were heading down the steps to the river path. More birds were flying low over the river, on their way to wherever home was. Not many other strollers were on this side of the river, although on the other side the path was busy with bicycle and foot traffic.

"She started coming to the center again," Adele said, walking slowly in the golden light. "First she just sat in on the group therapy sessions, but then she began helping out. Every year we have two sessions of self-defense classes for women. She attended. She said she was so out of shape, she had to start getting some muscles back."

Adele lapsed into silence again for several seconds, then said, "Howie Steinman is the martial arts instructor, and Howie fell in love with Connie." She sighed. "He was born to suffer, and he'd be the first to tell you all about it. It seems he has one unfortunate fixation after another, a visiting professor once, a singer with the opera company who moved on and Connie. Always the star on the Christmas tree, unattainable and irresistible. He was madly in love again."

Adele spotted a bench ahead and motioned toward it. They sat down and listened to the music of the river for a minute or two. "That last Friday," Adele said, keeping her gaze on the water, gold ripples on black now. "After the class Connie came to the office. She asked what she should do about Howie. He had started sending her little presents, flowers, candy, a book of poetry. She was embarrassed and didn't know how to handle it. I told her to tell him to get lost," Adele said dryly. "Well, she decided to go have coffee with him and be gentle, and tell him to get lost in a nice way. She called Eve from the office to say she'd be around on Saturday, that something had come up." Adele closed her eyes. "That was the last time I saw her."

Barbara let the silence stretch out long enough to assume that Adele was not going to break it. Then she said, "Jay said that she was suicidal."

"Bullshit! He called people who hadn't seen Connie for a couple of years, not since she'd seemed suicidal, and they backed him up."

"He called you?"

"Yes. I told him it was bullshit."

"From all indications, he was frantic."

"So they say." Her tone had been reflective, melancholic, tinged with regret and unhappiness, now it became hard, even bitter. "Look, Barbara, I knew Jay years ago, when he was married to Stephanie and I haven't had a thing to do with him since. For all I know, he changed, became a new man, or some damn thing, but the Jay I knew never cared about anyone except Jay."

"Tell me something about him," Barbara said. "He accused my client of stealing a valuable gold boat. That's not a trifling matter."

"God help your client if he took it, and if Jay was in any position to follow through. All that Egyptian stuff was collected by his grandfather, passed on to Jay's old man and then to Jay. And anything that was ever his was meant to stay his until hell does its thing."

"Can a leopard change its spots?" Barbara murmured. "Tell me more about the Jay you knew."

"Okay. His grandfather built the house, and he set rules that Jay's father had to follow, and Jay saw nothing wrong with those rules and kept them when it was his turn. The kids weren't allowed in the front rooms of the house unless he summoned them to display for guests. His living collection. They were beautiful children. They still are, in fact. Anyway, they weren't allowed to speak at the table unless in response to an adult. Then it was to be 'Yes, ma'am,' or 'No, sir.' Respect authority, and he was the authority. Obedience required at all times. No outdoor shoes inside. Take them off at the door. Come and go by way of the back door. Use the back stairs. Keep your toys in your own room or the den. If he found one out of place he threw it away. And he was miserly. He spent lavishly on his selected guests, but the kids had to earn every cent that came their way." She drew in a long breath, then laughed in her peculiar barking mirthless way.

"You might gather that I had little use for him. Damn right. A tyrant at home. He had a circle of friends that he cultivated the way a pot grower might cultivate a planting, always aware of the usefulness of individual plants, nurturing those of value, culling out the inferior ones. His pals were those he saw a use for immediately, or a possible future use for, directly or as a means to get to someone else. He had a box at Autzen Stadium, and he hosted events there, bigwigs, corporate visitors, people like that. Useful people. He had the biggest TV screen in the area, and invited his pals over to watch sports, football games, basketball games, golf tournaments. Drink a lot, good food, make contacts. Locker-room humor. Good old boy stuff. Everyone was a contact. Gung ho for development. More strip malls, more subdivisions, more business. Land-use laws were the work of the satanic tree huggers, who should be pinned to their beloved trees and used for gun practice. A real sweetheart." She stopped because she had run out of breath.

Barbara laughed. "In a minute you'll tell me what you personally thought of him. But it's curious that first Stephanie married him, and later Connie did."

"Stephanie was young and stupid," Adele said promptly. "And Connie was out of her mind. Stephanie got married and a year later there was Eric, and then Eve. She felt trapped by then. You know, for the sake of the children. Everyone could tell at an early age that Eric was gay, years before he realized it, in fact. And Eve…she was not quite right from five or six on. We could see that, too. Stephanie was trapped. Or thought she was."

Barbara knew that story well. She had heard it from too many of her own clients. "Sometimes they break loose," she said. "Sometimes they find the courage and take off."

"Stephanie would have stuck it out longer for Eve's sake," Adele said after a moment. "She knew what was in store for the kid—doctors, hospitals, home care or institution. Jay was bitterly disappointed in his children, and then disappointed in Stephanie. They were her fault, of course. His mother had always deferred to his father, he expected as much from his own wife, but she got involved in the shop, and she sided with the kids, and he could see that he was losing control. When he couldn't deny Eric's homosexuality, he booted him." She nodded, as if to herself.

"That was the key to Jay—control. A place for everything, and everything kept there. Control of his family, his home, his business. He had to be in charge. First Eric. He couldn't control his homosexuality, so out. He couldn't control Eve's mental illness. Out. Then Stephanie. He forced her out, too. He knew that if he made Eric leave, she would go, too. In his own way, he was still in control."

The light had changed again. The gold was gone, the river black now, with shimmering ever-shifting reflections of the path's lights dancing on it. Abruptly Adele stood up. "We'd better go. It's getting cold."

They started back the way they had come. "Was Connie breaking away from him?" Barbara asked when they reached the steps heading up.

Adele stopped and said slowly. "I don't know. A few weeks ago she said she was grateful that I made her come back from the dead because Eve needed her, what she could do for her. That was the key to Connie. She had an overwhelming need to be needed, not just donations to worthy causes, but personally needed. And she had lost the only ones she felt had truly needed her. Now there was Eve. I don't know if she still felt that about Jay. But if she wasn't breaking away yet, it was coming, and sooner rather than later."

Back in her apartment Barbara put on coffee, then made copious notes, most of them seemed unrelated to the case she was dealing with. But they were connected, she told herself. Everything is eventually.

When done, she stood holding her coffee in the darkened room and watched the reflection of lights on the swimming pool in her apartment complex. They had cleaned and opened it during the past week. The lights moved slowly up and down, an undulating motion under a slight breeze, and she considered what Adele had told her about Jay.

Meg had been dead-on, she thought then, to be afraid for Wally. If Jay hadn't been killed, he would have pressed charges. No doubt, Jay would have brought in a number of witnesses to testify to his good humor, generosity, benevolence, his civic-mindedness, but losing a valuable art object, a family treasure, could not be tolerated.

She trusted Adele's assessment of Connie's mental state. She said Connie had not been suicidal and Barbara believed her. And that meant a double murder as the most likely alternative. Someone in a black van took Connie to the coast and killed her, and a week later drove the same black van to Jay Wilkins's house and killed him. That would make the boat matter irrelevant, since it was found at the house. Wally would be out of it. Forgotten.

But if the investigators wrote Connie's death off as a suicide, and had only one murder to solve, Wally's name would be high on their list of suspects. Trying to avoid a prison sentence was a damn good motive for murder.

ELEVEN

On Friday, Bailey called. His contact had checked in. Connie Wilkins's death occurred between Saturday, the nineteenth, and Monday, the twenty-first. Death by drowning. Most likely a suicide. The nineteenth was the Saturday that Jay took her to the airport in Portland.

When Barbara left the courtroom the following Tuesday, she paused in the corridor to check her cell phone, and found a message from Maria. She called back.

"Mr. Lederer phoned to say the police were there with a search warrant," Maria said. "I knew I couldn't get you so I called your father."

"Good thinking. I'm on my way. Call Martin and tell him I won't be around. See you later." Her client, who had been given a suspended sentence, community service and probation, was in tears at her side. "Emergency," Barbara told her, patting her shoulder. "Just stay the hell away from that discount store in the future." The young woman nod-. ded and tried to smile through her tears.

Barbara was seething when she retrieved her car from the lot across Seventh, and cursing under her breath as she drove through town. Bastards, they timed it for when they knew she'd be in court. It meant they were going to write off Connie's death as a suicide and would not be investigating a possible double murder and anyone who might have had a motive for killing them both. Keep it simple: one suicide, one murder. One easily understood motive, to avoid prison. One prime suspect.

She pulled into the driveway in twenty-five minutes, five minutes less than her previous trip had taken. To her relief she saw that Frank's car was in the driveway, along with a police car and an unmarked car.

A uniformed officer was on the porch watching her as she approached. "Holloway," she said. "Attorney of record for Mr. Lederer." Without waiting for any response she walked past him, opened the screen door and entered.

Meg and Wally were side by side on the sofa, Frank in a straight chair nearby. Meg was pale and thin lipped, but Wally greeted Barbara with his big toothy smile and appeared quite comfortable. One detective was standing near the fireplace as if guarding the evidence bag on the floor at his feet, the other one sat in another straight chair. They were both young, late twenties, early thirties.

The furniture had been moved away from the walls, which had been painted with undercoat. The dismal moldy peach color showed through here and there. Tarps were on the floor, and cans of paint and a ladder near one wall.

"For goodness sake!" Barbara said cheerfully. "You're

having a party and you didn't invite me! For shame. And what on earth are you doing in here? Do you have any idea how many toxins are in the air from fresh paint out-gassing?" She shook her head. "Neither do I, but it's a lot, and poor Meg looks like she's ready to keel over from it. Meg, this can't be good for your sinus condition, and I know it's not good for my father's heart."

She ignored the detectives' scowls as they exchanged furious glances.

"I suggest we move the party to the den," she continued, "where we can all be comfortable. Meg, why don't you and Dad go put on some coffee, whip up a batch of brownies or something. We can't have a party without some nibbles, now can we?"

"Ms. Holloway, I would like to ask your client a few questions," the cop who had been seated said in an icy tone.

"And I want to assist you in every way possible," she said. "But I insist on cleaner air. It's bad enough to fell a horse in here. Come along, gentlemen. This way, I believe."

Wally was already on his feet, and now Frank held out his hand to Meg. "You do look a bit peaked," he said. "Come on. Coffee's a fine idea."

"Your house is looking better and better," Barbara said to Wally as they walked to the den. The two detectives followed. There, Barbara motioned toward the comfortable furnishings. "See, didn't I tell you it would be better in here?"

In the kitchen Meg said in a shaky voice, "She's… she's…"

"She's mad as hell," Frank said, grinning. "Let's make coffee. I'm afraid we'll be here quite a spell after she runs your other guests off."

"Wally," Barbara was saying at the window in the den. "Those new shingles look like scars!"

"Andy, the roofer, said after a few weeks of rain the moss will spread and they'll blend in," he said doubtfully. "I hope so. They sure do look bad now."

"Mr. Lederer, let's get back to it," the detective with a notebook snapped.

"I don't believe I caught your name," Barbara said.

"Jankow. Stephen Jankow. That's Marvin Trusdale. Now, Mr. Lederer, about Saturday, April 26, you said you were out cutting brambles all afternoon. Wearing jeans."

"Poor dear," Barbara murmured to Marvin Trusdale. "He's trying to tame blackberries by hand labor."

Trusdale grinned slightly. Jankow was not amused. His face had turned a darker shade of red than it had been only seconds earlier.

"Mr. Lederer, when you finished for the day, did you keep those jeans on?"

"I already told you all this," Wally said. "They were covered with stickers, leaves, junk, just like they are now." He pointed to the evidence bag. "Meg won't let me wear them inside."

"Detective Jankow, is this a formal interview?" Barbara asked. "I didn't see a stenographer around, but if you trust your memory enough… Anyway, if it is a formal interview and you'll require a signed statement afterward, then I should get out my tape recorder and we should start over. I always tape-record formal interviews. Didn't they tell you that at the office?"

Jankow gritted his teeth, then closed his notebook. "I think we've finished here," he said.

"I suppose you provided a receipt for whatever you intend to take away," Barbara said, pointing to the evidence bag. "Just a formality, we all understand, but routine."

"I gave your father a receipt," he said. He nodded at his partner. "Let's go."

Barbara and Wally walked to the door with the detectives, and she waved when they got inside their car and left with a squeal of rubber. The police car followed.

"Good riddance," she said when they were all out of sight. "What were they after?" she asked Frank, who had come in from the kitchen with Meg.

"Any denim items, shoes and the floor mat of his car."

"They made me change my jeans," Wally said, pointing to the chinos he now wore. "And they took all my shoes." He was wearing slippers. He reached for Barbara's hand, lifted it to his lips and kissed it. "Tiger," he said. "I salute you."

Meg said, "I had no idea you could just make them leave like that."

"They're flunkies," Barbara said. "Did you make coffee? We have things to discuss."

Seated at the old scarred table in the kitchen with coffee before her, Barbara said, "Since they were after denim, we have to assume that they found fibers at the scene of Wilkins's murder. I don't know what all they have and won't know unless and until there's an arrest and I get discovery. That's the evidence they've collected so far. They've had weeks now, so there's going to be a lot. And it appears that they've eliminated other possible suspects to their satisfaction. Meanwhile, you're not to say a word to them unless I'm there. Not the time of day, not your name. Nothing. Tell them on instructions from your attorney you're not to talk to them except in my presence, in my office. Then clam up.

"Next," Barbara said. "I'd like for you to write down everything you can think of concerning Jay Wilkins and those two meetings you had. There has to be a reason for him to have invited you to his place."

"Actually, I started doing that last night," Wally said. "I remembered a couple of things I didn't mention before. More might come to mind. When Jay opened that case to show off the Egyptian stuff, I remembered a time when we were just kids, fourteen, fifteen years old. He sneaked a couple of us into the study once to show off the gold. He told us not to touch anything, his old man would blow if he saw fingerprints on anything. He was scared when he took us in there. Then, that night when he fished out a key ring to open that case, I had the feeling it was just to show that he was master of the keys now. It was all his. He put his whole hand on the glass front, as if to show he was boss."

"And the bar," Meg said. "Remember how he went on about it, how his father had bought it in New Orleans from a brothel, had it dismantled and shipped home and set up. He never was allowed in that room, he said, and now it was his."

"The point is," Wally said, "he hadn't really mentioned his wife until Meg asked if he had heard from her yet. Just bragging about what was his now right up until then. After that, she was all he talked about."

Barbara nodded. "See? As you jog your memories, more and more little bits might come to mind. Just write them all down and we'll see if they are useful later."

For the next hour Barbara outlined what they should expect in the coming days and weeks—possible arrest, arraignment, booking, bail bond hearing. "We'll walk you through every step. And I want you in the office for a long afternoon of my own interrogation later this week." She consulted her calendar. "Let's make it Friday afternoon. And," she added when Wally glanced at his slippers, "I'll get your shoes back. They don't have any possible use for all of them even if they find something suspicious on one pair."

"It's the boat, isn't it?" Meg said. She looked agonized. "That made them turn their attention to Wally."

Barbara nodded. "Maybe. Just remember this, Meg. You saw someone else's car there, and whoever that was either hasn't come forward, or if he did, they're keeping it under wraps. I'll know more after I get discovery. If that person was the murderer, he may be just as afraid as you are. And probably he can't identify you. If he saw you inside the house, it was just for a second or two. For now, we keep it under our hats. Wait and see."

"If he has told the cops," Wally said, "and if they use that against me, that *I* was seen, so be it. *I* took the damn boat back. A practical joke that soured. You remember that, Barbara."

He looked fierce and determined, and Meg's anguish only deepened. Barbara nodded. She would remember.

TWELVE

On her way back to the office, Barbara made a mental list of all the things she had to wrap up in the coming days to clear the decks, get ready for anything. It was a long list, and the first thing on it was marching orders for Bailey.

At seven, her stomach making ferocious noises, and a faint headache coming on, she thought about lunch. She had skipped it, and then she thought about dinner, closed the folder in front of her and got ready to leave. She paused. Darren. She was supposed to let him know. He had asked her to go with him and Todd to a friend's place on the coast. She would have her own room, he had said, and the friends kept horses, theirs to ride all weekend. She placed the call.

"I'm sorry," she said. "I really can't. I'm totally swamped. I'll be working late and on through the weekend, I'm afraid."

After a long pause he said he was sorry, too. "Another time," he said. "I'll be in touch."

She closed her eyes and nodded. Another time. A mix of regret and relief left her feeling more confused than ever.

When Meg and Wally arrived Friday afternoon, he was wearing work boots. He held up his foot to show her. "I sort of like them. Just the thing for those brambles out back."

She laughed and motioned toward the seating arrangement at the coffee table. "As it happens," she said, "I have your shoes. Five pairs? Is that right?"

"That's what they took," Wally said. He and Meg sat side by side on the sofa and Barbara in the wing chair. She started what she knew was going to be a long, grueling afternoon.

When Wally began to talk about his cell mate from years ago, Meg said, "When Joey died, the chaplain wrote to Wally and thanked him for giving comfort during Joey's last years. The warden signed it, too."

"Bring it next time," Barbara said. "Anything that you have. A complete video of the show Wally does, anything like that."

She kept them until a little after five. After she saw them out, she sent Maria home. "I'm going to make notes for another hour, but you don't have to stay." She had made a few notes as Wally talked. But she wanted as full an account as possible while it was all fresh in her mind.

It was a little past seven when she leaned back, stretched, then cleaned off her desk, and left the office. When she pulled up in front of her apartment building and got out, the sun was still shining and the air was still warm. It was the perfect time of day for a walk, but she was too tired to make the effort.

She came to a stop when she saw Darren sitting on her front step. "What are you doing here?" she demanded.

"Waiting for you. Have you eaten?"

She shook her head.

"Neither have I. Let's go eat."

"I thought you were heading out to the coast."

"Tomorrow. Todd's invited a pal and he can't get away until about ten in the morning."

He took her arm, and turned her around. "Want to show you my new car, and if you're as hungry as I am, you're more than ready for some food."

She resisted only for a moment, then made up her mind. After they ate, she would tell him this had to stop. She could not stand being so confused—eager to see him, then backing away, wanting to go to bed with him, knowing it would be a mistake. An affair with him would be tantamount to a commitment, and she wouldn't, couldn't make such a commitment. The tension was there, almost palpable, and it was making her crazy. It had to stop. She couldn't think how to tell him, but words would come after she ate something. She would know by then.

THIRTEEN

"Todd wanted an SUV so we could haul a dozen of his pals at a time," Darren said, getting behind the wheel of his new car. "I drew the line. Four's the limit. I don't know yet what all the buttons and dials are for, but Todd does. He informs me in a pitying tone."

He drove easily, talked easily. Barbara leaned back in the passenger seat and listened.

"He's getting quite a circle of friends who seem to need constant driving here and there, so the truck just didn't work any longer...."

She closed her eyes and let herself drift to the music of his voice. When they stopped, she felt herself stiffen, and gave him a swift glance. They were at the Italian restaurant they had gone to once before, barely on speaking terms. He seemed oblivious.

Even the same table, she thought with dismay when they entered and were seated. She could remember nothing of that meal except that they had argued throughout dinner. From the start they had been wary of each other, as if they had both recognized from their first encounter that the other was a force to be reckoned with. She had cleared him and Annie McIvey of the murder of Annie's husband, but instead of expressing anything like gratitude, he had picked a quarrel. Or she had. She couldn't remember how it had begun, only that it had persisted throughout dinner.

He ordered a bottle of Soave as soon as the waiter appeared. "And focaccia, for starters," he added, then picked up his menu.

She consulted her own menu. They had started off arguing, but they wouldn't finish that way, she thought furiously. Keep it light and friendly, no arguments.

The wine and bread arrived and they ordered. "Sicilian halibut," Barbara said. After the waiter left she said, "I have no idea what I just ordered. Life's just one big gamble, isn't it?"

She began to talk about her new client. "He's incredible. A reformed pickpocket, with a highly paid act that uses his skill. Truly ambidextrous apparently. He shakes your hand with one of his, and steals your wallet with the other."

Darren laughed. "That would be pretty useful for some of my clients. This one guy had an accident, mountain climbing, that left him paralyzed in his right arm, his dominant arm. It took him six months of arduous therapy to retrain his brain and muscles in order to switch to a lefty, a pretty awkward lefty at that."

"Wally's going to give me a tape of his whole act," she said. "I'll put on a private viewing, a few invited guests.

See if any of us can spot him in the act. I couldn't in the demo." She stopped abruptly and looked away, regretting her words. Darren refilled her glass, then leaned back as the waiter came with their dinners.

A few minutes later, Darren said, "It isn't fair that you know all about my family and I know so little about yours, except for your father, I mean. My old man, a crooked cop who dropped out of sight to mingle with the great nameless masses and never surfaced again, sister married to a gangster, mother now married to a good, square-headed Dutch farmer who drinks whole milk with every meal. Tell me something about your mother."

Barbara looked at him in surprise. It was true, she had never really talked about her mother, it had been too painful. Slowly she said, "She was wonderful, beautiful, warm, nurturing, generous, and she ran the household like a drill sergeant. Often, when Dad was working late, you know, caught up in a case and not minding the time, she made dinner and took his to him while it was still hot. Sometimes I went with her." A vivid memory of wandering in the corridor outside his office rose in her mind. She had looked in the library, some of the other offices, and she had known that was what she wanted. She would be a lawyer, like her father.

"They gardened together, except when he got busy and didn't have time and she just did it. I can't remember that she ever complained, not then, not later, never."

"Maybe that explains his garden now," Darren said when she paused. "Making up for the times he didn't. Something like that."

"So we seek redemption. Maybe. I know he loves it.

And he takes the time. When I was very small I wanted to be just like my mother. She was the perfect wife, perfect mother, a perfect role model."

"For someone else," Darren said. "Not for you."

Barbara laughed and sipped her wine. "Right. I'm opposite her in every possible way."

"Was she happy?"

"I think so. When I went through my teens I thought she was a patsy, a doormat. Later I realized that she had what she wanted. She was indispensable to my father. She tried hard to teach me how to cook, how to sew, how to become more feminine, I guess, but I failed her miserably and she accepted me exactly as I am. So of course I felt guilty for not trying harder, and ashamed." She shook her head and said almost brusquely, "Enough. What's going on at the clinic these days?"

He told her some of the current gossip. The conversation moved easily to other topics as they finished their meals. After the table had been cleared, the waiter brought the dessert menu. Barbara waved it away. "No way. Not another bite."

"Tiramisu," Darren said. "We'll share it. And coffee for two."

They ate the sinfully good dessert and drank their coffee in near silence. It was a perfect ending to their relationship, a good evening, good talk, nothing mean or hateful to regret later.

Not in the car, she decided as they drove back to her apartment. For once she would ask him in. The first time.

At her door, before she could find the right words, Darren said, "I want to come in with you. We have to talk."

"I know we do." She unlocked her door.

Inside her apartment she switched on a table lamp and dropped her purse and briefcase on a chair. He set her laptop down.

She drew in a long breath, then said, "Darren, this is hard, harder than—"

He put his finger on her lips. "Didn't your mother teach you to let the guest go first?" He took her hand in a firm clasp. "You know I love you. I've loved you for a long time. I thought I could win with patience and cunning and good planning. I was wrong."

She tried to pull away, but his grip was firm and unyielding. "I'm sorry," she said. "I think I love you, too, but—"

He touched her lips again. "I'm not done," he said. "I think you love me, and I think if we got married we would both be happy for a time. It wouldn't last. Your sense of duty and responsibility would tear you apart. You would change. You're your mother's daughter, but also your father's child. And that mixture is the woman I love, not the one you might try to become. I don't want to change you in any way."

"I'm sorry!" she cried. "I love you but I can't marry you. I can't marry at all. I'm not the marrying kind, but you are. You need a stable relationship, companionship, everything a good marriage provides, and I can't do it. I'm selfish. I want my own life too much, my life, my work. I can't help it!"

He drew her close and held her, his cheek against her hair. "Don't define my needs," he said softly. "What I need is a deep, lifelong friendship. One that won't erode and turn bitter, trust and openness, someone I can confide in, who will confide in me. Someone I can count on. Who will call me if I'm needed. That's what a real friend is all about. We can't have a conventional friendship. The girl next door, childhood friend, friends forever. That isn't for us. There's too much sexual tension between us. The air crackles with it. It would drive us both mad. Maybe it already is driving us mad."

She could feel hot tears gathering but he was holding her too tightly to wipe her eyes. He loosened his hold and, keeping her hands in his, his gaze intense as he watched her face, he said, "Conventions say such a friendship must be platonic, but who wrote those rules? When have you ever accepted conventions as your guide? We can have the friendship we both need, without ties, without guilt, without being pulled apart in two directions, just an acceptance of each other. That's what I'm proposing, Barbara. A lifelong, very special friendship." He touched her cheek. "I've never seen you cry before. I want to make love to you."

Silently she nodded.

FOURTEEN

"I gazed into my crystal ball and came up with a probable time line," Barbara said on Sunday evening. "Tomorrow Wally gives his formal statement. I'll be tied up with a plea bargain Thursday, and they'll just happen to arrest him on Thursday."

"And I'll just happen to be batting the breeze with the fellows at the station when they bring him in," Frank said. "They might hold him overnight, but by Friday he'll be back at the homestead."

She nodded. "God, I'll be glad when Shelley's back."

"We'll have a welcome home dinner."

"Wally's going to bring me a couple of videos and some letters or something. We'll have a private video show. I'll invite Darren and Todd if that's okay with you."

He nodded, waiting for more, but she was off on another topic already.

"I wish I knew Wally better," she said. "I still don't

know how much of what I see is his performer's face, how much is his own."

Frank was gazing at the cats, sprawled in the sunlight like two road kills. "I can tell you this much about him," he said. "He is almost exactly the same as when he was a kid. Same big grin showing every tooth in his head. He took his punishment without a whimper. He got caught and expected more punishment than he got and he was grateful for that. He also refused to betray his accomplice. His attitude was fair's fair, and I'm pretty certain it still is. But keep in mind that he is more devoted to Meg than most men who have been married for forty years. And he absolutely won't let her go through any of the hell he's been through with the law."

Barbara nodded. "Aye, and there's the rub. If he says he took the damn boat back, the odds of being convicted for murder shoot up sky-high, and he knows it. To date, what Meg has told the police is that they worked all day on the house, ate dinner and watched a movie. So she hasn't actually lied yet."

"Once they arrest him, she'll be out of it," Frank said slowly. "And she certainly won't be called as a witness."

They regarded each other soberly for a few seconds. Then Barbara raised her glass in a semi-salute and drained it.

Her prescience proved flawless, and by two o'clock Friday afternoon, it had all come to pass. Wally and Meg were on their way back home. Barbara was in her office scanning the day's mail when there was a tap on the door. It opened and Shelley said, "Got a minute?" Barbara had never been so glad to see anyone.

She rushed to embrace her. "You look wonderful! Why are you home? We didn't expect you yet. How was the cruise?"

Laughing, Shelley led the way to the sofa and they sat down. She had a deep glowing tan and her hair had bleached out to a pale gold. It was shorter than it had been. And she was radiant.

"Alex was sketching a lot, but not finishing anything, and I kept wondering what was going on here, and we both said, 'Let's go home.' So here we are. It was a fabulous trip, fairy-tale stuff, but even Adam and Eve must have wondered what was on the other side of the wall. We wanted to come home and go back to work. I have tons of pictures and a few things I brought back. Alex has stacks of mail, e-mail messages, letters from his agent. It will take him weeks to plow through it, and he told me to beat it before you left for the day. So I did." She said this in a rush with no pauses. "What's been going on?"

"Too much to cover in a few minutes," Barbara said. "A new client, murder charge, like that."

Shelley caught in her breath. "I just knew it. Tell me about it."

Barbara started. At four-thirty Shelley stopped her and said, "Remember how we used to get take-out food, burritos and stuff, and take it to your apartment to eat while we talked? Let's do that now. I told Alex I might run late and he said good."

After Barbara cleaned off her desk, they went to Taco Loco, ordered far too much food, and took it to Barbara's apartment where they sat at her small table and proceeded to eat most of it.

"That was so good!" Shelley said, leaning back. "You can't get a decent chile relleno on a single island in Hawaii."

"Too many coincidences," Barbara said, bringing her account up to the present. "Connie Wilkins vanishes and ends up in the ocean, her husband is killed, and on the same day his daughter has a psychotic break." She scowled. "And the cops aren't even considering a double murder, one killer."

"I see your point," Shelley said. "Then, there's the boat. That's the problem, isn't it? Do you think Jay Wilkins would have pressed charges?"

"From what little I know about him it seems likely." She got up to make coffee. "I think the real question is why did Wilkins set up Wally. And I haven't come up with anything that remotely resembles an answer.

"Anyway, I'll be getting discovery next week and maybe a whole raft of suspects will come to light. And I have to find a way to meet and talk to Stephanie Breaux and her family, even if I can't question the daughter."

"I know Stephanie Breaux," Shelley said thoughtfully. "She's a very good shopkeeper. I go in there now and then. She remembers her customers' names, their taste, more or less their measurements."

"What else? What's she like aside from running a good shop?"

"Tall, a little taller than you, very dignified, elegant in an old-world sort of way. Dark hair turning a little gray, in a chignon, reserved in her manner and conservative in her clothes. Just elegant and refined. Want me to talk to her?"

Barbara shook her head. "I'd better do it. It might make

a difference in that you're a customer. I don't want to talk to the saleswoman, but to the ex-wife of Jay Wilkins and the mother of his two kids, whom he apparently despised. What I really need to find out is something about the daughter. How passive is she during her psychotic breaks?"

"Dr. Minnick," Shelley said promptly. "You know that was his specialty for most of his career back in New York, treating mentally disturbed youngsters. He knows all about schizophrenia."

"Bailey's due on Monday, discovery will start coming in, and we'll go on from there. Next Sunday, Dad's house for a celebratory dinner, and Dr. Minnick is invited. We'll have a private showing of Wallis Lederer, the great sleight of hand artist."

"Not much yet on Wilkins," Bailey said on Monday, as gloomy as usual, and as thirsty. That time of day he settled for coffee, although any time after three he headed straight for the bar. "Neighbors thought he was a pain in the neck, complained about kids leaving stuff in sight, an old truck, a bicycle too close to the street, things like that. He liked his neighborhood kept neat and clean. He was ready to sue at the drop of a soda can. People at the dealership were pretty tight-lipped, but he was not universally loved there, either. A stickler for keeping things clean, following rules, his rules. Not motives for bumping him off, just a general attitude that suggests they aren't going to spend a lot of time grieving. When guys begin bumping off bosses they don't like there'll be a real shortage of management. He was involved in a deal to get his hands on two other lots, used cars here in Eugene, a lot for used SUVs, trucks, vans in Salem. It would have taken a million up front to close the deal."

"He didn't have a million up front," Frank said. "Millions in possessions, nowhere near that kind of cash at hand. Like farmers, land rich, cash poor. Or at least not rolling in it."

Bailey consulted his notebook. A folder he had placed on the table had his full reports with details. "No big black car yet," he said. "Not one that belongs to anyone involved, or else is unaccounted for. No autopsy yet for Connie Wilkins, full name Constantina. Why would anyone hang a name like that on a helpless baby? She was pretty battered by rocks and stuff, wave action. It's going to take a few more days, a week. A special FBI pathologist was called in. Her sister will fly in to claim the remains and take her home."

Jay's only living relatives were his two children, and one distant cousin in New Hampshire, Bailey continued. "The Gormandi and Breaux shop is solvent, not making a fortune, but providing an okay living for the two partners after a couple of rough years during the recession. And no one at the Cedar View hospital will even admit that Eve Wilkins is a patient from time to time. Period," Bailey said, closing his notebook.

"And for this I pay your outrageous fees," Barbara said. "Okay. I'll have more in a couple of days, probably."

He helped himself to more coffee.

"Anything about the people who sued Wilkins?"

He shook his head. "The sales manager got canned, and walked into another job just like the last one. Seems innovative sales managers are in high demand. The guys who sued got a small settlement and moved on. And that's it."

Later, Barbara sat at her desk thinking about various things Bailey had reported. Adele, she decided.

"I understand that Connie Wilkins's sister will fly out to claim her body and take her home," she said. "Will you be seeing her when she's here?"

Adele hesitated, then said, "I've talked to her. She's pretty torn up over this, blaming herself and her brother for not doing something when they could have. She'll stay at my place while she's in town. Why do you ask?"

"I want to talk to her," Barbara said. "Like you, I think the idea of suicide stinks to high heaven."

"That really doesn't answer my question," Adele said after another hesitation. "What does Connie's death have to do with you, and Jay's death?"

"I honestly don't know," Barbara said. "My client is accused of killing him, and I know he's innocent. I want some answers, too. Maybe we can help each other."

"I'll see what I can do, but no promises."

"Good enough. Thanks, Adele."

She hung up and thought some more. After another moment, she placed a second call, this time to Randolf Berman, who had been Jay's attorney and was now in charge of the estate.

"Ms. Holloway, what can I do for you?" he asked in his best lawyerly manner.

"As you may know, I am the defense attorney for Wallis Lederer, who has been charged with the murder of Jay Wilkins," she said, just as smoothly. "I understand the scene of the crime has been unsealed by the investigators and is under your supervision. I want permission to inspect the scene."

His voice was noticeably cooler when he said, "I'm afraid that would be very inconvenient at this time. There are two estates to settle, and at present an inventory of the house contents is underway. On completion of that both estates require appraisals, and this will all take a good bit of time. If I can get back in touch with you at a later date?"

"I'm afraid that won't do," she said. "As the defense attorney in this matter I cannot be denied permission to inspect the crime scene, and I want to do so before anything is changed. As you know, I can get a court order to accomplish this, however I much prefer not to have to go that route."

When he spoke again his tone was so icy she could almost feel the chill on her receiver. "The inventory should be completed by tomorrow. I shall speak to Eric Wilkins about this. He can accompany you. He knows that nothing is to be removed or even handled. I trust you will honor that condition, as well."

Send the enemy to keep me under surveillance, she thought. "Fine," she said. "I'll give him a call tomorrow to arrange a time."

After hanging up, she muttered, "Stiff-necked bastard, don't talk to me about convenience when my client's life is at stake."

FIFTEEN

Tuesday evening Eric Wilkins stood by his mother at the kitchen sliding door and watched Eve in the garden. "She's okay now?" he asked.

Stephanie nodded. Eve, dressed in shorts and an old T-shirt, was on her knees attacking weeds with fierce concentration. "The same as ever. Earlier she scolded Reggie for letting the snails get out of hand. Tomorrow they'll go to the garden center and get bait of some sort."

Eve treated each plant as an individually prized treasure, noticed if a brown spot occurred on a leaf, or if a hole appeared. She tried to track down each offending critter to dispatch it, or used a soap spray, or put down bait. Nothing toxic was allowed, no weeds.

He turned away and said, "Mother, let's talk a minute before I go out and say hi."

She nodded toward the table where she had been looking at the drawings Eve had made since she had come home. It was always like that. She returned wan and list-less, the only energy she had was when she used her pastel sticks and drew. The pictures were always the same, colors without edges, a semicircle of a wall of color, with streaks of fire-red throughout. Centered in the foreground was a single object, disproportionately small, colorless. Sometimes it looked like a rock, sometimes a human figure without any real definition. The pictures had movement of their own, the wall was advancing, threatening…

Stephanie moved the half-dozen new pictures aside. "You look harried," she said, regarding her son.

"Meetings with lawyers. Connie's and his. Berman gave me a key to the padlock on the house, with strict orders not to take anything out. There's an inventory, he said, as if he's afraid I'll go in with a gunnysack and raid the place. Appraisers will come in next week. He told me that the defense lawyer for the guy charged with the murder wants to have a look, and it's my duty to accommodate her. It would not be convenient for him to do it."

"You don't have to do it," she said quickly. "It isn't your duty."

"It's not a problem," he said. "I'm taking all my days off now, vacation time, sick leave, all of it. I can't work anyway while so much is going on. Berman's arranging for a memorial service. He said the community expects it. He wants me to be there." He smiled his crooked little smile and turned to gaze at his sister. "I'll wear jeans and a T-shirt, if I go at all. And it seems the heir to Dad's estate is named Sylvester Wilkins."

"He's Jay's third cousin or something like that," Stephanie said absently.

Eric looked at her with an ironic grin. "Isn't he going to be surprised when he finds out he's inherited a million or more! At least it won't go to a dog or cat hospital."

Stephanie bit her lip. Eric turned back to gaze at his sister and she asked, "What was on the mind of Connie's lawyer?"

"He said Connie's sister is coming to claim the body and take her home, and while she's here she should go to the house and put aside whatever personal effects she wants. That was in Connie's will, that she's to have first pick of things like that, jewelry, clothes, photographs, whatever. He asked me if I would go with her, since Connie spoke to her about me, about all of us, and I would be sympathetic. She can't take anything away, just put it in a box or something. Nothing can be removed until the estates are probated." He stopped abruptly and went to the sink to get a glass of water.

"I like that lawyer, Stan Konig. I asked him to represent me through this. He knows I can't pay him until it's all straightened out, but he said that's okay," Eric said.

He was too young, she thought, for this kind of burden. Too young to be slapped across the face by his dead father and his mean-spirited will.

"Have you told Eve anything yet?" Eric asked at the sink.

"Only that they are both dead. We haven't talked about it. I'm not sure she really comprehends it yet."

"When it sinks in that Connie's gone, she'll take it hard," he said. "Well, I'll go say hi."

She followed him out and watched as brother and sister greeted each other.

"Hey, pig, finding any truffles?" he called, approaching Eve. They always had been like that, teasing a little, close, loving, accepting.

Eve stood up, looked at her knees crusted with dirt, and held up her grimy hands. She smiled the same crooked smile as his. She was so thin, Stephanie thought with a pang. She came home thinner every time. Eve drew near Eric and reached out. Before he could duck, she had taken his face in both her hands, and deliberately dragged them across his cheeks, leaving streaks of dirt.

"Why should I be the only dirty one around here?" she said, and laughed.

He was laughing too as he backed away. "You little devil. I'll get you for that."

"I'll wash up and, Eric, darling, I think you should do likewise. Your face is dirty."

Still laughing, she went to the door, stopped and turned back, all traces of amusement gone. "Did you know Connie's dead?" She directed her question at Eric. He nodded. "Dad killed her," Eve said. "He knew she liked us and he hated her for it so he killed her. I hope he's burning in hell now and forever." She entered the house.

Stephanie sank into a chair, stunned, and Eric was too shocked to speak.

Then he said, "Comprehend, hell. For God's sake, she can't go around saying that!"

Stephanie nodded, moistened her lips that had gone stiff and strange, and said, "I'll talk to her."

When Barbara reached the Wilkins mansion that Thursday, she spotted Bailey's vintage green Dodge already parked on the street. He said his car was meant to blend in, not be noticeable, but it was so old that people interested in antiques probably regarded it with awe, wondering how it managed to keep rolling, unaware that the engine and other moving parts were top of the line and recent. Bailey was taking exterior photographs. She stopped to wait for him.

When he got into his car and started it again, she drove slowly up the semicircular driveway. Rhododendrons were in full bloom in the space between the drive and the street along with two dogwood trees, already past their blooming season and other bushy plants. Eric Wilkins's little black car, garish with decals, was parked at the entrance. It would never be mistaken for a van, no matter how rainy and dark. She parked behind it with Bailey right behind her.

A covered, ten-foot wide portico, paved with brick-red flagstones with several shallow steps, extended from the house to the drive. On the topmost landing was a massive dark door with a stained-glass light. She rang the bell.

Eric Wilkins opened the door. He looked younger than she had expected, Barbara thought as she introduced herself and Bailey. Young and very good-looking with dark hair that was thick and down slightly past his ears. His eyes were dark blue, and skeptical as he looked Bailey over. Barbara couldn't blame him for that. Bailey didn't look like an investigator or a photographer, either. He looked like a bum. And Barbara, dressed in blue jeans and a T-shirt, had to admit that she didn't look much like an attorney.

"As I mentioned on the phone," she said, entering the house, "I'd like to get some pictures, if you have no objection."

He waved his hand in a general manner. "Whatever."

The foyer floor was a continuation of the unpolished flagstones that had acquired a faintly glowing luster over the years, with shadowed hollows and gleaming highlights. Centered was a deep green, plush floor runner with gold leaves twining the length. It ran through the spacious foyer, up wide stairs to a railed landing. Two magnificent Chinese vases in the same green and gold were against one wall, a long wooden bench along the other. A few scenic tapestries were the only wall decorations.

"I'd like some shots from the balcony, or landing, whatever it is, if that's okay," Barbara said, thinking of what Meg had said: it had been dark up there, and in the back halls by each side of the stairs. She wanted shots from both of those sides, too.

Eric shrugged. "Sure."

"And the study? Maybe we can have a look first, then let Bailey go to work with his camera."

Obligingly, Eric motioned toward a door about twenty feet down the foyer. Beyond it was another door, and the flagstones appeared to end just past it. Eric noticed her interest and said, "Guest lavatory. Want a look?"

She nodded. It would have been shadowed, too, she thought. Someone could have stepped in there, could have glanced out to see Meg. Eric opened the door to the lavatory. It had rich gold carpeting, pale gold twin washbasins with gold spigots, a crinkled-glass partition screening the toilet. Pale gold hand towels with dark gold monograms matched the decor. Even the soap, in the shape of leaves, was gold.

"My forebears liked the color of gold," Eric said dryly, standing at the door. "My great-grandfather came west and made like Paul Bunyan. New money, spend it big. Build a mansion. I guess by now, three generations later, it would be considered old money."

They went back to the study where the carpet was russet, but the drapes were pale gold. Barbara walked across to the glass-fronted case on one wall. "Is that where the boat was?"

"Ever since I can remember," he said, leaning against the door frame. "Afraid I can't open the case for you. Different circuit on the security system and I don't have the key or the password for it. They changed the one for the front door so I can get in, nothing else. I can still look but can't touch."

She looked at him swiftly, but could detect no bitterness in his voice or his expression. He appeared more amused than bitter, in fact. She glanced over the other objects in the case, ancient Egyptian for the most part, and probably the whole collection was worth a fortune.

The desk was L-shaped with a computer and printer on the short side, the keyboard on a sliding shelf. On the right side, the side nearest the foyer door, there were three drawers.

Come in the front door, twenty feet or so to this spot, open the bottom drawer and drop in the boat, head back out. Less than a minute, just as Meg had said.

"Okay," she said. "Onward. The bar room."

It was across the wide foyer, the door a few feet farther back than the study door. No one in it would have been visible to Meg that night without going to the door. Inside, she said, "Oh, my." The room was very large, the paving stones continued inside as far as the bar extended, about twelve feet, then more gold carpeting. A long, curved sofa in cream-colored leather was back twelve feet or so from a giant television screen. The sofa had cushions of red and black piled on one end. Several other upholstered chairs in the same creamy covering flanked it, and there were two glass-topped tables with their own chairs with red or black seats. Gold drapes were wall to wall, with filtered light showing through them. Even the lighting in the room had taken on a golden hue.

"You expect to see the furniture pushed back and a bright and shiny Buick on display," Eric commented, then walked behind the bar. "Teak," he said, pounding the countertop. "Stools, too. Heavy as sin. Black as sin."

A brilliant brass foot rail gleamed against the black teak. The rungs of the bar stools were of the same heavy brass, the swivel seats were black. Barbara's gaze lingered on a gold-and-white antique telephone. So far that was the only thing she had seen that she might covet. The bar was as well stocked as any commercial bar she had ever been in.

"You want a drink?" Eric asked. "Name it, bet I have it back here somewhere."

Barbara smiled and shook her head, and Bailey said, "Thanks, but I'd better get some shots now." She thought he showed incredible self-control.

"You want to keep an eye on me?" Bailey asked, setting his duffel bag down.

"What for? Go shoot away," Eric said.

Bailey ambled out, and Barbara said, "Mr. Wilkins, I really appreciate your cooperation. It must be difficult since I'm the defense attorney for the man charged with killing your father."

He smiled, "Eric, just Eric. Funny, I haven't been in this

house for over ten years, but nothing's changed, not a single thing. It's exactly the same way it was the day I walked out. Here he was always Mr. Wilkins, and I was just Eric. That hasn't changed, either." He pulled a bar stool closer and sat down, put his forearms on the bar, then said, "Ms. Holloway, I know who you are and what you do, your interest in this case, all that. I want to tell you frankly that if your client did kill my father, I know beyond a doubt that he had a good reason. I wouldn't lift a finger to help convict him. In fact, I'll do anything I possibly can to help you. If you get him off, more power to you and to him."

SIXTEEN

When Bailey returned, Barbara was on a stool by the bar, Eric on the other side. He broke off what he had been saying and leaned back as Bailey entered.

"Let's move out of the way," Barbara said. "Let him get some shots of the bar." They both moved away to watch him. When he was done, he snapped a few pictures of the rest of the room. Then Barbara said slowly, "Eric, maybe you'd like to step out a few minutes. I want to see how the crime was actually committed, as well as I can, anyway."

He shook his head. "I'm okay. I'll keep back and watch."

She took the police photos of the scene and put them on the bar and she and Bailey examined them.

"This stool was leaning against that one," Bailey said, positioning a stool. "And that one was all the way down. That's what he hit when he fell. It broke his neck." The autopsy report said the blow to the head had not been fatal, but would have had sufficient force to stun him, even render him unconscious. Bailey frowned at the picture again, then at the repositioned stools. "How the devil…?"

"Start further back," she said. "Bark mulch was tracked in, about here. They are close to each other and the assailant reaches for the pitcher, swings it and hits him in the temple." She frowned, too, then. "And what is Wilkins doing while the other guy arms himself? Just waiting?"

"Let's try again," Bailey said, standing both stools upright. "They're going at it. One guy is backed up to the bar." He stood with his back against the bar. "Okay. He reaches behind him and grabs the pitcher and swings it before the other guy can duck." He reached for an imaginary pitcher and followed through with the motion. Then he took the victim's role. "So he's hit and reels back, and bumps the first stool as he's falling." He twisted himself and hit the stool hard enough to make it tilt over. "He keeps twisting, maybe trying not to fall, and goes down. But he lands on the other stool rung and it gets knocked down, and also breaks his neck."

They both looked at the police photograph again. This time Barbara nodded. "That must be it." She looked closely at the bar stool, now on the floor, imagining a head coming down in such a way as to fall between the seat and the brass rung. There was plenty of space, and the brass was thick, the legs of the stool heavy teak wood, it could easily have broken his neck if he fell hard enough. "I think that's it." She and Bailey exchanged a look and he nodded. Neither of them mentioned that in the photo Jay Wilkins's head was free of the stool. It appeared that he had been moved after he died.

Eric had watched the reenactment with fascinated horror as the attorney and her investigator dispassionately played out the death scene. He turned away.

"Okay, Bailey, you're done here," Barbara said briskly, standing the stool upright again. "Get me copies as soon as you can."

"Okey dokey," he said. "See you." He picked up his duffel bag, and ambled out.

Barbara replaced the photographs in a folder, put it back in her big bag, then said to Eric, who was still facing away, "Are you okay?"

Not looking at her, he said, "Sure. I was just thinking how much it would have meant to a kid to watch *Star Wars* on a screen like that. I was never allowed in here in those days, and now you couldn't pay me to sit on that sofa, watch that TV." He turned around. He was pale, his jaw rigid. "I put a six-pack in the fridge when I got here. Let's go out to the kitchen."

He led the way through the halls, past closed doors, another hall, then into a huge kitchen with enough cabinets to have served a restaurant.

"You want a beer?" he asked, going to the refrigerator.

"Thanks, but no. I'm fine."

"Coffee? How about a double espresso over ice? Good summer drink."

She started to say no again, but then, understanding that he wanted something to do for another minute or two, she said that sounded great. She walked to a back door and gazed out over a small, beautifully landscaped area. Behind it Hendricks Park climbed the butte, topped with a wonderland of rhododendrons.

When the coffee was ready and they were seated at a big kitchen worktable, Eric opened his beer and took a long drink.

"You were telling me about the wills," she reminded him.

"Yeah. Both lawyers said it could be months before everything's settled. There are legal issues with the dealership, others involved or something. Mother can't believe it, and won't until transfers are made and money's in the bank. I can hardly believe it, either."

Suddenly he grinned and said, "We're out of it, the murder, I mean. The police checked. My partner—" He stopped, keeping his gaze on her intently, then said, "You know about me? I'm gay?"

She nodded.

Apparently he was waiting for a reaction. When there was none, he continued. "Paul, my partner, turned thirty that week and we had a party for him that Saturday. Big thirty. Celebrate or mourn? He wanted to mourn and we wouldn't let him. Lots of food, beer, music, a couple of downloaded videos, and then a bunch of us sat up talking for hours, settled all the world's problems, and conked out around dawn." He drank again.

She knew exactly what kind of party he was talking about since she had attended many just like it at his age.

He was going on. "Mother's completely out of it, too," he said. "Eve had a break that evening. Mother calls them episodes, but they're psychotic breaks even if she can't admit it. Eve just collapses. Wherever she is, whatever she's doing, doesn't matter. She sinks down into a fetal position and she'd stay like that for days, maybe until she died, if someone wasn't there to help her. She can't move by herself, can't control her functions… Anyway, she's never left alone, especially when she's helpless like that." More softly he said, "I don't think Mother's had a real day off for more than ten or twelve years."

He talked for a long time that afternoon while he sat at the table, sometimes looking at Barbara, then at the view outside, but most often, she thought, gazing into a troubled past. Much of what he told her was little more than a different viewpoint of what she had heard from Adele, but some of it was new. His grandmother, Jay's mother, had been demented, he said. She heard voices, gradually began talking back to them, and by the time Eric was five or six, she was screaming obscenities at the voices only she could hear.

"I didn't know an old woman like that even knew those words. I had no idea what a lot of them meant. They put her away. The story was that she'd had a debilitating stroke, was vegetative, but that was a lie. She was psychotic." He turned to gaze outside.

"That's what scares Mother the most, how that old woman lost it. The doctor says it isn't going to happen to Eve. She's being treated, monitored, and the fact that she went two whole years without a break is an excellent sign. They never had a doctor for Grandmother, no treatment, just put her away, out of sight, out of mind, too shameful to admit. And *he* called us *Mother's* twisted children." For the first time he sounded bitter.

"There's a genetic tendency, and it comes from his side, not hers. But the line stops here. It's for sure I'm not going to have any kids, and neither will Eve. End of the line."

In a dispassionate tone he told her about Jay's will. "I'd be willing to bet he hired someone to look up that branch of the family in New England, make sure their blood was pure, no sign of mental illness, or other weirdness." He finished his beer and got another one.

When he talked briefly about Connie's death he showed more emotion than his father's murder had elicited. "That's shitty. She made a real difference in their lives, Mother's and Eve's. This past break was the first time Mother didn't have to borrow money to pay the hospital bill. And later, there's going to be plenty to make sure Eve will be taken care of as long as she lives. She'll never have to end up in an institution. Just knowing that makes a huge difference."

When Barbara asked if he thought Connie might have been suicidal, his answer was quick and emphatic. "No way! She had a deep sadness, you could see it in her expression sometimes, but I think Eve made a difference in her life almost as much as she did in Eve's. She seemed determined to help my sister and seemed to love her without reservation. That's…so much more than my father ever did."

He told about the past Christmas, when Connie had brought Eve a thick book about fashions through the ages, how Reggie, Connie and Eve had sat thumbing through it, and breaking up in schoolgirl giddiness over the bustles.

"I wondered how long it had been since Connie had laughed like that," he said softly. "I think a long time." He laughed. "I didn't want to meet her. Mother sort of coerced me. I was all set to dislike her. After all, she had married my father, what could there be to like? But I did like her a lot. She was great. Eve is going to miss her."

In the pause that followed, a distant clocked chimed four and, apparently startled, Eric checked his watch. "I have to go," he said. For a moment he looked awkward and boyish. "I didn't realize I wanted to talk like that. Thanks for listening."

Barbara shook her head. "I'm grateful to you. I needed a better picture of your father and you've been helpful."

The picture she was forming, she thought as she drove back to the office, was of a complex man who had been terribly afraid of mental illness and homosexuality, who valued possessions over persons, who had a compulsive need to be in control, and if he lost control, wanted the unmanageable object or person put away.

Something Eric had said about Eve came to mind: she had to fight to keep control of all visual input, to maintain the world she saw as made of distinct and separate objects. Things rushing at her, like a beach ball at one time, a cluster of leaves caught in a gust of wind, anything rushing at her made the control slip and she fled in the only way she could, mentally. Both of them with the same need, expressed in very different ways, but basically they had shared the same need to maintain control.

A question followed swiftly. Had Jay Wilkins recognized that he was losing control of Connie?

She was very thoughtful when she reentered her office. What all that other business had to do with Wally or with Jay's murder she couldn't have said, but there was a connection, she was sure.

On Saturday Darren called. "Can you drop in for some dinner this evening? Todd's at his mother's this weekend."

"I can't," she said. "Too much to do, I'm afraid."

"Barbara, you have to eat. We can do it together. I'll make something quick and easy. I have something to show you."

"For just a short time," she said. But she felt awkward when she rang his doorbell that evening. She knew Darren had reservations about making love to her if Todd was home, and she would have refused anyway, but she had not expected to feel anything of the same reserve knowing his son was in Springfield. She had not asked him into her apartment again. They had not even been together since then.

"Hi," he said, opening the door. "Come in." He took her hand and walked into the living room with her. "This is it," he said, handing her a beautiful little sapphire-blue glass box.

Her first reaction was to refuse it, but the box was rectangular, not a ring box. She opened it. There was a single key on a white satin lining.

"What's it for?"

"The apartment over the garage. I'm giving it to you. Yours to use whenever you want, however you want, for as long as you want. Come on up. Have a look."

He took her hand and they went through the house, out the back door, crossed the patio, and up the stairs to the apartment. He held the screen door open and she entered.

It was a small apartment, with a living room and a galley-sized kitchen separated by a folding screen. The screen was partly open. A little table had been set with a white cloth, dishes for two, flowers and candles. Not saying a word, she turned and looked at the living room with a sofa, comfortable chair and lamps. The end table held a larger bowl of flowers.

It was only a few steps to the bedroom. More flowers on the bedside table, and across the foot of the bed a white summer-weight robe had been laid out. It gleamed like silk.

"I thought you might want to have a few of your own things up here," Darren said. His voice was husky.

"It's too much," she whispered.

"Excuse me a second." He left, and returned almost instantly. "Turned off the oven. Casserole. Salad and wine chilling. I knew it would all keep okay."

"It will keep," she said, reaching for his hand.

SEVENTEEN

Barbara walked through Frank's house that Sunday, dropped her purse onto a kitchen chair and continued out to the back porch, where she stopped moving. "What in God's name is that? And what are you doing with it?"

Frank looked at her crossly. "It's a fire ring, and that's a paella pan, and I'm trying to get this blasted thing to work." The contraption had two rings, a couple of inches apart. He lit a match and held it close to the lower ring. Yellow and blue flames shot up several inches high. He jerked back, muttering under his breath, then reached to the side of the device and did something out of sight. The flames died.

Thing One and Thing Two were crouched on the other side of the porch, in a ready-to-bolt position, their ears laid back, eyes slitted, as if they knew they might have cause to flee. She gave Frank a closer look; his eyebrows did not look singed.

The fire ring was on a metal stand, connected to a propane tank. Frank made an adjustment to a knob, then struck another match. Again he had to back off and turn a dial. He made another adjustment. The next time he tried to light it, there was a slight hissing sound, followed by a pretty blue flame that raced around the ring to complete a circle. He stood over it a minute, grunted, then turned to her with a grin.

"And that's how it's supposed to work."

"Where did it come from?" she asked.

"I borrowed it from Martin. I asked if he happened to know who might have one, and it seems he thought he might, and here it is." He had set the burner close to the table they often used for summer meals. It held a platter of finely cut onions, carrots, garlic, mushrooms, and a mammoth iron woklike pan. He picked it up and carefully positioned it over the top ring, which held it above the flame.

"Good," he said in satisfaction and added oil to the pan, watched it for a moment, then scraped in the onions and garlic. After stirring them a minute or so, he added the other ingredients. "We're having paella for dinner."

She nodded gravely. "I didn't think it was going to be turkey. Shelley and her crew will be here in about half an hour. Are you going to be busy cooking while we have our talk?"

"No. I'll get all this started, add the rice and broth and let it simmer until five. Turn it off, and it won't take more than fifteen minutes to finish. Everything else is done."

How was it that the men in her life could do that and she couldn't, she wondered, but she didn't spend a great deal of time worrying about it. Just a fact of life.

"Wally's coming in tomorrow. There are several things in his minute-by-minute playback of the two times he saw

Jay Wilkins that I want to go over with him. Free in the afternoon? Want to sit in on it?"

"Indeed I do. Nothing in sight yet?"

She shook her head. "I've scanned most of the discovery, not close reading, understand, but the general sense of it. A few people they questioned might warrant a second look, but that's a stretch." She frowned. "The one I really want is the person who parked a black van or big black car in that driveway. Whoever that was can clear Wally and as of now I don't see anything else, or even a hint there could be anything else."

"And that guy could put a noose around his own neck," Frank commented.

"Always a catch, isn't there?"

"You could set the table," Frank said, stirring the pan as he added saffron dissolved in water. "Not the plates. Stack them on the kitchen table. I'll serve the first go-round and folks can come get their own second helpings. That pan isn't going to be moved again until it's empty."

By five the table had been set, rice and broth added to the paella pan, and Shelley, Alex and Dr. Minnick had arrived. Frank's timing had been exactly right. He turned off the fire ring, covered the pan and went in to wash his hands.

Alex had a deeper suntan even than Shelley, and he seemed idiotically happy. Dr. Minnick was beaming as only a proud parent could, and it didn't matter a bit that he was father to neither Shelley nor Alex.

Frank offered drinks and after they had all been served, Alex said, "What I'm going to do is settle down with this beer on your back porch and draw the cats. I never had a cat to study and draw. I have a sketchbook full of dogs and I want to add to my menagerie."

"I told him we'd be having a conference and he was not invited," Shelley said, smiling at Alex. He smiled back at her.

"I thought we might go to the study to talk," Frank said. He picked up his iced tea and led the way.

Seated in a comfortable chair, wine at hand, Dr. Minnick said to Barbara, "You know I can't give a diagnosis of anyone I haven't seen and examined. So presumably all you want is an educated guess, and that's all I can provide."

"That's what I'm after," she said. "Let me describe her, tell you what others have told me, and then ask a question or two. Okay?"

"Fair enough."

She told him everything she had heard about Eve Wilkins. When she finished, Barbara said, "Remember, I haven't talked to her doctor and doubt that he would tell me anything in any event. I know this is too scant for a real medical evaluation, but if you could give me a general opinion based on so little, I would appreciate it."

Dr. Minnick nodded. "That was a good summary. I have a pretty good idea what's involved here. What is your question?"

"First. According to her brother, the doctor seems to think that Eve is making good progress. Yet, there is this break. Would you agree that two years between incidents indicates progress, or was that simple encouragement."

"It's progress," he said. "There will not be a cure, but the medications are improving constantly, and the most that can be hoped for is an ever-closer approach to a normal life. She will need a companion for the rest of her life, someone to ensure that she is protected when and if these incidents recur, and they could. She is receiving the optimal care, the best home care, the finest medical care there is, and I agree that there is hope that she can become self-sufficient and fairly independent if she has the ability to monitor her medication, be unfailing in regular evaluations and lab tests, and so on."

"She's smart," Barbara said. "She reads only for information, not for pleasure. Fiction disturbs her, but she kept up with Eric's math and science throughout his schooling. And she's something of an expert with horticulture. She draws and paints. She's had little social development, excessively shy, unwilling to meet new people. Just not socially well adapted, I guess."

He nodded. "It's part of the pattern, and it isn't likely to change much. She evidently doesn't cope with unpredictability, and human encounters are all unpredictable. Numbers are stable, she can grasp them, manipulate them, and they do what she expects them to. Self-expression through art is also predictable, even the attempts to communicate the chaos she experiences. She is trying to understand them through art."

"Is there a possibility that her behavior might vary when she's having one of her psychotic periods? Could she become violent? Aggressive?"

"Those are two different concepts, not to be confused. Let's take aggression first. I can't say absolutely not," Dr. Minnick said. "We never use absolutes where human behavior is concerned. But the chances are so slight, so close to nil that for practical purposes you can treat it as a negative. Her coping mechanism is to retreat into infantilism. She tried simple passivity, but when the blessed hormones came alive at puberty, it was the tipping point. Passive resistance was not working so she had to withdraw further. Infantilism, catatonia, mutism, loss of body functions, total helplessness. A retreat to the womb, if you will. In such a state there is no aggression."

"But she struggles if anyone tries to pick her up, or in any way handles her roughly," Barbara said.

"That isn't aggression by any means. It's an attempt to preserve the safety that has been interfered with. There's no directed violence, no intent to do harm, but communication of another sort that is crying out to be left alone." He paused for a moment, then said, "A screaming infant will not subside if it is slapped or shaken, but if it hears a soft voice, a mother's lullaby perhaps, feels gentle hands, frequently its struggles and cries cease. It doesn't understand the words, just the tone, the tactile gentleness, and it responds with docility. As does the young woman we are discussing. She does know the words, and her hearing is not affected. She responds docilely, albeit passively, as long as she does not feel forced to return to reality, her safety is not being threatened."

He paused again, regarding Barbara with a somber expression. "However, I must also add that since we are not talking about an infant, but rather a young woman who has achieved her full growth by now, depending on her physique, her physical strength, her struggles could result in doing harm to anyone trying to manage her or to herself. Not in directed aggression, but by striking out blindly, kicking violently, trying to maintain the safety of an egoless withdrawal. The one trying to handle her might label it violent aggression and, depending on who that person might be, could adopt even harsher methods. And that could force her into retreating further, beyond where she could hear and comprehend the words, and respond violently only to the tactile sensations she experiences. Or she could fail to respond to any outside stimulation. It could reach a point where she might be seen as irrecoverably, violently insane when not heavily tranquilized or deeply sedated. She could become totally catatonic, vegetative. Electroshock or a lobotomy might be seen as the only options in that event. That's a dangerous road to start down."

"You treated patients like that?" Barbara said softly.

The pain in his expression was answer enough. "I did. Sometimes we could save them, sometimes we couldn't." He drank the remaining wine in his glass. "Was there any other question?"

She shook her head. "Thank you, Dr. Minnick. This has been extremely helpful."

"In that case, I'll go out and help Alex study the feline form." He left swiftly, as if fleeing the memories that had been awakened.

"Barbara, are you really thinking that Eve…?" Shelley asked in a low voice.

Almost absently Barbara said, "I'm exploring avenues, just exploring." She shook herself and really looked at Shelley then. "I learned at the knees of a master," Barbara said, nodding toward Frank, "to look first at the ones with most to gain. Wally certainly, if he thought it meant keeping out of prison. And the ex-wife and her family. Eric may be out of it. Eve certainly had a big stake whether or not she was aware of it."

"But if she was helpless, lashing out more or less blindly… I just can't see it working," Shelley said. "Besides, they didn't know about the wills."

"We don't know that," Barbara said. "We know they make that claim, but we don't know for certain how much Connie told any of them. I'm inclined at this point to agree with you about Eve. A fetal position on the floor, maybe kicking out or something, or else fully responsible, backed up to the bar and reaching for a weapon. Can't have it both ways."

"And that leaves her mother," Frank said bluntly. "She's devoted her life to her daughter's care and she's in her fifties. The girl is twenty-three. Who's going to take care of her in ten years, twenty years?"

Barbara nodded. "That leaves Stephanie Breaux."

EIGHTEEN

When they left the study, Darren's son, Todd, was walking in from the breakfast room. "They're in there playing chess," he said. "They said I could play the winner, but I don't think they'll finish before next week."

Shelley hurried off to the breakfast room and Barbara followed. Frank said to Todd, "Did I hear you volunteer to help out here?"

"Sure."

"You can carry this out to the table and I'll bring these." He handed Todd a platter with what looked like a mountain of assorted seafood under a plastic cover and he carried a bowl of chopped cilantro and another of snipped parsley. At the fire ring he adjusted the burner and uncovered the seafood. As soon as the rice came to a simmer again he began adding chunks of halibut and salmon, shrimp, mussels and clams.

"What's that?" Todd asked pointing.

"Mussels."

"Why are they black?"

"Because nature made them that way."

Todd looked skeptical but made no further comment. Others had come to watch and sniff. "You could take the salad out," Frank said to Barbara, "and the wine could be uncorked. This will be ready in about five minutes. Bread's on the counter."

A few minutes later he began filling their plates. When Todd held his out he said firmly, "Please, no black mussels."

Evidently the boy had decided that nothing edible came in shiny black cases.

If getting up to serve themselves seconds indicated a successful meal, Frank admitted to himself as they ate, his dinner was a tremendous success. Todd, he noticed, went for a third helping, but no black anything appeared on his plate.

After dessert of strawberries with crème fraîche, a very contented group was prepared for the entertainment of the evening, the videos of Wally at work. He had given Barbara two.

Barbara had not told anyone what was on the videos, only that it was a performance by her client. The first one was the act for which she and Frank had seen the demo. This version was complete with sound.

The M.C. was on stage, music faded and he said, "Ladies and gentlemen, prepare to be amazed!"

There was a drumroll, then lively music as the spotlight focused on Wally as he wound in and out of the tables, greeting people. Music faded as the M.C. asked for volunteers, and rose again as the scantily clad women brought out the table and arranged the cloth. The male volunteers walked on stage and stood in a cluster looking awkward as Wally made his way up, then left again as soon as he was handed a microphone.

He approached a nearby table, where he stopped, reached down and untwisted the microphone wire from his leg. He had the woman at the table introduce herself, held the mike out to the man who said he was her husband, then somehow managed to get the wire twisted again, as he coaxed the woman to be his volunteer and gallantly escorted her to the stage where he made a show of seating her at the head of the table.

It was all engaging, his smile was charming, and his act with the cord very convincing. His timing was perfect, and he seemed every bit a born performer.

The last time he got the cord twisted, he looked exasperated, held his hand over the microphone, motioned to the stagehand and held a whispered conversation with him. The stagehand left, then returned with a lapel mike, took the other one and walked off shaking his head.

"Look, Meg, no hands!" Wally said, finally going to his volunteers, where he continued a fast-paced banter as he had them introduce themselves, and seated them ceremoniously one by one. One, a newlywed, received especially solicitous care.

He began to talk about driving to Canada to get cheaper drugs and at that point he happened to find the belt in his pocket. He held it up with a surprised expression.

The young man half rose, clutching his pants, and Wally tossed him the belt. The audience was laughing raucously. "Cut him a little slack, folks," he said. "After all, he's on his honeymoon.

"So we were all the way up in Michigan before someone on the radio said they were talking about *prescription* drugs. What's this?" He pulled out a wallet. It was fast action then as he pulled one item after another from his pockets, eyeglasses, a watch... "I've noticed that as we make our way through life, we sort of accumulate things, a lot of stuff seems to come our way and stick." He pulled out a necklace. "You wonder, how'd I manage to get so much stuff." One last wallet. He turned out his pockets then held out his empty hands.

Both audiences were delighted.

Wally invited the audience members to claim their possessions and explained the woman volunteer's role, to verify the owners of the purloined items and return them. He thanked his volunteers for being good sports.

When everything had been retrieved, he treated his last volunteer as if she were a queen and escorted her off the stage. He bounded back to give the uniformed men a chance to pat him down. He gave the M.C. a bear hug and lifted his wallet at the same time, returned it to even more applause and laughter, and was gone.

"How does he do that?" Shelley gasped through her laughter. "He's wonderful!"

"Nothing short of genius," Dr. Minnick said, grinning.

Although Frank had been watching closely and knew what to watch for, he had not spotted Wally in the act a single time. He nodded at Minnick's assessment, genius.

"Maybe the next video will show us a little of how he does it," Barbara said, putting the cassette in the machine.

The video started with Wally moving easily among an assembled group of men and women and a voice-over.

"The video you are watching was made at the University of Ohio, in Columbus. The event was a weekend symposium on urban crime, the attendees were mayors, city managers, chiefs of police, sheriffs and other law enforcement officials. Tonight's guest speaker is Mr. Wallis Lederer, who is an expert in one aspect of urban crime. No other details about his expertise have been revealed. None of the action has been rehearsed, none of the participants is acquainted with Mr. Lederer."

There were a few other details, and during it the video camera followed Wally, sometimes fairly closely, other times at a slight distance, but he was in the frame at all times. He greeted people, shook hands, bumped into a few, helped avoid spilled drinks and, except for the fact that he was not carrying a drink, he was just like any other member of the crowd. They were all wearing name tags.

There wasn't a sound in the living room as they all watched intently.

The camera followed Wally to the stage and he was introduced as the assembled group found tables and chairs.

Wally took his place behind a small podium to the side of the panelists' table. There was a smattering of polite applause.

Wally's smile was as big and open as it had been when he was entertaining at the casino, but he became sober-faced quickly. He thanked the audience and the host, then said, "I want to talk about a crime that is committed every day in every city on earth. It takes place at fairs, malls, subways, busy crosswalks, ball games, any place where a number of people gather and mingle. It is the crime of the pickpocket. And I'm something of an authority, since in my youth, and as a young man, I was one of them.

"I served time," Wally continued. "And a wise old man taught me to value the gift I had, but to put it to good purpose instead of using it to exploit my fellow travelers through life. I took his advice. Tonight, ladies and gentlemen, here among the most alert and aware members of society, there has been a crime. Check your pockets and purses, check your wrists for your watches. As I was mingling with you, introducing myself, meeting you good people, I was also robbing many of you."

Wally smiled, moved to the table, and started to empty his pockets and put the stolen goods on it. "Mr. Rowlands, if you would be so kind as to ensure that these all get back to their rightful owners, I would surely appreciate it." The host came quickly to the table. Wally stepped back and said, "As soon as all stolen property has been returned to its proper owner, I want to show you a video. Thanks to modern technology I can do this. Ever since I entered this hall I have been on video. Please welcome my assistant, Mr. Carl Hanrahan." He did not appear on camera, but there was more applause, and now people were reclaiming their wallets, a watch or two, a necklace. Some of them were grim, others grinning, shaking their heads sheepishly.

"Mr. Hanrahan will show the video he has been making. Most of it will be speeded up in the interest of saving time, but now and then it will be shown in slow motion," Wally said, paying little attention to those trooping onstage and leaving again. "Each time I committed a crime I signaled to Mr. Hanrahan and he noted where to slow the action to show it in real time, and then reverse it to show again in very slow motion."

The last person, a woman, picked up her wallet, glared at Wally and walked off the stage. He smiled. "I don't blame her. I'd be sore, too. I think Mr. Hanrahan is ready to show the video. If we could dim the lights a little."

The video was little more than a blur as it sped through the opening. When it slowed, Wally, off camera now, said, "Here it comes, first in real time." It looked as if he had accidentally bumped into a man, apologized, moved away. The film stopped, blurred as it was reversed, then started again in the slow mode.

"Watch my left hand. First the bump, followed by what is actually a prolonged apology and an attempt to help the victim regain his balance, always suspicious, by the way. But, as I'm steadying him with my right hand, my left hand is at his back pocket. There it is, and into my pocket it goes."

The video sped up again. "Now the bump into someone who is not the victim." Again the action was shown in real time, then in very slow time. "See, her companion has been bumped, and while she is distracted by this, and he is steadying himself with my help, I am in her purse." He lifted her wallet and put it in his pocket. In slow motion it appeared so obvious that it was a wonder that he had gotten away with it. In real time it had been imperceptible.

One by one he demonstrated maneuvers a pickpocket might use. When the video stopped, there was some applause, and the camera was focused on Wally again. He was leaning against the podium looking relaxed and amused.

"You just saw a few tricks of the trade," he said. "There are many more tricks up the pickpocket's sleeve. I've made

available a much longer video, on cassette or DVD, of the
tools in his toolbox. It's priced at the cost of the cassette
or disk, plus mailing and handling. Available only to legitimate law enforcement officials." He grinned broadly. "I
don't want to be held responsible for starting a school for
thieves. During the intermission Mr. Hanrahan will be glad
to take orders, or you can pick up an order form and mail
it in. And that concludes my presentation for this evening.
Thanks for your attention."

There was thunderous applause. He waved, his big smile
in place, and the video ended.

There was a flurry of movement among the home view-
ers, and many comments as they began to leave their
chairs.

"He's a magician."

"...total concentration every single second. Yet he
looked so relaxed."

"He has complete control of both hands at all times."

"Getting the watch was the neatest part. Man, oh man,
if I could do that."

"Even showing how he does it, it still looks impossible."

"Anyone want more coffee, another drink?" Frank asked.

No one did. They began to thank Frank for a marvelous
dinner, and Barbara for the great entertainment, and it was
not very long before everyone was gone and she and Frank
returned to the kitchen to finish the little bit of cleaning up.

"He'll make a fantastic witness," Barbara said, after
putting away the dishes from the dishwasher. "I just hope
he doesn't come across as too slick for his own good."

Frank nodded, then said, "I think Wally knows exactly
how to please whatever audience he has."

She decided she didn't want to think too deeply about what that meant.

"You know Meg writes all his material," she said, "except for the ad-libbed parts, I mean. He's great at ad-libs, and his delivery is top-notch, perfect timing. But her material is first-rate, too. She could have had a real career as a writer, comedy, children's fiction, I bet whatever she turned to."

"I suspect that's very much on Wally's mind. Why he's so determined not to let his predicament get in her way again," Frank said.

"Even to the point of facing the gallows for a killing he didn't do," she replied glumly.

NINETEEN

"Okay," Bailey said on Monday morning. "Not much, but here it is. I talked to some of the guys at the dealership. They all hated him, but not enough to haul off and take him out. And they aren't going to volunteer anything. New management is coming in from corporate headquarters and they don't know where they stand, they aren't taking chances."

"Nothing concrete, just a general hatred?" Barbara asked.

"Could be nothing more than the hired hands complaining about the boss. One kid, part-time after school and weekends, opened up a little. He was there for a year. Wilkins was on his back a lot. It's in there." He tapped a folder he had put down on the round table.

She nodded. "Some names for you to check out. People who were at the party they gave for Eric Wilkins's boyfriend." She handed him a list. "Any of the people at the dealership own a big black car or van?"

He shook his head. "Nothing there. One, but it's accounted for. At the coast with a bunch of kids."

"Anything new about Connie Wilkins?"

He shook his head again. "I bet I know as much as they do, and it adds up to zilch. Or else they're keeping a tighter zip on it than ever."

She spread her hands. "I guess that's it for now. Get me copies of these and you and Hannah might want to watch them. Wally's act." She handed him the two cassettes.

And that was it, she repeated to herself after Bailey left. If nothing broke, that's all she would have: a lot of people who had disliked Jay Wilkins, and no one who had had an immediate cause for wanting to kill him.

When Wally and Meg arrived that afternoon, he looked far too happy for a man facing a murder charge, Barbara thought, a bit sourly.

She introduced Shelley and they all seated themselves on the sofa and comfortable chairs around the table.

"You look like a man who just won the lottery," Frank commented.

"Almost that good. I talked to my agent this morning. He's lined up four bookings for me in Vegas. I had to turn down one for October. Told him I'll be tied up." He flashed his smile at Barbara. "But I'm on for November, January and February."

She thought he was perhaps too optimistic. His trial was scheduled for mid-October.

"I guess I'm about as retired as you are," he added to Frank. "But that's it, three, four gigs a year. Meg might go to some of them, maybe not, depending on what she's up to. Now, with a real home roost, there's not much appeal to flying off to Vegas. Rest of the time, home. I'm thinking of setting up a little woodworking shop in the barn, might be fun to fool around. I was pretty good once."

Frank thought he sounded a lot like a boy with a new bicycle.

"We watched your show," Shelley said. "It's really great!"

Wally bowed his head and thanked her. "Now, about our minute-by-minute account," he said to Barbara. "You said you have some questions about those two nights."

"I do, but Meg first. When you first spoke to Jay Wilkins that night in the casino, you said you mentioned that you had run out of quarters and wanted to go home. Was there more than that?"

"I guess so, but it was like that." She thought a moment, then said, "I think it was something like I ran out of quarters and since my limit to lose was ten dollars, I was done for the night."

"Do you remember how you were dressed? Jewelry? Dressed up?"

"We never dress up much when we go to the casinos. Except when Wally's got a show."

"When he asked you where you had been all those years, can you remember exactly what you said?"

Meg was looking bewildered. "Just around. I said we had moved around a lot and wanted to settle down. Oh, I said we had bought this old farmhouse that we were fixing up."

"You didn't say restoring, just fixing up?"

"That's how I think of it," Meg said. "What are you getting at?"

"I'm still trying to understand why he invited you to his house. From everything I've heard and read about him, he had two modes of dealing with people. He apparently was quite charming with those he considered important. With anyone he thought beneath him he was anything but charming. Brusque, even rude at times. They weren't people he would spend an extra minute with. I wondered where you fit in."

"You just described his old man," Wally said.

"You weren't dressed up much, either?"

"Slacks, sport jacket, Hush Puppies shoes. Nothing fancy. We didn't look anything like his high-rolling buddies." He held up his hands. "Look, calluses. A laborer's hands, that's what he saw."

"So he wouldn't have thought of you as influential, or prospective customers," Barbara said. "It just doesn't mesh with what I've learned about him."

"He was setting me up," Wally said.

"The real question is why. Anyway, you looked him over closely, and he backed off a little. Did his expression change? Did he look you over? Exactly what was his reaction?"

"He'd been sort of not very interested. We shook hands. At least we touched hands, but his hand was a little swollen, he said arthritis, the rain made it act up, and it wasn't much of a handshake. His eyes were roving as if he was checking on who else might be around. You know, the way you do when you don't want to hang around long. You're looking for someone more interesting. Then he looked…" He paused as if thinking. "Maybe tighter, more aware of me than he'd been. That's when I told Meg I'd cash in my chips and she should wait by the door while I went out to bring the car around. That's when he invited us to the house."

"Why did you tell her that?"

"I thought it was raining again. It had been raining off and on most of the day. It was pouring when we left the restaurant and went back to the motel to change. We were pretty wet. I didn't see any point in both of us getting wet again. If the rain hadn't stopped earlier, we wouldn't have gone back out that night. But it did, and I thought it must have started again."

"Why did you think so?" Barbara asked. "There aren't any windows in casinos."

"Jay's slacks were wet below the knees," he said promptly. "He had gray slacks, and the legs were darker low down, not dripping, but wet, and I thought he had just come in because his hair was sort of matted down, the way it gets when you wear a cap or hat."

"What else did you notice?" Barbara asked. None of this was in the written report they had made.

"Sand in his shoes, on the laces, and in the seams. Not a lot, but some. I thought he might have been walking on the beach and got caught in a new squall or something. And that's about it."

"So he invited you to his house. Did he say anything else?"

"Just what I wrote down for you. With his wife away, it was lonesome in the big house. It would be good to talk about old times. And he said for me to keep my hands in my pockets. He sort of laughed, but it was a dig." Wally shrugged. "We'd already said okay, so I just let it go. We went to cash in, and he kept walking the other way. That was the end of it."

"Was it raining when you left?"

"Nope. We went out together, got in the car and drove to the motel. The car wasn't even wet."

"Did you notice the time?"

"Not then. We got back to our room at twenty minutes before eleven."

Barbara flipped the pages of the report they had given her and stopped at another place she had highlighted. "At his house, when he put his hand on the glass case, did he say anything about it?"

Wally shook his head. "Not in words. But his attitude, his expression was like, see, it's mine now and I can smear it up all I want to."

There were several other points she had either Meg or Wally go over, and when she was done, she didn't know if she had learned anything useful or not.

After Wally and Meg left, Shelley said, "I talked to the two used-car dealers Wilkins was negotiating with. They're both disappointed that he's out of it. And between them it would have taken about a million up front to close the deals."

"Remember, he didn't have a million up front, or out back either," Frank said. "His wife did, he didn't. He hadn't run the dealership into the ground, by any means, but neither was it a gold mine. And he lost a lot in investments these last couple of years."

Friday evening when Barbara got home, she hit the play button on her answering machine to listen to messages while she put away a few groceries. Tomorrow, she was thinking, rest, cookout with Darren and Todd, then not much. On Sunday Darren and his son would leave for two weeks on their ghost town expedition.

She stopped moving when Adele Wykoph's voice came through the machine. "Barbara, call me. Whatever time you get in, give me a call. I'll be up and waiting." She sounded enraged.

She called back. "Thank God you're not gone for the weekend," Adele said. "Sonia's here and we have to see you tomorrow. The cops are giving her the runaround, all but patting her on the head. There, there, we'll take care of it. Bullshit! They want her to go away and leave them alone, that's what they want."

"Adele, slow down. Take it from the top. Who's Sonia? What's going on?"

"Sorry. I'm spitting nails I'm so mad. She's Connie's sister. They called her to tell her they're ready to release Connie's remains. She flew in on Tuesday, and since then she's been on a merry-go-round, lawyers, funeral director and police. She'll have a cremation, receive the ashes on Monday and fly home on Tuesday morning. Tomorrow morning she's meeting Eric at the house to sort through Connie's personal things, and that means that tomorrow afternoon is about the only time she'll have to consult you. On Sunday she wants to go to the cemetery to pay her respects to David and Steven."

"What do you mean, consult me? What does she want?"

"Some advice from someone who knows criminal law and how to go about seeing that they don't let the death of her sister fall between the cracks."

"She agrees that it wasn't suicide?"

"Absolutely. She thinks someone murdered her, and she wants some answers no one is giving her. Tomorrow, Barbara, as soon as she gets done at the house. One or two."

"Will you be home? Should I come over there?"

"No," Adele said sharply. "This isn't going to be a social call. She wants to talk to you as a professional criminal lawyer. Your office, one or two."

TWENTY

Sonia Carrolton looked very much like the photographs Barbara had seen of her sister, Connie. A physical description of one would have fit the other, five foot five, one hundred thirty pounds, fit, blond hair, brown eyes. Next to Adele in her peasant skirt and overblouse, Sonia appeared even smaller than she was.

Her voice was low pitched with the accent that Barbara thought of as Southern aristocratic, and was pure Virginian.

After the introductions Adele said, "Sorry if we've kept you waiting. I thought we should get a bite to eat and let Sonia relax a little." It was a few minutes after two. Sonia had spent several hours sorting through her sister's possessions.

"Forget it," Barbara said, but she wished she had stopped for a sandwich. "Please, make yourselves comfortable." She motioned toward the clients' chairs and took her own chair behind her desk. "What can I do for you, Ms. Carrolton?" she asked when they were all seated.

"I want to retain you to be in charge of an investigation into the death of my sister," Sonia said.

"You know I'm already involved in the case concerning the murder of Jay Wilkins?"

"Yes. Adele told me. She told me a lot about you, Ms. Holloway. I don't see how this could interfere with your defense in that matter." She drew in her breath. "I can't very well oversee a private investigation from three thousand miles away. I need someone to represent me here. Someone who knows good investigators, who can direct them, assess their reports and keep me informed."

Barbara studied her thoughtfully. She was drawn and looked very tired, but she also looked angry. And Adele was furious. Everything about her posture, the set of her mouth, the way she was watching Barbara so intently, attested to her fury.

"You're not satisfied that the police are doing their own thorough investigation?" Barbara asked.

"Not at all. There are two possible scenarios that they are considering. One is that my sister was so despondent that she was suicidal. In that one, they say she packed her bag and told Jay she was planning to visit me. They say that possibly at one time Connie really intended to fly east, but she changed her mind. She asked someone to meet her at the airport and give her a ride to the coast. Maybe the friend has a cabin over there where Connie asked to remain for a few days. Then, at the coast, she either fell into the ocean accidentally, or else she deliberately threw herself in. The friend, they think, is too fearful of being involved to come forward."

Although Sonia's voice shook a little as she talked, she maintained her composure.

"The other scenario?" Barbara asked.

"I suggested that perhaps she was never taken to the airport in the first place, and they said they had considered it, and investigated Jay thoroughly as a matter of routine, and ruled him out as a possible suspect. And no one else had the opportunity. No one had a motive. She had no enemies."

"They chose the easy way out," Adele said furiously.

Sonia glanced at her and said, "Please, let me."

Adele leaned back in her chair.

"They had one of the investigators talk to me, report what they had learned, what Jay had told them." She told it briefly and succinctly.

The investigators were satisfied that Connie had slept in her own bed on Friday night, and that she had showered on Saturday morning. She had bought a ticket to Roanoke on the Internet. Her husband had taken her to the Portland airport on Saturday, April 19, and she got out of the car and was walking toward the entrance when he left. He never saw her again. His movements were all accounted for from that moment until Monday night.

"They said he called many people using his cell phone asking about her, including me on Sunday night and again early Monday morning. They said she died between Saturday and Monday." This time when her voice faltered, she stopped speaking.

Barbara nodded. "Ms. Carrolton, why do you rule out the possibility of either suicide or an accident?"

"We, that is my family, were taught from childhood that there are certain moral codes that we must adhere to. We were taught that suicide is a mortal sin, excusable only in the event of a terminal illness with intolerable pain and suffering. I believe in those codes and so did Connie. At one time she wanted to die, during the months following the deaths of David and Steve, but it was passive waiting. She made no move toward it. She called me in late March and she was not suicidal then. And she would not have fallen into the sea. She was a mountain climber, athletic as a girl, and an athletic woman. It is inconceivable that she might have fallen into the sea."

She would do, Barbara thought then. Sonia looked soft and easy, but her low lilting voice and charming accent were misleading, she had steel inside, showing in her eyes, in her every utterance. "I'll do what you ask," she said. "Did the police give you the autopsy report?" Sonia said no. "All right. I'll need a letter authorizing me to receive any documents you're entitled to, any reports, and so forth. It's a power of attorney concerning this matter. We'll have to have your signature notarized. I'll call my secretary to come in to do that. Will you be up to more questions? An hour or longer possibly?"

"Of course," Sonia said. "Thank you, Ms. Holloway."

"You have to understand that if in time I see myself on a collision course with the defense of my client, I will have to withdraw to avoid a conflict of interest." Sonia nodded. "All right, I'll call my secretary and prepare the letter."

Barbara wrote the letter and made the call. "While we're waiting, you might as well let go," she said to Adele. "What's got you so pumped up?"

Adele was more than ready. "That scumbag Jay told the cops that I had Connie under my thumb, under my control. He told them I made her give up her medication and that she spent her nights pacing and crying because she couldn't sleep. She wanted her medicine back because she couldn't stand being so depressed all the time, but she was afraid of me! He said she told him it was too hard to keep trying to put on a brave front, but I said it was the only way to deal with depression. If he was in any shape to take it, I'd sue the bastard for defamation or something, if I didn't haul off and shoot him first."

"Did they tell you that?" Barbara asked Sonia.

"Yes. I told them I didn't believe it, and they said everyone they had talked to except Adele agreed that she was suicidal. And," she added slowly, "they found a letter on the computer that they interpret as a suicide note. They gave me a copy."

"May I see it?"

Sonia took a manila envelope from her purse, withdrew a letter and handed it to Barbara. "I also have a copy of her will," she said. "I haven't read it, but her attorney told me the terms." She cast a swift glance at Adele.

"Maybe I should take a little walk," Adele said.

After a perceptible hesitation, Sonia shook her head. "You might as well hear the rest of it." She put the will on the table. "Apparently Connie went to her former attorney in February to discuss a new will. He had urged her to do so soon after the accident, but she simply couldn't cope with it. He said that a year ago, Jay Wilkins's attorney got in touch with him to inform him that he now represented Connie. He sent a copy of a new will that she had signed. In that will her entire estate was bequeathed to her husband, Jay Wilkins. No bequests to charities, no mention of family, nothing else. At that time Mr. Konig destroyed Connie's old will. He said that was customary."

Adele made a low throat sound that could have been a curse.

Sonia ignored her, and kept her gaze on Barbara. "When the attorney mentioned the new will in February, Connie had no memory of it." She closed her eyes briefly and drew in a long breath. Her voice was steady when she continued a moment later. "That day they hammered out a draft will that Connie signed before she left the office. The attorney advised her to do so." Again she paused, then she tapped the will on the table. "This is what they came up with. One half of her estate was to go to her husband, the other half to be divided among Eve and Eric Wilkins and her Virginia family. She restored the various charitable bequests she had designated previously."

"How much money are we talking about?" Barbara asked.

"About eight million dollars."

Barbara nodded, and Sonia went on in a lower tone. "The will was finalized in March. Connie signed it, and that was that. But in early April she returned to the attorney with handwritten notes about further changes she wanted. He had her sign the notes while she was there. She said she realized that she had not provided sufficiently for her stepdaughter, and wanted to set up a trust exactly like the one she and David had set up for their son, Steven, years before.

"He asked if she still had a copy of the trust they had established before, and she said she was sure she did. It would expedite things if she found it and they used that as a model, he suggested, and she told him she would look through the boxes of papers in her possession and they left it at that. She never got back to him," Sonia said faintly.

"That was it, handwritten notes?" Barbara asked.

She nodded. "Connie didn't realize that he had destroyed the old will when Mr. Berman sent him a copy of the new one. Apparently she assumed that he still had it and it would be a simple matter to change a few details and be done with it."

"Do you know what terms she was talking about?"

Sonia nodded. She swallowed hard, then said, "She wanted to put one half of her estate, but not less than four million, in the trust fund to provide for her stepdaughter for the rest of her life, and the other half was to be divided four ways among the stepchildren, Jay and her Virginia family."

This time Adele erupted. "Jesus! Eight million, slashed to four million, then less than one million!"

Both Sonia and Barbara gave her sharp looks, and she said doggedly, "And then it would have been zip. She was going to dump him within the next six months. I saw the signs. It was coming."

"Cork it!" Barbara said sharply. She looked at Sonia. "What else did her attorney say?"

"He knew I was going out to the house to see about her personal effects. He had suggested it, in fact. He told me to concentrate on documents, anything to substantiate what she had written, referring to the old trust fund. He said if we could back up her written notes, he would defend them as a codicil in probate court."

"And did you?"

"No. There wasn't a scrap of paper, no old cards, no notes, no old e-mails, nothing. We corresponded a lot about the trust at the time. They were modeling theirs on the one we established for our own children fifteen years ago, but there wasn't anything." She leaned forward and her face flushed. "In early April she had boxes of papers, this morning nothing! She always kept everything, exactly the same as I did. We all do. We're pack rats, my whole family. We keep every card, everything. And there wasn't a scrap."

"Do you know if Connie told Jay what she was doing?" Barbara asked before Sonia could continue.

"She would have told him. She's…she was so honest it wouldn't have occurred to her to keep it from him. Besides, he changed his will at about the same time she did, in March. She must have made him do that, or at least talked him into it. Eric told Konig that Jay's original will left one thousand dollars to each of his children, the rest to that distant relative. He changed his to reflect hers. Half to her, the other half divided three ways." She took a deep breath, then said clearly, "That distant relative is named as the main beneficiary in the event of Connie's death preceding Jay's."

Abruptly Sonia stood up and leaned against the desk, her hands white from clutching it. "If Jay Wilkins is the heir to her estate, my sister's money will go to some distant relative of his that no one ever heard of before! She intended to help that child, her stepdaughter, exactly the way she would have provided for her own child!"

Adele looked ready to explode, her face was fiery red, and a vein was throbbing in her temple. "Just hold it," Barbara snapped at her. "Let me think a minute." She waved Sonia down, and leaned back with her eyes closed. Then she said, "Ms. Carrolton, you say you had a great deal of correspondence about the trust years ago. When you go home, find everything you can to support what your sister intended. If a handwritten codicil is backed up with anything to substantiate it, the probate court will have to consider it. There's no guarantee how they will decide the issue, but they will need more than a few notes. The immediate family's demands will carry more weight than a distant relative's, especially if you can document her intentions from the past and she referred specifically to the past."

Sonia nodded and sank back down into her chair. Barbara picked up the computer-generated letter she had referred to and scanned it. It was less than half a page of printout.

I can't take it much longer. Please, God, how much longer must I endure? Pretending, always pretending. J tries so hard to help, but it's no use. He doesn't understand. Adele doesn't understand. No one does. I hate being alive. I don't want to live. I'm ready

There was no salutation, no end punctuation, and although the lines had no printed date, someone had penciled in a date, March 27.

"I can see why they interpreted it as a suicide note," Barbara said. "While we're waiting for my secretary, I'd like to take your statement about the phone call Jay Wilkins made to you back in April. Maria can notarize your signature when she gets here. I'd also like a statement from your brother about the call Jay made to him later that day. It should be notarized, too." Sonia nodded.

Barbara was still at her computer keying in the statement when Maria arrived. She finished it, Sonia read it over and signed it, and Maria notarized it and the power of attorney.

Maria made copies of the will and the note, and started a pot of coffee. "Just in case you want it later," she said.

After Maria left, Barbara motioned toward the sofa and

upholstered chairs, and they all moved across the room. "You mentioned that your sister called you in March," she reminded Sonia.

"Yes. I was overjoyed that she had called. There was no communication at all from her after the accident, no e-mail, letters, nothing, and then the call. I urged her to come home, but she said there were things she had to attend to first. She said she would come later. She told me a little about her stepdaughter, Eve."

For the next hour or two Sonia talked about her sister. Sonia had wanted to meet Eve for herself, to understand what had drawn Connie to her. It had been an emotional meeting, she said.

Adele added, "They both cried like babies."

"She's a lovely girl and very brave. She understands how ill she is, and she's coping with it as best she can. No whining, no self-pity. I can see why Connie was so taken with her, not just the transference of love for her own child, although it might have started like that. But as her own person, a young woman who is determined to make the most of the life she has…"

"One last thing, not a real question, something to ponder," Barbara said. "If it turns out that my investigator can come up with no more than the police have, I'll do my best to make them consider this an unsolved criminal act, not a suicide or accident. I would want your permission to go public, if that is the case. Or if I feel confident that I know who committed this act, but can find no way to produce enough evidence to justify an accusation, I will inform you of exactly what I have learned and why I reached my conclusions, but I won't be able to go beyond that in any formal sense. Can you accept either of those two possibilities?"

"He did it!" Adele blurted. "You know it and I know it. Jay Wilkins killed her!"

Carefully Barbara said, "Listen, both of you. It's almost impossible to charge a dead person with a crime unless there are eyewitnesses. If the police decide this is an unsolved homicide, it would be difficult to bring any charge. The accused is always granted the opportunity to offer exonerating evidence attesting to innocence."

"Just don't let them say or imply a suicide and close the books on it," Sonia said fiercely.

Alone again, Barbara sat at her desk for a long time making notes, two lists of tasks, one for Bailey, and one for herself. She read the will, then reread the handwritten notes more slowly. It could go either way, she thought.

She was still at her desk when the sound of the doorbell startled her. She glanced at her watch and frowned. No one came calling on an attorney at seven-thirty on a Saturday night.

Angrily she went to see who was out there, and she was even more startled to see Darren. He was carrying a paper bag.

"What on earth? Oh, God, the cookout! Darren, I forgot. I got busy and forgot."

He came in. "I figured as much, and your car's still out there. So I brought you some dinner. Coast clear?" He nodded toward her door.

"Yes, they left a little while ago. Darren, I'm sorry—"

"Shush. I'll just put this down." He walked past her to her office where he cast a sweeping glance over the cups, the papers on her desk, her yellow pad. "Just how I thought it would be," he said. "I won't stay. Todd looked over my supplies and said I forgot a few things. New shopping list to fill. Things like chocolate-milk mix, cookies, peanuts, chips."

He was walking back to the outer door as he spoke. "He's packing his gear and when I get back we'll load up the truck so we can take off early." He stopped at the door. "It's all right, Barbara. It's okay."

She shook her head. "It isn't. It isn't fair."

He kissed her lightly. "Let me decide. See you in two weeks. Don't overwork, remember to eat and sleep. Get some exercise. I love you." He didn't wait for her response, didn't seem to expect any, and he left.

She locked the door behind him, then stood with her forehead pressed against the door. God, she thought bleakly, is this what I want?

TWENTY-ONE

"I don't like it," Frank said on Sunday evening. "You can't take two different paths and do justice to either one. They might draw farther and farther apart with every step, and you aren't obligated to Sonia Carrolton the way you are to Wally. Also," he added darkly, "I hope you realize that if you try to bring charges against Jay Wilkins for the death of his wife, you're killing the best chance Wally's case has. No more double murder with one killer. Keep them separate."

"I know all that," she admitted. "But maybe the paths separate to get around a roadblock. Maybe they come back together on the other side of it. Maybe Jay had nothing to do with Connie's death. However that goes, I don't think the two cases are totally separate. There's a connection."

Frank shook his head.

"Dad, we have to face it. If I don't find something, Wally's going down."

* * *

As Frank sat in stony-faced silence while Barbara briefed Shelley and Bailey the next morning, it was clear that he didn't like it on Monday any more than he had on Sunday.

"She's willing to spend a bundle and end up with an unsolved murder rather than accept accident or suicide," Bailey said in a disbelieving tone. "Just to get out from under a load of guilt and remorse over not doing something."

"She doesn't believe for a second that it could have been an accident," Barbara said. "And she can't let herself believe in suicide. Not just guilt and remorse, but the certainty that her sister would suffer the torments of hell for eternity if she took her own life. Belief systems are hard to argue with."

"You're the boss," Bailey said. "You want me to go over the same territory the cops have covered? Time, men, money involved. Not a done deed by Friday."

"I'll see what I can get from the official investigation. If they stonewall, that's how it will have to be. I'll ask Adele for a list of people who knew her back when she was at her lowest, the ones who maintain that she was suicidal. I want to know when they last saw her. And, the flip side, more recent contacts who were around her after she began making a comeback. And the doctor's name, the one who prescribed the drugs in the first place. Were there follow-up exams, lab tests, automatic refills, what? Dosages, interactions, everything you can find out."

She turned to Shelley, "Dr. Joan Sugarman, the one who detoxed her. A statement, if she's willing to make it. And the martial arts instructor, what he told the police."

She thought a moment as Shelley made notes. "Finally, what medications Jay Wilkins was taking, dosages, when filled and so on. I'm sure Eric Wilkins will be cooperative and let you have a peek at his medicine cabinet. That should be quick, before anyone starts clearing out the mansion."

They discussed it a while longer, then Bailey slouched out morosely, and Shelley stood up. "You think it's all connected, don't you?" Her eyes were shining with excitement.

"I think they could be connected," she said slowly. "But it's just a hunch, nothing more than that."

"Good enough for me," Shelley said. "I'll get right on this stuff."

Frank was last to leave. At the door he regarded her soberly. "I hope you haven't bitten off more than you can chew. I used to wonder where that phrase comes from. Maybe a plug of chewing tobacco, poison."

Thursday at two, Barbara walked into the police detective unit at city hall, where she was supposed to meet with Lieutenant Vern Standifer. He was not waiting for her in the hall. She opened the door to the big office, crowded with too many desks, and noisy with several detectives going about their business, conferring with one another, on phones, talking to citizens, who for the most part appeared to be nervous. No one looked up when she entered, and no one seemed aware of anything beyond their own tight circle of activity. She approached the nearest desk and interrupted a detective who was on the phone.

"I'm looking for Standifer. Is he here?"

At another desk, Milt Hoggarth turned around. He had been engaged in conversation with a seated woman.

"This way," he said to Barbara, jerking his thumb toward a closed door. He was a stocky man in his fifties; a fringe of faded red hair, shaggy eyebrows equally faded, florid complexion, and a bright red dome of a bald head was description enough to single him out in any crowd.

"It's always a pleasure to see you, Lieutenant, but I'm really looking for Standifer."

"You'll settle for me," he said, crossing to the door. He opened it and motioned for her to enter.

The room was cramped and small, more crowded than the outer office, with file cases, folders and stacks of papers piled on a desk, boxes on the floor and so little floor space that he had to sidle between boxes to get to his desk. He pointed toward a metal chair opposite his own.

"Now you tell me in twenty-five words or less what you want, I tell you why you can't have it, and we can both get back to work."

"I want to talk to the lead detective in the disappearance and death of Connie Wilkins. And you're not he."

"Captain Smiley said since we have a good working relationship I should be the one to talk to you." He face was expressionless, but his voice was heavy with sarcasm.

"Oh, dear. Does he know about your ulcer?"

"I don't have an ulcer."

"And I don't want to be responsible for causing one. Why can't I see Standifer? Is he afraid I'll bite him?"

"Cut the crap, Holloway. Why? What's your interest? I have that file, and I've been assigned that case, as if I needed another case. Isn't defending a murderer enough on your plate? You talk to me or beat it."

"I must have been absent the day the professor taught

that an attorney can have only one client at a time," she said. She took Sonia Carrolton's notarized authorization from her purse and handed it across the desk to him. "I've been retained to represent the interests of the family in the investigation. I want the autopsy, and whatever information you have to date, and especially why you are jumping to the conclusion that it was a suicide."

He skimmed the letter and tossed it back to her. "I'll have a copy of the autopsy sent to your office. And you know damn well I won't tell you anything about an ongoing investigation. But we have a good case for suicide. We know where she holed up on the coast and we're looking for the pal who drove her over and as soon as we locate her and have a talk, that case is closed."

"Hoggarth, I want details. Unless you give me full details of what evidence you are basing that conclusion on, with an opportunity to either accept or refute that evidence, I'll hold a press conference and blow your closed case so wide open you'll still be scrambling to find pieces a week after Christmas."

He glowered at her and she smiled. "You know I'll have Bailey follow your tracks to hell and gone to find whatever you already have. You know that Bailey has an uncanny knack for finding odds and ends that your own guys somehow missed. And, finally, you know damn well that I won't settle for a Daddy-knows-best answer. Give."

"One," he said, "she left a suicide note."

"Unsigned, computer stuff that anyone could have keyed in."

"Two, she was being jerked around in too many ways. Wykoph on one hand, her husband, and that insane Wilkins girl. She wanted out from under all of them. And she wanted her dope. You don't call an addict clean after a few months. They crave the dope and if they can't have it, most of them cave. If they stay off a few years, maybe, not a matter of months. And we have a list of folks who know she was suicidal."

"Two years ago, not recently. Wykoph was her friend, and Connie loved Eve Wilkins. It stinks, Hoggarth."

"Also, we know who has an isolated cabin in the Bandon area, a pal of hers. She bought her own one-way airline ticket, tourist, but she always flew first-class. She was willing to spend a few hundred bucks to make it look good, but not a couple thousand. She didn't want her husband to go in the terminal with her, and didn't even want him to take her to the unloading area. She got out and walked."

"You know what he told you," she commented. "A shame he can't be cross-examined."

"We found stubs, receipts. We talked to Realtors. We can account for his time right up until he turned his car over to valet parking on Saturday night, and again on Sunday and Monday. By then she was in the ocean."

"He provided himself with an alibi before she was even reported missing? That's interesting."

"I said we found the stuff in his wallet, his car, here and there. Credit card purchases. He wasn't thinking alibi."

"Right. Or, maybe while he was going through all the motions, accumulating a raft of such receipts to prove his innocence, someone else was busy transporting a dead body to the coast and getting rid of it."

"Jesus Christ! Don't try to spin a conspiracy out of this!"

"Then a week later the other guy went to Wilkins for

more money, they got into a shoving match and Wilkins ended up dead. I can make that case sound as good as the one you've got. Did you find any hard physical evidence to prove she stayed in a cabin on the coast?"

"We know who killed Wilkins," he said angrily. He stood up and she did, too. "I'll see what kind of details we're able to include with the autopsy. A day or two."

"You didn't find anything like that, did you?" she murmured. "You're waiting to find her driver and ask questions. Is that it? Hoggarth, what happens if you don't find her?"

"She's out there, living in a cloud of sweat, waiting for the knock on her door," he said. "We'll find her and she'll tell us what we need to know. We're done here. Why don't you take off and let me get on with my business."

Driving again, Barbara had to admit that they could make a persuasive case for suicide. And meanwhile, until they sent material to her, all she could do was wait. Stephanie Breaux, she thought then, was involved in both cases; it was time to talk to her.

Stephanie had not been enthusiastic about seeing Barbara, but she had agreed to a meeting, and at ten the next morning Barbara pulled into the driveway and parked behind an old light blue Camry. An even older Civic, much battered, was next to it. The houses were set back from the street thirty or forty feet, with shrubs and trees in abundance. The grass needed mowing in Stephanie's yard.

Built in the fifties, the house was modest in all ways. White with blue trim, it had a driveway that sloped down steeply to a garage that was under part of the house, one of countless split levels that were then in style because they were inexpensive to build, and took up less land space than most four bedroom houses. Barbara went to the front door and rang the bell.

Stephanie opened the door almost instantly. "Ms. Holloway," she said. "Please come in. I'm Stephanie Breaux."

There was a small foyer with stairs at one end, a closet and an arched doorway to the living room. The light green wall-to-wall shag carpeting probably had been installed when the house was built. It was badly worn. "I appreciate this opportunity to talk to you," Barbara said as they moved on to the living room. "Thanks."

"Adele called me. She told me what you're doing for Sonia Carrolton. Of course, I'll help in any way I can."

She was a tall woman, slender, almost too slender, and very straight, but it was her face that was striking, with high, finely chiseled cheekbones, smooth skin the color of ivory, deeply set dark blue eyes. Her dark hair was streaked with gray, pulled back in a chignon, but soft around her face. Hers was the kind of face that appears on cameos, Barbara thought. And she could have modeled for a classic Greek statue, or be featured on a modern runway modeling the latest fashions. She was poised and, as Shelley had said, elegant in an old-world way, cool and self-possessed. The black jeans and simple T-shirt she was wearing did not detract from her elegance; it was innate, in her posture and graceful movements.

Stephanie motioned to a wing chair by a picture window and went to a matching chair with a small end table between the two, but before either of them had sat down, two young women came down the stairs, then stopped at the arched doorway. They were both carrying several books.

"Ms. Holloway, Reggie Johanssen, and my daughter,
Eve. This is Ms. Holloway," she said to them. Reggie came
forward eagerly with one hand outstretched.

"Ms. Holloway! I follow all your cases in the newspapers. You make me wish I had gone into law instead of just
liberal arts, but I doubt that I have enough mental discipline
to do what you do. I'm very happy to meet you." She was
amply built, with curly auburn hair, a wonderful broad
smile and a sprinkling of freckles across her nose. She
pumped Barbara's hand with enthusiasm.

Eve did not leave the archway. She looked frightened
and did not smile, but she was lovely with the same fine
bones as her mother. There was little other resemblance.
Her hair was wheat-colored and her eyes a much lighter
blue. She looked more like a teenager than a young woman
in her early twenties, small, even fragile. The grip on the
books was white-knuckled.

"Hello, Eve," Barbara said, rescuing her hand from
Reggie.

Eve did not respond.

"We're off to the library," Reggie said. "Back in a couple of hours. Come on, Eve, let's beat it."

Eve was out the door before Reggie got there.

"Your daughter is very lovely," Barbara said when they
were gone.

Stephanie nodded. "She's beautiful."

They both sat down and Barbara said, "Did Adele tell
you that the police are trying to make a case that Connie
Wilkins committed suicide?"

"Yes. But I don't believe it."

"Will you tell me about her? How she changed from the

time you first met her until the end? What she was like with Eve?"

Stephanie nodded. "She was almost as shy as Eve the first time she came. Recently, she talked about taking Eve to Portland, to the museum, let her see museum art. She thought that Eve is quite talented, and that her talent should be developed. Connie said she would rent an SUV with plenty of room in the back, that we could all go, Reggie and I, pack a nice box lunch and find a quiet place…" She looked past Barbara and became silent for a moment. "Connie said if that worked out, maybe later this summer we could take a train trip to San Francisco. They have small compartments for families. Eve would never have to leave it for meals or anything else. And we would rent another van down there, avoid taxis and buses…"

She paused, and looked down at her hands. "Connie believed Eve had to get out into the world more often, that she should not be allowed to become too reclusive. Eve's doctor agreed. I was always afraid to subject her to chance encounters. I thought I was doing the right thing."

Abruptly she stood up. "Ms. Holloway, would you like a cup of coffee? It won't take a minute to make."

Barbara nodded and stood up. "May I come with you? Would you mind if I have a look at Eve's garden. I've heard a lot about it."

Stephanie looked surprised. "Of course. That's how Connie began with Eve, just talk about the garden. And then Sonia. She's a professional landscaper." She motioned for Barbara to come along and led the way to the kitchen. It was small, with eating space at one side, and beyond sliding glass doors was a patio and the garden. Barbara went through the kitchen and out the door.

Half the patio was covered with latticework and vines. On that side was an exercise bicycle, a table and several lounge chairs. It had a concrete slab floor, and already that morning the uncovered half was sizzling hot in the sun. Two bicycles were leaning against the house. Not a gardener, Barbara had to admit that this one was very nice, if a little too neat. It seemed that every plant had its own space surrounded by dark mulch. Not a weed was visible. Stephanie joined her.

"Eve planned it and the girls planted everything, but Eve does most of the real work, and all decisions are hers."

"You can almost see an overall pattern," Barbara said after a moment.

Stephanie glanced over the garden and nodded. "I'm sure she has a pattern in her head. Anyway, back to Connie. After Jay was killed, a detective came to talk to me. They implied that someone in town was hiding Connie. I think for a time they believed she killed Jay. I told them that was absolute nonsense. She had no reason. She could have walked out if she wanted to."

"Do you know why she didn't?" Barbara didn't look at Stephanie as she asked, but kept her gaze on the garden as if still trying to figure out the pattern.

"I have no idea," Stephanie said. "We never talked about him. I don't think either of us ever mentioned his name. But she had been healed as early as Christmas, I think. She changed a lot then, began to laugh and joke with the girls, and by spring she was thinking about future trips. She wasn't sick, and she didn't have to kill him to get away."

She went inside to get their coffee and they sat on the patio as she continued to talk about Connie. "She was very patient and gentle. I could see the pain in her eyes and on her face sometimes when she looked at my daughter, as if she yearned to hold her close, but she never made a motion toward doing it, as if she knew intuitively how to act. And Eve grew to love her."

"Did she ever mention her will, providing for Eve the way she did?"

Stephanie shook her head. "Not a word. I still don't really believe it, and probably I won't until it actually happens. I don't know how she got Jay to agree to go along with it, but it seems again to demonstrate that she was well and strong."

Taking a chance on ending the conversation prematurely, Barbara said, "You know I'm also representing the man accused of murdering Jay Wilkins. Can you think of anyone who might have had reason enough to want to murder him?"

"No. A lot of people disliked him. He was not a likeable person although he could be charming and amusing when he saw an advantage to it. I suppose at one time I could have qualified, but that was a long time ago. There had been no contact between us from the day I walked out of his house."

"I suppose the police asked if you could account for your time on that Saturday night." She said this as casually as she could keep it and it appeared that Stephanie had not taken offense.

"Of course. I was upstairs working on the store books when it began getting dark and the wind started to blow. I came down to check on Eve. She had been riding the exercise bike. She does that every day unless they go out on their bikes. I found her on the floor. I imagine a gust of wind had blown something into her face and she fell off or slid off." She remained composed, but her voice changed subtly, became lower pitched and the words came more slowly, as if it was painful to utter them. "Eric told you how it is with her?"

"Yes. Ms. Breaux, I'm so sorry."

She closed her eyes for a moment, then said, "Thank you. It can be difficult. It's more difficult for her."

A short time later when Stephanie looked at her watch, Barbara took it as a cue that the conversation was to end. She stood up and said, "Thank you for giving me this time. Later, if the police persist in trying to make Connie's death a suicide will you give me a formal statement to the effect that in the last months Connie was hopeful and making future plans?"

"Of course. They must not label it a suicide. That's too heavy a burden for her family. And it isn't true."

After seeing Barbara out, Stephanie returned to the patio to pick up the cups, but instead she sank into one of the chairs and closed her eyes as a sharp memory of one of her last meetings with Connie surged into awareness.

Adele had called to say Connie wanted to have Stephanie join her and Adele at lunch. She had resisted. "Why? We have nothing to talk about."

Adele had snorted. "Don't kid yourself. The most important person in your life is Eve, and more and more that's what Eve is becoming to Connie. The most important person in her life. That's what you have in common."

Connie and Adele were already seated when Stephanie entered the Bon Marche restaurant a week later. It had been awkward, with nothing but the weather to talk about for what had seemed a very long time. Then over salads, Connie had said, "There's something I wanted to bring up, but…" She had not taken a bite, just moved salad greens around on her plate a little. She picked up a roll and started to crumble it, put it down almost guiltily and, gazing out the window at rain, she had said, "There's something I'd like to do, but only if it's okay with you."

What she was proposing came out in a rush then, a studio for Eve, sharing Reggie's studio perhaps, supplies, a worktable, an easel. But most of all a mentor, someone to guide her, to help her realize how very good her art was, to help her develop her own style even more than she had done alone, to teach her how to mount her art, ready it for display, arrange gallery space, a show…

What Stephanie remembered most clearly was Connie's intensity, her passion, what had appeared to be almost a desperate need to be allowed to do this for Eve.

"I'll find someone who understands, who won't try to impose her own will on Eve, who will recognize her talent and encourage her. I used to know artists… If not someone from here, then someone from San Francisco, or New York, anywhere. It has to be exactly the right person."

She had stopped abruptly. "She doesn't have to know I'm doing it," she had said after a moment, picking up the ruined roll again, adding to the scattered crumbs on the table. "I mean…I don't want to seem like I'm trying to take over, take charge, trying to take your place."

But she was, Stephanie had thought then, and she would.

Eve, totally dependent on her mother, would gradually transfer that dependency to Connie, her benefactor, with her overwhelming need to mother another woman's child. She studied the younger woman's face and knew that Connie was as aware as she was of the implications, and Connie was as helpless as she was to resist. She could not refuse such an offer, and Connie could not step back.

Stephanie knew without a doubt that she would risk everything, life itself, and worse, even risk losing her daughter if it added to Eve's chances of achieving a decent life, and in that moment she realized that the same thing could be said about Connie.

TWENTY-TWO

"Just more of the same, nowheresville," Barbara told her crew on Monday morning. "Wally's case hasn't moved an inch, and Hoggarth's been put in charge of the Connie Wilkins business. He's going along with suicide, of course."

"He's a good man," Frank said. "He goes where the evidence takes him."

"Maybe. That hasn't always been my experience with him." She turned toward Bailey who was slouched down in his chair with a coffee cup precariously balanced on the arm of it. "I want a three-hour period when Jay Wilkins couldn't account for his time with credit card purchases, receipts or real estate agents."

"You can't make a case against him simply by wanting to," Frank said.

"Three hours," she repeated. "That's about how long it would take to drive from Florence to the Bandon area and back to Florence. No one can account for every minute of a whole weekend and on into the next week. But he did apparently. It stinks."

"Three hours," Bailey muttered. "Right. Martial arts guy—Howard Steinman—full report or shortcut?"

"Short."

"He's a nut. Fully accounted for that whole weekend."

Shelley nodded. "He lives in his own fantasy world. I imagine he sees himself as a Samurai or Ninja warrior or something. He's very soulful," she said gravely. "Very sensitive. He told me so. And he adored Connie Wilkins, worshipped her. When they went out for coffee on Friday, the last day of the class, she was mournful, almost tearful that this was the end for them. She told him to get on with life, to put her out of mind, forget her. He said it was not just a casual goodbye, it was *The Long Goodbye*. Lots of emphasis."

Shelley thought a moment, then said, "He has a smattering of Eastern philosophy, talks about wholeness, oneness, finding oneself in the infinite void. And suicide is the ultimate statement of fearless selfhood."

"Good God!" Barbara muttered. "Did he cry on your shoulder, want to hold your hand?"

"Close," Shelley said. "But he's also very brave, he told me that, too. He'll suffer this loss bravely. She would have wanted him to be as brave as she was."

Bailey was gazing at her aghast. He got up to refill his cup. "It's a good thing you're the one who had to talk to the spook."

"You would have loved him to death," Shelley said. She went on with her report. "Dr. Sugarman has a cabin out near Bandon. She never loaned her key to anyone, and she was at the hospital or on call that whole weekend, so she couldn't have found the time to drive Connie over. She was pretty annoyed with the detectives who kept hinting that she and others had secreted Connie away. They were not friends, but had a patient-doctor relationship, period. She's really sore because they got a search warrant to go through the cabin and she had to take time off to watch. They didn't find a thing. She gave me a list of Connie's original medications, dosages and such, and her own prescriptions. Dr. Minnick helped me sort them all out."

"Did you get her statement?"

"I taped it. I'll transcribe it and take it back for her to edit. She says exactly what's on her mind, but it wouldn't do for a formal statement, we both agreed." She dimpled saying this, and Barbara could imagine how Joan Sugarman had expressed her annoyance.

"Finally," Shelley said, "I met with Eric Wilkins at the big house and got a look at Jay Wilkins's medications. High blood pressure, high cholesterol, aspirin therapy and sleeping pills. The same doctor treated him and his wife until she switched to Dr. Sugarman."

"Good work," Barbara said. "Did Dr. Minnick go into the effects of mixing those drugs on Connie's list?"

"Yes. He was surprised, for instance, that she was still on muscle relaxants as well as pretty strong sleeping pills. He said the sleeping medication likely was no longer effective, that after a time the patient develops a tolerance and has to stop or keep increasing the strength, but there it still was. He also said that she must have been numb in the head from all that stuff, unable to read a complete sen-

tence, or think through a complete idea. It's all in there."
She pointed to a folder she had placed on the table.

"Great."

"Almost forgot," Bailey said when Shelley leaned back,
finished. He reached into his duffel bag to get Wally's
videocassettes.

"Bailey, for God's sake, hold that cup or put it on the
table," Barbara snapped.

He looked at her, then at the cup in surprise, but he put
it on the table, and tossed the cassettes down. "And the two
copies," he said, adding them. "We watched them over the
weekend. The guy's good, real good. It's all a matter of distraction, just little distractions, enough to divert attention.
Like the chair nearly knocked over. While two guys grab
and steady it, he's picking a third guy's pocket. Really neat."

"That's it," Barbara said suddenly. "Distraction. That's
what the invitation was all about, to give Wally something
to distract him from whatever he noticed about Jay Wilkins that night. Give him something bigger to think about,
like going to prison."

"What are you talking about?" Shelley asked.

"The reason Jay Wilkins asked Wally and Meg to his
house for drinks. The reason he planted the boat on Wally.
A distraction."

"Thirty thousand smackeroos," Bailey said. "Not exactly a little distraction."

"Connie Wilkins's estate will come to eight million,"
Barbara said softly, "and he expected first to get it all, and
then at least half of it. And no doubt he fully expected to
recover the boat." She noticed with satisfaction that Frank's
skeptical expression had changed to a very thoughtful one.

* * *

When she was alone again Barbara pulled open the folder with Wally and Meg's minute-by-minute account of their meeting with Jay at the casino. She made notes as she read through it. At nine-thirty or so the rain had stopped and they'd decided to go to the casino. But Jay must have been out in the rain before it stopped, and his pant legs were still damp when Meg met him at about twenty minutes after ten.

The drive from Bandon to Florence would take about an hour and twenty minutes. Six-thirty on, she thought grimly. He had checked in at his hotel at about six-thirty, changed clothes and left again. Where had he been from then until twenty minutes after ten? She thought of what Frank had said, she couldn't make a case against him simply because she wanted to. "But maybe I can," she told herself. "Maybe I can."

She started to close the folder again, then stopped and jotted: arthritic hand, swollen. But he had not been on anti-inflammatory medication, or pain killers.

Barbara left the office early that day after telling Maria to take off whenever she wanted to. "I'm going for a long walk," she said. "Too much sitting around spreads the human body in unsightly ways."

Maria laughed and waved goodbye, and Barbara headed to a supermarket for salad greens, then drove to the riverside park. It was a warm day, a touch too warm in the sun, but pleasant in the shade. The river flashed silver and black. Birds skimmed the surface of the water they way they did. There were kayaks, a flotilla of inner tubes with kids, not too many people on the bike path, a few romping dogs that were supposed to be kept on leashes, picnickers, kids at play. Everything was normal, placid, as it should be on a summer day. And her head remained as empty as she walked as it had been when she started.

There was no good place to launch anything like a defense. Testimonials, references by distant people, the videos. And denial. Period. She frowned and sat down on a bench. "That damn boat," she muttered. That goddamned boat. It kept coming back to that pretty little gold barge.

A canoe passed by with three young men and not one of them wearing a life jacket. Fall in and drown, she thought darkly at them. It happened every year in spite of all warnings. Show how brave and daring you can be, fall out, get swept away, drown. Help out the gene pool, get rid of the stupids.

She started to walk again, and then thought bitterly that she might solve the mystery of Connie Wilkins's death, but it was the wrong murder.

She reached her car, where the salad greens were wilting in the heat, and she headed for Darren's house, telling herself firmly that she was done with thinking for the day.

TWENTY-THREE

Hoggarth had sent over a packet for her. It contained Connie Wilkins's autopsy, photographs and a written report and, to her surprise, it also included a typed sheet of paper with Jay Wilkins's movements starting on Saturday morning, and continuing until Tuesday morning.

After a brief glance at the autopsy pictures, she turned them facedown. Too gruesome. The sea, waves and rocks had savaged Connie's body cruelly. Instead, she began to read through the other typed pages. Exactly what Hoggarth had said, every minute practically accounted for with receipts, credit card purchases, Realtor statements… She read slower when she came to the time she was interested in: six-thirty on for Saturday night. He checked into the Sand and Surf resort hotel about six-thirty, got directions for a bar and grill called The Waves and went out for dinner. Credit card purchase of two drinks at The Waves. Arranged for the group who played that night to call the next week for an engagement in Eugene. The casino a little after ten, turned his car over to valet parking at eleven-fifteen. Picked it up the next morning at ten, then with another Realtor until two…. Home on Sunday, phone calls from a cell phone, the last one at midnight to his business manager.

She put the papers down, frowning. His time had been accounted for almost minute by minute. And that was just too damned unnatural. Too damned convenient.

And why a call at midnight to his manager? What had been so important that it couldn't keep until the following morning? She started to look up the number to call him, then changed her mind. She would just drop in, she decided.

It was a short drive to the dealership on Good Island Pasture Road, where a number of car dealerships were clustered like covered wagons getting ready for the assault. When she walked into the showroom, a salesman met her at the door. She smiled and shook her head. "I'm looking for Mr. Levinson. Is he around?"

He was and, summoned by the salesman, he approached her, beaming. "What can I do for you, young lady? A coupe? Convertible?"

"Sorry," she said. "I'm not buying. I'd like to talk to you for a minute or two if you have the time. Barbara Holloway. I represent Wallis Lederer, who is accused of murdering your late employer."

His smile vanished and a wary expression took its place. "Oh. I already talked with someone you sent over."

"I know. I have only one question, actually. Just to clear up a detail. I was in the area and decided to ask in person."

He glanced in annoyance at the salesman, who was hovering nearby. "Come on, my office is over here."

Inside the office he motioned toward a chair and sat behind his desk. "Okay, ask your question."

"It's been reported that Jay Wilkins called you at midnight on April 20, a week before his death. Can you tell me why? What was so important that it couldn't wait until working hours?"

"Nothing," he said. "It wasn't about anything. I got out of bed. You do, you know, when the phone rings late at night. When I heard who it was I let him talk to the answering machine. He said he wouldn't be in on Monday, he was waiting for his wife to check in. And he said a music group would call him and I should tell the receptionist to transfer the call to me. He had listened to them play, thought they were good and that they would work out for the dealers' meeting we were to host in September. And he told me to e-mail him the weekend activities on Monday. That's it. And it could have waited until morning."

"Was that usual for him, late-night calls, and to arrange for a group to play like that?"

"First time ever for either one. I arrange everything—meetings, company dinners, entertainment. The meetings rotate among the northwest dealers. Our turn this year." His words were precise and his voice completely neutral then as he added, "Mr. Wilkins delegated tasks and never gave them another thought unless they were not carried out to his satisfaction."

"Well, as I said, I had one question, and you answered it. Thank you, Mr. Levinson."

In her car, she put in a call to Bailey on her cell phone.

"Drop in if you're anywhere nearby. Otherwise, in the morning. I'll be in the office until about six."

When two people act out of character, she thought, driving, you want to know why. Hoggarth being so cooperative was out of character, and it could mean that he was as dissatisfied with the case being made for suicide as she was.

And Jay Wilkins acting out of character and arranging for entertainment himself. Why?

Bailey arrived at ten minutes after five. He headed straight for the little bar that he claimed was his, and helped himself to the Jack Daniel's that she kept just for him.

Slouching down in his chair, holding his drink, barely discolored with water, he regarded her with his usual morose expression. "What now?"

"I might have found the three hours I wanted," she said, taking the account of Jay Wilkins to the round table to show him. "Credit cards, personal reports, all tallied, except for this period. He checked in at his hotel at about six-thirty. Then nothing until the credit card payment for two Bloody Marys at a tavern called The Waves, no time given, and the casino a little after ten. No credit card or cash receipt for dinner that night."

He shook his head. "You don't down two drinks like that in a couple of minutes. Not like quick shots."

"Check it out," she said. "Did he actually talk to the group playing there? Was he there for their entire performance? Where did he have dinner? You know the drill."

He drank thoughtfully, then shook his head. "A group like that, playing in a place like Florence months ago? They could be scattered to the wind by now. And who's going to remember who ate what and when back in April? You don't think you're chasing a dead horse that's just laying there rotting away?"

"Check it out," she repeated. "It's the only three hour period there is. Bailey, he asked directions to the tavern at the hotel desk. He already knew what he had to do. He was covering his tracks. He went out again. But when he met Wally and Meg, his pants were noticeably wet from the knees down and there was sand on his shoes. If he'd been in a bar for a couple of hours, doesn't it seem likely that the pants would have dried by the time he got to the casino, when it was no longer raining? And where did he run into sand in a restaurant and then in a bar? Check it out."

He drained his glass and set it down. "Okey dokey. That group might be playing in a beach cabana in Tahiti by now."

"Make sure your passport is in good order."

TWENTY-FOUR

"Still nothing," Barbara said glumly on Frank's porch that Sunday.

"Doesn't it always seem that way along about now?"

"God, I hate waiting for other people!"

He sighed and stopped trying to be reasonable with her. He knew how much she hated having to wait for others, but there was little to be done about it. Nothing new was surfacing on Wally's case. Bailey was tracking down a bunch of musicians.

Barbara had drawn back from a question she wanted to ask, aware of the line around him that she dared not cross. Had her mother ever mentioned a career of her own, a life of her own? Had she really been content to sacrifice her own life in order to take care of her husband and child, especially since neither of them had needed such care? It seemed incredible to Barbara that Stephanie had little life beyond caring for her daughter, and that Meg had spent forty years existing in Wally's shadow and was finally having the role reversed. Wally was determined to enthrone her even at the risk of prison. One after another eclipsing their own lives for others. And Darren? She forced her thoughts away from that direction, determined not to go there.

One hot day followed another hot day and she only grew more restless. Sonia Carrolton sent a packet of papers by FedEx and Barbara had a delivery service take them to Stan Konig, Connie Wilkins's attorney. He was delighted with them.

There was nothing to go to court with, she told Frank. *I didn't do it.* That was all she had. Wally's denial. It didn't help her mood an iota when Frank commented that you go with what you have or you take a plea bargain. Or else you tell the police what evidence you're sitting on, and why you didn't disclose it earlier. Let them go after the black van or car.

She wanted to kick one of the cats.

Then, in late July, Bailey came in as unkempt as always, but he was looking self-satisfied, perhaps even happy, and that was so rare that Barbara felt her pulse quickening. He helped himself to the bourbon, slumped down into a chair and grinned.

"Got it," he said. "What the doctor ordered. Signed, sealed and now delivered. Long or short?"

"Just tell me, for heaven's sake. Don't make a production out of it."

He tossed a folder down on the table, took a long drink and told her. "Okay. I located that group. A trio, two brothers and a sister, citizens, parents from Brazil. They call themselves the Amazonians, and they play a bunch of weird instruments that no one ever saw before. Just starting out. I tracked them to Falls City, Idaho, and talked to them."

He took another drink. "On the nineteenth they got a card from Jay Wilkins. He wrote, 'Great show! Call early next week for an engagement in Eugene.' They showed me the card. They were all atwitter, figure it's the kind of break they dreamed about."

"Did he talk to them?"

"Nope. They never laid eyes on him. Just the card. So I went looking for the cashier who delivered it to them."

He finished his drink and held up the glass in an inquiring way, as he always did for the second one. She nodded impatiently.

"She remembered him," he said. "And she remembered the group because the guys were so cute, with thick wavy hair and big brown eyes, and the neatest accent. Just quoting, just quoting," he said, stilling her impatient protest. "They play mambas, sambas, maybe sousas for all I know, and the joint was packed, and rocking with people dancing their legs off. Jay Wilkins went to the cashier's station and said he'd had two Bloody Marys and lost the tab but he paid up and gave her a tip for the waiter, if she could find him. And he gave her a ten spot to deliver the card. She said he was really nice, to pay up like that when he could have just walked out with no one the wiser. And, naturally, she read what he had written on the card, and was impressed that a rich Buick dealer had spent time listening to the group, and so on."

Barbara let out a long breath. "You done good, kid," she said. "Have another drink. Have three. You gave me the three hours I needed."

"I always do good," he said amiably. "You just don't show the kind of appreciation a guy needs from time to time."

"Now just shut up. No dinner receipt, a sham at that bar. He killed her, and that's when he had time to dispose of her body. After carting it around all day in the trunk of his car, I guess."

Bailey shuddered and took a very long drink.

As soon as he was gone, Barbara called Milt Hoggarth and was put on hold until he got off another line.

"What do you want, Holloway?" he snapped. "I'm busy."

"Ten minutes of your time," she said. "I have something for you."

"I'm tied up and will be till hell freezes over. Just tell me."

"Nope, not on the phone. I'll spot you to some lunch tomorrow. Here in the office. Sandwiches and coffee. Deal?"

He hesitated, then said, "Twelve-thirty. It better be good. I'm swimming in stuff to get done yesterday."

"It's good. See you tomorrow."

"Pastrami on rye. Two. With pickles. Iced coffee." He hung up.

Grinning, she called Frank. "I'm having an office party tomorrow, twelve-thirty. One other invited guest, Milt Hoggarth. Care to join us?"

"What have you found?"

"Tomorrow. I promised Hoggarth two pastrami on rye sandwiches. Place your order."

"I'll pick them up on my way over. You sound pretty pleased."

"Bailey delivered the goods," she said. "He's really not a bad sort."

* * *

Hoggarth was hot, his face as red as his scalp; he was rumpled and tired, and he was bad-tempered when he appeared the following day. Frank had arrived minutes earlier looking cool and neat as only an affluent attorney could manage to do in the heat.

"Lieutenant, iced coffee coming up," Barbara said cheerfully. "Get comfortable."

He muttered something in a growly voice and sat down after a curt nod to Frank.

Barbara passed two sandwiches to him, put iced coffee in front of him and sat on the sofa with an iced coffee of her own. "I understand how limited your resources are these days," she said. "Budget cuts, vacation season, vicious crimes being committed right and left. I had Bailey do your work for you. No cost to the department or the city."

"Cut the comedy and get to it," he said unwrapping a sandwich.

"I suppose they're still looking for the mysterious driver who secretly drove Connie Wilkins to Dr. Sugarman's cabin and left her there, then went back a few days later to clean up any evidence that she had been in the place. And when they exhaust that option, they'll move on to an alien abduction," she said meditatively.

Hoggarth's face went shades darker and he looked as if he might grab his food and march out with it.

"Down, Hoggarth. Down," she said, and told him about the wills, and what Bailey had found. He attacked his sandwich savagely as he listened, and was unwrapping the second one when she finished.

"And not a shred of proof," he said.

"That's it and you know it," she said flatly. "There's the will business. From eight million down to four, then probably less than one million. The so-call suicide note on the computer that he conveniently wrote for her. Tourist class ticket. She didn't give a damn about money, but he did. Scouting out the tavern ahead of time, that very careful day full of alibis, all those phone calls to make sure everyone knew how concerned he was that she was suicidal. He checked in at his hotel at six-thirty and no one saw him again until ten. He had it planned to the minute. Even the Bloody Marys. Not the kind of drink you turn bottom's up and have another, not shots you can drink in a couple of minutes. You take your time over drinks like that. Proving he was in the tavern for a long time, when everything we know about him said it was the last place where he would have spent a second. Loud music, frenzied dancing, noisy. Not his kind of thing. Your boys swallowed it all, suicide, his alibis, everything he tossed out, I'm afraid."

"What about her brother?"

"He saw her two years ago, after her first husband and son were killed, just like all the others they talked to, and not since. And on the phone he told the detective who called that he didn't believe it when Jay said she was suicidal. That his family aren't the suicidal types."

She gave him a searching look. "Why didn't you swallow it, Lieutenant? Your people took it hook, line and sinker, but not you. Why not?"

"I'm Catholic," he said. "She was Episcopalian, what we call Catholic lite. She might have thought of it right after the accident that got her husband and kid, but not years later."

"Did you read her autopsy report? There was bruising on her right temple. She was pretty battered, but you don't bruise after you're dead."

"They figure she hit her head on rocks when she jumped."

"Or he slugged her and drowned her in the bathtub. Did they think to check the water in her lungs for fresh water? Of course not. You fish a drowned person out of the ocean, that's that."

Frank had not touched his own sandwich, nor had Barbara, and he had remained silent throughout, but now he said, "Milt, tell me something. Did they hand you a package all wrapped up as a suicide? Confirmations on those receipts, credit card purchases, all of it?"

"Something like that," Hoggarth admitted after a moment. Then he said bitterly, "You don't backtrack and double check on a colleague. It will go down as an unsolved murder. You know how welcome an unsolved case will be, new investigations, the works? And what's the point in charging a dead man with murder? Especially when it's circumstantial? It's going to rot in the unsolved file, most likely."

"Do I have your assurance that it will be called murder?" Barbara asked softly. "Can I tell the family that?"

He nodded. "We'll check on the tavern, the group, first, all that, of course, but it was murder. There are others who have to be checked out, you know. The kid, Eric Wilkins, the ex-wife."

Frank didn't know if Hoggarth was aware of Barbara's satisfaction with his answer, and he thought that was what she had been after: an unsolved murder on the books. That explained a little about why she had left Wally out of it, what he had seen that night, how he had put her on the right track. Later, he thought. Talk about it later.

She began to eat her chicken salad on wheat. "He had to do it before those notes were incorporated into her will, that's why the fake suicide note appeared on the computer when it did. He was starting to set the stage in March at about the time she was making her notes."

"Will notes like that hold up in probate?" Milt asked Frank.

"Your guess is as good as mine. But there's no doubt he would have contested it if admitted as a codicil, with a coin toss as to winning. I expect he wasn't looking to get murdered himself."

Hoggarth finished the last of his sandwich and coffee, wiped his mouth and hands carefully, crumpled his napkin and tossed it down. He stood up, and for a moment he looked awkward. "Thanks, Holloway," he said. "For the sandwiches. They were good. I've got to go."

She walked to the outer door with him, and when she returned, she commented, "Well, as his captain said, we have a good working relationship. Sometimes. For a second there, I thought he might even call me Barbara. One step at a time."

"What are you up to?" Frank asked.

"Just doing the job Sonia Carrolton hired me to do."

"You know that none of this business about Connie Wilkins will be allowed in Wally's trial."

"I read the rule book, Dad. It's been a while, but I really did read it once. I know the rules."

He finished his sandwich in silence. She knew the rules, and she would not hesitate to take a battering ram to them

if necessary, and if that wasn't enough, resort to dynamite.
But the judge always had the last word.

Barbara began to gather up the sandwich wrappers. "I'll
call Sonia in a few minutes and drop in later if you'll be
around."

No more talk about rules, he well understood, or what
any of this had to do with Wally's case, but it was just as
well. What was there to say?

TWENTY-FIVE

"I'll see Berman this week," Barbara said Sunday. "Get this codicil business settled."

Frank scowled.

"Dad, if I can't link the two deaths, Connie's and Jay's, do you have any other suggestions?"

He had none. He had not voiced any doubt about the outcome of the trial, but doubt persisted and grew, then grew again. Denial was not enough. He also knew that if he was prosecuting this case, Wally would go to prison. Opportunity and motive, and both easily proved, would be more than enough. Strangely then, it wasn't Wally's face that he was seeing in his mind's eye, but Meg's. She had aged during the past few months, almost as if stricken with a deadly disease that was ravaging her system. He shook his head to get rid of the image.

"Next week I want to talk to Wally and Meg," Barbara was saying. "I'll take a run out to their place. Want to go?"

"Yes. I'd like to see how much they've done to that place." Even as he said this, he realized that he really wanted to see how Meg was doing.

Randolf Berman's attitude was glacial when Barbara sat across his desk from him. "Of course, we'll contest it," he said. "Those brief notes can't be accepted as a valid will."

He was tall and thin, with a comb-over that she hated on sight. She regarded him levelly, and said, "If you do, Connie's family is prepared to press a murder charge against Jay Wilkins. I gave them my assurance that I would represent them in such an event. Are you certain Mr. Wilkins's distant cousin will be prepared to use whatever inheritance he derives from the estate to defend such a charge? It seems more likely that he'll be delighted to receive whatever he can, since he couldn't have expected anything at all. Would the corporate coowners of the dealership go along with another very long delay in freeing the assets of the estate? I understand that they are anxious to reorganize at this time."

"That's preposterous! On what grounds could anyone bring a murder charge? She was all but declared a suicide."

"No, Mr. Berman. It appears that the investigators have been purposely vague on that score. They are still calling it an ongoing investigation, but it was murder, and they know that. Connie had no enemies. Jay had a great financial gain at stake. I'm very much afraid there is no other suspect to turn to."

Berman looked ready to erupt in anger, and she said, "I believe one of the interesting questions that might come to light publicly is how it came about that a reputable local attorney allowed a woman obviously under the influence of prescription drugs to so alter a will that her natural family was excluded along with a dozen charitable organizations she had previously supported both in works and with generous donations, and to which she had previously made substantial bequests."

A deep flush suffused his face and scalp. "I could have you brought before the bar for making such an implication. I'm a member of the board and we deal harshly with those who overstep."

She shrugged. "I imply nothing whatsoever. I merely state a fact. That the will you prepared for her does make those exclusions is a fact. That she was rendered temporarily incompetent through the overuse of prescriptions drugs is also a fact. As it is that her condition was clearly visible to any observer." She stood up. "I believe we have concluded our business, Mr. Berman."

At the door she paused and turned to look at him. He had not moved. "I was taught in law school that the most valuable asset any attorney has is his or her personal reputation. That we should always guard it zealously. Good day, sir."

On Thursday that week Barbara and Frank drove to Wally and Meg's house. It had been painted a pale yellow with white pillars, and it looked handsome, with no sign of its previous disrepair. Inside, it was just as beautifully redecorated. The living room was creamy white, and a luxurious rug with a dark red floral pattern was on the floor. Barbara had never seen a rug like that outside a museum. The fireplace insert was ornate black cast iron, finished with a dull glow.

"It's lovely," Barbara said. "You've done a beautiful job."

Wally looked like a man without a care in the world, happily welcoming them with a broad smile. Meg looked tired and almost haggard. Her smile was as welcoming as his, however.

"Gradually we'll replace every stick of furniture that's too modern," Wally said, gesturing toward a glass-topped coffee table. Two books were on it, the top one was *Woodworking Projects for the Home Craftsman.* "Everything should be a period piece. It will take time, but we'll have time."

Then, seated in the living room, Barbara said, "We have to start thinking of the trial. Six weeks and counting. I want to fill you in on how it will go, what to expect and so on."

"You don't have anything new, do you?" Meg asked. She was both hopeful and anxious.

"I'm afraid not. Nothing's come to light. Have you thought of anything you can add? Anything about the van or car you saw that night?"

Meg shook her head.

"Okay. First, I'll want you in the office for a few hours immediately before the trial. I'll want to go over your testimony step by step, Wally, minute by minute practically. It's laborious and tiresome, but it has to be done. After I'm finished, Dad will tear into you from a prosecutor's angle. Just to give you an idea of how the cross-examination is likely to go, prepare you for tough questions."

Meg paled a little as she heard this.

Barbara gave her a sympathetic look and continued, "And for the trial itself, I think we should plan on Bailey picking you up every day, just to make certain you arrive on time. And we'll stay together for lunch and other breaks." She had a few more details.

"What I think we should do is hang out at a hotel from Monday night through Thursday," Wally said. "Long drive out here and back every day. The Hilton, walking distance to the courthouse. Okay?" he asked Meg.

She nodded. "It will remind us of the life we're missing these days." She gazed around the room. "Weekends will be like parties after a few days in a hotel again." She looked as if she were already missing their new home.

"Meg," Barbara said then, "no one is going to ask you a single question, and if any reporters approach, your only answer is no comment. We're going to keep you all the way out of this. I won't call you and neither will the prosecution."

Wally looked satisfied, and Meg looked miserable.

"So I won't have to lie under oath," she said faintly. "You're not going to tell them I was there, what I saw?"

"If we had been able to find that car or van, it would be different, but Bailey's good, and if he hasn't found it, no one else will, either. It can't be verified, and can only add to the prosecution's case."

When Barbara finished what she had to say, Frank leaned forward. "Wally, there's one more thing that has to be considered. There's always the possibility of a plea bargain, right up until the trial starts. This is a case that's purely circumstantial, but you have to recognize that a verdict can go either way. A plea bargain always results in a lighter sentence than a trial that ends up in a conviction."

"You know, the pen is full of guys who didn't do it," Wally said. "They'll tell you so, you and anyone else who will listen. Funny thing is, some of them really didn't. But there they are. A plea bargain would get me ten to fifteen, guilty probably fifteen to twenty-five, since there was no intent to do murder. I'd hate to be one of those whiners who tells everyone who comes along how innocent he really is. Nope, I'm in it all the way." He flashed his big smile. "Besides, I'm counting on Barbara to clear me."

He stood up. "You want to see the woodworking stuff I've got already? Not done by a long shot, but a good start."

Frank looked at Barbara, and she spread her hands. "We're done. I'll chat with Meg while you admire the newest in saws or something."

"Lathe," Wally said indignantly. "My newest tool is a lathe. Come on, Frank. I think my first real project will be a desk for Meg. I'll start with something smaller, just to get the feel..." They walked out as he talked.

"I don't think I can bear it," Meg said in a low voice when they were gone. "We've been fighting. Something we never did before. He swears that if I say a word, he'll simply write out a confession and be done with it. And he means it."

"Don't fight with him, Meg. You can't help by talking, and you could do him harm. You have to believe that."

"I'm the only person on earth who knows, absolutely knows, he's innocent. You can know only what we tell you, but I know, and I know whose fault it is, and I can't speak."

"Are you sleeping? Writing?"

She shook her head. "I can't write a thing, and I wake up in a cold sweat again and again. I'm so afraid."

"Do you have a contract yet?"

"Yes. It always takes so long to work out the details, back and forth, back and forth. But it's done."

"So they'll be back in print. Congratulations."

Meg nodded in a distracted way, then said, "If I told them and took a lie detector test or something wouldn't they have to believe me?"

"No. They might use a lie detector to corroborate their own suspicions, but never to refute them. Give it up, Meg. Accept it."

"You don't understand," Meg cried in anguish. "It would kill him to go back. I know him. I know what it would mean to him."

They heard the men returning, Frank's deep chuckle, Wally's running chatter. Barbara put her hand on Meg's arm. "Don't fight with him, Meg," she said softly. "He needs your support, not anger or tears or regrets. And not your fear."

Startled, Meg studied Barbara for a moment, then nodded. "I know," she said.

In the car heading back to town, Frank said, "He told me that if he loses, he wants her to rent out the house, or even to sell it, and move to town where there will be people around. Make friends, have a life. He asked me to represent her, take care of the details. That's one reason he's been working his tail off, to get it ready if the need arises." His head was turned as if he were gazing out the side window, fascinated by the landscape of an industrial complex.

Her hands tightened on the steering wheel. How many times over the years had he cautioned her not to let herself become involved emotionally with her clients, how it could result in heartbreak? They both knew that if Barbara lost the case, more than one life would be destroyed.

TWENTY-SIX

"Five weeks and counting," Barbara said on Monday. "And nothing new. So you're on your own, guys." She scowled at Bailey's coffee cup balanced on the arm of his chair. He hastily picked it up and put it on the table. Just as well, she thought darkly. She was in a mood to start throwing things.

"I'll have a couple or three pretrial hearings and that's that," she concluded.

On Friday, in Shelley's doorway, Barbara said, "When you wrap it up at Martin's, you might as well just go on home. Nothing for you here. I'll go over the notes for Monday's pretrial hearing, and I'll take off."

Shelley looked as disconsolate as Barbara felt. The hearing was to decide her motion for dismissal of the charges against Wally. It was doomed from the start, but she had to go through the motions, give it a try. She spent the afternoon reviewing her notes, and at four-thirty, she told

Maria to close shop. "I'll be leaving in a few minutes. Go get a head start on the weekend."

At ten minutes before five Bailey called. "I have something," he said on the phone. "Ten minutes."

It was a long ten minutes.

When Bailey arrived he headed straight for the bar and poured himself a generous bourbon, touched the water, as if duty required it, and sat down at the ornate round table.

"Give," she said.

"Right. I got to worrying that you weren't even sniping at me and decided to do something about it. I miss it when you just glare at me without a word."

"For God's sake, it's not a theatrical production. What do you have?"

"I'm getting to it," he said, evidently enjoying himself. "I kept thinking about that van or car. Double checked every lead I had, same as before, no dice. Then I wondered, hey, what if it was rented? For a week, a weekend, a month, something. Hadn't thought of that before, since no one involved needed to rent anything, but what's to lose? I began checking." He grinned and drank all his bourbon, held up his glass the way he always did, and ambled to the bar for a refill when she nodded, with impatience that was choking her.

"And what do you know? I found it," Bailey said. "Three rental places have black vans for hire. I had a look at the records, and there it was."

"I'm going to kill you as you sit there, if you don't stop this and get on with it," she said.

He grinned. "That's the Barbara I know," he said. "So there it was. Seems that a van went wonky back in February, threw a cylinder, cost more to repair than to replace, something like that. Old model, time to upgrade anyway, and the owner put in an order for a new van just like the old one, bought, registered, the works by March 5. It was a custom job, interior to order, racks, shelves, things like that, and it takes time to get it delivered. Old van out of commission, they rented a temporary fix. Black unmarked van would do okay until the new model was delivered, on April 27."

She was advancing toward him with her hands clenched and he held up his own hands in mock surrender. "I give. Gormandi and Breaux. Registered in the name of Diane Gormandi. She has a better credit record than Stephanie Breaux. They both have keys. They keep the van parked at the shop and use their own cars for daily use. By the time I got on the trail, they were using the new one for business, trips to San Francisco, Seattle, L.A. I saw that it was new and I checked it out, but since it was bought and registered on March 5, and was exactly like the old one, white with blue lettering, I never gave it another thought. My fault."

Barbara sank into a chair, feeling as if she had been sandbagged. Stephanie Breaux!

There was a long silence. Bailey finished his drink and set his glass down. Finally he cleared his throat and she pulled her gaze back from space to look at him almost blankly, as if she had forgotten he was there.

"I'll be heading out. Anything else for me? How about on Monday?"

"No. I'll give you a call." She could hear her own voice as distant, remote, and shook herself. "That was a good piece of work, Bailey."

He heaved himself upright, ambled to the door, and paused. "Yeah. Why do I have the idea it's a piece of work you wish I hadn't got around to? I'll be home if you decide to call." He saluted and left, closing the door quietly behind him.

After a moment she rose, went to the outer office to make certain the door was locked, then returned to her own office to put things away. When done, she left and drove to her apartment, where she carried her things upstairs, then walked out again, this time heading for the river and the bike path.

It had rained in August, an almost unheard of event in Eugene, and then again at the beginning of September. The world had turned darkly green. With dormancy broken unexpectedly, surging life showed in every bush, every tree, every blade of grass. Almost like a second spring, she thought, walking. Then she forgot the greenery. Repeatedly she told herself to rethink her case. Think.

Her head remained empty. She kept walking until the park lights were coming on, the trail lights flicked on, and approaching bicycles glowed like Cyclops, one after another. She had accomplished nothing, she realized in disgust. Just exhaustion. Her legs were throbbing when she entered the rose garden on her way home again. The fragrance was stronger in the evening air than it was in daylight, intoxicating, nearly overwhelming. She almost dared anyone to accost her, to give her the opportunity to release her frustration and her fury.

In her apartment, she went to her desk and sat in the dark with her eyes closed for a long time, and she began playing again and again in the private theater of her mind, the murder of Jay Wilkins. She changed details the way a film editor might, adding some, removing some, changing the order. Over and over she started and ran through it until, finally satisfied, she opened her eyes and turned on the light. It was ten-thirty.

Her stomach felt hollow and a headache had started to pound behind her eyes. Belatedly she remembered that she had meant to go to the little get-away apartment, have dinner with Darren… "I told him not to wait, not to expect me if I didn't show, and for God's sake not to bring me something to eat," she muttered. She forgot him and checked the clock again.

It was too late to call Stephanie Breaux. Let her get at least one more night's sleep.

TWENTY-SEVEN

Barbara made her call at eleven on Saturday morning. "Ms. Breaux, there are a few questions I would like to ask you regarding the murder of your former husband."

"I don't see why," Stephanie said. "I don't know anything about that. I'll be at the shop all day. Maybe you could drop in around two?"

"No, Ms. Breaux. This really should be a private conversation. I'd like you to come to my office where we won't be interrupted."

Stephanie's tone became much more distant and formal when she said, "I fail to see why I should accommodate your schedule, Ms. Holloway. Saturdays are very busy for us. It really would be most inconvenient."

"I'm very much afraid this can't wait for a convenient time. I want to talk to you about a black van, Ms. Breaux. In my office."

There was a long pause. "I'll come by at one. Where is your office?" Her voice was little more than a whisper.

At twenty minutes past one Stephanie arrived, and once again she was the cool and controlled woman Barbara had met a few months earlier. Not a sign of agitation was visible when she sat down and regarded Barbara with an appraising look. "I don't see why you thought this was necessary. I have already told the investigators everything I can, and I repeated it to you. I was home with my daughter the night Jay was killed and I know nothing about the matter." Her poise was perfect, her manner that of a patient shopkeeper dealing with an irritable customer.

"There are a few questions, however," Barbara said conversationally. "Why did you wait until Monday to take your daughter to the hospital? Were you hoping a bruise on her back would fade? Or possibly one on her arm? I can subpoena the doctor and the admitting nurse, you know, to testify about such bruises. They don't fade in a day or two, I'm afraid. Or should I pose such questions directly to Eve? Or petition the court to have her questioned by a psychiatrist?"

Stephanie's color faded, leaving her more ghostlike than ivory-toned. "I won't permit anyone to question my daughter," she said. "She is not to be approached by you or anyone else."

No longer the patient shopkeeper, her voice had an intensity Barbara had not heard before, each word clipped and hard.

"That may not be your decision," Barbara said. "This is a murder case. My client is falsely accused of murder, and I intend to know the truth about what happened that night.

From you, here in this office, or from you on the witness stand under oath."

"She can't tell anyone anything. She has no memory of that Saturday, and her doctor will affirm that she had an attack on Saturday. They can tell by her state of dehydration."

"Which brings us back to my first question. Why did you wait so long before you took her to the hospital? Ms. Breaux, if the spotlight becomes focused on you for any reason, there will be very difficult questions asked, both of you and of your daughter, and, if forced, I will see to it that the spotlight is turned to you. The court will not accept the word of a private doctor in such a matter. They will want their own evaluation, made by a neutral psychiatrist, in their own facility. Your pleas will not change that fact. You were there. You drove a rented black van to Jay Wilkins's house the night he was murdered. That's the starting point of this conversation. We can conclude it here, privately, or through the courts in public."

Stephanie moistened her lips. "I was there. You're right. I used the van and went there. Eve fell off her exercise bike and I put her to bed. I knew she wouldn't move again and I went there to plead with Jay and Connie for financial help. He…he was on the floor dead, and I panicked and ran away."

Outwardly Stephanie was not very different from before. Her voice was the key, Barbara thought. Although her voice had dropped to a near whisper, she appeared unaware of the change.

Barbara shook her head. "They'll trip you up a dozen different ways with a story like that, and then they'll still want to question Eve."

Stephanie stood up and crossed the office to the window.

She moved the blind aside and gazed out. With her back to Barbara she said. "I killed him. Connie wasn't there and I asked him for help. He laughed at me and said my crazy daughter belonged in the nuthouse. He was in my face, threatening, pushing me back into the bar. I hit him with the pitcher and he fell and hit his head on the stool. I wiped off my fingerprints with a towel and ran away." She sounded as if she were reciting lines from a play that held little interest to her.

"It might fly," Barbara said thoughtfully. "Of course, there are details that don't quite work, but it's closer." She went to Stephanie and took her arm. It was as rigid as steel. "Come sit down and let's really talk. She was there, wasn't she? How did she get there? Why did she go there? Did you take her?"

Stephanie wrenched away from her. "Stop it! As soon as anyone tries to ask her a question, that's the story I'll tell. They will accept it! I did it! I killed him! That's all they need to know! She was bruised when she fell off her bike. She doesn't know a thing about this!"

Stephanie looked desperate, even her lips were pale.

"How did you manage to leave the house without having it recorded by the security system? Why did you take a red Afghan out with you? The housekeeper's statement reported it missing. Stephanie, they'll trip you up over and over."

Barbara took her arm again, and this time there was no resistance. She nearly pushed Stephanie down into a chair. "Now, just tell me what really happened. Eve hit him, didn't she? Does she know?"

In a dull voice Stephanie said, "She doesn't know a thing about it. She had been so restless. For nearly two years she had been well, and she wanted a job, something to do. Just more and more restless and feeling capable of actually doing something besides stay home or ride with Reggie." Her voice broke and she said raggedly, "She just wants a real life."

Barbara did not say a word and Stephanie drew in a long breath, then continued in what sounded like the voice of a robot, without inflection, dull and lifeless, the voice of complete despair. "Connie called on Friday to say she'd be there on Saturday and Eve was waiting for her all day, watching for her car, looking out the window for her. She was so disappointed, she hardly ate any dinner. Nothing I said seemed to reach her, and she went out to the exercise bike. She was riding it when I went up to work on the store books.

"Then she called me on her cell phone, but all she said was that she was at Connie's house. He must have grabbed the phone away from her. He told me to come get my crazy kid. I could hear her calling for Connie. He yelled at Eve to shut up and she said, 'I came to see Connie.' And she called her name again. Jay was yelling at her, cursing her. He said, 'She isn't here! Can't you get that through your thick head? She's gone. She isn't coming back! Stop that! I told you to stand still….' Then he said, 'Jesus Christ! She's taking off her clothes,' and he must have put the phone down on the bar. That's where I found it. He didn't disconnect. I heard Eve scream and Jay shouted something and she cried out again. I heard a crash. I grabbed my raincoat and ran out to the garage to get my car. I saw that her bicycle was gone. I realized she had ridden over there so I went to the shop. I had to use the van to take her and her bike home."

In the same lifeless way she continued as if the lines had played through her head repeatedly until one word followed another automatically.

"I pulled into the driveway and saw her bike against a tree. And I saw that the front door wasn't closed all the way. Her shoe was wedged in it. He always made them take off their shoes before going inside. She must have dropped it when he opened the door. The other one was by her side in the bar room. She was on the floor, still holding the pitcher. I had to loosen her fingers... He had fallen with his head against the stool. He was dead. She was soaked through. She had a head scarf, and it was soaked. She was shivering. I got her to her feet and wrapped her in the Afghan and took her to the van and put her on the backseat and covered her up. I was going to go back for her things when another car pulled in, and I ducked down out of sight. Someone went inside. I couldn't see who it was, just someone in a long black coat. I was terrified, and knew I had to drive straight to the hospital where Eve would be safe, but before I got back in the van, the other person came out again. I didn't move until the other car left. Then I went in for her jacket and shoes and cell phone. He was holding her jacket. When I pulled it free, he shifted and fell down from the stool. I nearly fainted when he moved, and grabbed onto the bar to steady myself, and that made me think about her fingerprints. I took a towel and wiped everything I thought we might have touched. I picked up her other shoe on my way out, got her bike inside the van and drove home and put her to bed. She had a bad bruise on her back, another one on her arm where he must have grabbed her, and he had slapped her. Her cheek was red and swollen. I was afraid to take her to the hospital because they would wonder how she got so beat up. But on Monday I couldn't wait any longer. I told them she fell off her bike on the patio. They accepted that."

As though exhausted, she leaned back with her eyes closed when she finished.

Barbara stood up and paced the office a minute or two, then she said, "It was clearly self-defense. He was attacking her and she defended herself."

"What difference will that make?" Stephanie said without opening her eyes. "You know they'll demand a psychiatric examination in a state institution, and that will kill her as surely as putting a bullet through her head. She won't be able to tell them anything, and they might even label her schizophrenic with homicidal tendencies and lock her up for treatment. If a single question comes up concerning her, I told you my story. I'll stick with it and make them believe it. I killed him in self-defense. I was afraid he would make Connie stop helping to support Eve. I wanted the money for her. I'll make them believe me, and I'll deny this conversation. I'll do whatever I have to do. They must not get near my daughter."

"What if the label fits? You weren't there. You don't know exactly what happened? Only what you infer."

"You don't understand!" Stephanie cried, sitting upright. "She was fine throughout that, her call to me, calling Connie, taking off her wet jacket, all of it. She hit him when he attacked her, and she was still fine. Then he must have fallen on her, or lunged at her, or something. That's when her episode started. Until then she was just defending herself. It's the only hopeful thing about it, that she was in control until then."

Barbara stood up. "Sit still, Stephanie. I'm going to put on coffee."

And she needed a moment to think, she realized, measuring the coffee. She could easily visualize the scene she and Bailey had reenacted, the blow to the head, Jay falling, twisting. If he had fallen toward Eve, grabbing her jacket, that was enough to have set her off apparently. No matter what Stephanie confessed to, they would want to question Eve. It would seem too obviously a case of a desperate mother trying to protect her ill daughter. And Stephanie was right, they would demand an examination by the state. It was routine. Dr. Minnick's words came to mind. She could be forced to retreat even further, back so far she would be irretrievable.

When the coffee was ready she took it in. Stephanie had not moved.

"Does Eve accept that story, that she was riding her exercise bike and fell?"

"Yes. She never remembers the hours before an episode, during it and for a day or two after she comes out of it. We always try to tell her what happened, as much as we know anyway."

"And you can't ask her why she was out on her bicycle that evening?" Barbara murmured. "Why she went there?"

"No, I can't." She drew in a shuddering breath. "When the rain started, she might have been closer to Jay's house than ours. She knows that whole neighborhood well. Maybe she just wanted to ask Connie for a ride home. I don't know."

"Have you talked this over with Eric?"

Stephanie shook her head. "I haven't told anyone." She

picked up her coffee, then put it down without tasting it. "What are you going to do?"

"I don't know," Barbara said. "An innocent man's life is at stake."

"My daughter's life is even more at risk," Stephanie said, in an anguished voice. "She is twenty-three years old! And equally innocent."

"Well, go on home, Stephanie. I won't do anything until I think a long time. I really don't know."

"Before you, I don't know, before you tell, before you subpoena me, I don't know what I mean. Will you tell me first?"

Barbara nodded. "Yes. I'll tell you." She knew that Stephanie would rush Eve to the hospital as soon as she heard that Barbara had to tell the authorities. And she knew that would not protect Eve. A private hospital could not resist a court order to allow questioning of a patient, questioning under the standard rules.

When Stephanie reentered her house that afternoon, she could hear Eve laughing on the back patio. She stopped moving and closed her eyes for a moment, then went up the stairs to wash her hands and face. Later, she told her image in the mirror. Later you can cry, but not now. By the time she went down and joined Eric and Eve, she was smiling.

"What's the joke?"

"We're playing school, the way we used to do when we were kids," Eve said. "He's the teacher and I have to do his assignment. I don't know what a dingo looks like, and he keeps telling me it's a cross between a dog and an evil dwarf. Liar!"

"What I told you, dear deaf pupil, is look it up in the encyclopedia or on the Internet, or go to the library. I've done the best I can with my description."

They were both in high spirits, with laughter ready to erupt any moment. Eric looked at Stephanie and said, "I start classes on Monday. Or did I already tell you about it?"

"Several times," she said. "You're practicing being back in class, are you? Will you be here a while longer? I didn't get to shopping yet. Let's order something in for dinner, and I promise to cook a start-of-classes feast tomorrow." Inside her head, she kept hearing, *Later, later.*

That afternoon Barbara pulled off the coast highway at a motel with a Vacancy sign. Go think, she had ordered herself. Walk on the beach, and think. She had left a message for Frank not to expect her on Sunday, she would see him after court on Monday.

"Think," she muttered to her brain. Her brain was paying very little attention.

Sunday afternoon, Barbara was sitting on a log gazing at the sky and the gray ocean. It was as if space had doubled over and there was no clear beginning of either sea or sky, only a continuous gray expanse that began somewhere overhead and ended where waves tumbled, frothed and shot geysers of spray around black basalt columns and rocks jutting out of the water. She had checked out of her motel, and she knew she had eaten since she was not hungry. She had bathed; there were moist towels to prove that. She had left the bed a jumble of sheets and blankets, attesting to a restless night, either dream-laden or with long periods of staring into darkness.

That morning she had been jolted awake by a nightmare. Bound to stakes, both Wally and Eve were watching her. He was smiling; Eve looked terrified. Sticks and twigs were heaped to their knees and higher, and she held a burning fire stick. She had to light the fire or be consumed by the flame she held. She couldn't move and the flame in her own hand burned lower and lower. She desperately tried to fling it away but she was frozen, watching the flame. She had to light one of the pyres. Her cry of protest awakened her and she jerked out of bed in darkness. She had not even tried to sleep again.

And, she thought bleakly, she had gone around and around and around and was no nearer an exit than ever. Stephanie's story would not hold up; they would question Eve. They would learn about the bruises and see Eve exactly as Barbara had visualized her, pressed back against the railing of the bar. Criminally insane? They would demand their own evaluation, their own observation in their own hospital, and Eve would probably never leave it. She'd be labeled criminally insane, homicidal, dangerous.

In her mind's eye she saw the girl again, timid, shy, frightened, then her quick bolt out the door clutching her books. She was hardly more than a child.

Both women, she thought then, both Stephanie and Meg had lived their lives in shadowed lands, lands of self-denial, and both had seen the doors open to the sunshine, a new life, new beginning, a return to her career for Meg, a return to the land, to a little place in the country, and a life she had yearned for. And freedom from fear for Stephanie, that ever-present fear for her child. Now with her daughter's future secure, a chance to develop as an artist, to make a real life for herself, the doors were drawing closed again. A glimpse of freedom, of sunlight, then back to the shadows, deeper than ever, blacker than ever.

Eve wasn't her responsibility, she told herself harshly, as she had done many times since checking into her motel. Wally and Meg were. But he was strong, prison would not kill him. Eight, ten years would pass and he could be out again. And Meg had waited before and had used the period to launch a whole career. She could do it again, resume the career, pick up where she had left off. It wasn't as if she would be widowed, left destitute and homeless. Besides, they had had a good life. She thought of Wally's words, if found guilty, fifteen to twenty-five, and almost violently she shook her head, banishing the words again. She remembered what he had said about his old cell mate. "He told me I'd be back here just like him, old and dying."

The image of Meg's tormented face, drawn and pale, kept recurring. Could she pick up where she had left off? Begin again? She had glimpsed the sunlight beyond the newly opened doors, and she too had been plunged back into shadows, deeper, darker than ever. Could she emerge again?

Then, suddenly Barbara was thinking of her own mother, whose face had grown haggard and drawn with illness. The door had never opened for her, she thought, and shook her head again, more angrily than before. This wasn't about her mother. It had nothing to do with her. Even as she thought this, she knew it was not true. For whatever reason it was all tied together and she could not separate one from another. Her own mother had lived in the shadowed lands without questioning why, and she had died there, never glimpsing the sunlight beyond the doors that never opened for her. She had been about Meg's age when cancer struck, Barbara realized. And the doors had closed forever.

Had she ever wondered what else she might have done? Barbara had never asked her that question, had never even thought to ask, just accepted her mother's role in life. Had it been enough? She bit her lip.

An erratic wave raced inland and crashed, sending a spray high onto the cliffs, catching her in an icy shower. The tide had turned. It was growing dark, and now the sky and sea no longer formed a folded gray blanket, but a blacker, denser substance, still without edges, without definition, and the blackness carried a chilling misty rain and ocean spray that felt like ice particles being driven into her face, blinding her. The rain tasted salty, like frozen tears.

TWENTY-EIGHT

"Your Honor," Barbara said on Monday, "I move to dismiss all charges against my client, Wallis Lederer. We all know how impossible it is to prove or disprove a circumstantial case, and this is a blatant example. The prosecution has no motive for Mr. Lederer, there is no witness, no physical evidence, no forensics linking him to the crime scene, no smoking gun, but there is the lack of an alternate suspect, and I submit that that is insufficient grounds for bringing a charge of murder. It was simply a matter of convenience to name Mr. Lederer."

The prosecutor sputtered in anger. Warren Dodgson, fifty-eight years old, was one of the older assistant district attorneys. With a florid complexion, a bit overweight and dark hair that had a suspiciously even color without a sign of fading or graying, he tended to sputter and speak in loud, rapid, not always coherent, or complete, sentences. He had been around the block more often than she had, and he knew how to turn his anger on and off like a flashlight.

Evidently Judge Hiram Wells knew what to expect from him. "All right, counselor," he said patiently. "Your turn. But keep it down."

"The defendant had a powerful motive. He wanted to avoid a prison term. He was convicted and sent to prison for stealing, and he did it again, and this time, as a habitual criminal, his sentence would have been much longer. He took that boat and when he returned it, Jay Wilkins said he intended to press charges. He killed him to prevent that. As good a motive as you'll find. Home with his wife. Not even an alibi."

"Your Honor," Barbara said, "it is the defense position that there has been a double murder committed. First Connie Wilkins, then a week later her husband Jay Wilkins. We will maintain that there is a single murderer responsible for both of those deaths, and Mr. Lederer is not that person."

This time Dodgson's anger could have been real, she thought. He gaped, then exploded, "That's the most preposterous statement I've heard in a decade. There is no, absolutely no, connection between those two deaths, and she knows that as well as I do."

"What I know is that for weeks the investigators assumed that Connie Wilkins committed suicide, and by the time that assumption was abandoned, Wallis Lederer had been arrested and charged with murder. Instead of admitting that they were mistaken, they have gone ahead with this procedure. What I also know is that Lieutenant Milton Hoggarth, the lead detective in the death of Connie Wilkins, told me in person that it is an open case, with an ongoing investigation, and that it is officially recognized as an unsolved homicide. I maintain that Jay Wilkins's death is also an unsolved homicide."

* * *

"It went on from there," she told Frank at lunch. "Back and forth. In the end, of course, the motion to dismiss was rejected. But I planted a seed in Judge Wells's mind."

"And in Dodgson's," he said. "He'll report back, word will get around." He narrowed his eyes, frowning. "You want them to charge Wilkins with her murder?" he asked after a moment. "Is that the game plan?"

"If they do, it will make it a snap to show that the boat issue is a charade and without that, there's no case against Wally."

And that could be the best chance her case had, he knew.

"Hiram Wells is a good man," Frank said after a moment. "He's been on that bench thirty years, I'd guess. I've tried cases before his court. He's fair, and probably rankled as much as most judges are these days by having sentencing orders imposed, jury instructions dissected, just being under the microscope of the far right out for blood. He could swing either way, give you a little space, or clamp down tighter than a vault door."

"Holding pattern," she said. "We wait and see."

They left the restaurant and separated on the corner, Frank turning to go home, and Barbara to the Gormandi and Breaux shop two blocks away. She had committed herself with her court appearance that morning. And now she was on her way to cementing that commitment. She had not told Frank about Stephanie's disclosure, and she did not intend to tell him. It would not lighten her own load one bit, and would only put an equal burden on him. Let him keep his innocence, she thought derisively.

A light rain was falling, hardly enough to pay attention

to and, in fact, few people were bothered. She did not have an umbrella with her, and her head was bare, but she was no different from most others on the sidewalk. Visitors, tourists, outsiders marveled at the acceptance of a little rain most Eugeneans displayed. Oblivion is the best defense seemed to be the attitude.

Few retail shops remained in downtown Eugene; most had joined the lemminglike rush to the sprawling mall across the river, but Gormandi and Breaux had stayed, as if to announce that theirs was not a shop meant to attract groups of restless teenage girls with five dollars between them, or budget-strained housewives, or casual shoppers with an hour to kill before a movie. Inside, the racks were not crowded, and each item was unique.

"Clair de Lune" was playing softly in the background when Barbara entered. Stephanie was with two customers comparing one white blouse with another. She looked up when Barbara came in, and if she stiffened or paled or had any negative reaction, it was not visible. She nodded.

Barbara returned the nod, and began to look through a rack of tailored suits. She should shop in a place like this, she thought, dress her part for a change, but she knew she wouldn't. Shelley always said Barbara was not a shopper. She knew what she wanted, went to a store that had it, bought it and left, all as quickly as possible. That's not shopping, Shelley often said.

A sale was concluded, the customer paid, and Stephanie carefully wrapped the purchase in tissue paper, put it in a bag, and the customer left with her companion. Stephanie did not move from behind the counter as Barbara approached.

"I'm not going to call you," Barbara said. "And no one is going to bother Eve. You should know that."

Stephanie bowed her head a moment, then looked up. "Thank you," she said faintly, and now Barbara could see the pallor that had spread across her classic features.

Barbara nodded, turned and left the shop. Signed and sealed, she thought. Doubly committed.

Meanwhile, she had a case to prepare, one that could swing in two completely different ways, and she had to be ready for either one.

On Thursday, Hoggarth stormed into her office. He was red-faced and furious. "What are you trying to do, Hollo-way?" he snapped, ignoring her motion for him to take a chair. "You know damn well that he killed her. What's this crap about a double murder?"

"Lieutenant, let me tell you a little story," she said calmly. "There was a rabbi being held hostage and his enemy said, 'If you can explain the Torah in thirty seconds I'll spare your life.' He was flourishing a great, long sword, swishing it back and forth. The rabbi said, 'Easily done, my friend. Do unto others as you would have them do unto you. All the rest is commentary.' That's my philosophy, Lieutenant. All I know is the official word, which is that Connie Wilkins's death is an unsolved murder. All the rest is commentary, opinion, speculation, or call it what you will."

"I've seen you pull one fast one after another, extortion, blackmail, right under my nose, but it isn't going to work this time. You think you'll force our hand," he said in a mean low voice. "And you think wrong. We don't charge anyone without proof and we're in the process of finding the proof. Until we do, zilch."

"Very commendable," she said. "I heartily approve of your approach. I wish you had applied it to Wally Lederer, but I guess we can't have everything we wish for, can we?"

"And get this," he said, more red-faced than he had been only a second earlier, "Dodgson is on to you and your tricks. He's going to swat you back in your cage every time you even think double murder."

"He's coming armed with a whip and chair? Oh, my. I'll be sure to wear my tiger mask. Anything else on your mind, Lieutenant? It's always nice chatting with you, but I am a bit busy these days."

He glared at her, turned and walked out stiffly.

Three weeks and counting. On Friday night she told Darren, "I won't be back until the trial is over."

"You should get away from it all now and then if only for an hour or two at a time. You need to relax a little," he said, rubbing her back.

"Can't," she said. "Just the way it is." She was surprised by a flush of annoyance brought on by his words.

The following Tuesday Eric came to the office without calling first. "I had to tell you something," he said when Barbara went to the outer office to see him.

"Well, come on back and tell me," she said. She stopped by Shelley's door and looked in. "If you're free, Eric has something to tell us." She motioned for him to come along back to her office. Shelley followed.

Eric was nearly dancing and clearly had no intention of

sitting down. "Probate okayed the handwritten codicil! Everything's going ahead now! Konig said you did it, you and Sonia. And he said you must have twisted Berman's arm. He isn't going to contest it, out of respect for the family, and he'll start liquidating Dad's estate. But Konig said we don't have to wait for that. He told Mother she could start looking for a bigger house, with space for a studio or something for Eve, whatever she needs!"

Shelley was laughing along with him, and he grabbed and hugged her and then to Barbara's surprise, he hugged her, too.

"In like a whirlwind, out like the same," Barbara said through her laughter when he rushed out. "When's the last time you saw anyone as excited as he is?"

"Maybe it's a first," Shelley said, grinning broadly. "Made my day, I'll say that." She waved and returned to her own office, and Barbara resumed her seat behind her desk.

Every day she was searching the newspapers, listening to the radio news, watching local television newscasts almost compulsively, for any indication that the police would name Jay as Connie Wilkins's murderer. There was nothing. The story had died in the media, old news, no developments; with an election approaching, an unsolved murder did not rate a column inch. She still had two cases prepared, and felt as if she were doing a balancing act on a tightrope without a safety net, ready to swing down on either side of it. Or fall flat on her face on either side, she amended.

Wally and Meg came in on Wednesday morning the week before the trial. He was as affable and relaxed as always, and she looked haunted.

"You're welcome to stay," Barbara told Meg, "but this is going to be a long grueling day. If you have shopping or something else to do…"

"I'd like to stay," Meg said. "I won't butt in or say a word, promise."

They started. There was a brief break for lunch, brought in by Maria, and they returned to it. Then Frank started his cross-examination.

Meg looked more and more strained as the day wore on, but she was true to her word and remained silent. Wally's good humor was unshakable. At five, Frank leaned back in his chair and said, "You'll do fine, Wally." Barbara seconded that.

She went to the bar and brought out wine, bourbon and water. "Now, relax, and let's just talk a few minutes," she said, although she thought if Wally relaxed any more he would start snoring.

"It's going to take longer in court," Barbara said after passing out drinks, "because there will be objections, arguments, God knows how Dodgson will play the game, and I'll show your two videos, another couple of hours, plus recesses. We'll run into two days, but basically that's it."

"They're letting you show the videos?" Wally asked. "I thought they might not."

"Well, we talked about it a while," she said. "But yes, I'll show them."

Frank suppressed a smile. What she had said that day was that Dodgson had gotten so loud that Judge Wells had come to a decision in her favor just to shut him up.

"And you don't want me to mention anything about the wet pants and sand in his shoes," Wally mused. "Any reason?"

"It's immaterial to the case I'll be building. Jay was a man worried about his wife's safety. That's the issue. We'll go along with that."

He regarded her shrewdly, nodded and sipped his drink. "I think he killed her," he said, "and somehow he was using us to cover himself."

"Whatever you think, keep it to yourself," Barbara said sharply. "You don't offer a word beyond whatever answer the question demands. No volunteering anything."

"Gotcha," he said. "You're the boss. But that's what I think. Anyway, we'll check into the hotel Sunday and be on hand bright and early Monday morning."

"In that case, come on out to the house for dinner on Sunday," Frank said. "You can tell us your stories, and I'll tell you some of mine. Deal?"

Wally grinned. "Deal."

After Wally and Meg left, Barbara said, "I'm worried about him, Dad. He's too carefree and calm. It's unnatural."

"I think he just has faith in you," Frank said. "He's a born optimist. That and his belief in you will see him through it without ruffling a feather. Wish I could say the same about Meg."

"He's the optimist and she's the realist," Barbara said. Or, she added to herself, he's the skilled performer and Meg's his audience.

That Sunday night at dinner, Wally told them one of his stories. "So there I was with three handguns on the table. Two guys came to claim theirs, but no one would come up for the last one. So a detective took it and they ran it through the FBI lab testing for matching bullets, and came

up with an armed robbery, unsolved. They had been looking for that particular gun for a long time. And I had the
guy on a video. They used that video in court and got a conviction." Wally leaned back in his chair smiling broadly.
"I was hero of the day."

"You picked the pockets of FBI agents, detectives, sheriffs, without anyone noticing that you were stealing their
guns? Good heavens!" Barbara said, awed. "And there was
a ringer in the group! Incredible."

"Yep, there he was, playing cops and robbers, seems he
liked to play both sides. Sometimes a cop, sometimes a
robber. He should have stayed home that night."

Frank had made a leg of lamb, boned and stuffed with
a savory chanterelle stuffing, and no one at the table was
in a hurry to move after his dinner.

"Your turn," Wally said to Frank. He poured himself a
little more wine.

"Well, this is about one that got away," Frank said.
"Some years ago I had this client, charged with drunken-
ness, rowdiness, breaking up some furniture and starting
a brawl. He and his buddies all testified that they were the
innocent, sober bystanders when a bunch of outsiders came
to break up the wedding party they had attended earlier that
afternoon. Lunch recess came and my client took off with
his pals, but when court resumed they weren't there. Half
an hour later, after the bailiff went looking for them, they
came staggering back, drunk as lords, each and every one
of them, singing in the corridor. The judge was pretty sore
about it. Lost that case," Frank said, shaking his head.

"And now you make your clients stay in sight during
lunch," Wally said. "I thought there might be a reason."

One of the cats strolled in. He stood up with his paws on the table and sniffed. Frank told him to beat it. "That's Thing One," he said.

Barbara gave him a skeptical look. She no longer could tell one from the other and she doubted very much that Frank could, either.

"We'll get a cat after… Later, we'll get a cat," Meg said. "And a dog. A big dog to guard the chickens. I imagine there are coyotes out around us. I haven't seen any, but I know they used to be all over the place."

"They still are," Frank said. "You're going to have chickens?"

"I know. We started wanting just a house in the country, and now it seems I want a kitchen garden and I want chickens. Remember, I grew up on a real farm. Mom had a job in town and I rode in with her to go to school, but I was a farm girl. I guess I'm reverting to type."

Barbara began to clear the table. She had heard a note of defiance in Meg's tone, and recalled what Frank had said, that Wally wanted her to rent the place or sell it if he was found guilty. Meg was telling him no, Barbara thought. All those years living in city apartments, hotels, hungering for a farm, a few chickens, a little garden.

After they ate blackberry cobbler and had coffee, Meg offered to help clean up and Frank said absolutely not. They didn't stay much longer. At the door Meg took Barbara's hand and held it for a moment, then closed it.

"Starting tomorrow, he's in your hands," she said. "Good luck."

Barbara didn't open her hand again until she was back in the kitchen to help load the dishwasher. Frank drove her home as soon as they were done. At her door he said, "Bobby, she put him in good hands. It's going to be okay." But when he got home and sat down with his crossword puzzle, he wished fervently that he really believed that.

Jury selection did not take long. Wally objected to two prospective jurors, and Barbara added them to her single choice to exercise her peremptory challenges. She trusted his judgment in sizing up people. Dodgson challenged two, and it was done. The jury was made up of six women, six men, the youngest was twenty-two, the oldest seventy-two, two black men, one black woman, one Hispanic woman. A good cross section of the county, Barbara thought.

Dodgson's brief opening statement had no surprises. The most persuasive statement he made in Barbara's opinion was when he said, "Ladies and gentlemen, the reason the defendant took the boat doesn't matter. A practical joke, greed, revenge for a long-nursed grievance, it's all immaterial. No one can point to a different thief and a different murderer. He alone had the opportunity to take the boat, and no one except the killer had the opportunity to return it. The theft of that boat provided the sole motive for the murder of Jay Wilkins."

When it was her turn, Barbara concluded by saying, "This is a circumstantial case with no direct evidence, no forensic evidence, no eyewitness, nothing of substance to point to in charging Mr. Lederer. The defense will offer an alternative view of what happened, and if that case is as plausible as the case the state will present, you must ask yourselves if there is a reasonable doubt in your minds as to the guilt of Mr. Lederer. It is not your task to question if he did not do it, then who did, as the state implies. That is not your job."

And here we go, she thought when the prosecution called its first witness.

Mrs. Wanda Haley had been the housekeeper for Jay Wilkins for eleven years. She was sixty, pleasant-looking with a placid expression, a bit overweight, and that day she was nervous at her role on the witness stand. Most witnesses were.

She recalled the day of April 22 and gave a brief account of her morning. "I got there at nine like always and started right in on the kitchen. Put dishes in the dishwasher, cleaned the stove and polished it, and the faucets, the refrigerator door, just all the usual things. Then I took my vacuum and cleaning supplies to the study. That's always next, and I was surprised to see Mr. Wilkins was in there again. He had stayed home on Monday, too. He went to the bar room and began talking on the telephone in there. I cleaned the glass for the cabinet with the cars, and was going to do the other one when I saw that it wasn't closed all the way. And I saw that the little boat was not where it belonged. So I went to the bar room and asked Mr. Wilkins if I should close it. He was real upset and looked at the door and called his insurance man. He was cursing, really mad. And in a little while the insurance man came with a policeman, I guess. I was back in the kitchen by then, though."

Dodgson nodded. "When Mr. Wilkins was in the bar room talking on the phone could you hear what he was saying?"

"Yes, sir. Some of it. He was yelling at someone and said his wife was in danger and he wanted an investigation. He said to send someone over right now to get her picture and get it posted. It was things like that."

"All right. And when he saw that the boat was missing, what exactly did he say?"

She looked uneasily at the jury. "Well, like I said, he was cursing. He said, that goddamn son of a bitch stole it! Thumbing his nose at me in my own house. I'll see the goddamn bastard back in prison. It was things like that."

"Then what happened?"

"Well, he yelled at me to go do the bedrooms or something. And that's what I did. And just before I was ready to leave, a detective came to the kitchen. I had just mopped the floor. I always leave that for last thing, and he said he was sorry to be tracking it up again. He was real nice. He asked me to go with him to see if Mrs. Wilkins packed a suitcase or something, and we looked in the closet where they kept the suitcases and I saw that a little roll-on suitcase was missing. And he asked me how her health was, and I told him it was fine. She'd been real sick the year before, but in the fall and over winter she got well and she was fine."

"Did he ask you anything else?"

"He wanted to know if she'd talked about going away on a trip, and I told him no. And I asked him if she'd gone off and he said yes. And that's all. He said I could go on home and I did."

"All right," Dodgson said. "Now let's move forward a week to Monday, April 28 Do you recall that morning?"

Mrs. Haley nodded, then said yes. She did the kitchen and took her gear to the foyer. She looked into the bar room, saw the body, and ran back to the kitchen to call 911. She told them to send someone to the back door and she waited for the police in the kitchen. Two officers came, called for others and pretty soon, she said, the house was full of detectives.

"They told me to wait in the kitchen, and then one of them asked me questions. Like could I tell if he had eaten at home on the weekend. There was a plate with a steak bone on the kitchen counter, and spare ribs and slaw and stuff still on the table in the breakfast room, like he had take-out food. A skillet had some egg sticking to it, open bread loaf, the kind of breakfast he fixed for himself sometimes."

"What else did they ask you?"

"They had me check out the silverware and things like that to see if anything was missing, but it was all there. There was one towel gone from the downstairs bathroom and a red silk Afghan from the bar room."

Dodgson produced one of the gold towels and asked her if the missing one was like it and she said yes. He finished with her very soon after that.

Barbara stood up and greeted Mrs. Haley pleasantly, then said, "Early in your testimony you said you had a routine that you always followed in your daily job at Mr. Wilkins's house. You said that you cleaned the stove and polished it, and the refrigerator door and faucets. Did you do that every day?"

"Yes, I did."

"And did you clean the glass doors of the locked cabinets every day?"

"Yes. And the bar, and all the mirrors, the television screen, everything that had a finish that would show smudges or fingerprints, water spots, or anything like that. He told me to when he hired me. And I did."

"Did all those surfaces need such meticulous cleaning on a daily basis?"

"No. You couldn't tell the difference from one day to the next, but it's what he wanted, and what I did. And the bath-room wastebaskets. They had to be cleaned and polished every day."

"I see. What did he do if he spotted a smudge?"

"He left me a note on the breakfast room table. Like, 'Clean the refrigerator,' or 'The mirror is streaked.' But it didn't happen much. I was careful."

"On Monday, April 28, you didn't follow your usual routine, did you? You didn't go straight to the study after doing the kitchen. Why was that?"

"He'd been home all week, in a bad mood, and I wanted to keep out of his way. If he'd been in the bar room I would have gone to the study. I was just checking first."

"During that week did he tell you why he was in a bad mood, what was on his mind?"

"No. He never talked to me about anything. I read it in the newspaper."

"He never talked to you? Not about his missing wife, or the missing boat?"

Even as Mrs. Haley shook her head, Dodgson objected. "Your Honor, this is all irrelevant."

"Withdraw the question," Barbara said equably. "When you called 911 why did you tell them to send someone to the back door? Why not let them ring the bell and admit them at the front?"

"I couldn't open that door," Mrs. Haley said. "He told me never to open that door or he'd know. He kept chang-ing the password and I had to keep mine written down just to remember it. The password I use is different from the front door."

Barbara nodded. "I see. Did Mrs. Wilkins talk to you?"

"Yes, she did. She'd ask about my husband and kids, and she showed me her sweatpants and shirt and said she intended to get back her muscles. She was real friendly. She said that when her exercise class was over, she'd get a bike and start riding with her stepdaughter."

"You said that Mr. Wilkins was in a bad mood all that week. Can you tell the jury how that showed? In what actions or speech?"

"Well, like I said he didn't talk to me, but he stormed around the house, and he was on the phone a lot, sometimes yelling on the phone. It sounded like someone at the dealership might have been who he called sometimes, the way he was giving orders. And I heard him tell someone that he couldn't sleep, he was so worried. But usually I tried to keep out of his way that week and he left me alone."

"You testified that over the weekend he had eaten in both nights. What about the rest of that week? Had he been having his meals at home, either cooking something or ordering in?"

She nodded. "Every day there were boxes, or cartons, things from take-out food. I don't think he ate out a single time that week."

When she thanked Mrs. Haley and resumed her seat Barbara was aware of the slight puzzlement on Dodgson's face, as if he were wondering why she was bolstering his case of a man worried about the safety of his wife and the theft of a valuable art object. You paint your picture of Jay Wilkins, she thought, and I'll paint mine.

At that time the judge called the luncheon recess.

"Well, we got us the beginning of a motive, and we got

us a corpse," Wally said in the car heading for Frank's house for lunch. "What's next?"

"They'll probably call the medical examiner," Barbara said.

"And he'll say, Yep, he was dead all right," Wally said. He sounded altogether too cheerful, but Meg groaned.

The state's next witness was Lawrence Trelawney, who identified himself as a representative of the company that had carried Jay Wilkins's home owner's insurance. A well-dressed man, even a little dapper, in his middle years, he had been easy to talk to when Barbara had met him months earlier. He was at ease on the witness stand.

"Will you tell the jury what transpired on the morning of April 22?" Dodgson asked.

"Yes. Mr. Wilkins called my office and said that the boat, Cleopatra's Barge, had been stolen, and that he knew who took it. He was infuriated and demanded that I come to his house to tell the police about the value of the item. He said he would see to it that a police officer was there to take details. Of course, I did so."

Dodgson produced the boat then and had Trelawney identify it. He did not pass it to the jury to examine, but had it entered as a state exhibit.

"What is the value of that boat?" Dodgson asked.

"On today's market it would be worth roughly twenty-five to thirty thousand dollars."

Dodgson repeated the figure in an awed tone. "Did Mr. Wilkins tell you who he suspected of stealing the boat?"

"Oh, yes. More than once. He accused Mr. Lederer and told us why. He said that the boat had been in place on

Monday night, that no one but Mr. Lederer and his wife had been in the house, and the boat was gone Tuesday morning. And he said that Mr. Lederer had been arrested in the past for robbery. He showed us his security system and said he had made certain it was turned on Monday night."

"Did he say more than that?"

"Yes. He said they had examined the boat and that Mr. Lederer was still holding it when he, Mr. Wilkins, took Mrs. Lederer's arm to escort her to the bar room, and that Mr. Lederer followed a minute later."

Dodgson looked very grave when he turned to the jury and said, more to them than to the witness, "And he was certain that no one else had entered the house that night?"

"He was quite positive about that. In fact, he said his security system proved it."

Dodgson was content to let it rest there, the identity of the thief had been established beyond a doubt, was his attitude.

Barbara said good afternoon to Mr. Trelawney, and then asked, "You said you launched your investigation. What did you do?"

"I looked up the history of the boat, the appraisal, things of that sort. Two days later I accompanied a police officer to the home of Mr. Lederer to ask him if he knew anything about the boat. He denied any knowledge about it."

"Mr. Trelawney, were you very concerned with the theft of such a valuable item since your company insured it?"

"Not at that time. Of course, no one knew then that Mrs. Wilkins had already been murdered herself."

Dodgson roared an objection. "Move that comment be stricken as not relevant to this trial." It was sustained.

"You weren't overly concerned. Why was that?" Barbara asked then.

"Mr. Wilkins was very agitated, but he said that his wife was also missing, and that he feared for her safety. I'm afraid I assumed that this was an instance of a domestic quarrel. In my experience the departing spouse frequently takes a prized object away, and eventually that spouse returns, there is a reconciliation and the object reappears. This matter seemed very much to fit that scenario. I advised Mr. Wilkins to await the return of his wife before taking any further action."

"Did he accept that advice?"

"No. He called me a day later to see what I was doing about it. A day or two after his death was discovered I was notified that the boat had reappeared. After that it was no longer my concern."

The next witness was the officer who had made the initial report of the theft of the boat. He added little to what Trelawney had already testified to.

Then Barbara asked, "Why did you ask the housekeeper about Mrs. Wilkins's state of health?"

"Well, Mr. Wilkins said she was suicidal, and I thought if she was disturbed, maybe she took the boat just to get even or something. People do that sometimes. But the housekeeper said she was all right."

"Did your department start a formal investigation at that time?"

"No, ma'am. We wanted to wait until Mrs. Wilkins came back and ask her about it. We did a routine background check on Mr. Lederer, but that's all."

The medical examiner was next. His testimony was so

precise and matter-of-fact that he made a death by murder
seem almost prosaic. The deceased died between nine and
midnight the night of April 26. He suffered a blow to the
head that was not fatal but most likely rendered him unconscious, and death was caused by the severance of his
spinal cord at the first and second vertebra. Such severance
caused death to occur instantly. He identified the pitcher
that had been used as a weapon. It still had Jay Wilkins's
hairs in it.

Dodgson had him fill in some details, how they knew
when death occurred, had the body been moved after Wilkins broke his neck, was there any indication of drugs or
alcohol, and a few others.

Barbara had no questions.

In rapid succession the first police officer to respond to
the 911 call testified and described the routine in homicide
cases, which he had followed. Barbara had no questions.

Forensics would be next, Barbara knew, and she did
have a lot of questions, but before Dodgson could call on
the first witness, Judge Wells adjourned for the day.

"It's been a long first day," he said to the jurors. He instructed them not to read about the case, watch any newscast that referred to it, or discuss it with anyone, including
one another, and that was the end of day one.

In the corridor outside the courtroom, Meg drew in a
long shuddering breath, then said, "Thank God they're
done with the boat business."

Barbara did not contradict her, but she knew they were
not done with it yet.

TWENTY-NINE

The first witness the following day was Detective Sergeant Donald McChesney, the lead detective of the investigation. He was tall and lean, almost to the point of emaciation, with sharp cheekbones, a long pointed nose, dark hair and eyes and a swarthy complexion. He looked as if an incipient beard was close to emerging.

He described the investigation in specific details to go along with photographs of the crime scene as well as a schematic of the front of the house, the entrance, foyer, the bar room and the study. Pointing to an enlarged photograph of Jay Wilkins's body, he described the same scenario that Barbara and Bailey had enacted. Then he said, "There was hemlock bark mulch on the floor here." He positioned the schematic on the easel and pointed again. "Bark mulch was on the doorjamb, and small amounts here and here." He pointed to them on the foyer floor. "Outside, on the front entrance stones, more bark mulch.

It is used extensively in the foundation planting all around the house.

"We recovered no fingerprints, except some of Mr. Wilkins's. From Mr. Wilkins's fingernails we recovered some denim fibers, and there were some yellow cotton fibers on the bar stool, the bar and on the floor.

"The television was turned on but it was muted. When we examined Mr. Wilkins's desk in the study, we discovered a gold boat in the bottom right drawer. It had been wiped clean of all fingerprints.

"We called the security company to come turn off the system, and they recovered a tape, a log of the past month with a record of all the times the system had been turned off and on."

Dodgson stopped him at that point. "Will you explain the system to the jury so we'll all understand just what you mean?"

He gave a detailed account of each opening and closing of the outside doors.

Dodgson produced a sheet of paper and showed it to Judge Wells and Barbara, then passed it to the officer to identify.

"It's a printout of the log for the period starting Sunday, April 20, to Monday, April 28."

Dodgson had a second sheet entered and asked him to describe that one. "That's the log for the back door that the housekeeper uses."

"In other words," Dodgson said slowly, speaking to the jury now, "we know every single time an outside window or door was opened and when it was closed again. We know that Mr. Wilkins returned from the coast on Sunday evening, ordered a meal and remained home that night. On Monday he turned the system off to admit the defendant and his wife, and turned it back on when they left. On Tuesday he admitted the police officer and his insurance agent. And no one entered or left that house again except for the housekeeper or someone delivering food until the night that Jay Wilkins admitted his killer." He turned to the witness. "Is that a correct summation of the logs?"

The officer confirmed it was.

Now the boat business was wrapped up, Barbara thought, at least for now. Every juror's gaze shifted from the sergeant to Wally. She heard a soft moan from Meg, sitting behind her, and she hoped that Frank was holding her hand, or patting her or something. At her side Wally was looking thoughtful.

Dodgson then asked, "You said you found yellow cotton fibers. Did you find the source for them?"

"Yes, sir. They match the towels in the downstairs bathroom."

"Also, you found denim fibers. Did you locate a source for them?"

"Yes, sir. We obtained a search warrant for the defendant's house and a pair of denim jeans was located. On examination, the fibers matched the denim in the jeans."

Dodgson opened a plastic bag and carefully removed a pair of jeans. They were worn and faded, with thorns and dirt still clinging to them. "Are these the blue jeans you found when you searched the defendant's house?"

The sergeant looked them over, then said yes.

"And the fibers at the crime scene matched the denim in these jeans. Is that correct?"

"Yes, sir."

Dodgson walked to the jury box with the jeans. "I won't pass them among you," he said. "As you can see they are soiled." He held them up for the jury to look at, then returned them to the plastic bag and had them entered as a state exhibit.

"Sergeant McChesney," he said, "is it your practice to try to reconstruct the events of a crime like this? To give you a direction for your continuing investigation?"

"Yes, sir. We generally do that."

"Will you tell the jury how you reconstructed this crime?"

"We believe the assailant stepped into the mulch and picked up a stick. There are quite a number of them. They break off with winter rains."

Barbara objected. "You Honor, this is merely speculation, guesses as to what happened. The detective has no way of knowing if what he is suggesting actually occurred."

"We said it is speculative," Dodgson said smoothly. "This is a common procedure in a serious investigation. It is merely used to give the investigators a sense of what might have happened."

The judge nodded, then regarded the jury and said, "It must be clearly understood that any speculation done by the investigators is not to be considered evidence. It is speculation only." He overruled, and the detective continued.

"The assailant rang the doorbell and Mr. Wilkins opened the door. His assailant put the stick in the doorway to keep the door from closing, and followed him into the bar room. He left bark mulch in the foyer, and on the floor in the bar. They stood in front of the bar. The assailant picked up the pitcher and struck Mr. Wilkins, then probably knelt down to see if he was dead. In feeling for a pulse, he caused the body to shift. He put the pitcher down, went for the towel and wiped all fingerprints off the bar and the pitcher. Then he wiped the boat and went to the study and put it in the drawer."

"Objection," Barbara said. "Move that the last remark be stricken as moving beyond speculation concerning the act of murder. No evidence has been presented to indicate such action."

It was sustained.

Unperturbed, the sergeant continued. "We assume he picked up his stick on the way out and tossed it back into the plants and left the scene."

"And how do you account for the denim fibers?"

"When Mr. Wilkins was falling, he likely grabbed at something for support and his hand raked down the assailant's leg."

"Why do you say the killer put the pitcher down instead of just dropping it?"

"If he had dropped it, it would have broken on the stone flooring, or at least chipped or cracked. It didn't do that. If he intended to use it again, he would have kept it. Since Mr. Wilkins's neck was broken on the stool's rung, the murderer didn't need the pitcher, so he put it down."

Dodgson finished soon after that and Barbara stood up. "Detective McChesney, just to clarify some of the assumptions you made, do you know how bark mulch was deposited in the doorsill?" He said no, and she went down the rest of the assumptions, each time getting the same answer: no. He didn't know how long the assailant and Wilkins remained at the bar before the attack. He didn't know why the pitcher was not cracked or broken. He didn't know how the body got moved. When she finished that line she asked, "Is there anything unusual about the security system at the Wilkins house?"

"It's standard, with an added feature," he said.

"What is that added feature?"

"Keeping the thirty-day log. Not many private systems do that."

Pointing to the schematic, Barbara asked where the outside keypad was located. He pointed to it.

"Is it plainly visible?" He said yes.

"Where is the inside control panel with the switches?"

"On the foyer wall."

"Is it plainly visible?"

"No. It's located behind a wall hanging."

"Are the cases in the study connected to the same security system?"

"They're tied in to the system but on a separate circuit. It has to be turned off and the cases unlocked with a key. They have to be operated manually."

"Does the log include them?"

"Yes."

"And what does it tell about when they were opened that week?" She picked up the printout and handed it to him.

"It shows that the case with the gold objects was opened on Monday night at six twenty-five and closed on Tuesday at two-thirty in the afternoon."

"You mentioned bark mulch in the doorway. Just to clarify what you meant, is this the kind of object you were talking about?" She went to her table and Shelley passed her a door threshold—a metal strip as long as the door was wide, with raised rubber running the length of it.

When the sergeant examined it he said it was just like the one at the Wilkins house.

"What is the purpose of it?" Barbara asked, handing it to the foreman of the jury. He looked it over and passed it along to the other panel members.

"It closes the gap at the bottom of the door to make a tight fit," the sergeant said.

Barbara retrieved the threshold and, pointing to it, she said, "The raised top is ridged, and there appears to be a metal strip. Exactly where was the bark mulch found?"

"On the extreme left as you enter."

"About the door itself, is it spring loaded or weighted in such a way that it automatically closes after being opened?"

"No."

"If it's pushed open, it stays open until someone closes it. Is that right?"

He hesitated a moment, then said yes.

"In other words it does not need to be propped open with anything. Is that correct?"

"Yes, but someone might not have known that."

"I move that the last part of his remark be stricken," she said, glancing at the judge.

He nodded. "Everything after the word 'yes' will be stricken."

"Sergeant, what is the lot number of the blue jeans you examined?"

"I don't know. There's no lot number on them."

"When were they manufactured?"

His answer was more brusque. "I don't know."

"Do you know where they were manufactured?"

He said no.

"Exactly what were you basing your conclusion on? That the fibers matched that particular garment?"

"The fibers are old and frayed and faded just like the jeans, obviously as old as the jeans. They are a perfect match."

"I see." She walked to her table and Shelley handed her a man's denim jacket. It looked to be as old as the jeans, as faded and just as frayed. She held it up to the sergeant. "Would those fibers match this jacket?"

"I would have to have it examined under a microscope to be certain," he said.

"Did you examine the jeans under a microscope?"

He hesitated, then said no.

She put the jacket down and held up a child's coveralls, in the same condition as the jacket and the jeans. "Would those fibers match this material?"

"I don't know," he snapped.

"All right. Would it be correct to say that the fibers you found are frayed and old, very faded, and that the jeans are in the same shape, and that's just about all you can say about them?"

Dodgson objected, but Judge Wells overruled and after another pause the sergeant said that was a fair statement.

"Did you go to Mr. Lederer's house yourself with the search warrant?"

He said no. Two detectives on his team did that. They had stipulated as much at a pretrial hearing, she just wanted to make it clear now.

"But you can answer for them," she said. "Is that correct?"

"Yes."

"Where were those jeans that day?"

"He was wearing them."

"So they asked him to change his clothes, is that right?"

"Yes."

"Where was he when he took off his jeans?"

"On the back porch by the door. He put on a robe and slippers there."

"Was the robe already by the door?" He said yes, and he said yes when she asked if the slippers were already there.

"What else did they collect that day?"

"His shoes."

"Did they examine his car and remove the floor mat?"

"Yes."

"Was there any bark mulch on his shoes?" He said no. "Was there any in his car or on the floor mat?" He said no again.

"After the jeans were examined, what did you do with them?"

"We put them in the evidence bag, and they've been there ever since until today."

"I see. I noticed that when Mr. Dodgson removed them earlier, he was careful not to turn the evidence bag over. I'd like to remove them again at this time." She did that, then carefully held the plastic bag close enough for him to see inside. "What is that in the bottom of the bag, Sergeant?"

"There's some dirt, maybe some thorns, just debris from the jeans."

"What was Mr. Lederer doing the day your officers collected the jeans?"

"He was clearing brambles off his property."

Barbara walked in front of the jurors, showing them the dirt in the bag. Then she replaced the jeans and returned it to the exhibit table.

"Did you find any dirt, thorns or debris like that at the crime scene?"

"No."

She moved to the schematic and pointed to the floor in the foyer and then to the bar room where bark mulch had been found. "Do you know how that bark mulch was left in those places?"

"No."

"All right. Previously you made many assumptions about what happened that night. Did you make any assumptions about how the bark mulch was left on the floors?"

"We assume it was on the defendant's shoes."

"Was there any bark mulch in the study?"

"No."

"Was any found anywhere else besides where you indicate here?" She pointed to the schematic, and he said no.

She asked if they'd found any yellow fibers in Wally's car or on his clothing, and the answer was no. She asked the same question about red silk fibers, and got the same no for an answer.

When Barbara said she had no more questions, Dodgson in his redirect examination simply reinforced the fact that the security log showed that no one had entered the house after Wally and Meg's visit on Monday evening until the next day after the boat was discovered to be missing, and that the boat had reappeared after someone murdered Jay Wilkins.

Judge Wells called for a brief recess then. When the bailiff escorted the jurors out, Wally leaned over the rail behind the defense table to take Meg's hands. "I told you
Frank wouldn't have given her a thumbs-up if she wasn't
good. She made a monkey out of that guy. Let's go get a
soda or something."

"I'll come, too," Frank said, and the three of them
walked out of the courtroom together.

After the recess Dodgson called Sergeant William
Henry. His duty, he testified, was to do a background check
on the associates of Jay Wilkins, look into his business affairs, examine his computer, to try to determine if there had
been a problem serious enough to consider it a motive for
murder. He had the appearance of a million-dollar account
manager who would reconcile the statements down to the
last penny.

"As part of this investigation, did you do a check on the
defendant?" Dodgson asked.

"Yes."

"Please tell the jury the findings of your check."

Since Wally had used his prison experience in his own
video, Barbara had agreed not to challenge having it
brought up in court. The sergeant told of his results, the
youthful pickpocket arrest, and later the arrest and subse-
quent prison sentence.

"And did your investigation reveal any serious problem
or altercation involving Mr. Wilkins?"

"No, sir. Mr. Wilkins's business affairs were in good
order, there were no threats, no enmity among associates
or the people who worked for him."

Barbara watched Dodgson with great interest. He had to ask the next question no matter how reluctant he was to bring up the name of Connie Wilkins. A missing wife, a missing boat and a dead husband couldn't be left hanging without some explanation.

He asked it. "Did your background checks include one concerning Mrs. Wilkins?"

"Yes, sir. We had the report that he had called in to say she was missing, and we checked it out. Eventually we concluded that it led nowhere and we abandoned that line of inquiry."

When she started her cross-examination Barbara asked, "Sergeant Henry, you stated that your investigation of Mrs. Wilkins led nowhere. Can you explain what you meant by that?"

He glanced at Dodgson, then said, "We ruled her out as a suspect."

"But please tell the jury why she was a suspect to begin with, suspected of doing what?"

"There was the possibility that she had taken the boat herself," he said deliberately.

"Did the department at any time consider her a suspect in the death of Mr. Wilkins?"

"At one time or another we considered almost everyone who knew him, including her."

"I see. Exactly when did you abandon that suspicion?"

"Around May 8."

"Sergeant, please tell the jury why you abandoned that line of inquiry at that time."

Dodgson objected, then said, "Your Honor, may I approach?"

Judge Wells looked resigned when he motioned them both forward. "All right, counselor," he said to Dodgson.

"Your Honor, the death of Connie Wilkins is irrelevant to this trial. There is an ongoing investigation into her death, and to bring it up in this context could compromise that investigation, and it would certainly muddy the waters and confuse this jury."

"I would think that a missing wife, a missing prized object and a murdered husband has to be explained," Barbara said. "If that is considered entirely irrelevant and outside the scope of this trial, there is no reason for the jurors not to look it up for themselves. And that could leave them even more confused when they learn that her death by murder occurred a week before that of her husband. They just might start talking about it in the deliberation room, wondering on their own if there's a connection."

"He could instruct them not to look her up or discuss it," Dodgson said in a voice that threatened to break into a thunderous roar any second.

"Not if it's irrelevant," Judge Wells murmured. "What next? They can't look up the national debt? This matter is going to be referred to again. I think it's better to clear the air here, today. Overruled, Mr. Dodgson. Let's get on with it."

When they were back in their places, Barbara said to the police officer, "Would you like me to repeat my question?"

"No. The body of a drowned woman was recovered from the ocean and on May 8 she was identified as Connie Wilkins."

"When did she die?"

"Between April 19 and April 21."

"She died a week before Mr. Wilkins. Is that correct?"

"Yes."

"Was her body in the ocean for all that time?"

He said yes again.

"Have the facts of her death been determined?"

"No. There's an ongoing investigation."

"What department is conducting that investigation, Sergeant Henry."

"The homicide unit."

She thanked him and said she had no more questions. When Dodgson got up for his redirect, he gave Barbara a venomous look before turning to the sergeant.

"On Saturday, the nineteenth of April, did you determine the activities of Mr. Wilkins before his encounter with the defendant at the casino?"

"Yes." In a flat, dispassionate voice he recounted Wilkins's movements for the weekend.

"So his time was all accounted for from the nineteenth until the twenty-first of April?"

"That's right."

When Sergeant Henry was dismissed, Judge Wells called for the lunch break. In the car, heading for his house, Frank said cheerfully, "The trial was just lengthened by a day or two. Now they have to switch to game plan B."

He glanced at Barbara, who appeared oblivious. "I think I'll leave you guys to your lunches," she said, "and take a walk."

"Is anything wrong?" Meg asked anxiously.

"Nope," Frank said. "She does that. Walks and thinks during breaks. She'll catch up with food in a bit."

But something was wrong, he knew. He had sensed an

undercurrent of wrongness for days, and while the trial was going almost exactly how they had expected with no surprises yet, the feeling of something wrong persisted.

THIRTY

"They'll try to stay with game plan A," Barbara had said a week before the trial started. "Keep it simple. Boat, motive, opportunity, there's your case. Verdict, guilty. If they have to go to game plan B, they'll want to demonstrate that Jay was an outstanding citizen, liked by all, with absolutely no enemies, a man, furthermore, who was devoted to his wife and deeply concerned that she had become suicidal."

And so it came to pass, she thought that afternoon in court when Dodgson called his next witness, a stockbroker, a man of substance and wealth, with an impeccable reputation. He was the first of a succession of such witnesses, each with variations of the same testimony. Jay Wilkins was an all-round great guy, a good sport, generous, easy to get along with. He had dropped out of their social circle when he remarried and devoted his time to caring for his ill wife. It was inconceivable to think that he might have had a real enemy.

Barbara had the same question for each of them and, with variations, the answer was the same.

"Were you an intimate friend of Mr. Wilkins, with a confidential personal relationship?"

"No. He was one of a group of us who got together. We all shared the same interests in sports, or politics, or whatever."

The last witness of the day was Oliver Schaefer, the president of a local bank. In response to a question by Dodgson, he said, "I saw him in March, around the middle of the month. It was a meeting with a representative from the Small Business Administration. Afterward I talked briefly with Jay. I mentioned that I had heard that his wife's health had improved greatly, that someone had seen her out and about. He became very disturbed and said that she was making every effort to resume a normal life, but it wasn't working. He didn't dare leave her alone in the evening, for instance, because that was when she lapsed into the deep depression and despondency that was so alarming. That was the last time I ever saw him."

When Barbara stood up to cross-examine, she returned to her point. "Mr. Schaefer, were you an intimate friend of Mr. Wilkins? One he shared confidences with?"

"No, not really. Ours was a friendly relationship, but hardly in the category of a very close personal friendship."

She had no further questions.

It was a few minutes after five when Judge Wells adjourned for the day.

The jurors filed out behind the bailiff and then the courtroom emptied. Not very many observers had been attending the trial and only two reporters, who had not yet tried to corner Wally or Barbara.

In the corridor, Wally stopped their group and said to Frank, "I've got to hand it to you. In there today, it hit me what a great job you've done bringing up your kid." He took Frank's hand to shake it vigorously. At the same time, he passed a note to Barbara with his other hand as he continued to speak earnestly, "She walks like you did years ago, and even talks like you—calm and cool, and as honed as a rapier." He grinned and stepped back. "Just wanted you to know," he said. Taking Meg's hand, he turned and they walked out together.

"What was that all about?" Frank asked when they were out of hearing range.

Barbara read Wally's note, then said, "He wants me to meet him in the lounge at the Hilton in twenty minutes. Don't know why."

It was happy hour, and the lounge was crowded when she entered. A piano player was going through a jazz medley. The acoustics in the room were good, though, and the table she spotted near the far wall would do. She had to wait only a few minutes before she saw Wally come in. His mop of glowing white hair made him stand out in most crowds. She waved, and he made his way to the table. A waiter arrived at his heels.

"Pinot noir," Barbara said.

"For me, too," Wally said. When the waiter left he said, "You'd think, leading the life I've had, I'd be a boozer, but nope. I was afraid to start when I was a kid. My mom would have had my scalp. You remind me of her in some ways. She was focused, like you are. I'd make up an elaborate story about something or other and she'd listen, and then home in on the one weak spot, and before I knew it, I'd be saying, 'Mom, I'm sorry. I'll never do it again.'"

He chatted easily until the waiter returned with the wine, then he moved his own aside a little and leaned forward with both hands on the table. "I've been looking for a way to get you alone for a few minutes, but Meg's sticking to me like a burr these days. I gave her a foot rub, and she agreed to lie down while I shmooze with guys at the bar for a few minutes. I'm worried about her, Barbara. I know I've handed you a rotten case without much to work with and I just want to say that if it goes sour, that's the way she blows. But, if that happens, I'd like to know that someone's looking after Meg. I keep thinking about last Christmas. There we were in a hotel room, a nice room, mind you, but like a thousand others. We had a little tree that we decorated." He held his hands about a foot apart. "A real little tree. We began to talk about our Christmases at home, the trees we had, the smells, family, candy and cookies. You know. Anyway when she said let's get a house in the country, it was as if a hammer had banged my head."

His voice was low, but so intense that the other bar sounds, the voices chattering, the piano, seemed to fade, and all she could hear was Wally.

"I realized what I had done to her all those years, and how much she had wanted a little farm, a little garden. A home. A real home. She never said so, and I never gave it a thought, never a thought. But there it was, and once you know it, you can't just let it go. You know?"

She nodded.

"So, anyway, that night I swore that I'd make it up to her, spend the rest of my life making it up to her. Not out loud, mind you. She wouldn't have stood for it. I thought it would be a sacrifice to move out to the country, out of the limelight and glitter, and I wanted to make a sacrifice, absolve myself, but you know what? I love it as much as she does. And I can still go do my thing now and then. It's been good out there, and it gets better. It's something we could have done twenty-five years ago, but I was too stupid to realize it. Except for this hell we've blundered into, it's worked out perfectly."

He stopped to sip his wine, and Barbara took her first sip of her own. She had felt immobilized by his words and his passion.

"She's strong," Wally said. "But this is too much. She has too much guilt over that goddamn boat. After…I mean, in case it goes the wrong way, your dad said he'd help her with financial decisions, things like that, but she's going to need a friend or two besides. She doesn't deserve this now. She never deserved anything like this, but especially now. Seeing a dream come alive, then having it snatched away again, mixed with such guilt… It's a bad combination."

Before she could speak, he glanced about then said in a lower voice, "There's something else. You know, I told you and Frank that I play cards now and then. Remember?"

She nodded.

"Yeah. Look, it used to bother Meg, but it was never enough for her to get in a panic about or anything like that. But sometimes the stakes got pretty high. Real high. You know, the way we traveled, one section of the country after another. I opened bank accounts here and there. She doesn't know a thing about them. I kept thinking the day would come when I wouldn't be able to do my act, arthritis, an accident, something, and I wanted something extra put away, just in case." He glanced around again. "Anyway, these past few months, I've been closing those accounts, getting cashiers checks, and I stashed them away in a safe deposit box. We opened it together when we came home, but she forgot all about it, and I got hold of her key and kept it. The checks are there, and she'll need them if… Anyway, she might need them, but funny thing is I can't give her the keys right now. You know how she is. She might think… It might alarm her. I want to give the keys to you, for her, just in case." He drew an envelope from his pocket and put it on the table. "The keys," he said.

When she didn't move, he said in an intense voice, "Put them in your purse, Barbara."

She picked up the envelope and dropped it into her purse, and he lifted his wine and took a long drink. "Thanks." He put his wineglass down.

She reached across the table and put her hand on his. "Wally, we'll never abandon her. I promise. But you can't lose hope. It always looks bad at this stage when the prosecution seems to have all the aces, but I haven't even started my case. Please, don't lose faith now. It would be demoralizing for all of us, you, Meg and me, Wally. I need your faith in me."

He lifted her hand to his lips and kissed it. "I said, just in case. You know, a contingency plan, a backup. That's all I mean. I've seen you home in on the weak spots, kid. And you're good, even better than my mom was." He smiled his big gleaming smile. "I'll get on up to the room. See you in the morning, counselor." He picked up the tab, and left swiftly.

She took another sip of her own wine, but she didn't want it now. She stood up and walked out. Wally was already out of sight.

She drove to her office, let herself in and put the envelope in her safe, and afterward she went to Frank's house to tell him about the meeting. She left again almost instantly, without waiting for a comment, without adding one of her own.

It smelled like rain when she unloaded her briefcase and purse at her apartment. It was too early for the leaf-stripping fall rain that generally came around the end of the month, to be followed all too soon by the fogs that persisted through the end of the year. But everything else had gone crazy, she thought, unlocking her door. Why not the weather, too?

She walked from her little office to the kitchen, back, more times than she could count until, exhausted, she sank down into her good chair. Wally's words kept playing in her head: if it goes sour, just in case... Over and over. When the rain started, she got up and watched out the window. It was like an end of the month driving, pounding rain that left the world sodden and beaten down, the summer flowers in tatters, blackened and done for, the trees stripped bare. Then, finally, she thought about something to eat.

Although less than a week ago Frank's stuffed lamb had been delicious, that night it was tasteless, and after a few bites, she gave it up, and drew a bath. Tomorrow, she told herself. Concentrate on tomorrow, the trial. Wally's words kept repeating in her head.

THIRTY-ONE

Two more upstanding community leaders testified the next morning attesting to Jay Wilkins's virtue. Wally passed Barbara a note: "Is the Pope on the witness list?" She suppressed her grin and asked the witnesses the same two questions she had asked the day before. Was either of them a personal friend of Jay Wilkins? She got the same answers: No.

After the midmorning break Dodgson called John Levinson, the general manager of the dealership.

"Was Mr. Wilkins a fair employer?" Dodgson asked.

"Yes. As long as you did your job and followed the rules he left you alone."

"Was he generally on the job? I mean, was he an absentee employer, or right there doing his own work?"

"He was almost always there. And when he wasn't, we kept in touch every day, either by phone or by e-mail. He wanted to know what was going on all the time. He kept a close watch and a close ear on the operations." His tone was completely neutral, revealing nothing of what he was thinking as he answered the questions.

"Under Mr. Wilkins's leadership was the company considered a major community asset?"

"Yes. It was, and it still is."

Dodgson nodded. "Do you recall the week of April 21 through April 26?"

"Yes."

"Was Mr. Wilkins there during that week?"

"Not a single time."

"And did he keep in touch, explain his absence?"

"Not at first. He called and left a message not to expect him on Monday of that week, and a couple of days later he called to tell me he'd be out a few more days, until he heard from his wife."

"How did he sound when he talked to you?"

"He was anxious. He said he was very worried about her, and if she called him at the dealership, to let him know instantly. He said he wouldn't be leaving his house and I should get in touch day or night if I heard from her."

"Mr. Levinson, did he say why he was worried about her?"

"Yes, he did. He said she was too sick to be out wandering around alone." Levinson sounded so bland that he might have been talking about wallpaper he had seen one time or another.

When Barbara stood up for her cross-examination, she said, "Good morning," pleasantly, and he inclined his head slightly but made no other response.

"I'd like to clarify a few of the things you've referred to," she said. "What did you mean when you said Mr.

Wilkins kept a close watch at all times? A close watch on what?"

"Everything," he said. "The salesmen, the mechanics in the shop, the secretary, the boy who cleaned things. Everything."

"You mean he checked things personally?"

"Yes. He checked the restrooms, and the cars that had been test driven. He kept an eye on the desks. No food or drink was allowed outside the lounge. And the shoes. Anyone who went out to the shop had to change shoes when he came back. No tracking grease or oil into the showroom. He kept tabs on everything."

"And what did you mean by a close ear on everything? He listened to the salesmen?"

"He could monitor them from his office. The closing room, the showroom, the shop, the lounge. He listened in from time to time."

"Was everyone aware of this?"

"Yes. He laid it out when you were hired. You knew the rules, and that he might be listening and watching."

"What were some of those rules?"

Levinson was trying to maintain his neutral, even stoical tone, but his resentment was starting to show as he said, "You had to clock in and out for breaks, lunch, starting and closing times. If you were late more than fifteen minutes you were docked an hour. No food or drink, not even water, outside the lounge. Employees had to use the bathroom off the lounge, not the one off the showroom. You couldn't leave a soda can or dirty cup sitting around anywhere. No smoking anywhere on the property. No profanity. The telephone wasn't ever to ring more than three times before someone answered it. You had to clean the microwave after every use. Every car that a customer entered had to be cleaned afterward, the steering wheel, dashboard, the glove compartment, the floor mat cleaned with a hand vac. He didn't want to see fingerprints or smudges on anything. There were others, but I can't remember. They were written down and posted in the lounge."

Dodgson was on his feet. "Objection! This is all irrelevant. I move that it be stricken. Many work places have strict rules as a way to enforce discipline."

"Your Honor," Barbara said, "Mr. Wilkins has been portrayed as an easygoing, congenial man, but he was more complex than that, as most human beings are. I argue that it's fair to show more than one aspect of his character."

Judge Wells overruled.

"Mr. Levinson," Barbara said then, "are you saying that Mr. Wilkins personally enforced his rules? The microwave, for instance, what if he found it soiled?"

"He did once and he had it removed for a week," Levinson said. He had regained his neutral voice. His answer was uninflected.

"In what ways did the dealership prove to be a community asset?"

"We support local groups, the university, for example. We have a box at Autzen Stadium, and give generously to the university as a whole. Kids sports, other charitable organizations. We host many meetings with out-of-state visitors, officials from Washington, other businesses from around the West Coast."

"I see." She paused for a moment. "In your testimony

you said he left a message for you not to expect him on Monday, April 21. Will you tell the jury about that call?"

"Yes. He called my house at midnight on Sunday and left the message on my answering machine. He told me to e-mail him about the weekend activities, that he would not be in on Monday and that he had asked a group of musicians to get in touch about an engagement and I should take their call."

"Was that unusual, for him to make a late-night call?"

"It was the only time he ever did."

"Later in the week when he said he would not be in until he heard from his wife, was that unusual, for him to mention his personal affairs?"

"Very unusual. That was the first time he had ever mentioned her to me."

"When he was not at his job, you said you kept in touch. How did you do that if he was out fishing with friends?"

"I reported in by calling his cell phone. He wanted daily reports."

"What was the penalty for someone who broke his rule about smoking on the premises?"

"The first time they were reprimanded, if it happened again, they got fired."

"And if they were late?"

"Same thing. Once or twice, a reprimand, a third time, fired."

"Mr. Levinson, were there others employed at the dealership who had been there as long as or longer than you?"

"No."

"As the general manager, are you aware of the tenure of most employees?" He said yes. "And how long did most of them stay on the job?"

His voice was almost robotic when he said, "About two years usually."

She thanked him and said no more questions.

"They just have a few more witnesses on their list," Barbara said when they broke for lunch that day. She, Wally and Meg were in Frank's car, heading for his house, where he had promised hot soup and sandwiches. It was raining. Not a pounding rain like that of the night before, but steady and cold.

"Then it's your turn to start your defense case?" Meg asked.

"Yes. Probably in the morning." Her first witness would be Adele Wykoph. And she'd better not cause trouble, she added to herself. She had had a stormy session with Adele when they discussed her testimony. The scene played in her head.

"What do you mean I can't say he killed her? He did and you know it."

"We have to stick to this case, and she's not part of it. Her death is separate from the murder of Jay Wilkins, and the prosecution will keep it that way."

"Bull! It's part and parcel of the whole picture."

"Adele, please listen to me. All you have to do is answer the questions, nothing more. And I can't imply anything about her murder. I can't bring it up except in the most general terms."

"Jesus! They're calling the tune and you're dancing to it!"

"For God's sake! Look, I don't tell you how to run your center. Don't you tell me how to conduct my case!"

"They're going to whitewash him, and you're letting—"

Adele stopped abruptly and when she spoke again a second later, her voice was different, the intense fury replaced by a softness, compassion and understanding. Her professional counselor's voice. "Barbara, are you in trouble? You are, aren't you?"

"And don't start analyzing me!" Barbara snapped, then drew back, startled by the vehemence of her own voice.

"Well, here we are," Frank said, bringing her back to the car, the house, the falling rain.

Inside, while Meg commiserated with Frank about the state of his petunias that had succumbed to the numbing cold rain, Barbara fled to the second floor.

The first witness of the afternoon session was Officer Amelia Martinez, a solidly built Mexican American, forty-seven years old. She had been with the domestic disputes department for sixteen years.

"On the night of Sunday, April 20, did you have occasion to speak with Mr. Jay Wilkins on the telephone?" Dodgson asked.

"Yes, sir."

"Do you recall what he said?"

"Yes, sir, and I have my notes."

"Please tell the jury about that call."

"He said his wife had gone missing and he was anxious for the authorities to start an immediate search for her. I asked for the details, and he told me she had not gone to her sister's house in Virginia, that her plane had landed on time and all, but she hadn't been on it. When he said that it transpired only the day before, I told him that he should wait another day or two. Flights are delayed, maybe she

missed her connection, or something like that. But he was
agitated and said she was in danger. That her life was at
risk. When I asked him what he meant he said that she
might be suicidal. I told him our policy is not to declare
someone missing in such a short time, just twenty-four
hours or so in his case, and he became angry. He said it was
our job and he wanted someone to get on it immediately."

Dodgson stopped her. "What were his words when he
said she might be suicidal?"

She scanned her notebook, then read: "'You don't understand. She's sick, depressed, and she might even harm
herself. She could kill herself.'"

"No more questions," Dodgson said. He nodded to Barbara. "Your witness."

"Officer Martinez, was Mr. Wilkins's call alarming or
unusual?"

"No. We take calls like that a lot. They have a quarrel
and someone goes off and the other one gets in a panic. I
thought it was just like those other ones."

"How long do you usually wait before you issue a missing person report?"

"Several days when it's an adult, especially one who
packed her own suitcase and said she was taking a trip."

"Thank you, Officer. No more questions," Barbara said.

Dodgson had her repeat what Jay had said, then he
called in quick succession three women whom Jay had
called to make inquiries about Connie, and each of them
verified that she had believed that Connie had been suicidal.

Barbara asked each in turn when was the last time she
had talked to Connie, and the answers were all similar: two
to two and a half years ago.

Dodgson called Detective Edward Jarrell, who said he was a computer technology specialist. He was in his thirties, pale and intense, with straight blond hair, and a slight build.

"Did you examine Mr. Wilkins's computer following his death?"

"Yes, sir."

"Is that routine?" When he said yes, Dodgson asked, "Exactly what do you look for?"

"Any threatening e-mails, chat-room discussions that might have aroused hostility, electronic relationships that might have developed. Things like if he was into Internet gambling, or pornography. Anything that might have a bearing on the murder."

"Did you find anything of that sort?"

"No, sir. It appeared that he used his computer mostly for business, to manage his financial affairs, to keep up with the stock market, the automotive industry, all things of that sort."

"Did you find anything out of the ordinary?"

"One drive was password protected, and his wife used that one."

"Detective, please explain to the jury exactly what you mean about a protected drive."

He cleared his throat as if preparing for a long spiel and that's what he gave. He explained about partitioning a computer hard drive, about the use of passwords to protect certain areas, like Internet banking. "Drive F was dedicated to her use," he said when he finished.

"But you were able to open it and examine the files in the folder. Is that correct?"

"Yes sir. I was." He sounded very confident and even a little proud as he said this.

"What was in the files?"

"There were two. One was the purchase of an electronic plane ticket to Roanoke, Virginia, using a credit card. The purchase was made on April 14. The other file was titled, 'Late Night.' It was just a few lines, like the beginning of a longer piece that she didn't finish."

Dodgson showed a printout to the judge and to Barbara, then handed it to Detective Jarrell. "Do you recognize this?" he asked.

"Yes, sir. It's a printout of the piece on the computer."

Dodgson asked him to read it aloud, and he did in a lugubrious tone. "'I can't take it much longer. Please, God, how much longer must I endure? Pretending, always pretending. J tries so hard to help, but it's no use. He doesn't understand. Adele doesn't understand. No one does. I hate being alive. I don't want to live. I'm ready'"

"How did that handwritten date, March 27, get there?" Dodgson asked then, retrieving the printout.

"I added that, to indicate the date that it was written. That's always recorded, of course."

Dodgson nodded as if to agree, of course. He took the printout to the foreman of the jury and solemnly handed it to him, then stood by as it was passed from juror to juror. After he had it admitted as an exhibit, he asked, "Were any of the other drives protected with a password?"

"No, sir."

"Does that indicate that Mrs. Wilkins had access to the entire computer, but Mr. Wilkins could not access her private drive?" Jarrell said yes. "So it was like having her own private computer that he could never see. Is that right?"

"Yes, sir. They were the only two to use that computer and there wouldn't be any point in having a password and telling him what it was. It was her private drive."

When Barbara cross-examined, she asked, "Detective Jarrell, did Mr. Wilkins have voluminous e-mail, from friends as well as business associates?"

"No. It was all business."

"Was he signed in for any chat rooms or forums?"

"An automotive forum, and a financial forum, that's all. No chat rooms."

When he was dismissed, Dodgson asked the judge if he could approach, and they both went to the bench.

"I have another witness to call," Dodgson said. "Unfortunately his name got dropped from our list. I apologize," he said to Barbara.

His contrition was as phony as a snake oil salesman's guarantee. Barbara made a rude sound and drew a reproving glance from Judge Wells.

"Who is it?" the judge asked Dodgson, evidently as annoyed as Barbara.

"Howard Steinman," Dodgson said. "His statement was included in discovery," he added.

"Your Honor," Barbara said, "I am unprepared to cross-examine Mr. Steinman without the opportunity to review his statement. I'm not even sure we have it with us. May we have a recess at this time?"

"We'll recess," he said. "Tell the bailiff if you have to send for the statement. Otherwise, half an hour."

As Barbara returned to her table she saw Adele Wykoph

in the back of the courtroom. She nodded, then said to those at the defense table, "Recess. They're calling Howie Steinman. Do we have his statement? I don't think we do."

The judge tapped his gavel, made his announcement, repeated his admonition to the jurors not to discuss the case and walked out. After the bailiff led the jury out, Barbara and Shelley started going through the various thick binders.

"I don't understand what's happening," Meg said plaintively. "Why do they keep bringing up Connie Wilkins? What does she have to do with anything?"

"Let's go to the coffee shop downstairs, and I'll explain Barbara's strategy," Frank said. Wally and Meg left with him.

After a few minutes, Shelley said, "I'll go get it."

"Don't break the speed limit or anything," Barbara said. "We'll have at least half an hour after we get our hands on it. I'll go have a chat with Adele."

Shelley put on a shocking pink raincoat. "I can't believe they're actually calling him," she said. "He's such a flake."

"Maybe we'll get our chance to demonstrate that," Barbara said.

She went to speak to Adele as Shelley walked out.

"What's going on?" Adele asked. "They can't be serious using that fake suicide memo. She didn't write it."

"They say she did. Now they're calling Howie Steinman without prior notice. They're really trying to show that Jay was concerned about Connie, believed she was suicidal. Anyway, we weren't prepared for Steinman. So they're giving us a little time. I doubt that I'll be able to call you today."

Adele's look was incredulous. "Howie Steinman? Good God! Barbara, you have to give me an opening to blow him out of the water. You have to."

"Let's go out and have a little talk," Barbara said.

They left the courtroom and walked to the end of the corridor, out of hearing range of those coming and going. Then, standing before a tall window, Barbara said, "The prosecution's case rests on two major premises. One is that Jay had no real enemies, no one with enough motive to resort to murder except Wally. And the other one is that Jay honestly believed that Connie was suicidal. If they can convince the jury of just those two points, they probably will get a conviction. I have to work with that scenario, otherwise, Wally Lederer is going to be found guilty, and I know he didn't do it."

Adele was watching her intently, listening. "You *know?*"

"Yes."

"You know who did, don't you?" Adele asked in a near whisper.

"I didn't say that. I said Wally didn't do it, and that's all I said."

"You know," Adele repeated, almost as if to herself. "Why didn't you tell me in the first place?"

"I couldn't. But since they're bringing Steinman into it, I can ask you about him. But, for God's sake, don't perjure yourself, or leave yourself open to a defamation of character charge."

Adele gave a snort of laughter. "Honey chile, I've testified before. I know the ropes, how far I can go, when to draw the line. Trust me."

Barbara wished she could. She felt as if she had drawn a wild card and had to play it.

THIRTY-TWO

With dark blond hair down past his ears, pale blue eyes, dressed in a tan sport jacket over a forest-green turtleneck sweater and blue jeans, and wearing a gold medallion on a chain around his neck, Howie Steinman was thirty-six years old and unmarried. He had an intense way of watching Dodgson, almost a hypnotic, fixed stare as he detailed his background. He wrote a monthly computer column, he was a Beta tester of many computer programs, both company sponsored and freelance work, and he taught several classes a week in various martial arts.

"During the past spring did you conduct a martial arts class at the Women's Support Center in Eugene?" Dodgson asked.

"Yes, an eight week self-defense class that incorporated some tai chi and aikido along with a few other techniques."

"How many participated in your class?"

"Usually there are between ten and fifteen. I believe it was twelve women last spring."

"Was Connie Wilkins a member of that class?"

"She was."

"Will you please describe the relationship that developed between you and Mrs. Wilkins?"

"Complete trust and honesty," Steinman said without hesitation. "I asked all of them to say what they expected out of the class, and she said she had let her muscles become lax following a long illness. She hoped to regain good muscle tone and self-confidence. We became friends, or more than friends, more like spiritual intimates. A deep mutual attraction was there from the start, and it grew and strengthened as the weeks went by, but, of course, we both understood that it was a doomed attraction, destined never to be fulfilled. I admired her spirituality, her resolve, her valiant efforts to overcome a deep-seated death wish, and I struggled to find a way to alleviate her pain."

It was eerie the way he kept his gaze focused so intently on Dodgson as he spoke, and the prosecutor was starting to look uncomfortable. He held up his hand to stem the flow of words. "Mr. Steinman," he said, "please tell the jury about the last time you saw Mrs. Wilkins."

"We agreed to have one last intimate meeting," he said. "Just the two of us. Over a cup of tea. She said it was our final farewell, that I would never see her again. She was fearless, but gentle and caring, unafraid for herself, but concerned about me. She pleaded with me to put her out of mind, to think of her as a passing dream that had eased my own path, and she said it was time for me to get on with life and live it to the fullest, with every day a blessing to be savored. She said we would never meet again in this realm, but perhaps in another one day. Her eyes were awash with unshed tears."

Dodgson stopped him again, then asked, "What was your understanding of her words that day?"

"She was preparing me to learn of her coming demise. She wished to spare me the agony of hearing it from another, to tell me she would face her own transition with a calm spirit, that she was ready and unafraid."

"You thought she was telling you that she would die? Is that correct?"

"Yes. She had a complete grasp of our relationship, and she knew the torment I would suffer afterward. It was her last gift to me, her affirmation of her own spirituality and her desire to elevate me to the same level of revelatory acceptance."

Dodgson was walking back and forth before the prosecution table, as if trying to escape that unwavering stare. His voice was brusque when he asked, "What was the date of that meeting, Mr. Steinman?"

"The last full day of her life, late in the afternoon, with the sun setting over the distant hills, and the air fresh—"

"I just want you to tell the jury the date of that meeting," Dodgson said in a grating voice.

"April 18."

"Thank you. Your witness," he said to Barbara, and he took his seat frowning.

"Mr. Steinman, do you usually wear glasses?" Barbara asked easily when she stood up and he fixed that same steady gaze on her.

For the first time he looked surprised at the question. "No."

"Objection," Dodgson said belatedly. "Irrelevant."

"Withdraw the question," Barbara said. "I just wondered." She smiled at Dodgson and then at Steinman. "Mr.

Steinman, please tell the jury the titles of several of the computer programs you tested in the past two years."

"The White Prince and the Monster from Nowhere, The White Prince Returns, The Kingdom of Fear, The Sword of Proelis."

She held up her hand and he stopped. "Are those what they call heroic adventure games, fantasy games?" He said yes. "Are those the same kind of programs you write a monthly column about?"

"Yes, but you have to understand that they all require the same meticulous vetting that the most intricate financial program demands. It is not a frivolous endeavor."

"I understand. Moving on, how many times did you and Mrs. Wilkins meet over a cup of tea, or anywhere else outside class?"

"Just the one time. It was a very special occasion, and—"

"That's enough. You answered the question," she said. "That's all that's required." She smiled at him. "You said that meeting was her last gift to you. What other gifts had she given you?"

"Her presence in the class, her cooperation and striving to achieve, her concentration, her existence."

Barbara nodded gravely. "I see. Did she ever give you a material gift of any sort?"

"She understood that materiality was the least significant thing one can give to another."

"Do you mean she never gave you a material object of any kind? Just a yes or no, if you will."

"No, of course not. It wasn't necessary."

"All right. When you asked the class as a whole what

they expected to get out of it, exactly what did Mrs. Wilkins say? Just her words, please, Mr. Steinman."

"She said she had let her muscles get lax and she wanted to regain muscle tone. And that she wanted to regain self-confidence."

"Are those her exact words, that she wanted to regain self-confidence? Did others hear her make that statement?"

"She didn't use exactly those words, but that's what she meant."

"Was that the first time you had met her, that day in class?"

"Yes, but sometimes you don't need—"

"Thank you. The answer is yes. How could you tell exactly what she meant if she didn't say the words, if you had never met her before, had no idea of her history, or anything else about her?"

"I have learned to listen with more than just my ears," he said. He was still staring, and now he was leaning forward a little bit, as if to draw closer to an object he had to observe closely.

Barbara nodded gravely. "Just what other sense do you use for listening?"

"I have learned to sense, to feel the currents issuing from another person. They are like magnetic waves, or radiations, and with discipline one can master the art of tuning in to them and interpreting them. I could read her radiations clearly."

"And put into words what those currents signify? Is that what you mean?" Barbara asked.

"Exactly that."

"You said a mutual attraction developed. Was Mrs. Wilkins also adept at reading radiations?"

"No, she lacked the training that is required."

"If you didn't meet with her outside of class, how did she become aware of your growing attraction to her? Did you tell her in front of the class?"

"No. I sent her little tokens, white roses once, a box of chocolates, a book of poetry. She understood what they meant."

"Did she keep the items?"

"She took them to the center, to share with others and to declare in public what was happening between us. It was her subtle way to let others know."

"Did you make other efforts to signal your interest? Call her, or write notes?"

"Objection!" Dodgson called out. "Your Honor, may I approach?"

Judge Wells beckoned them forward. "Well?" he asked. He sounded peevish.

"She's making a mockery of this witness, taunting him, ridiculing him. This is an unfair cross-examination and she knows it."

"He's a romantic, narcissistic fool, the hero of his own fantasy," Barbara said calmly. "Furthermore, he's your witness. I wouldn't have touched him with a ten-foot pole, but since you called him, I have the right to reexamine every single statement he made in his direct, as you well know."

"Peace, both of you," Judge Wells said. "You're over-ruled, Mr. Dodgson. She's within her rights, as she says." Then he said to Barbara, "But, Ms. Holloway; do finish it soon. You've made your point, I think, and it's getting late."

She nodded. "I'll try, Your Honor. He doesn't make it

easy." She did not miss the glint of amusement in the judge's eyes when he waved them both away.

"Mr. Steinman," Barbara said, when they resumed, "would you like to have the question repeated?"

"I heard what you asked," he said. "I called her a time or two, and I sent her a note or two."

"And how did she respond?"

"She asked me not to do that again. I understood very well what she meant. It was not necessary any longer. She recognized what was happening."

Barbara looked from him to the jury where several of the women were smiling, although the youngest one, Mariann Matthews, age twenty-two, looked intrigued and fascinated. But Barbara knew she would be safe even if she contrived a meeting, simply because she likely was attainable, and Howie Steinman fixated on the unattainable. Barbara turned once more to meet Steinman's penetrating gaze.

"You said that Mrs. Wilkins had a deep-seated death wish. Please tell the jury if she ever said that in words, or if you interpreted that from her radiations."

"Every living organism has its own distinguishable band of radiations. The higher the organism, the more complex the harmonic mixture becomes. There are the simple rhythmic ones that are easily interpreted, such as happiness, anger, the readily visible emotions, but there are also deep underlying pulsing rhythms that set the pace for all the rest. I could sense in her the deepest of them, the unyielding death wish."

Barbara nodded. "I see. In the class of twelve women, you could single out her radiations clearly enough to interpret them and translate them into language. Is that correct?"

"Yes. With sufficient training and discipline that art can be mastered. I mastered it."

She nodded again, returning his steady gaze with one just as unwavering. "Now, on the day you shared a cup of tea with Mrs. Wilkins, you said she told you to put her out of mind, that you would not meet again, and so on. You also said she told you to get on with your life. Mr. Steinman, is it possible that what she actually said in spoken words was for you to get a life?"

There was a ripple of laughter in the courtroom and Judge Wells tapped his gavel lightly. At the same time Dodgson objected in a very loud voice that it was a leading question. It was sustained.

Steinman's gaze did not flicker for a second. He looked at Barbara almost pityingly, and before she could ask another question he said, "No matter how she actually communicated with me, I know what she meant."

This time Dodgson bellowed an objection. "Move that the comment be stricken," he yelled. It was stricken.

Barbara shrugged. "No more questions." When she turned to resume her seat, she glanced over the courtroom and was startled to see Stephanie Breaux in the back row of spectators.

Dodgson made a heroic effort to salvage his witness. "Mr. Steinman, was it your sincere belief on that afternoon of April 18 or any other time that Mrs. Wilkins was suicidal?"

"She knew she was doomed, and whether by murder or suicide, she was prepared for the coming transition."

"Objection, move that the answer be stricken as not responsive to the question," Dodgson cried out, enraged.

Barbara stood up also. "The witness answered the question to the best of his ability."

"The answer will be stricken," Judge Wells said. "Mr. Steinman, just answer the question."

"I believed she was suicidal," Howie Steinman said clearly, to everyone's amazement.

The next witness was Mrs. Elizabeth Ogden, a stout, broad-faced woman, forty-three years old. Her hair was graying and thin, and her makeup looked as if it had been applied by someone unused to using lipstick or eyeshadow. She had on too much of each.

While she was being sworn in, Barbara glanced again at the spectators. Stephanie was gone. The newspaper had reported that the defense would start its case that day; possibly that had drawn her. And she might be back, Barbara thought then. She might sit through the entire defense. What difference could it make, she demanded silently. But it mattered even if she couldn't understand why. She forced her attention to the witness who was answering a question.

"...not really on the corner, you know. But there's nothing between our house and Owl Creek Road except an empty lot that used to be an orchard, but it's not been tended for twenty, or maybe that should be more like twenty-five, years, and it looks like we're on the corner."

Dodgson held up his hand. "I'd like to introduce a schematic of the area, just to locate the properties we're talking about here." He showed it to the judge, and then to Barbara.

"Objection," she said, getting to her feet. "May I approach?" she asked. The judge waved them both forward. Barbara picked up her own two maps of the area and followed Dodgson to the bench.

"Now what?" the judge asked. He glanced at his watch.

"His schematic is so simplified that it is meaningless," Barbara said. "It gives no idea of the growth in that area or the distances involved. I have here two USGS topographical maps, one is of the entire area, and one is an enlargement of that particular area. If you will compare them, you'll see that his schematic misrepresents the neighborhood."

Judge Wells looked resigned as he said, "Let's have all three." He spread them on his desk and peered first at one, then another. When he finished he said to Dodgson, "I'll allow you to use your schematic, with the understanding that when she cross-examines, I'll also permit her to introduce the government maps. Or you could agree to use them in your direct, if you choose." He rolled Barbara's maps and handed them back to her.

"She can't introduce new evidence in cross," Dodgson said aggrievedly. "There's nothing wrong with using schematics in such a case. It isn't as if we're trying to sell property here. Besides, this witness has trouble reading a real map."

"It's hardly new," Barbara said. "It's making sense of a child's drawing. And she's your witness. You should have tutored her."

"Enough," Judge Wells said sharply. "You have my decision. It's four now. Will you finish your last two witnesses today?" He handed Dodgson's map to him.

Dodgson looked sullen as he took his own schematic back. "I'll be done. She's the one delaying things here."

"And will you be prepared to begin the defense in the morning?" the judge asked Barbara.

"Yes, Your Honor. But if he can't rein in this witness, I suspect it's going to be a late adjournment today."

The judge waved them both away.

Dodgson used his own simplified map. On it, there appeared to be only the few houses on Owl Creek Road, and the single Ogden house on Hunter's Lane and nothing else between Eugene and the coast. It was not fast or easy, but Dodgson got Mrs. Ogden to describe their farm as forty acres, with a wheat field across the road from the house, apple and pear orchards, a large garden and cornfields. They had lived in the area all their lives, and she knew all the people who lived on Owl Creek Road.

"Are you familiar with their habits, their comings and goings, things of that sort?" Dodgson asked.

She looked surprised at the question, nodded, then said, "Well, you do, you know, with neighbors you've known for years. Be hard to surprise any of us I guess."

Dodgson got to the night of the murder quickly as soon as the background was out of the way. "Do you recall that night?" he asked.

"Oh, yes indeed. It was my daughter's birthday sleepover. Not that her birthday was on the weekend, because actually it was on Tuesday that week, but you don't have a sleepover with teenage girls on a school night. They don't sleep at all, you know. Up all night, and eating all night. So we let her have her friends over on that Saturday night, and I made cake and fried chicken for their supper, with sweet potatoes topped with marshmallows, the way kids like it…"

She would have gone on, but Dodgson held up his hand and interrupted. "All right. Please tell the jury what you observed that night at a little after nine o'clock."

"You can't believe how tired I was," she said. "All that

cooking, and shopping earlier, and trying to feed four girls. People think boys eat a lot, but believe you me, girls can match them bite for bite, and then some. I told them I'd clean up the kitchen, you know, let them have a real party without chores or anything, and that's what I did. And they went on to the den to do their things, you know, fix their hair, try on clothes, things like that. My husband went to Bend to visit his folks. They retired over there, but they don't much like it. Too cold, but he just didn't want to be home when they were gong to sleep over. They scream, you know, and that bothers him, so he went over to see his folks, and I cleaned up the kitchen and all."

"Then after about nine what happened?" Dodgson asked, not raising his voice, but unable to conceal a hint of impatience that sharpened his tone.

"I'm coming to that," she said. "See, I was tired, dead tired, and I just plopped down on the sofa to watch television. Usually I shut the draperies, but I didn't think of it, I was that tired, and I turned on the television. We have a remote, you know. You don't have to get up to do anything, and I guess I wouldn't have got up no matter what, once I settled down. And headlights hit me right in the eyes."

"Headlights," Dodgson repeated. "Did you notice what time it was?"

"Yes. There's a clock on the television, green numbers that glow in the dark and all, and it was a quarter after nine. I thought it was funny for anyone to be leaving that late on a rainy night. Sometimes weeks go by without anyone going out at night. You see them coming home sometimes, but not going out. And it raining and all."

Dodgson finished with her soon after that, and Barbara stood up and introduced her own map and placed a transparency over it. Mrs. Ogden looked at it with a blank expression when Barbara pointed to it and said, "Can you recognize your own house on this map?"

She couldn't.

Carefully Barbara circled the house. "And this is the corner lot that's going wild," she said, tracing its outline. "Then Owl Creek Road, and the residences on it." She pointed out each one, then circled it. "So you know everyone on that road, and have known them for years, all except Mr. and Mrs. Lederer. Is that right?"

"I know them," Mrs. Ogden said. "They're all good friends, except like you said, Mr. and Mrs. Lederer, and I hardly know them at all, but they've been so busy—"

Barbara interrupted her. "All right. Now let's look at Hunter's Lane. Here's Highway 126, and your wheat field, your house, and then there's a curve in the road and Owl Creek Road on the left. The curve continues for a time, and there's another household about a mile and a bit up here. Do you know the people in that house?"

"The first house up that way?" Mrs. Ogden asked. "Sure, that's Sam and Mary Lewiston. They been there for twenty years or more."

"How about the next household?" Barbara asked, tracing Hunter's Lane for another half mile or so. Mrs. Ogden knew them also. And the next family as well, but after that she shook her head.

"On up farther there's the Arnold family. I know them," she said helpfully. "Maybe a couple more up that way."

Barbara nodded. "So there are a lot of families who live

in the area who might drive on Hunter's Lane routinely. Is that right?"

"Not usually late at night, and in the rain like that," Mrs. Ogden said.

"All right, let's talk about the lights you saw. From your living room can you see Owl Creek Road?"

"Not from there, but from the kitchen, or outside the house. Our garage is in the way, and the empty lot with all that wild growth."

"Does your living room look out over Hunter's Lane?"

"Yes. That's out front."

"For lights to come into your living room, the car had to be on the curve, didn't it?"

"I guess so," Mrs. Ogden said uncertainly.

"It had to be facing your house, the lights aimed at your house or the lights wouldn't have hit you in the eyes. Is that correct?"

Again Mrs. Ogden's uncertainty was clear as she agreed that was right.

Well, Barbara thought then, she wasn't trying to convince Mrs. Ogden of anything. This was for the benefit of the jurors, who were watching attentively.

"All right, and then, when the car finished the curve and straightened out, the headlights would have been on the road, no longer on your house. Just lights on the road. Is that right?"

"I didn't keep seeing them come in like that," Mrs. Ogden said.

"What did you see?"

"Just lights. There's no streetlights out that way, you know. So it was just lights on the road, like you said."

"Did you see a car?"

"I couldn't. Dark, raining and all, and no streetlights or anything."

"Thank you," Barbara said then. "No further questions."

As Dodgson started his redirect, in spite of herself Barbara was thinking about Stephanie's presence in court again. Did she have suitcases packed, cash in hand, ready to grab Eve and bolt if Eve's name came up? Did she believe the prosecution offered no threat, but she couldn't be sure about Barbara? What would satisfy her? The quick conviction that was predicted?

Dodgson called his final witness. Detective Stephen Jankow, who was just as intense and hungry looking as he had been the last time Barbara had seen him, when he had been sent to collect evidence from Wally's house. He would burn out young if he didn't lighten up, she thought fleetingly, as he told about his history as a homicide detective.

"Are you familiar with the area of Hunter's Lane and Owl Creek Road?" Dodgson asked.

"Yes, sir. I was out there two times, first to collect evidence from the defendant, and the next time to ask questions of his neighbors."

"And what was the result of your questioning of his neighbors?"

"I asked each one if they had seen any car leaving the area the night of April 26, and no one had except Mrs. Ogden. And I asked each one if they had driven out that night at nine or later. They all said no."

"What else did you do following the questioning of the area residents?"

"I drove from the defendant's house to Mr. Wilkins's house and timed the drive. It took thirty-five minutes."

Dodgson started to return to the prosecution table, then paused and asked, as if it were an afterthought, "Detective Jankow, precisely when is the homicide unit called to investigate a case?"

"Whenever there's a violent and/or unexplained death," he said promptly.

"Are all those instances determined to be homicides?"

"No, sir. Sometimes it's decided they were accidents, and now and then one's determined to have been a suicide."

"When is that determination made?" Dodgson asked.

"Sometimes not until the investigation is completed, sometimes right away, depending on the situation."

"Is the investigation concerning the death of Connie Wilkins still under investigation?" Dodgson asked.

"Yes, sir. It's ongoing."

The Prosecutor nodded and took his seat. "Your witness," he said to Barbara, almost casually.

He looked smug, as well he should she thought. That was a good move, one that constricted her chest and made her mind race for a way to counter it. They were fighting a silent duel, out of sight of the jurors, but they both knew exactly what he was doing, disproving her theory of one killer and two murders, driving home the idea that Connie's death could still be called a suicide, and Jay had had cause to fear such was the case. She nodded to him slightly, acknowledging the ploy, but before facing the detective, and before she could prevent it, she cast a quick glance over the spectators. *Stop it,* she thought, furious at herself.

"Good afternoon, Detective Jankow," she said, looking

at him. His entire body seemed to stiffen and his nod was little more than a twitch. "Have you ever worked with Lieutenant Hoggarth in the homicide unit?"

"Once or twice," he said.

"Is Lieutenant Hoggarth the lead detective in the Connie Wilkins case?"

"I think so," he said cautiously.

"Detective Jankow, the homicide unit surely isn't so big that you can't keep up with who is in charge of different cases, is it?"

Dodgson objected and was sustained.

"Rephrase your question, counselor," the judge said.

Barbara nodded. "You said you've been with the homicide unit for seven years. Is that correct?"

He said it was.

"And in all that time have you ever known Lieutenant Hoggarth to have investigated anything other than murder cases?"

"I only know the cases I was on," he said after a pause. "They were both murder."

She regarded him for a moment, then said, "Do you know if the death of Connie Wilkins has been determined to have been a murder?"

He paused longer this time, cleared his throat, then said, "I don't know. I'm not on that case."

Her first impulse was to pound on him. He did know. Everyone in homicide knew. But she stilled the question already forming as a cautionary instinct seized her. Although she didn't know what the trap was, she suspected that she had been led to one. She nodded to Jankow, as if satisfied with his answer, then asked, "Did you ask Mr.

Lederer if he had driven out on Hunter's Lane on Saturday night, April 26?"

His quick glance at Dodgson was enough to confirm that her trap warning had been on target.

"Yes."

"And what was his response?"

"He denied it."

"Just like everyone else? Is that right?"

Dodgson objected in a loud voice and it was sustained.

Moving to the map still on the easel, Barbara pointed to the first house past the Ogden house on Hunter's Lane. "Did you ask the inhabitants of this house the same question?"

He said yes. "No one from there left at that time."

"And this one?" she said, moving on to the next house. It was the same answer.

She continued up Hunter's Lane for another mile and a half, and his answer was unvarying. After that, he said he had not asked anyone else on the road.

"I see. Where does Hunter's Lane end, Detective Jankow?" she asked then.

"Up around the Alvadore community."

"Did you canvas that area to see if anyone had driven out that way that night?"

He flushed slightly and said no.

"Can you describe the Alvadore community for the jury?"

"Farm country, orchards, things like that."

"Is there a general store?"

"I think so."

"A gas station or two?"

"I think so."

"A school?"

"Yes."

"Some businesses? A commercial nursery, for instance?"

"Yes."

"In other words it's a real community with over a hundred inhabitants, a nursery, greenhouses, businesses. Is that correct?"

He clipped off an affirmative answer.

"Detective," she said then, "if someone from the Alvadore community wanted to drive to Veneta, or to the coast, or even to west Eugene, how do you suppose they would go?"

Dodgson called out his objection. "That's a hypothetical, and irrelevant."

She shrugged when it was sustained. The jurors would have the map; they could figure it out for themselves when they deliberated. She had no more questions.

Dodgson kept his redirect short and to the point and the detective left the stand. Then Dodgson said, "The state rests, Your Honor."

"And that's their case for better or worse," Barbara murmured to Wally.

The court adjourned, and when Barbara's group gathered in the corridor for a few minutes, she was already sorting out the testimony, starting to think of her own witnesses and trying harder to keep her thoughts about Stephanie's presence at bay.

"As soon as we get out of here tomorrow," Wally said, "we'll head out to the house. Anything I should do over the weekend?"

"Rest, relax," Barbara said. "I'll begin working on my closing statement, but the evening before I call you we should spend a little time going over a few points."

"And I'm going to plant garlic," Frank said. "Rain or no rain, it's time."

Meg appeared startled. Then, with a faraway look she said, "I forgot about that. We always planted garlic in the fall. Like tulips and daffodils." She turned to Wally. "Tomorrow, when we drive out, we have to stop at the nursery to buy garlic, and a few tulips and daffodils."

"I guess I know what I'll be doing over the weekend," he said with a grin.

As they walked out, Frank said to Barbara, "Good job, dodging that bait he was dangling."

"What was he up to?"

"I've been keeping an eye on that case and no announcement's been made yet, but the preliminary determination was suicide, before Hoggarth got involved. I think he was going to go there and there's no way you could refute it since that's all they've put out."

She felt a chill. It would have been damning if she had been the one to force the state's witness to state under oath that he had seen a report calling Connie's death suicide.

Shelley touched her arm and said slowly, "They don't really have much of a case, do they?"

"I just wish Cleopatra's barge had sunk on its maiden voyage, no reproductions, no copies, no little boat to gum up the works. Well, onward. See you in the morning," Barbara said.

In her car a few minutes later her hands tightened on the steering wheel when she realized how much Stephanie's appearance had shaken her, how she had lost focus, and how close she had come to sinking the one hope her case had.

THIRTY-THREE

When Adele came forward to take the stand the next morning, she was resplendent in a dark red skirt that reached the tops of stylish leather boots that added an inch or more to her height. She wore a hip-length black silk jacket embroidered with red and gold roses, and under it a light red silk blouse. Several heavy gold necklaces finished her outfit. Queen of the Amazons, Barbara thought as Adele was sworn in.

Adele recounted her background. She had a double major in psychology and sociology from Johns Hopkins, and she was currently the director of the Eugene Women's Support Center, a position she had held for twenty-one years.

"Please tell the court exactly what the support center does," Barbara said.

"We offer counseling service of all kinds—psychological, emotional, financial, nutritional. We offer family planning, family and marriage counseling…"

Dodgson stood up. "Your Honor, I object to this line of questioning as irrelevant to the trial at hand."

Barbara turned to Judge Wells. "May I approach?"

He motioned them forward. "Does this have relevance?" he asked Barbara.

"Yes. Ms. Wykoph is a trained psychologist with decades of experience in counseling troubled women. She will testify that Connie Wilkins was not suicidal, and that there was no reason for anyone to assume she was. And that goes to the heart of the defense."

The judge's scrutiny of her was shrewd and knowing. "Very well. You may proceed. Overruled."

Barbara next asked Adele, "Do you routinely offer a physical fitness class, or self-defense class?"

"We offer it twice a year, in the spring and again in the fall. We engage Howard Steinman to conduct those classes."

"Do you offer courses in philosophy or religion?"

"No. Now and then we have workshops in meditation or yoga, but not on a regular basis."

"Does Howard Steinman teach philosophy along with his fitness routines?"

"Never. There is little or no discussion of any sort in his classes except about the techniques, and as soon as the class is over the women go to the dressing room, and he leaves the premises."

"In your opinion, does Mr. Steinman have the training or education to assess the emotional or mental condition of his students?"

Adele's lip curled slightly. "No. His training is in martial arts and computer programming. He has no advanced degrees and absolutely no training in psychology."

Barbara had Adele describe her long association and friendship with Connie Wilkins.

"Is two years an excessive period of time for grieving?"

"There is no norm. For some people it is a few months, for most it persists for over a year, into the second year and even beyond." Adele paused, then said, "Often the holidays, Christmas or an anniversary, for example, prove to be very difficult. That often persists for many years."

"Do you recall when Connie Wilkins lost her family? Her first husband and her son?"

"Yes. It was three years ago in March. The accident took place on March 25, and the funeral was March 29."

Barbara nodded. "What was Mrs. Wilkins's mental and emotional state during the past winter and spring?"

"She was starting to resume her volunteer work, and she had developed a keen interest in her stepdaughter and was making plans to take her on trips to museums, galleries, things of that sort. She was very forward looking and busy again."

"When was the last time you saw Mrs. Wilkins? Can you tell us about that occasion?"

"It was Friday, April 18," she said slowly. "It was the last day of the self-defense class and she came to my office for advice. She told me that Howard Steinman had asked her to go to a nearby coffee shop with him, and she didn't know how to tell him to stop wasting his time. She didn't want to hurt his feelings, but neither did she want his attentions."

"What was your advice?"

"I told her to tell him to get lost," she said. "I told her he always fell in love with someone out of reach, that it was not a new thing with him, and just to tell him to knock it off."

"Did she indicate that she would take your advice?"

"She said she'd tell him much the same thing, but find a nicer way to say it. We were both laughing."

"Did you know that he was sending her little gifts?"

"Yes. She brought them to the center and put them down in the general room where everyone wanders in and out. She wanted no part of them."

"Ms. Wykoph, in your professional opinion, was Connie Wilkins suicidal in April?"

"Not in April and not ever. She was never suicidal. She was grief-stricken, but her religious upbringing, her personal philosophy was such that she never once contemplated suicide."

"Thank you, Ms. Wykoph," Barbara said. She turned to Dodgson. "Your witness."

"Ms. Wykoph," he asked, "during the last few months that Mrs. Wilkins was a regular attendee at your center, were all your contacts with her during daylight hours?"

"Yes."

"You were never with her in the evening?"

"No, I wasn't."

"So you only know the face she presented to the world during those few daylight hours when you saw her. You can't say how well she was coping with the after-dark hours, the night hours?"

"She had no 'face.' She was very transparent," Adele stated.

"Move that the comment be stricken," he said. Judge Wells said it would be stricken. "Let me rephrase the question," Dodgson said to Adele. "All you can really know about her behavior is what you observed during the few hours she was at the center. Is that correct?"

"No, it isn't," Adele said. "As a clinical psychologist I am often called on to make a judgment about behavior that I don't see directly, based on the observations I make at other times."

"Ms. Wykoph, is it not true that people who are in mourning can and do hold down positions of responsibility and carry out their duties more than adequately if that is necessary? Teachers, teach. Doctors see their patients. Sales people serve their customers. And as far as the world is concerned they are as normal as ever. Please, just a simple yes or no answer. Is that not correct?"

She hesitated for a moment, then said, "That is correct."

"Is it not true that many people have different roles depending on circumstances? The same person may seem one way with some groups, and altogether different with others?"

"It is true that some people have alternate personalities or personas that become dominant depending on circumstances and the situation. But those are not consciously assumed roles, they are integral to the psyche of the individual," Adele said.

Dodgson looked disgusted with her response. He moved in closer and asked in a grating voice, "Are you prepared to state positively that you know exactly how a person will behave when not in your presence?"

"No one could make such a statement," she said coolly.

He looked at the jury, spread his hands, shrugged, then turned his back on Adele and walked to his table, waving to Barbara on the way. "I have no further questions of this witness," he said. His body language and expression both said it wasn't worth continuing.

Barbara started her redirect examination.

"Ms. Wykoph, you said that Mrs. Wilkins did not have a 'face,' and that she was transparent. Can you give us a brief explanation of what you meant by those terms?"

"Objection," Dodgson said angrily. "Another lesson in Psychology 101 is irrelevant to the case of the State versus Wallis Lederer. In fact, I object to this whole line of inquiry concerning Mrs. Wilkins as irrelevant."

"I believe that for those of us who haven't had that course in Psychology 101, the terms are not self-explanatory," Barbara said. "And Mr. Dodgson's other objection has already been addressed by the court."

"Overruled," Judge Wells said. But he sounded a little weary as if he would like to end this dialogue as soon as possible.

Barbara repeated her question.

"If I may use the example the prosecution used, what I mean is that in the case of necessity forcing the person in mourning to perform routine chores, or to carry on with a work situation, that person is behaving in the way that is acceptable to others, but it is an act. There is little or no spontaneity, and little or no initiative. A depression deep enough to bring about suicidal thoughts is also fatiguing, mentally and emotionally, and is reflected in physical fatigue, lassitude. Or, more rarely, it is reflected in almost manic behavior that appears hysterical on occasion. When not actively engaged in a required response, that person most often appears withdrawn and remote. When Connie Wilkins was in her deepest period of mourning, she had no interest in the world or in others, and she never pretended she did. When her recovery period began last fall, she began to take an interest again, and it showed in her actions toward her stepdaughter, and later in her resumption of volunteer work, in her interest in regaining muscle tone, in planning for the future. She regained the spontaneity she had shown previously, and she had a desire to start new activities. She never pretended anything."

"I see," Barbara said. "Will you also explain how it is that you can form a judgment about actions you don't observe directly, based on what you do see."

"It goes back to the points I just made," Adele said. "Spontaneity is not something one can pretend. Connie had recovered her physical and mental vitality, and those two attributes are impossible to sustain unless they are real."

"Earlier you said that even though one has recovered from mourning and has resumed a normal life, that person occasionally lapses into sadness again. Is it possible that Mrs. Wilkins became despondent and deeply depressed on a daily basis when she returned home after a busy day?"

"No. The reawakening of the feeling of loss is temporary and seldom lasts more than a day or two. It would not be a daily occurrence."

Barbara thanked her and said no more questions, and Adele left the stand. Every juror watched her as she left the courtroom. Also watching her, Barbara saw Stephanie again in the back row. Her stomach spasmed. If Stephanie felt trapped by testimony, would she leap up and make a dramatic courtroom confession? It would destroy her, her daughter, and it would destroy Barbara. But her desperation could easily override reason. Barbara turned to the bench again.

"Your Honor," she said, "at this time I would like to have

my colleague read two statements which I will then submit as defense exhibits. One is from Mrs. Wilkins's sister, and the other is from her brother. They both live in Roanoke, Virginia."

Dodgson was on his feet to object before she finished speaking, and Judge Wells motioned them both forward.

"Ms. Holloway, Mr. Dodgson, I intend to call for a recess, during which I would like to discuss this with you both in chambers. Please bring the statements with you, Ms. Holloway."

In his chambers, actually one large room with old furnishings, chairs covered with black leather that was showing cracks, a large globe on a stand and many pictures of young adults and children, the judge waved both attorneys to chairs. He was still in his robes behind a big, dark mahogany desk with many framed photographs on it.

He pursed his lips. "May I see the statements?"

She handed them to him. He motioned for her to sit and he began to read. When he finished, he leaned back and gazed at the ceiling for a minute or two, then said, "Mr. Dodgson, have you had ample opportunity to examine the two statements?"

"Yes. They are just more of the same. It's a case of he said, she said and adding on to it doesn't improve matters. Neither of them can be cross-examined, to find out what else they had to say."

"Your Honor," Barbara said quickly, "it is important to my case to demonstrate that those closest to Connie Wilkins and who knew her best, knew she was not suicidal. If Jay Wilkins was making frantic phone calls it was not because he believed she was. Also, Mr. Dodgson has had those statements since July. At any time he could have had his own depositions taken."

Judge Wells held up his hand. "What I propose is that you highlight the few lines that you think are indispensable at this time for your colleague to read. Mr. Dodgson, will you stipulate that the statements may be entered in their entirety, that the jury may read them when they begin their deliberation if they are so inclined?"

Dodgson looked doubtful and seemed ready to refuse when Judge Wells said, almost gently, "I advise you to so stipulate, counselor."

"Yes, Your Honor. No objection to that," he said.

He was objecting with every fiber of his being, Barbara suspected. When Judge Wells turned to her, she nodded. "I'll highlight the lines for Shelley to read."

He fumbled in a desk drawer and came up with a highlighter, and as she read over the questions and answers, he leaned back again with his eyes closed.

When she was done, he read what she had highlighted, then handed the pages to Dodgson, who read them with a fierce scowl. "Very well," the judge said, giving the pages back to Barbara. "Have those lines read. Who is your next witness?"

"The young man who worked at the dealership, Douglas Moreton."

"After your colleague reads the lines, I think it will be wise to have our luncheon recess. Clear the decks of this business, so to speak. Anything else?"

Neither had anything else to say and they were dismissed. Walking back to the courtroom, Barbara had to admire the judge. He was wise, patient and fair, just as Frank had said, and he also had his case completely under control and intended to keep it that way.

After the recess Barbara had Shelley read the question, then the answer. Sonia's was first. "He called me at seven-fifteen and I realized it was only four-fifteen in Eugene. He said he had been up all night, worrying, and he was afraid that Connie would harm herself, that she might be suicidal. I told him that was nonsense, and of course it was. She would never consider such a thing. I didn't take it very seriously, but I didn't know yet that she already had been murdered."

Nick Robbe's statement followed. "It was a little after four in the afternoon, and he repeated what he had said to my sister early that morning, that Connie might be considering suicide. I told him there was no way she would ever do that or even think that. He begged me to give him a call if we heard from her. He said she didn't have to get in touch with him or anything, but he had to know that she was alive and safe."

Both statements were entered as exhibits, and they recessed.

Phase one, Barbara thought, watching the jury members. Some obviously were bored or sleepy. Several of them had been shifting positions frequently, as if they were finding it difficult to be comfortable, although she knew the chairs were very comfortable. Her real worry was that they might dismiss everything they had been hearing as inconsequential.

THIRTY-FOUR

That day when they left the courtroom a reporter and a video cameraman met them in the corridor. While the videographer began taping Wally, the reporter asked Barbara, "Why all the attention on Connie Wilkins? What's she got to do with anything?"

Barbara laughed and waved at her team. "You go on, I'll catch up." The cameraman paced them, videotaping Wally as they walked. She said to the reporter, "You know I won't comment on what's developing. What I will say again is that Wally Lederer is innocent and by this time next week I'll have proven that." The video camera swung around to focus on her. She smiled at the lens. "I repeat, Wally Lederer is innocent. Wally will take the stand, probably on Monday, and we'll have a little theater of our own."

She walked to the tunnel entrance, with the camera on her all the way. Then she waved and descended the ramp and both newsmen remained behind.

When Barbara reached Frank's house, Maria was un-
packing hot burritos Mama had made. "She began to worry
that everyone was just eating bologna sandwiches or something like that," she said, smiling.

"Mama spoils everyone who crosses her path," Barbara
said, sniffing. "And you're getting more like her every
day," she added to Maria. The burritos smelled too good
to resist, but when she started to eat, she found that her appetite was gone.

Doug Moreton was a lanky, tall young man who had a
lot of catching up to do before his girth began to balance
his length. He looked as if he was still growing taller. His
neatly pressed jeans, although new looking, were a little
short. Fair, with gray eyes, he appeared younger than his
age, which he said was nineteen. He was in his first term at
Lane Community College, studying automotive mechanics.

"Mr. Moreton, were you previously employed at the
Wilkins dealership?"

He nodded, then said quickly, "Yes, ma'am." He was very
nervous, darting quick glances about as he spoke. He said
he had worked there for over a year, all through his senior
year at high school, and on into the summer. When Barbara
asked what his duties had been, he went over the same list
that the general manager had talked about. He cleaned the
sink, mirror, wastebaskets, the cars taken out for test drives…

"Was it a good workplace?" she asked. When he looked
puzzled she said, "I mean, did you enjoy working there?"

"I liked the hours," he said. "Twenty-five hours a week
and no night work. That was good. I was saving up to get
a car and go to LCC."

"What hours did you work?"

"Every day from three until six and five hours on Saturday and Sunday."

"Did the weekday hours interfere with your schoolwork?"

He hesitated, then shook his head. "I got by okay," he said almost defensively. "I went to North and it's not a bad bike ride, by the river, over the bridge and you're practically there. It's quicker than the bus. Except on some Thursdays when I had chemistry lab and sometimes we ran late, and then it was a hassle."

"Were you ever late?"

He nodded, then said yes.

"Did anyone say anything to you about it?"

"Yeah, he did. He bawled me out, Mr. Wilkins, I mean. He said, 'Boy, if you can't get here on time, just get out.' He took an hour off my paycheck. I thought I'd have to give up the chemistry lab, or else quit, and I hated that. But one of the mechanics said he'd clock me in on Thursdays if I didn't show up in time. He knew I wanted to be a mechanic. So that worked out."

"Were there other occasions when Mr. Wilkins bawled you out?" Barbara asked sympathetically.

"Yeah, a couple of times a week at least. He'd see me coming out of the bathroom where I'd be cleaning the sink or something and yell, 'Boy, get out there and clean up that car. I don't pay you to hang out in the toilet.' Or he'd yell, 'Get in there and clean up that garbage. Haven't you read the rules? Can't you read English?' I'd go in the lounge and couldn't see any garbage, maybe a Coke can or something like that, but that's all." His words came faster as he talked, as if things had been building for a long time. "He didn't want to see a water drop in the sink, or a smudge or fingerprint on the mirror or anywhere else. He was really on me after the closing of a deal. The desk in the office has a glass top and he'd go in and if he saw a fingerprint on it anywhere, he'd really yell. Everybody left prints on it. I mean, it was glass. I told the mechanic who clocked me in that Mr. Wilkins hated me and he said it wasn't just me. He hated all kids. He called them filthy animals, and if the customers brought kids in with them, he'd be on my back like a flash once they were gone to clean up their filthy fingerprints, clean the filthy bathroom, straighten out those magazines. I mostly tried to stay out of his way."

"Was that what he usually called you, just 'Boy'?"

"Yes, ma'am. I don't think he even knew my name."

"Why did you leave the dealership job after Mr. Wilkins was no longer there?"

"Some new people took over and they said they didn't need anyone cleaning all the time when there's a cleaning crew every night."

"Was there a cleaning crew every night all the time you worked there?"

"Yes, ma'am."

Barbara smiled at him and said, "Thank you, Doug. No more questions." His smile was tentative at best.

Dodgson had no questions. He had read the jury as well as Barbara had. Doug Moreton had won their sympathy and all Dodgson would do was reinforce it if he tried hammering at the boy.

Barbara called her next witness.

Mrs. Vanessa Littleton was beautifully dressed in a beige raw silk suit and matching blouse, with a single strand of pearls. She was forty-three, with makeup so discreet that it appeared at first glance not to exist, and hair so carefully coiffed that it appeared natural although its strawberry blond color did not come in nature. She was poised and relaxed as she was sworn in and took the witness stand.

"Mrs. Littleton, were you acquainted with Jay Wilkins?" Barbara asked.

"Yes. He was our neighbor."

"Were you friends?"

"No, simply acquaintances who happened to live in the same neighborhood."

"Do you recall an occasion when a boy had car trouble on your street and you came to his aid?"

"Yes, very well."

"Please tell the court what happened that day."

"I had been walking my dogs and was on my way home late one afternoon when I saw an old car pull into a driveway up our street. I thought it might be the Wilkins house, but I wasn't certain until I drew closer. I saw a boy trying to push an old car out of the driveway to the street. The drive has a slight incline, hardly noticeable, but too much for the boy to cope with alone. I stopped and asked him if he was having trouble, and he said he would have to leave the car and go call his father to come with a truck to tow him home. He had pulled into the driveway in order to turn around, and his car stalled and wouldn't start. He was about sixteen, the age of my youngest son at the time. I knew the nearest public telephone was five or six blocks away, and I started to invite him in to use my phone, but instead, I told him to give me his father's number and I would make the call. I advised him to stay with his car until his father arrived, and to explain to Mr. Wilkins what had happened if he came before the boy's father got there. He gave me a cell phone number and I continued walking home and called his father and left a message. He returned my call a few minutes later and I told him about his son and his difficulties."

"Mrs. Littleton, why did you advise the boy to remain with his car and wait for his father?"

"I believed that if Jay Wilkins came upon it, he would have it towed. I hoped the boy could explain the situation and prevent that."

"Had there been other similar incidents in the neighborhood to make you think that?"

"Not just like that situation, but there had been other incidents. Jay Wilkins would not tolerate disorder in our neighborhood, and he was quick to complain, and even to take action if he felt anyone was violating what he regarded as a covenant."

"Was there a written covenant governing what was appropriate and what was forbidden?"

"No. He took it on himself to decide. His family was the first to build in the area, and he seemed to consider most of the rest of us as upstarts who had to be taught how to behave." She smiled slightly, an ironic little smile. "Six or seven years ago, my husband and I bought a camper and had difficulty in maneuvering it around the house to park it. We needed to do some rather extensive landscape work first. Jay Wilkins threatened to sue us if we didn't have the camper removed. I knew that boy's old car would not last five minutes in his driveway if he saw it there."

"Do you know what the outcome of the incident was?"

"Yes. Jay Wilkins called a towing company and had the car towed away before the boy's father could get there."

"Thank you," Barbara said. "No more questions."

Dodgson rose and, without leaving his table, he asked, "Mrs. Littleton, is it possible that Mr. Wilkins was merely trying to protect the property values of the neighborhood?"

"That was what he claimed, but some of us thought it more important to protect human values," she replied coolly.

After the witness was excused, Judge Wells beckoned Barbara and Dodgson. At the bench he said, "Ms. Holloway is your next witness to be Mr. Lederer?"

"Yes, Your Honor."

"Since it is now almost four, I think that I'll recess at this time until Monday morning. I understand that Mr. Lederer's testimony will be lengthy, with the videos to display, and it might be best not to break it up with the weekend. Besides," he added with a smile, "it's a lovely day and the jury, and indeed all of us, might enjoy a little sunshine before the rains set in."

Barbara walked briskly hoping to clear her head, to go into the near meditative state she often reached when walking, leaving her feeling refreshed and alert. It was not happening. The thoughts that chased one another were meaningless, time wasters, a misuse of little gray cells.

A flock of seagulls wheeled overhead, their raucous screams discordant. The next wave of rain was coming, she thought distantly. The seagulls preceded a front.

The sun was very warm, the deep pools of shade welcome as she walked into and out of them. She had reached the footbridge, started across, then stopped to watch the speeding water carrying the land to sea grain by grain. Assembly line. Tireless, forever on the job. Her thighs were burning and she became aware of a throbbing pain in her heel. She turned to retrace her steps. She didn't even like to walk on the other side, where the trail was in the sun with no cooling caves of shadow. She should have gone home to change her clothes, put on good walking shoes. Her court clothes were not appropriate here. Rules. More rules. She began to limp.

She stopped abruptly in the middle of the path and shook her head. She had no idea of what had been running through her mind, no memory trace.

She thought of the news article that she had read that morning summing up the state's case. No one but Wally could have taken the boat, and the home security system proved that it had been returned the night of Jay Wilkins's murder. Only the killer could have returned it. In cold black-and-white print the conclusion had been inescapable. The person who stole the boat killed Jay Wilkins. It was as simple as that. The reporter had finished with a quote from an "expert." It was a waste of time to try the case, a waste of taxpayer money, a waste of court staff and facilities already overburdened with more pressing demands… She shook her head, trying to clear away the words.

She began to walk again. She had to write her closing statement. Her only witness from here on out was Wally himself, and a handful of letters, plus the videos. Nothing. And what had she accomplished to date? Again, nothing. Refuting the state witnesses a little was not enough, and half of her refutation could be used by Dodgson to drive home his own point that Jay Wilkins would have followed through with charges against Wally even if the boat had been returned. Wilkins had believed in sticking to the rules, and the rule was that if you stole, you went to jail. No exceptions, no excuses.

The pain in her heel was getting worse with every step. As soon as she got to the park, she sat down on the nearest bench. What she wanted to do was ease her foot out of the shoe, but she was afraid she might not get it back on.

Phrases various people had said kept repeating in her mind:

If it goes sour.
She's only twenty-three! She just wants a real life.
Sometimes we could save them, sometimes we couldn't.
Just to know someone's looking after Meg.
Infantilism, as helpless as a new-born.
It will kill him to go back!
They'll kill her...

Even as the words reverberated silently, the faces of Meg and Stephanie formed, faded and formed again in her mind. Meg, anguished, drawn and hollow-eyed, her jaw clenched so hard it looked painful, and Stephanie as frozen and pale as marble, two equally terrified, equally desperate women. And everything depended on their not losing control, keeping silent. If either of them broke, it would all go up in flames; the woman would be destroyed, the ones she loved would be destroyed, and Barbara herself would be destroyed.

She was shivering. Three egrets skimmed the water, no longer gleaming white in sunlight, but ruddy, and the shadows had lengthened and merged until now there were few patches of sunlight even on the other side of the river. She looked behind her at the park in surprise. It was almost empty with just a few people remaining, and no boys throwing Frisbees.

It wasn't that she had never lost a case, she thought clearly then. She had. And it wasn't that she had not worried right up until the verdict was delivered; she always did. Juries could be mercurial and unpredictable. But in the past she had always thought she had conducted the best case, if not the only case, she could manage. In the past she had always tried to find the truth and reveal it.

You made a decision, she told herself harshly. How many times had she counseled a client: you made the decision, and you have to live with it for good or bad.

She stood up and started to walk. The pain in her heel was excruciating. She returned to the bench, then eyed the grass between herself and her car at the far end of the park. She would destroy her panty hose, she thought as she took off her shoes. *Good! Destroy them all and be done with it.*

"You made the decision and you have to live with it," she repeated as she started to walk across the grass. It was cold and wet.

"But what if you can't?" she said under her breath. "What if you can't?"

THIRTY-FIVE

After all his guests had gone on Sunday night, Frank didn't even pretend to work the crossword puzzle. He sat brooding about Barbara, who looked too tired, and about the coming week. He was very much afraid that the entire trial now depended on how well Wally did on the stand, and the strength of her closing statement.

He was picturing the expression on Meg's face when she said, "I didn't realize how good it was to get your hands in the dirt."

"Mud," Wally had said, showing every tooth he had. "She was like a kid with a brand-new mud puddle."

"It was good," Meg said softly. "I planted tulips, too, and daffodils, crocuses, hyacinths. Wally doesn't even know what a hyacinth is."

"I held the umbrella," Wally said. "We made a deal. I'll dig or till, whatever, and even help with weeding, and I'll hold the umbrella, and let her play in the mud."

For a brief moment, they had both looked very happy.

"He'll be great on the stand," Frank said to Thing One, the cat on his lap. Thing Two tried to climb aboard with him.

"And damned if I could see any other case she could have tried to make," he told them. They listened attentively the way they always did.

Wally was as good as Frank had expected. He told his story simply. He was one of four children, father worked in a mill, after-school job, his first and only girlfriend, who had been his wife for forty-two years.

Barbara stopped him to ask, "When you worked at the dealership did Jay Wilkins also work there?"

"Yes, he did."

"Were you friends?"

Wally shook his head. "He was the boss's son, learning the business from the ground up, and I was the flunky who cleaned the bathroom and kept the cars clean. We knew each other, that's all. He had a car and raced the gut on Saturday night, ran with a different crowd."

Barbara smiled. "I think some of the jury members might not know exactly what you mean when you say he raced the gut. Can you tell us what that means?"

Some of the older jurors were smiling. They remembered.

"Kids with cars would drive up and down Willamette for three, four hours every Saturday night. I don't think they're allowed to do that these days. People complained a lot even then." In answer to her question he said that he had not owned a car.

In the same simple, direct way he told about his first arrest when he was seventeen, his probation and community service afterward until he was twenty-one.

They had the morning recess then, and Barbara couldn't tell how the jury was reacting. Sympathetic, suspicious, impassive perhaps. But they no longer looked inattentive or restless.

After the recess Barbara asked, "Did you continue to work at the dealership?"

"No. I was fired. Jay's father gathered everyone and told them to check their wallets because they had been rubbing elbows with a common thief, and he told me to get out. That was that."

"When was the last time until this past spring that you saw Jay Wilkins?"

"At our graduation. I never saw him again until last April."

She let him talk about the next few years without interrupting him.

"All right," she said. "So you and Meg were married and you moved to San Francisco. Then what happened?"

"I was standing by the jewelry counter in a department store…" He continued on to the arrest.

Barbara stopped him. "Why were you in the store?"

"That's where Meg worked and I was waiting for her to get off. I worked in the Sears loading dock on the other side of the mall and got off about a half hour before she did."

"Mr. Lederer, did it occur to you then, or at any time, that that might have been a case of entrapment? Having the purse so conveniently left open, and the store detective right there?"

"Not at the time," he said. "Later, I thought it might have

been. I guess I looked pretty suspicious, dressed in work clothes, beat-up sneakers, jeans. Whether it was a setup or not, I shouldn't have done it and I knew that. I deserved to be punished."

"What was your punishment?"

"Five years in prison."

"Do you believe that serving that prison term rehabilitated you?"

"Two things straightened me out," he said. He told the jury about Meg's promise to wait for him, and her threat to leave him if he ever crossed that line again.

"And the other thing that straightened you out?" Barbara asked when he paused.

He talked at some length about his cell mate, Joey. He did not mention learning to play cards.

"So, when I was released," he continued, "I worked on an act. I did my first big performance two years after getting out."

"Your Honor," Barbara said, "at this time I would like to show the court a video of Mr. Lederer's performance."

Since it had already been decided that it would be permitted, Dodgson did not object.

A television was set up and the bailiff loaded the cassette. Several attendees in the courtroom moved to more favorable viewing positions, the reporter among them, and the video started.

Barbara watched the jury as the tape played. Stony-faced at first, slight bewilderment followed. They didn't know why they were viewing it, what it had to do with the trial. Then, when Wally began to unload the various items he had lifted on his way to the stage, a few smiles appeared.

The foreman chuckled and someone else laughed discreetly. Several of them laughed when Wally handed the M.C.'s wallet back to him at the end. After the television was wheeled out again, they were studying Wally with renewed interest.

Judge Wells called the luncheon recess. He was not smiling, but he had watched the video with interest as keen as that of the jury, and Barbara could see the glint of amusement was back in his eyes.

When they left the courtroom, the reporter who had approached Barbara the day before grinned and gave a thumb's-up sign, as he spoke on his cell phone.

The temperature had dropped overnight after the rain front passed. It was very cold outside. In the car Wally said, "Honey, there goes your garlic."

"It's exactly where it should be," Meg said, and Frank, said "Amen."

That day Maria spread the table with luncheon meats and cheese, three kinds of bread, and all the condiments anyone could think of. There was also an assortment of do-it-yourself salad makings.

"Are you all right?" Meg asked Wally. "It must be hard, up there so long on the witness stand."

"Honey," he said, "this is the first time ever that I got top billing. Star of the show. The one they came to see. It's okay." Then he laughed. "Let's eat."

After lunch, with Wally back on the stand, Barbara asked, "Have you continued to perform through the years, Mr. Lederer?"

"About thirty years," he said.

"Did you keep in touch with your old cell mate, Joey Washington?"

"Up until he died, about eight years after I got out. I sent him cards, notes, clippings, things like that. He didn't write back, but he had crippling arthritis, and I never expected him to. And, although he wouldn't admit it, he was illiterate."

"Mr. Lederer, did you also provide some financial support to Mr. Washington?"

He shifted a bit, then said yes. "I figured he was responsible for my getting my act together. I thought I owed him something for that. He was old and sick and he didn't have any family to give him anything."

"Exactly how much money did you send him over the years?"

"Ten percent of what I made, same as an agent's fee. He had earned it."

She nodded, and walked to her table where Shelley handed her the letter from the prison chaplain. After Wally identified it, she showed it to the judge and then to Dodgson.

"At this time," she said, "I would like my colleague to read that letter to the court." She waited for Dodgson's objection. It came swiftly.

"I object. This is highly irregular. It's prejudicial, an unprecedented attempt to influence the jury." He would have continued, but Judge Wells held up his hand to stop him.

"Your objection has been noted," he said.

"I have cites to reference such a request," Barbara said. Shelley was unloading books from a large bag and stacking them on the defense table.

"We'll discuss this in chambers," Judge Wells said. He

called for a recess and minutes later Barbara walked into his chamber with her pile of books. There were nine of them.

That day Judge Wells asked his secretary to bring coffee, and he settled behind his desk without another word and began to read the cites. The secretary, a bald man of middle age, brought in a coffee tray and left, also without a word.

"Help yourselves," Judge Wells said, without looking up. "I take it black, half a spoon of sugar. If you will, please." Barbara glanced at Dodgson, who was slouched in his chair, scowling. She poured the coffee and took Judge Wells his the way he liked it, then poured for herself, and glanced at Dodgson again. For a moment he looked as if he might snarl at her, but he shrugged, then nodded. She poured a cup for him and sat down.

The judge read each cite carefully, made a few notes of his own, then sipped his coffee.

"Do you have a list of the cites for Mr. Dodgson?" he asked Barbara.

"Yes, Your Honor. The letter was included in discovery, of course. The letter is not without precedent. Usually outside documents are introduced only to refute a witness, to impeach a statement, but at times they are also used to substantiate a statement, which is the case here."

Dodgson objected again, this time in a louder voice, "And I say it's too prejudicial."

Judge Wells gave him a warning look. Evidently it was enough. Dodgson subsided.

"As you say, Ms. Holloway, there are precedents. I will allow you to go forward. Overruled, Mr. Dodgson."

Quickly Barbara said, "Thank you, Your Honor. After

Mr. Lederer's second video has been shown, I will ask for the same ruling in order to present additional affidavits about the effect of his training film. I believe the same cites apply to them. May we discuss that now, instead of when it arises in court?"

"Let me see them," Judge Wells said. He finished his coffee and held out his cup for her to refill. She did so, added the half spoon of sugar and returned it, then she brought out the letters from her briefcase.

"I provided Mr. Dodgson with copies of the letters," she said when she handed them to the judge.

He thanked her absently for the coffee, then started to read the letters. There were a lot of letters and they added up to nothing less than a glowing endorsement. Dodgson knew this as well as she did, and he was seething, red-faced.

Her coffee had grown cold, but she did not get up to replenish it. She watched the judge read.

When he finished, he regarded her thoughtfully for what seemed a very long time.

"Every one of those letters has been authenticated, certified by the signatories. If I can have Mr. Lederer identify five or six of them and have them read, I would be willing to refer to the others, have them admitted as exhibits, and move on, since they tend to get repetitive. Otherwise, as a separate issue, I will enter each one of at least twelve such letters to substitute for character witnesses."

"My God!" Dodgson roared. "If that isn't a threat to lengthen this trial, I don't know what it is."

"You took two days with character witnesses," she said hotly. "I have every right to take as long as I need to do the same thing for my client."

"Peace, both of you," Judge Wells said mildly. "Ms. Holloway, I won't decide that issue until it arises in court, presumably sometime this afternoon after our recess. I imagine Mr. Dodgson will object then, and I will have a decision." He turned to Dodgson. "If I rule in her favor, are you willing to stipulate that the other letters be admitted as exhibits for the jurors to examine later?"

Grudgingly Dodgson agreed to stipulate and they were dismissed. On the way back to the courtroom Dodgson said furiously, "Next you'll want to give him the Medal of Honor while's he on the stand."

She laughed. "That's an idea. I'll take it under advisement."

When everyone was back in place, Barbara reminded the jury of the letter that Wally had identified, then asked Frank to read it. He would read all the letters written by males. As he read, she recalled sitting in the back of the courtroom observing him when he argued cases at a time that seemed so remote now. How impressed she had been then, how proud. He had a fine voice, and his timing was perfect.

"Dear Mr. Lederer," he read, "it is my unhappy duty to inform you that Joseph Washington passed away at three-thirty this morning. He died quietly in his sleep. I was with him during his last hours and he asked me to tell you how grateful he was for your generosity, and that he regretted not writing to tell you that personally. You made a difference in the last years of his life. Your gifts provided him with a few comforts as his illness progressed, and I want to add that he shared those gifts with others as unfortunate as he was...."

Frank read the signature, then said, "There is a hand-written note added at the bottom of the letter."

"Mr. Lederer, I want to add my thanks to that of our chaplain. Joey was a good influence on many of our inmates, including you yourself, and your gifts to him were very important in the last years of his life." It was signed by the warden.

After the letter was added as an exhibit, Barbara said to Wally, "When you received that letter did you consider your debt to society paid in full?"

He shook his head. "I worried about it. I got the idea of an exhibition for law enforcement officers to help them spot pickpockets and nip it in the bud. I made a training film."

"At this time, Your Honor," Barbara said, "I would like to show the jury the video Mr. Lederer prepared to introduce his training film."

As before, the television was wheeled in and attendees jostled for a better place to view it. The reporter managed a front row position this time. Again Barbara watched the jury as the video played. In many ways it was more impressive than the entertaining one had been, if only because Wally was picking the pockets of police officers, some in uniform, some in plainclothes. When the motion was slowed, some of the jurors were leaning forward with intent looks. She suspected that they, like the group in Frank's house months earlier, had been trying to catch Wally in the act, and failed.

When it was over, Judge Wells called for the afternoon recess. Barbara left the defense table to walk in the corridor for a minute or two, and the reporter caught up to her. "Ms. Holloway, are those videos for sale? We'd like to buy one or both, play excerpts on the evening news maybe."

Smiling, she shook her head. "Later. Ask Wally himself later, after this is all over. You saw the announcement at the end of the training video, available only to authorized law enforcement people."

"The guy puts on a good show," he said.

She smiled again. "You bet he does." She returned to her table to pick out the best of the many letters of appreciation. She got right to them when court resumed.

"Mr. Lederer, do you recognize this letter?" she asked, handing him the first one. He identified it. It was from the chief of police in Tucson. She asked the judge for permission to have it read, after passing it to him and then to Dodgson, who made his objection known. Judge Wells beckoned them forward.

"Ms. Holloway, you may have your client identify all the letters, and have them admitted as defense exhibits. But then limit the reading to the four you consider representative. As you stated, they are very repetitious. Overruled, Mr. Dodgson."

One by one Wally identified the letters and then Frank stood up to read four of them. They all expressed appreciation and went on to order the training video. In various ways the letters all said the video would be a valuable training tool.

When that was done, Barbara asked, "Mr. Lederer, if you planned to make a longer training video, what was the purpose of the one we just saw?"

"Just to demonstrate that no one is immune, including the police. To give an idea of what kind of training might be helpful, a few of the tricks to be on the watch for. In the video you just played, no one knew ahead of time what I was going to do, but I couldn't very well go out and pick the pockets of unsuspecting strangers. I had to use actors for the training video." For the first time since he had taken the stand he smiled broadly, the same smile he had used in the videos, and he added, "I might have been arrested, picking the pocket of an innocent bystander."

"Did the actors know beforehand what you were going to do?"

He shook his head. "I never told them. I just told them to go somewhere, like a subway or a street corner, and mingle, and pay no attention to me or the camera. After I did my thing, we would meet somewhere else and I'd give back whatever I had taken, and that was that. I never warned them what to expect. I had to use a lot of different actors," he added.

"Was your cameraman paid?" He said yes.

"In the video we just saw you say the training video is available at the cost of handling and mailing. Do you include the salaries of the actors and the cameraman in those costs?"

He shifted a little, then said no. "I didn't know how many I'd sell," he explained, "or even if I'd ever sell any. I wasn't sure how to include their costs, prorate them I guess, so I just didn't include them."

"The dates of those letters indicate that you have been putting on the exhibitions for about twenty years. How many a year do you usually do?" He said three or four. "And how many of the videos have you actually sold?"

"I think it's around three to four hundred by now. I'm not real sure. I don't handle them myself."

"Do you charge for the exhibitions?"

He shook his head. "They pay my expenses, a hotel room, like that."

"So your work with the training film, the exhibitions are all in the nature of a public service, donations of time and skill for the public interest. Is that correct?"

Wally looked uncomfortable. "I never thought about it that way. It just seemed like something I should do because I could and no one else was doing the same thing."

She nodded. "All right. You and your wife were traveling a lot, putting on the exhibitions, performing in Las Vegas or Atlantic City or other places, then what happened?"

"I think we just got a tired of it...."

It was four-thirty, and Barbara didn't want to get back to the reality of a missing boat and murder that day. Instead, she led him into talking about the old house they had found and how they had gone about making it livable. Wally was a superb witness. He grasped instantly what she was getting at, and he was voluble as he described the old house, what it needed and how they had worked on it.

At nearly five she asked why they had gone to the coast in April.

"The paint smell," he said. "It was getting to us. On clear days I'd go out and work on the blackberry jungle, but just sleeping with those fumes was too much. We decided to go breathe some fresh sea air and let the house get some air. We wanted to check out some of the places we had loved as kids. Agate Beach, the Devil's Churn, the toffee pulling machine at old Nye Beach. We wanted to see if it was still there."

At that point Judge Wells tapped his gavel and said court would recess for the day.

THIRTY-SIX

Barbara woke up with a start from troubled dreams that had involved being chased by an unseen enemy, struggling up a steep mountain trail, in as much danger from falling to her death as from being caught. It was still dark in her apartment. She turned over to go back to sleep, but as the dream images faded, her closing statement surged into focus. It was hopeless, she decided minutes later, her brain was swirling with worry and new phrases to add to her statement. She got up and pulled on her robe. It was five in the morning.

A long shower helped clear her head. A pot of coffee helped more. She sat at her desk and reread her statement, then began rewriting sections of it.

She printed out two copies of the statement, one for Frank. After dinner, she would try it out on him, the best critical advisor she could imagine.

"Hang in there," she muttered to herself. "Just a few more days."

That morning Wally appeared as relaxed as ever, and Meg looked exhausted. Sleeping as little as she was, Barbara suspected, and repeated her own advice, this time to Meg. "Hang in there. Just a few more days." Meg managed a weak smile and nodded.

A few minutes later, with Wally on the stand again, Barbara began.

"After you revisited the places you remembered, you ended up in Florence for the night. Is that correct?" He said yes, and she asked, "Why did you go to the casino?"

"I wanted to check it out. I thought if they did shows, maybe I could do my act there."

"Please tell the court what took place that night at the casino."

After he described the encounter, she asked, "Did Mr. Wilkins appear troubled, worried?"

"No. As I said, at first he didn't remember us. He looked and acted okay, a little stiff at first, then he got friendlier." Wally said he and Meg had spent the next day down around the dunes, and returned home Sunday evening.

"Please tell the court about your visit to Jay Wilkins's home on Monday," Barbara said.

When he got to the scene at the display case, Barbara stopped him. "I have the state's schematic of the room," she said. "And a transparency we can mark. Mr. Lederer, please show us exactly where the three of you stood when he opened the case."

Shelley put the room drawing on an easel and placed the transparency over it. Wally left the stand to go to the easel, where Barbara handed him a marker. "Just indicate where each of you was."

"Well, we moved back out of the way so he could open the case. He was here," he drew a circle near the case. "Meg was just about here, about four feet back, maybe five feet, and I was by her. He stayed at the case while we were looking at the boat. Then I gave it back to him and he put it down again and the three of us moved on out to the bar room."

"When he returned the boat to the case, did he close the door?"

"No. He just set it down and stepped away."

"Was the door opened wide?"

"Yes. Straight out. It's about two feet wide, out that far. He had to open it all the way to reach the boat."

After he was seated again, she asked, "While you were in the study, did you look over his desk?"

"I didn't pay any attention to it."

"Did he show you the rest of the house?"

"No. Just the entrance foyer, the study and then the bar room."

"Did he show you or tell you about his security system?"

"No."

"How did Mr. Wilkins appear? Was he relaxed, pleased to see you?"

Wally shook his head. "He didn't seem to be. I was thinking that maybe he regretted his invitation. He was nervous, a little abrupt, and he seemed preoccupied, not interested in us. He never asked us a single question all that evening."

"All right. What happened at the bar?"

"Jay went behind the counter and mixed drinks. But suddenly he began to talk about his wife. He said he was worried because she hadn't turned up at her sister's house in Virginia. I thought we had walked in on a family spat and were in the way. He went out to get her picture to show us, and kept on talking about her. She had been sick, and he was afraid she was suicidal, he said. I had never met her, and I didn't know anything about their private lives, and I began to think that we should just finish our drinks and leave. That's what we did."

"When was the last time you saw Jay Wilkins?"

"That was it. I never saw him again. We left and had some dinner and went home."

She had him recount the day the detective and the insurance agent had come to ask him questions. "Did the detective say to hand it over and they'd forget the whole thing?"

"He said that, and I told him I didn't know what they were talking about. I didn't."

"Did you hear from the insurance agent after that?"

"Yes. We read about Jay's murder in the newspaper, and a couple of days later the agent called and told me the boat had turned up in the house."

"Now, on Saturday, April 26, do you recall what you did during the day and evening?"

"Same as every day. When it wasn't raining I cut brambles. It was starting to get dark when I quit. I took off my shoes and jeans on the back porch, put on a robe and went to take a shower. We ate dinner, and we watched a movie until about ten or ten-thirty, when we went to bed."

"Did you always change your shoes and jeans on the back porch?"

"Yes. Meg made me. She said I was worse than Hansel and Gretel, leaving a trail everywhere I went. Sometimes the brambles were wet and a lot of stuff stuck to them, and it fell off as they dried."

"When the detectives arrived with a search warrant did you change clothes on the back porch again?"

"Yes. They said they wanted the jeans and I took them off and handed them over."

"When did you buy those jeans, Mr. Lederer?"

"Back in March. I didn't have anything to tackle those vines in and I knew they'd tear up anything, so I went to Goodwill and got the first pair I found that fit me. Dollar and a half. I didn't care if they got ruined."

"Did you own any other denim pants?"

"No. After the police took that pair I went back to Goodwill and bought another pair just about like them."

She nodded and went to stand by the defense table, "Mr. Lederer, you said that after you were sentenced to prison your wife told you if you crossed that line again, she would leave you. Have you ever crossed that line again?"

He shook his head. "Not once. I knew she meant it. Besides, I never was tempted again, I had a way to go with my life."

"When you first started to perform, were you making a living salary?"

"It took a while, two years."

"How did you live during that time?"

"My wife was working and she supported us."

"Exactly when did you send your first contribution to Joey Washington?"

He looked uncomfortable, the way he had before when talking about it, and that was what Barbara was after. She wanted to remind the jury that his gifts had been voluntary and that he in no way was boasting about them.

"We talked about it, Meg and I, when I got my first check, and she agreed that it was the right thing to do. It wasn't much, but I knew Joey could use it."

She paused a moment, then asked, "Mr. Lederer, did you steal that gold boat?"

"No."

"Did you kill Jay Wilkins?"

"No."

"Thank you," she said. "No more questions. Your witness, counselor."

"At this time we will have our morning recess," Judge Wells said before Dodgson could get to his feet.

After the jury was gone, Barbara turned to Meg. "This is going to be hard to watch," she said. "Are you okay for it?"

"Harder on him," Meg whispered, motioning. Wally had left the stand and was coming toward them. Barbara doubted what she had said was true. She moved out of the way for Wally.

"Honey," he said to Meg, taking her hand, "why don't you go buy me a shirt? I'll need a clean shirt before the week's over."

"Why don't you go pluck a duck," Meg said softly.

A huge grin spread across Wally's face, and Barbara suspected a private joke was responsible. Then Frank said, "Why don't we have something to drink? I'm taking orders. Shelley, want to come help carry things?"

"Just water," Barbara said. "I'll go wash my hands." She walked by Stephanie Breaux, once again seated in the back row, and her slight nod was not acknowledged. Stephanie did not move. She had lost weight, a few more pounds and she would start looking gaunt. She appeared not to have moved a muscle when Barbara returned.

When they resumed, Dodgson was more than ready. "Mr. Lederer, when you and Jay Wilkins were both boys, weren't you a bit envious of him? The boss's son, privileged and favored, with his path smoothed out by his father?"

"No," Wally said.

"You mean it didn't bother you that he had a car and you didn't? That he had better hours than you did? That he could take off when he chose?"

Barbara objected. "Multiple questions are difficult to answer. Heaping question on question is improper cross-examination."

"Sustained," Judge Wells said.

Dodgson asked the same questions, individually, and each time Wally said no. "Didn't it bother you that you had to clean the bathroom, scrub the sink and toilet after him?"

Wally shook his head. "I never thought of it that way. I was doing the job I was hired to do. That's all."

"And didn't it bother you that a schoolmate, almost exactly your own age, inspected cars that you had cleaned to make sure you had done a good job? That didn't bother you?"

"No."

"Did you use a time clock back then?" Wally said yes. "And if you were late were you in danger of being fired?"

"Yes."

"Was Jay Wilkins ever late?"

"Yes."

"Was he fired?"

"No."

"Was he reprimanded? Bawled out?"

"I don't know."

"Did you ever hear of him being bawled out?"

"No."

"And that didn't bother you, upset you, that he was allowed to play by different rules?"

Wally shrugged and said no in the same even-voiced way. Dodgson was looking more and more disbelieving, incredulous as he continued to try to get Wally admit to envy. His voice grew louder and he moved in closer as he kept at the same subject with more questions.

"Objection," Barbara finally said. "The prosecutor is asking the same question repeatedly with one variation after another because he doesn't like the answer he keeps getting."

Judge Wells sustained the objection and asked Dodgson to move on.

With a disgusted look at Wally, Dodgson stepped back a few feet and looked at the jury as he asked, "What crime had your cell mate committed to put him in prison?"

"Objection. Irrelevant."

"I don't think so," Dodgson argued. "Was he a con man, a murderer, a child molester? It matters who the defendant relied on as his mentor. Obviously it was a serious crime for him to have been convicted and sentenced to a very long term, a crime that would see him die of old age and infirmity in prison. The crimes committed and criminals convicted of them are a matter of public interest, in the public record. What other advice did such a sterling character offer?"

"That is prejudicial," Barbara snapped. "I move that the

prosecutor's remarks be stricken. Joey Washington's record is irrelevant to this trial," she said furiously.

Judge Wells beckoned them forward. "The objection is sustained and the comments will be stricken. I advise you, Mr. Dodgson not to refer to the matter again." He motioned them away.

Barbara was seething. The comments would be stricken, but the memories of the jurors could not so easily be wiped clean. The idea had been planted and would lodge that Wally had chosen a mentor who was possibly a child molester or a murderer.

Dodgson did not let up on the pressure until the luncheon recess gave them all a respite. That day, to Barbara's surprise, Martin showed up with a beautiful Greek salad and grilled salmon. His wife, Binnie, had added her specialty, raspberry tarts.

The strain was showing on Wally, now that he could relax a little, and Meg looked ready to fall over.

"A few more days," Wally said, putting salad and salmon on a plate. He set it down in front of Meg. "Next week we'll get to that henhouse, get it built. Do you buy chickens in the winter, or wait until spring?"

"Chicks in the spring," Meg said faintly. "And a warming box with a lightbulb for heat for them. That's how my dad always did it."

"And so will we," he said.

Frank began to tell about a case he'd had back in the early days that involved a dispute over a hen and a clutch of chicks. "Seems the hen took a notion to build herself a nest across a fence line on a neighbor's property and both parties claimed the chicks. Threatening lawsuits, probably oiling their shotguns, neither one willing to give an inch. And the chicks were coming right along, nice broiling size. Then a family of raccoons moved in and helped themselves to a fine chicken dinner. Case over. I was willing to share my fee with the coons, only I didn't get a fee. The old guy claimed it was my fault for not getting his chicks back for him while they were still real property."

Wally laughed and Meg smiled. Barbara was preoccupied but she did begin to pick at her food and even ate some of it.

"A clutch of chicks," Wally said. "A pride of lions, exaltation of larks, pod of whales. What else?"

"Pack of wolves," Frank put in. "Den of thieves. Warren of rabbits." They all became silent, thinking.

"A giggle of girls," Shelley said after a minute or two.

"You made that one up," Wally said, grinning. "I like it. There's a bevy of something, but damned if I can think of what."

Barbara left then. A few minutes later she heard Wally's laughter. She closed her eyes, recalling his words: "If it goes sour."

He knew, she thought, and he was trying his best to put on a cheerful face for Meg. He knew how near the edge she was.

THIRTY-SEVEN

That afternoon Barbara had to admit that although she despised the insinuating questions Dodgson asked, she admired his skill at implying more than the words he used. Even his body language was an accusation. He was standing before the witness stand, his arms folded across his chest, staring at Wally fixedly as he said, "Mr. Lederer, it is well-known that performers have to practice their craft continuously. Singers sing, dancers dance and so on. Does practicing your act rely on others who are both unsuspecting and innocent?"

Wally considered it for a moment, then said, "The final act does. When I was still—"

Dodgson cut him off. "You answered the question. You need unsuspecting and innocent people for your act to work. While practicing, did you say, 'Excuse me, sir, while I pick your pocket'?"

"Objection," Barbara said sharply. Without hesitation Judge Wells sustained it.

Dodgson left it at that, but he had made his point. He shrugged and shook his head. He asked, "When you were perfecting your act and your wife was supporting both of you, did you ever try to get a real job?"

"That's what I was doing all the time, preparing for a real job, a profession as an entertainer."

"Were you content to let her be the official breadwinner while you were *practicing* your craft?" He had made his point and the heavy sarcasm in his voice made it clear what he meant.

"Objection," Barbara cried. "Your Honor, the prosecutor is couching his questions in a manner that is both prejudicial and full of unwarranted implications."

"I just asked a simple question," Dodgson said, raising his eyebrows as if surprised at her indignation.

"Overruled," Judge Wells said.

"Were you content?" Dodgson nearly yelled the question at Wally.

If Wally was struggling to remain calm it was hard to tell, but his voice was firm when he said, "I was working to make a better future—"

"Move the answer be stricken," Dodgson said in a loud voice. "Not responsive."

It was stricken.

"Were you content? Yes or no."

"Yes."

"What was your wife's job?"

"Objection. Irrelevant."

"It's relevant," Dodgson said smoothly. "He was content for her to be the breadwinner. It's fair to know what she had to do to keep him content."

"Your Honor," Barbara said angrily, "I move that the prosecutor's comment be stricken and he be told to stop editorializing."

Judge Wells said softly, but in a way that suggested he was as angry as Barbara, "Sustained. Mr. Dodgson, ask your questions in a straightforward manner."

Dodgson spread his hands in a gesture suggesting he was innocent. He spent the next hour trying to get Wally to admit to envy of the wealth of the celebrities who frequented the casinos, their expensive jewelry, the retinues that accompanied them, their fat wallets. It was excruciating to watch. His manner, his looks of disgust and disbelief, of incredulity said more than the words.

Barbara well understood that he was trying to rattle Wally, make him lose his temper. And he was running out the clock. He didn't want to finish in time for Barbara to start her redirect. He wanted the jurors to take away the impression he was creating that Wally was a deceitful man, lying, secretly envious of others, and one who very likely used his skill as a pickpocket not only on the stage, but off, as well. Guilt by implication, by innuendo and insinuation. Plant the seeds of distrust and suspicion and let them take root overnight and send the roots deep into the jurors' minds where they would be hard to remove. Whether her many objections were sustained or overruled, Dodgson was undeterred.

At lunch that day neither Wally nor Meg had any appetite. Barbara took a sandwich and immediately went upstairs with Shelley. They had work to do.

Dodgson didn't get to the boat until late that afternoon. "Isn't it true, as Mr. Wilkins told the investigating officer, that he handed that boat to you and while you were look-ing at it, he escorted your wife to the bar room?"

Frank took Meg's hand and held it firmly. She was trembling.

"No, that isn't true," Wally said.

"Filled with envy for the boss's son who was now the boss, surrounded by luxury and comfort while you were struggling to make your house habitable, didn't it strike you as a way to get back, to even the score just a little bit by taking a prized possession of his?"

Barbara called out her objection before Dodgson fin-ished his question. "Your Honor, may I approach?"

He beckoned them forward.

"His questions are loaded with false implications and assumptions that have repeatedly been denied. Such ques-tions are on the order of when did you stop beating your wife? Mr. Dodgson is reinforcing again and again his own assertions about envy and jealousy that Mr. Lederer has re-peatedly disclaimed. I move that his entire line of questions be stricken."

"You're out of your mind!" Dodgson said, possibly even in real disbelief.

"I will take your motion under advisement," the judge said. "Mr. Dodgson, I have spoken twice to you about in-serting opinions and implications into your questions. If you persist, not only will I find you in contempt of court, I will order you to submit your questions in writing for my approval and have the court stenographer read them to the witness. Is that clear?"

Dodgson nodded, and Judge Wells said sharply, "I want an answer, counselor. Is that clear?"

"Yes, Your Honor."

"Objection sustained. Rephrase the question, Mr. Dodgson, and take my warning to heart."

In a series of rapid-fire questions, Dodgson forced Wally to admit that when Jay Wilkins moved from the glass case to lead the way to the bar room, there had been a time, however brief, that his back had been turned and he couldn't have kept his eyes on Wally during that period.

And so he had it both ways, Barbara thought. It didn't matter if Wally had handed the boat back or if Jay had replaced it himself, there had been an opportunity for Wally to take it.

Dodgson moved on to the day when the detective and the insurance agent had gone to ask Wally about the boat. "When the detective told you to hand it over and Mr. Wilkins would forget the whole thing, did you believe him?"

"I had no reason to believe or disbelieve—"

"Did you believe him? A simple yes or no!"

"Objection. The witness was trying to answer the question."

"No speech is called for," Dodgson said hotly. "He believed it or he didn't."

"He didn't know what the detective was talking about. He had no basis for belief or disbelief."

"Sustained," Judge Wells said.

"If you had taken the boat then would you—"

Barbara objected before he could finish. "Conjectural. A hypothetical question." It was sustained.

"Looking back now, from what you know about Mr. Wilkins, do you believe today that he would have forgotten the matter?"

She objected and it was sustained.

"Did you worry about that boat all week, what it could mean if a charge of grand theft should be filed with an expanded investigation?"

Wally said yes, he worried.

"Did you consult a criminal defense attorney during that week?"

"Yes."

"And on Saturday night, did you decide you had to try to clear up the mess, make amends, ask forgiveness—"

Barbara objected in a loud furious voice.

"Withdraw the question," Dodgson said. "Mr. Lederer, on Saturday night, April 26, did you leave your house at about nine o'clock and drive to the home of Jay Wilkins? Did you ask him to forget the—"

"Objection!"

"Sustained," Judge Wells said sharply.

Dodgson swung away from Wally abruptly and returned to the prosecution table. "No more questions," he said angrily. He looked as if he believed he was being thwarted by the legal system and the defense attorney, both intent on preventing his getting at the truth. He sat down with his arms crossed, glaring at Wally.

She could well understand why he had a string of successful prosecutions behind him. It was ten minutes past five and Judge Wells adjourned for the day.

The small group at the defense table did not hurry out. "Let's wait until the corridor clears a bit," Frank had suggested. Meg was very pale and shaking, and Wally, now that the focus was no longer on him, was little better. "You were really super," Frank said to him.

"You raised a live one," Wally said, nodding toward Barbara. "She's good." He had one arm around Meg's shoulders and she was leaning in toward him.

"The best," Frank agreed.

"I think what we'll do," Wally said, "is go to our room and have a good drink or two, and eventually order some food. And then," he said, giving Meg a little shake, "let's take in a movie. Game?"

"Whatever you want to do," she said in a low voice. She looked as if she would get to their room and weep for a long time.

"Okay," Barbara said, "let's make tracks. You were great, Wally. The best I've ever had on the stand. Now Shelley and I have work to do. Make the movie a comedy."

While Shelley transcribed the notes she had made all through Dodgson's cross-examination, Barbara and Frank started on her closing statement. They stopped for the dinner delivery later and got back to it. Shelley left at ten, and it was midnight when Barbara began to gather up her own things.

"Bobby, try to get a little sleep tonight," Frank said. But he knew she would go over the day's inquisition closely. They were both very aware that Dodgson had scored points that day. Sleep was not a menu item that night.

THIRTY-EIGHT

The next morning, Barbara started her redirect examination. "Mr. Lederer, you said you felt no envy toward Jay Wilkins when you were boys working at the dealership. What did you feel toward him?"

"I was sorry for him more than anything, when I thought of him at all. But I didn't spend much time thinking about him."

"Why were you sorry for him?"

"Well, we were both hired at the same time, at minimum wage, and I was working twenty hours a week, and he was working half that much, and sometimes even less. I had more spending money than he did even after buying my own clothes and things, and putting away a little for school. A lot of times he didn't have gas money, and once when he let his insurance lapse, his dad took away his car keys until he caught up. After I left the job every day, I could forget it, but he had to go home with his dad. I wouldn't have traded places with him for anything. I mean, his father had all those rules, and he made everyone follow them, and I guessed it was the same at their house."

She nodded. "The question was raised about how you practiced your act in the early years. Can you explain to the jury how you perfected your skill?"

He grinned. "I must have picked Meg's pocket a thousand times. Also, we got hold of a store mannequin and while she was working I practiced with it. We'd sit in a sidewalk café with coffee and I watched people, where they kept their wallets, the inside breast pocket, or hip pocket, or even in the side pocket of a coat. And one night at the restaurant where Meg worked I got to talking with the owner, Luigi Maggiore, and I told him everything, and what I was up to, but I needed some real live people and I was stumped. He thought it was pretty funny, and he suggested that he might be able to help. It was a neighborhood restaurant with a lot of regulars. He said he'd invite some of them over for an after-dinner treat and let me have a go at them. We talked it over and it seemed perfect.

"One night about eight people hung out after they ate, waiting for the treat. They all knew Meg—she was the cashier and hostess—and she took me around introducing me. Luigi didn't show up but his wife was there, in on it, and she invited everyone to have a drink on the house while they waited. So everyone was milling about, talking. Altogether it was half an hour or more before Luigi came in. He asked them all to be seated and said he'd explain what was in store. I started pulling things out and putting them on a table and his wife handed them back. The folks were all laughing, having fun. They wanted to do it again another time and I said it would be best if unsuspecting people were involved, and someone said, why not do it again next week and he'd bring in another couple and not tell them what was up. A few of them did that, and then the friends brought friends, and I got in a lot of practice."

"Did Mr. Maggiore provide free drinks for that event?"

"Well, we agreed that I'd pay for them, but he only charged me at cost, so it was okay. After the first time, most of them didn't take him up on it, when they realized what the joke was."

"Have you kept in touch with Mr. Maggiore through the years since then?"

"Yes. He's one of our good friends. He's in a nursing home now and we visit him two or three times a year."

"Did you keep in touch with any of the regular diners who were there in the first practices?"

"Quite a few of them. I send them passes for any show I'm going to be in and we get together when they can make it."

"After you started working at the casinos didn't you envy the wealth you saw all around you?"

Wally shook his head. "Those folks had their lives and we had ours. I liked ours. Those exhibitions took us all over the country, three or four different areas year after year. We had a camper and over the years we explored wherever we happened to be. Grand Canyon, the sequoia groves, the Tetons, old Williamsburg, Mammoth Cave, the museums in New York and Philadelphia. We liked our lives just fine."

"When you went to Jay Wilkins's house, did you feel a sense of injustice that he had so much and you had little in comparison?"

Wally shook his head. "It wasn't like that. I thought it

was a little pathetic that he was my age and living in his
father's house, while I had worked for my house and it was
truly mine and Meg's. We found exactly the house we had
come home for, and we love it. I thought there he was surrounded by things his father and grandfather had collected,
they weren't really his. It was more like he was the caretaker. And he was having trouble with his wife when my
wife was by my side, still my best friend. It was not envi-
able at all to see him so jumpy and nervous."

"Did you feel that you had to settle the score in any way?"

"No. There wasn't any score to settle. I thought his father had decided his future, and he had stepped right into
the role his father had chosen. I felt sorry for him."

She continued to cover some of the points Dodgson had
hammered on until the morning recess.

"I'll wrap it up in a few minutes and Dodgson will make
his closing statement, and either he'll stretch it out until adjournment, or he may stop early, hoping to break my stride
by adjournment. If he cuts it off between four and four-
thirty, I'm going to ask for an early adjournment. Meg, I'll
use you as a reason to stop early. I'll tell the judge you're
ill. Okay?"

"I don't think it would be a lie," Meg said. "By the time
that man finishes, I may be quite ill." She looked ill, pale,
with deep shadows under her eyes.

"We call what ails you a hangover," Wally said gravely.
"I poured gin and tonics into the old girl last night, had her
giggling like a kid." He grinned, but that morning his grin
looked forced.

When Barbara resumed, she asked, "Mr. Lederer, you
admitted that you were worried after the detective and the

insurance agent came to your house to ask questions about the boat. You consulted an attorney. Will you please tell the jury what advice you were given?"

"You said there wasn't a thing I could do except deny it. I didn't take that boat but there was no way to prove it. You said it is impossible to prove that you didn't do something if it seemed that you'd had the opportunity. You told me to be patient and wait for developments."

"Did you take that advice?"

"Yes."

She asked a few more questions to reinforce what he had said earlier, then she asked, "When was the last time you saw that gold boat before it appeared here in court?"

"That Monday night when my wife and I visited Jay at his house."

"When was the last time you ever saw Jay Wilkins?"

"That same night, Monday, April 21."

"Exactly what did you do from six o'clock on during the evening on Saturday, April 26?"

"I changed my shoes and jeans on the back porch, showered and had dinner with Meg. We cleaned the kitchen together, then settled down to watch a movie. When it ended we went to bed."

She nodded at him. "Thank you, Mr. Lederer. No more questions." It was five minutes before eleven, an hour and a half before the usual lunch recess.

Wally was excused and Judge Wells asked Dodgson if he was prepared to make his closing statement.

Dodgson spent the hour and a half extolling the virtues of Jay Wilkins, a man of integrity, with an impeccable reputation, a preeminent business leader who had been looked up to by the entire business community, and indeed the community as a whole. He had no enemies.

"He gave up his social life when he married Connie Wilkins and devoted himself to her care....

"And then, on a mission that was devoted to the future of his wife's health, a chance encounter brought him in contact with Wallis Lederer."

Barbara glanced at her watch, twelve twenty-five, right on time, she thought derisively. Judge Wells tapped his gavel a minute later and announced the luncheon recess.

"Sort of makes you want to go lay a wreath on his grave," Wally commented as Frank drove them to his house for lunch.

"Or drive a stake through his heart," Barbara said.

Her gaze met Wally's in the rearview mirror. His was shrewd and knowing. He believed Jay had killed Connie, and she had more or less confirmed his suspicion that she shared that belief. She turned away and did not try to modify what she had said.

Dodgson picked up where he had left off when he started that afternoon. "Jay Wilkins extended the hand of friendship and offered the hospitality of his home to the defendant....

"You have been entertained and amused during the course of this trial, but, ladies and gentlemen, this trial is convened for one purpose and one purpose only, to determine the guilt or innocence of the defendant. There have been many diversions from that one grim purpose, many side trips to distract your attention, and now you must refocus on the facts of the case.

"Jay Wilkins had no enemies with a murderous hatred in their hearts. He was well liked and respected. He set rules at his workplace, and he expected those who accepted the rules, his employees, to abide by them just as he abided by the rule of law.

"There was one and only one motive for his murder." He went to the exhibit table and picked up the gold barge, returned to stand close to the jury box, and held it up.

"It is a fact that this gold boat was in Jay Wilkins's house on the night of April 21. It is a fact that for a time, however brief, Mr. Wilkins's back was turned from the case and from the boat. Whether it was in the case or in the defendant's hands is irrelevant. We have all seen his skill at stealing, how fast he can move, as fast as a striking snake. The boat is small, not much bigger than a deck of cards. It could be slipped into a pocket in a second."

He slipped it into his own pocket where it made hardly a bulge. He took it out again and returned it to the exhibit table.

"It is a fact that after the defendant and his wife left Jay Wilkins, he closed the outside door, resetting the security system, and that system is mute evidence that no door in that house was opened again until the housekeeper arrived the following morning and discovered the theft. It is a fact that the defendant is a felon, twice convicted of theft. It is a fact that after being questioned about the theft of the boat the defendant was alarmed enough to consult a criminal attorney. He knew a third conviction with his criminal record would result in a much longer prison sentence than the one he had served in the past. He was told by the attorney that it would be impossible to prove he didn't take the boat, and we can surmise how much that must have added to his alarm.

"It is a fact that we know exactly when the house was entered during the days that followed the theft. And we know exactly who entered, when and when they left again, right up until the discovery of the murder of Jay Wilkins."

Dodgson went down the list carefully, detailing each time the door had opened and closed.

"It is a fact that no one had the opportunity to return the boat before the night of April 26, the night of Jay Wilkins's murder, and no one had the opportunity to return it after that murder."

He paused, then said, "There is only one conclusion that can be drawn from the undisputed facts. Only one person could have taken the boat and returned it. Only one person entered the house on the night the boat was taken, and that same person entered the house the night the boat was returned, and on that night Jay Wilkins was assaulted and killed. Only one person was there on both nights, the thief and the murderer. And that person was the defendant, Wallis Lederer. Why he took the boat makes no difference. Envy, malice, a vicious practical joke? It doesn't matter. The fact is that he alone had the opportunity."

The prosecutor began a meticulous and painstaking recapitulation of the night of the murder. After that he said, "You have heard much testimony about the dirt and debris found on the jeans the detectives collected from the defendant's house but, ladies and gentlemen, we have no way of knowing how much dirt was on those jeans on the night of the murder of Jay Wilkins. Perhaps the defendant wasn't cutting blackberries that day. We don't know, but ask yourselves, is it likely that Mr. Wilkins would have opened his door to admit a stranger off the street who just happened to be wearing jeans that were an identical match to those collected from the defendant?" He looked and sounded incredulous at the idea.

In the same vein he said, "And ask yourself if it isn't stretching coincidence too far to suggest that a car drove down Hunter's Lane at nine-fifteen, an event unusual enough to draw the attention of Mrs. Ogden. Is it a coincidence that that car left the area where the defendant lived at precisely the right time to arrive at the Wilkins house at nine forty-five on the night of April 26?" He shook his head and looked the jurors over as if expecting an immediate answer.

"You have the facts, ladies and gentlemen," Dodgson said. "You are required to consider them carefully when you begin your deliberations and put aside all the distractions that have been presented by the defense. The facts say one thing loud and clear—the defendant did steal the boat, and on the night he returned the boat, he murdered Jay Wilkins."

When he sat down Judge Wells said, "Is the defense ready to make its closing statement at this time?"

Barbara turned to Meg, who looked as if she might faint. "Your Honor," she said, rising, "may I approach?"

When she and Dodgson went to the bench, he looked smug and satisfied. She asked for an adjournment for the day. Dodgson protested vigorously. "It's just a waste of time, a delaying maneuver."

"Mrs. Lederer has been taken ill," Barbara said when he subsided. "I'm afraid she will collapse in court."

The judge looked past her at Meg, then nodded. "I think that's a reasonable request at this time," he said. "We'll recess until morning then. I trust that if Mrs. Lederer needs medical attention that will be taken care of overnight."

"Yes, Your Honor. Thank you. We'll see to it."

That was a sincere pledge, Barbara thought when she returned to her table. Meg needed a tranquilizer, or sleeping pills, or something to get her through the next day or two. She must have felt the knife twist deeper into her heart every time that damned boat was mentioned.

"Honey," Wally said, taking Meg's hand as soon as the jury was escorted out, "remember when you had the flu a couple of years ago? You had some sleeping pills. We still have them. Let's take a run out to the house, check things and get the pills. It would be a nice break, a drive out in the country, sit in our own nice chairs for a while."

"I'm all right," Meg whispered.

"You're not," he said flatly. He looked at Frank. "That's what we're going to do, head out to the house. I'm not taking a powder or anything. Don't worry."

"It's a good idea," Frank said. "I wasn't worried." At least, not about that, he added under his breath.

THIRTY-NINE

It was late that night when Barbara finally got to bed, only to drift into a restless sleep punctuated by dreams that woke her up but left little memory. Bad dreams, she knew, disturbing dreams. Hours too early she was up again, unrested and heavy-feeling.

That morning Meg looked as dopey as Barbara felt. "I'll be like this for hours," Meg said. "Sleeping pills." She grimaced. But at least she had slept.

Then the judge called on Barbara for her closing statement, and she felt the familiar surge of adrenaline.

"Ladies and gentlemen," she started, "the trial you have been witnessing involves a circumstantial case. I want to explain exactly what that means. There is no direct evidence, no indisputable facts that point to one person only as the perpetrator. No eyewitnesses. No fingerprints. No DNA samples to match.

"The only possible match the prosecutor has presented

proved to be inconclusive. The denim fibers could have come from any garment roughly of the same age, equally faded and with the same wear and tear evident. In our area, ten- or twelve-year-old denim jeans or jackets, or even children's garments, are not rare."

She was walking back and forth before the jury box slowly, emphasizing each point she made. "As it always happens with circumstantial cases, there are a few undeniable facts, and there is a great deal of speculation. What that means, ladies and gentlemen, is that the facts lead to opinions about their meaning. That is what speculation means in this context, an opinion, no more than a guess as to the meaning of factual evidence and its relevance. As we move along today, I want to make a clear distinction between the facts and the speculation about them. We all know that well-meaning people often have different opinions about the meaning of the same facts.

"In circumstantial cases such as this one it is important to know enough about each of the people directly involved in order to form your own opinion about the probability that any one of them would have behaved in the way the prosecution has speculated."

She paused a moment, then said. "I want to examine what has been testified to here in court about everyone, starting with Wally Lederer."

She did a step-by-step recap of Wally's life, then summed it up. "He committed two crimes and he accepted his punishment as just and deserved. He did not come away bitter and resentful. He confided in the restaurant owner who came to his aid, and they became lifelong friends. He valued friendship. He befriended his cell mate, an old man who was ill, because he valued the advice the man had given him. He put on exhibitions for nothing more than his expenses, and he made the training video for police departments all over the country to use and charged only the cost of handling and mailing.

"As a youth he was sentenced to do community service and today, more than forty years later, he is still doing community service because he recognized a need that he could fulfill."

She kept the focus on Wally until the morning break. When they resumed, she said, "The second person you must take into consideration is Connie Wilkins, the wife of Jay Wilkins." There were several looks of surprise.

"She's an important element in the tragedy that unfolded," Barbara continued. "She has been referred to many times during this trial, and her death has been referred to. She died on or about April 19 or 20 and her body was recovered nearly two weeks later. There is an ongoing investigation by the homicide unit concerning her death."

She had expected Dodgson to object, and almost obligingly he did so. "I move that the remarks be stricken," he said. "That is a red herring that adds a layer of confusion to this trial. It is irrelevant."

"Your Honor," she said quickly. "Insofar as Connie Wilkins's health was a major concern of Jay Wilkins and had a direct bearing on his actions, it is extremely relevant."

He overruled.

She recounted Connie Wilkins's history, then said, "With one exception, the witnesses who testified that she was suicidal had not seen her for more than two years. The other witness who testified that she was suicidal was the instructor who gave the exercise and self-defense class."

She shook her head. "He said he has learned to listen with more than his ears, and he had the ability to know what Connie Wilkins meant no matter what words she spoke...." She quoted a few of the things Howie Steinman had said, then added, "You must decide if she told him to get a life, or to get on with his life.

"You heard the testimony of Adele Wykoph, a psychologist with more than two decades of experience working with troubled women. Ms. Wykoph said that Connie Wilkins was never suicidal, she had been in mourning and she did not try to pretend otherwise.

"Connie Wilkins's sister stated that she was not suicidal. It was against her religious beliefs and, besides, she had been making plans for the future. Connie Wilkins's brother said the same thing. Neither of them accepted suicide as even a remote possibility."

She reviewed Adele's statements about a public face, and how impossible it was to maintain, and compared Connie's period of deep mourning with her recovery of vitality and optimism.

She began to walk back and forth slowly again, as she said, "And finally there is Jay Wilkins."

She quickly repeated some of what the businessmen had said about him. "But keep in mind that the box where he so generously entertained his guests was paid for by the dealership. It was a business expense. As were his contributions to the university, business expenses to be taken as such, reducing the company's tax liability. The meetings he lavishly hosted were business expenses, advertising and promotion expenses.

"His associates and business friends all said that Jay Wilkins had no enemies, but that has to be examined in the light of something else they all said. They were not personal friends. He did not have a confidential relationship with any of them. The most that can be made from their opinion that he had no enemies is that they, in the casual, group relationship they had with him, did not know of any enemies. And that is quite a different statement."

Judge Wells tapped his gavel at that point and announced the luncheon recess.

"Right on schedule," Frank murmured when Barbara returned to the defense table.

When they left the courthouse for lunch, Barbara said, "I'll take a walk and catch up to you in a while."

She was aware of Frank's anxious searching look, but she ignored it, waved and left them. She felt she could not bear Wally's forced good humor, or Meg's unfeigned despair.

That afternoon, Barbara continued, "The personality of Jay Wilkins that we have been considering was not an assumed public face. With his peers, his business colleagues, his equals, Jay Wilkins had the persona of a congenial host, easy to get along with, a man who enjoyed the tailgate parties and get-togethers to watch sporting events.

"But Jay Wilkins had a second persona that was dominant at other times with other groups. Again, it was not a temporarily assumed public face. That persona was also Jay Wilkins and it governed his behavior and every aspect of his being when it was dominant. The phrase Jekyll and

Hyde has passed from a literary work into the general consciousness. There are people who have different, distinct personas, and when either one is dominant, the person is exactly what that persona accepts as normal and reasonable.

"Jay Wilkins at the workplace was a man of many rules, and he enforced those rules personally and inflexibly." Item by item she reminded the jurors of the many rules and how Wilkins had enforced them.

"Jay Wilkins monitored his employees on the showroom floor, in the closing room and even in the employees' lounge. That goes far beyond maintaining discipline. It is accepted that the employee lounge is where they can relax and speak freely, but not if an inflexible employer might be monitoring every conversation.

"Aside from his many rules, Jay Wilkins showed what seemed to be an obsession about what he required of Doug Moreton. The mirrors, the washbasin and faucets, wastebaskets, the surface of the glass-topped table in the closing room, all had to be kept shiny clean at all times.

"When new management arrived, they let Doug Moreton go because they saw no need for such compulsive cleaning. There was a professional cleaning crew who came in every night, and that was sufficient, as it is with most establishments.

"Jay Wilkins did not confine his rule-making to the workplace. He tried to impose his own rules in his neighborhood." She talked about the boy whose car had been towed away and the threatened lawsuit over the camper.

"He was an impatient man who not only demanded that his rules be obeyed, but that obedience be instant."

She was moving back and forth before the jury. And

they were listening attentively, without movement, as still as statues, their expressions unreadable.

Barbara continued, "Jay Wilkins imposed rules in his house, as well. The housekeeper had to clean and polish the same things every day. Although he lived alone in that big house for a number of years, and he alone might have left a fingerprint here or there, she was required to clean and polish every surface that might have shown a fingerprint or smudge. On the rare occasions that he found fault with her, he left her curt little notes—clean the refrigerator, or clean the stove. She also said that he never talked to her. And Doug Moreton doubted that Jay Wilkins even knew his name.

"At his home, Jay Wilkins installed a state-of-the-art security system and he had a special feature added to it. He wanted a log to keep tabs on every single opening and closing of all doors. His trophy cases had their own separate circuits, thus they were doubly protected. He had a key for those cases, which made them even more guarded. He knew exactly when all the doors and windows were opened and when they were closed. He wanted to know not only when anyone entered his house but when anyone left it."

Barbara regarded the jurors soberly as she said, "Please keep in mind when you deliberate the characteristics of the three people involved in this trial. And keep in mind that the past actions of most people determine their current actions. As we examine the events that occurred between Saturday, April 19, and Saturday, April 26, the night of the murder of Jay Wilkins, ask yourselves is the allegation that has been made in character?

"We know from testimony that Connie Wilkins bought

her plane ticket for Virginia and packed her suitcase for the trip herself. Jay Wilkins drove her to the Portland airport on Saturday, April 19. She got out of his car to walk toward the departure gate and he left the airport and drove to the coast where he spent Saturday and much of Sunday on a preliminary investigation of property he would consider purchasing.

"We know that a chance encounter Saturday night occurred between Jay Wilkins and Mr. and Mrs. Lederer. On that occasion Jay Wilkins invited them to his home on Monday evening to discuss old times.

"We know that on Sunday evening Jay Wilkins returned home in anticipation of his wife's phone call from Virginia. And we know the phone call did not come.

"Sunday night Jay Wilkins checked the airlines and learned that his wife's flight had landed safely on time. He called his wife's sister and learned that she had not arrived, and neither was she expected. He then called the police to report his wife missing. The officer who took his call treated it as a routine case of domestic dispute. But Jay Wilkins continued to worry and at midnight he called his manager to say he would not be at the office on Monday. He had a cell phone, and there was the phone at the dealership where his wife could have called him, but he remained at home. And at four-fifteen Monday morning he called his wife's sister in Virginia again. He told her that he had been up all night, unable to sleep because he was so worried. And he voiced his fears that Connie Wilkins was suicidal and he feared for her life. Her sister rejected that assessment. She knew it was not true and she thought, as the police officer had, that Connie Wilkins simply wanted some time alone. She did not take his call seriously.

"Jay Wilkins made other calls that day, each time repeating his fear of suicide, and those he spoke to, people who had not seen his wife for years, accepted that she might have been suicidal. But Adele Wykoph, who had been with Connie Wilkins a great deal during the winter and spring, told him that she did not believe it. That afternoon Jay Wilkins called his wife's brother in Virginia.

"This time he pleaded with the brother to get in touch if he heard from her. He said she didn't have to call or anything, but he had to know she was alive and safe." She repeated the phrase, "He had to know that she was alive and safe." She paused then for a moment before continuing.

"Connie Wilkins's brother repeated what his sister had said earlier. He knew Connie was not suicidal, and he also did not take her absence seriously.

"But on Monday Jay Wilkins called the police again and this time he demanded that they begin a full investigation, post her picture and start a real search for her.

"Jay Wilkins had no reason to state that his wife was suicidal, but such a claim accounted for his panic about her disappearance. His panic went far beyond the worry that a domestic dispute might have caused.

"Then Wally Lederer and his wife arrived in response to his invitation to visit. He put on a public face, pretended for a time to be the genial host they would have expected and showed them his trophy cases."

She paused again. The jurors remained as still as wax figures, watching her intently. "Please picture that scene before the glass case," she said. "Jay Wilkins opened the door wide in order to remove the gold barge. He handed it to Meg Lederer. She in turn passed it to Wally Lederer. And here the two accounts diverge. In Jay Wilkins's account, he moved away from the case and took Meg Lederer's arm to escort her to the bar, leaving Wally Lederer holding the boat with the case wide-open. Ask yourselves if what you know about Jay Wilkins fits that scenario. He monitored his employees, even in the lounge, and he monitored the coming and going of his own household members. His house had the tightest security system possible. Is it likely that, knowing Wally had been convicted of stealing in the past, Jay Wilkins would have left him holding the gold boat, with other valuable objects accessible? Would that be in keeping with what you know about him?

"The other scenario is that Wally looked at the boat and handed it back to Jay Wilkins, who was still standing by the case, and he replaced it himself. Then the three of them moved on to the bar room. Ask yourselves if it is more logical for Jay Wilkins to have remained by the case until the boat was returned. I encourage you to act out the two scenarios during your deliberations."

She resumed her slow pacing back and forth as she said, "There are other considerations I urge you to discuss about the trophy case and its contents. The housekeeper testified that the door was closed almost all the way, so much so that she did not notice it was not entirely closed until she went to it to clean the glass. When did the door get closed that much? Jay Wilkins opened it fully, extending it about two feet. If he closed it most of the way, why not all the way? Was it on his mind that the boat was covered with fingerprints? Once the door was closed the security would reset and the housekeeper would not be able to open it. Knowing his obsession with fingerprints, an almost phobic aversion to them, does it seem likely that it was on his mind to clean the boat himself before closing the case?

"You have to consider whether Wally Lederer would have taken the boat in the first place. Wally valued friendship highly. He responded to acts of kindness with kindness of his own. He befriended an old, sick convict who had helped him regain his path. He became a lifelong friend with the restaurant owner who helped him along the way. He made no distinction. Acts of kindness were important to him and he repaid them. Jay Wilkins had extended hospitality and the offer of friendship. Do you think in light of what you have learned about Wally Lederer that he would have repaid that with an act of treachery, the theft of a valued object? He harbored no long-standing envy of Jay Wilkins. Rather, he had pitied him as a youth, and he pitied him as an older man, believing as he did that Jay Wilkins was having a marital dispute. He thought of him as the caretaker of his father's possessions, not a man to be envied or someone he would have wanted to wrong in any way.

"When they were in the bar room, Jay Wilkins dropped his pretense and began to voice his concerns about his wife and his fears for her life. He could no longer maintain the public face he had assumed. Having no desire to get involved in a family dispute, a marital problem, Wally and Meg left the house as soon as they could do so politely."

She stopped for a moment, then said briskly, "At the start of my remarks I mentioned that there are relatively few facts in this case, and a great deal of speculation. It is a fact that the boat was in the case on Monday evening, and that Wally and Meg examined it. It is speculation that it was taken at that time. All we can say for certain is that it was missing on Tuesday morning and it was found a day or two after Jay Wilkins was killed. But also, it had been cleaned of all fingerprints. Why?

"It is known that all three people handled the boat, Jay Wilkins, Wally and his wife. They all left fingerprints on it. There was no reason for Wally to have cleaned it since his fingerprints should have been on it. But we also know that Jay Wilkins had what could be called an obsession about fingerprints and smudges, both in his home and at his workplace. Of the three who handled it, he was the only one with any reason to have cleaned the boat. As you deliberate, ask yourselves if it is possible that Mr. Wilkins removed the boat after Wally and Meg left, and cleaned the fingerprints himself. Remember, he had been up all night worrying, and by then he must have been in a state of nervous exhaustion. In such a state people frequently do and say things that they don't recall afterward. We know that by midweek he stopped pressuring the insurance agent about it as well as the police. By then, his other fears might have made the boat seem irrelevant. Ask yourselves if he could have found it later, perhaps in his own pocket or even in the desk drawer, and instead of turning off the security system and unlocking the case to put it away, he decided it could be dealt with later.

"The prosecution also stated as a fact that the boat was returned on the night of the murder but, ladies and gentlemen, that is speculation, a guess. The investigators have no way of knowing when it was placed in the drawer. All they can state as factual is when it was found, after the investigation began. It could have been in the drawer ever since the night Wally and Meg Lederer visited Mr. Wilkins. There is no way of knowing when it was put there."

When she paused again, Judge Wells tapped his gavel and said they would recess briefly. He left, and moments later the bailiff led the jury out.

At the defense table Meg was regarding her with tears in her eyes, but Wally's gaze was appraising. "Are they buying it?" he asked.

Barbara shrugged helplessly. "I don't know." She waved. "See you in a few minutes," and she fled. In the washroom she splashed water on her face and blotted it dry. The impassivity of the jury was unnerving. Now and then a nod, or a frown was about the only reaction they had shown to anything she said.

Shelley entered the restroom. "Are you all right?" she asked.

"Right as rain," Barbara said. "Considering."

"Yeah. Me, too. What a bitch of a case."

And that summed it up, Barbara decided. It was a bitch of a case.

FORTY

Back in court, standing once more in front of the jury box, Barbara said, "There are a few things that we know about Jay Wilkins's activities in the days following Wally and Meg's visit. We know he called his insurance agent and the police about the missing boat, and he demanded an immediate arrest of the man he accused of taking it. We know that he demanded that the police intensify their efforts to find his wife. And they continued to regard her absence as voluntary."

She paused, then said slowly, "If Jay Wilkins had said that he feared his wife might have been murdered, the police would have acted swiftly and decisively in an effort to locate her. But he maintained that he was afraid that she was suicidal. His fear was real. His agitation and worry were real and the investigators thought he was overreacting to a commonplace domestic dispute, or they attributed it to the alleged theft of the boat.

"Then, curiously, by midweek, Jay Wilkins stopped putting pressure on the police about his wife, and he stopped pressuring his insurance agent about the boat. He stopped making frantic phone calls. He stopped all his activities. And he did not leave his house a single time that week."

She stopped moving and regarded the jurors as she said slowly and deliberately, "I suggest, ladies and gentlemen, that Jay Wilkins was behaving like a man in fear for his own life. We have no way of knowing why he stopped putting pressure on the investigators. All we can do is speculate."

She went on more briskly, "And now for the night of the murder. There have been very few facts introduced as evidence about the events of that night. What is known is that someone entered the house at nine forty-five and remained for one hour and five minutes, and during that time Jay Wilkins was hit in the head with a glass pitcher, and that he fell in such a way that his neck was broken and he died instantly. The house was not entered again until the housekeeper arrived on Monday.

"We know that Jay Wilkins had denim fibers under his fingernails. We know there was bark mulch on the threshold and in the foyer leading to the bar room, and in the bar room itself. We know that a hand towel was missing, and that a red Afghan was also missing. And we know nothing else about that night."

She paused, then said, "That's all we can claim to know about that night. What I am going to do is separate those few facts from the speculation surrounding them. First the bark mulch. The state has speculated that the assailant stepped into the bark mulch in order to pick up a stick, but there is no evidence to support that speculation. It is no more than a guess, an opinion. There are alternate guesses. That person might have walked through the bark mulch in the planting between the driveway and the house. He might have walked around the house in the bark mulch, perhaps trying to peer into a window. Or he might have stepped into the bark mulch for another reason altogether. There is no evidence to support one opinion over another. We don't know, and we can't know from the evidence.

"Next, there was bark mulch in the doorway." She walked to the exhibit table and brought out the threshold. "Where the bark mulch was found is most unusual, in the corner where the door meets the doorjamb and the floor. No one would have stepped on it at that place. To account for it, the prosecution has speculated that the assailant used a stick covered with bark mulch to prevent the door from closing. But why? It suggests premeditation, preparing for an undetected exit from the house. But again, why? If that person suspected or knew there was an elaborate security system, he would have known that Jay Wilkins had to turn it off in order to admit him. Would he have thought in advance that it would have been turned back on during his visit? If that person did not know about the security system, there was no reason to provide for an undetected exit from the house.

"An alternative speculation might be that the person who went to that door that night was unwelcome. You've seen the scenario in movies. The person inside tries to close the door, and the one outside puts his foot in it to prevent that. He puts his foot in the corner, exactly where that bark mulch was located, then forces the door open and enters. The door isn't spring loaded, or on any kind of automatic closing device. It would have remained open until someone closed it."

She took the threshold back to the exhibit table. "Ladies and gentlemen, the theory advanced by the detective explaining the mulch is speculation, not fact. The alternative I have suggested is also speculation, not fact. We can't say from the evidence how the bark mulch got there."

Barbara used the schematic of the front of the house, the entryway, the foyer and the rooms off it. "There was bark mulch here," she said pointing to the foyer. "And inside the bar room bark mulch was here."

Remaining by the easel, she said, "Please keep in mind where there was no bark mulch." Once more, as she spoke she pointed. "There was none leading to the lavatory. That is roughly a distance of thirty feet from the bar room. And there was none leading to or inside the study, and that is about twenty feet from the entrance door, or thirty-five feet from the bar room.

"The bark mulch was wet that night after intermittent rain for weeks, and rain that night in particular. It would have clung to anyone's shoes who stepped into it. And it would have been removed by the rough, unpolished stone flooring throughout the foyer. As the mulch dried, even more would have flaked off. The stone flooring goes past the lavatory, and it also extends into the bar room. The study has deep pile carpeting and it would have been even more efficient at rubbing mulch off shoes, but there was none on it. There is no evidence to indicate that the assailant walked anywhere except to the bar room. He left no traces anywhere else."

She moved away from the schematic, closer to the jury

box, as she said, "And keep in mind the other places where no bark mulch was found. None was found on Wally Lederer's shoes. Nor in his car.

"The next puzzle is what happened during the hour and five minutes between when the door was opened and when it was closed. The assailant went to the bar room where he stood in one place, according to the evidence. What was Jay Wilkins doing? Did he stand as still as the intruder for the next hour and five minutes? Why?

"And what happened to the red Afghan? We don't know. We do know that no red silk fibers were found in Wally Lederer's car or on his clothing. The bar room has the stone floor to the end of the bar, and the rest of it is carpeted with a pale gold, plush pile carpet. Anyone with bark mulch on his shoes could not have walked across it without leaving evidence. There was none. But the housekeeper testified that the Afghan was kept on the sofa across the room.

"You may start to speculate about what took place between Jay Wilkins and his killer, and how the Afghan played any part in the exchange. That's fair enough since the state's case is based on speculation. You may consider that Jay Wilkins himself walked across the room and brought the Afghan back to the bar with him. That it did play a part in whatever was being said at the bar. There is no evidence to support any speculation whatsoever, therefore the state left it out of their reconstruction of the crime. But is it insignificant enough to be neglected altogether? We don't know."

She smiled slightly. "It is always a matter of convenience to omit any facts that don't fit the speculative reconstruction you have arrived at."

Quickly sober again, she said, "But something happened that resulted in the assailant picking up the glass pitcher and striking Jay Wilkins with it. We don't know at what point in that hour and five minutes the attack occurred. A glass pitcher does not seem a weapon of choice if a murder is planned. In the state's reconstruction, the stick in the door implied premeditation, but why then was the killer not prepared to kill? Why was he without a weapon at hand?

"And why was the pitcher placed on the floor instead of being dropped? Did he keep it in hand to use again? Or did he put it down thinking to render aid, only to find that Jay Wilkins was dead? One opinion is as valid as the other because we don't know why. One guess is as good as another. But it does lead to another question.

"At what point did the assailant decide to get a towel and wipe off his fingerprints? Remember, no bark mulch was found leading to the lavatory and none was found inside it. Yet, he would have left traces of it wherever he walked.

"Yellow fibers were found on items in the bar room, but none were found in the study or in Wally Lederer's car or on his clothing.

"The investigators theorized that as Jay Wilkins fell, he reached out and raked the leg of Wally Lederer's jeans, and that accounted for the denim fibers in his fingernails. But we have demonstrated that the match was not conclusive. Any number of garments could have yielded such fibers. You saw Wally Lederer's jeans, and you saw the dirt and blackberry debris in the evidence bag. If fingernails had raked down those jeans, dirt and debris would have been loosened and come away with the fibers. Some of it would have lodged under the fingernails. Dirt and debris would have fallen to the floor. None was found. None at the immediate crime scene, none in the study, or in the foyer, none under the fingernails and none anywhere else on the premises.

"The prosecutor has suggested that perhaps the jeans on that particular day were not covered with dirt and debris, but that is more speculation. Wally Lederer testified that he cut brambles every day except when it was actually raining. He had two acres of brambles that he was clearing by hand. He changed his jeans at the back door and put on a robe and slippers that he kept by the door for that purpose because his wife made him. Would that particular day have been any different from all the others? Would he have kept wearing those jeans despite his wife's demand that he change and not track up the house they were so painstakingly restoring?" She shook her head. "Or did he change as usual, and later on change again and put the jeans back on in order to visit Jay Wilkins? That is even more implausible.

"Wally was not allowed to wear those jeans in his own house because he left a trail wherever he went. It is not possible that he could have been in the Wilkins house that night wearing those jeans without leaving some trace of blackberry dirt or debris, however slight."

"Then there is the matter of headlights," she said slowly. "Mrs. Ogden saw headlights, nothing else, at nine-fifteen on that night. And that's all we know about that. We don't know whose car it was, or where it was going, or where it came from. How many other cars in and around Eugene were being driven that night that could have arrived at the

Wilkins house at nine forty-five? We don't know that, either." She shook her head again. "As I said earlier, this is a purely circumstantial case with a great deal of speculation, and speculation is not enough to take the next step to certainty. If we don't know, we have to admit just that. We don't know.

"Ladies and gentlemen," she said slowly, "if the police had started their investigation with the death of Jay Wilkins, they never would have brought Wally Lederer's name into it. There is absolutely no physical evidence that leads to him, and in fact what evidence there is points away from him. And yes, they could have just as reasonably arrested a stranger, a passerby who happened to be wearing old, faded denims, and who happened to be in the area at the right time."

She was stopping more often now, and emphasizing her statements more forcefully, and she was holding the attention of the jurors.

"If the police had started the investigation with the death of Jay Wilkins, immeasurably more serious than the missing boat, they might have asked why he had appeared so nervous and why he had appeared to be living in fear of leaving his house. And why he had insisted, in spite of statements to the contrary, that his wife was in danger of taking her own life. As you deliberate, keep in mind two important facts about the many phone calls Jay Wilkins made over a few days. He told his wife's brother that he had to know if she was alive and well. The second fact to keep in mind is what he didn't say to any of the people he called. He did not say he had to remain at home in case she returned. He said he remained home in order not to miss a call from her, but with a cell phone he was never out of reach by telephone, no matter where he was.

"If the police had started with the murder, the investigators would certainly have discovered that second persona, the one who ruled his workplace with an iron first, who showed no tolerance or mercy toward his employees, the one who made hard and fast rules and swiftly punished anyone who broke them, the man who tried to impose his rules on his neighbors, and monitored his own household. And they might have concluded that *that* man had made enemies.

"If they had even considered the Jay Wilkins that Doug Moreton and Mrs. Haley, the housekeeper, knew, they might have concluded that the most likely person to have cleaned the fingerprints from the gold boat was Jay Wilkins himself.

"And they might have wondered if there was a connection between the two deaths when both husband and wife met such violent deaths within a week. And they might have theorized that one killer was involved, and that that person had nothing to do with a gold boat.

"But the state did not pursue that course for their investigation. Instead, they built a circumstantial case against Wally Lederer based on two assumptions, neither of which has been proved, or can be proved. They accepted the statement made by Jay Wilkins that the boat was stolen by Wally. And they assumed when the boat was found that the only time it could have been placed in that drawer was on the night of the death of Jay Wilkins. Both of those unproven and unprovable assumptions became fixed in their minds as facts. They constructed their case based on those two faulty assumptions.

"Those two assumptions are not facts, they are suspicions, opinions, no more factual than the stick in the doorway, or the reason for putting the glass pitcher down instead of dropping it. All you can say about any speculation is that it could have been this, or it could have been something else.

"Your task here is not to determine either the theft or the misplacement of that gold boat. You don't have enough information to form a conclusion about that because you don't know why Jay Wilkins appeared to be so afraid. Sadly, neither does the state. If one speculative explanation seems as plausible as another, you can't decide which to choose by the toss of a coin. You must be convinced that one is true, the other false, and if the evidence you have seen and the testimony you have heard does not allow you to be certain of the truth or falseness of either, you must conclude that neither has been proven beyond a reasonable doubt.

"It is not your task to determine who was responsible for the death of Jay Wilkins if not Wally. That is a task for the police investigators. Your only task at this court is to determine if you are satisfied that the evidence and the testimony that has been presented here has convinced you beyond a reasonable doubt of the guilt of Wally Lederer. If it does not, you must find him innocent."

She turned to look at Wally for a moment, then addressed the jury again. "When Wally came to me for advice about the accusation of taking the boat, I told him that he had to be patient and await developments. I said at that time that there was no way for him to prove he didn't take it. That same advice would apply to the death of Jay Wilkins. Wally had no way to prove his innocence. But, ladies and gentlemen, he didn't need to prove it. The state's own witnesses and the crime scene evidence proved it for him."

She looked at the jury members one after another, then smiled very slightly. "That concludes my statement, ladies and gentlemen. Thank you for your attention." She nodded at them, and to her relief there was a nod or two, and even a faint smile in return.

Judge Wells announced that court would recess until the following morning, gave his usual reminder to the jury not to discuss or read about the case, and left the bench. As soon as the jury was led out, Wally took Barbara's and held it. "You were swell," he said huskily. "I'll have something real to say tomorrow, but for now, just thanks."

They didn't linger long in the corridor that day. Watching Wally and Meg walk away hand in hand made Barbara want to weep.

"Bobby, let me drive you to my place, just leave your car wherever it is. Relax with some wine, and in a little while we'll get some dinner and I'll take you back to your car. Okay?" Frank said gently.

She shook her head. "Thanks. I think I'd rather just crash for a time."

"No. Not again. You need some decent food. We'll go someplace quiet and you don't have to say a word, and neither will I, and then you can crash. Come on."

She was too tired to argue and she knew that she needed to eat something and if she went home she probably wouldn't. As they walked to the tunnel, Frank said, "You did a wonderful job today, a superb job. With absolutely nothing to work with you spun gold. I'm very proud of you."

FORTY-ONE

The next morning the state and the defense rested. Judge Wells instructed the jury and sent them out to start their deliberations and announced a recess until twelve-thirty.

Wally and Meg had walked over from the Hilton. They had checked out and packed their things, left the suitcases in the car, and now they joined Frank and Barbara in his car to drive to his house. Barbara had left her own car there earlier.

"What now?" Meg asked on the way.

"Now we wait," Wally said. "That's it, just wait."

He said something else, or Frank did, but Barbara paid little attention. She had been plunged back into her days as a graduate student when a visiting lecturer had come to talk to them. A successful trial lawyer, with bushy black curly hair and an oversized mustache, she remembered his appearance but not a word of his formal talk that day. When it ended, he had looked at his watch, grinned, and said, "I still have a few minutes to keep all eyes on me. That's never a time to be wasted. I'll fill it in with a few more remarks, not footnotes, mind you, not even apropos of anything, just some random thoughts. You're going to find the longest day of any trial starts at the moment the jury leaves to deliberate. Whether an hour or a week, it's one long day of hell. And two things I should warn you about that you won't find mentioned in your law books. The two gods of advocacy. Yeah, they're real. The god of crowing and the god of despair. You start crowing too soon, celebrating your defeat of the enemy before the jury has delivered a verdict, the god of crowing will notice, and he's likely to strike you down faster than lightning hit the kite. And the god of despair is a jealous god, more jealous than most, I'd say. You try to encroach on his turf, decide for yourself when it's time to despair, he just might make sure that effort isn't wasted. Don't tempt him." He looked at his watch again, then waved. "I'm out of here. As the chorus girl said to the drunkard, see you at the bar."

The car stopped. They had reached Frank's house.

Shelley had gone to the office to check in with Maria. Meg and Wally went with Frank to inspect his "livestock."

"The best gardener's helpers you can find," he said leading them to the back porch. "Red wrigglers, world's greatest little compost machines."

Barbara drifted upstairs to stretch out on her old bed, the same one she had used after graduating from a crib until she left for college.

"The longest day," she repeated under her breath. No matter how often it came along, it was always the longest day.

She was too restless to stay still more than a few minutes. When she went downstairs again, Wally was standing in front of the fireplace, where a low fire was burning.

"Barbara," Wally said, "I want to tell you something. I've been around performers a lot, and I've seen magic acts of all kinds. But what I saw you do in court these last couple of days was real wizardry, nothing fake about it. You turned the case upside down and had the prosecution biting itself in the ass before you were done. That was magic, pure magic. The neatest verbal sleight of hand I've had the privilege to witness. And it was all done with words. No hands, no gimmicks, no props, just words. You're the tops, Barbara. I know we can't tell how the jury will swing. I've heard a lot about juries in my time and they can do anything from playing follow the leader, to dividing into unmovable blocks of granite, to swinging chairs at each other. They're beside the point right now. However it goes, I know I've had the best damn lawyer there is."

He was regarding her soberly, with no hint of his big smile or actor's flourish. "I knew my case was a loser from the start. I was going down with the ship. I don't know that now. Thanks."

She could find no words with which to respond.

Behind her Frank cleared his throat. "Coming through. Hot." He was carrying a tray with the coffee carafe and cups. "Meg's bringing sugar and cream," he said, putting the tray on a table.

"Someone's cooking something," Wally said, sniffing.

"Soup," Meg said putting down the creamer and sugar. "Frank and I decided some hot soup would be nice today."

"She said I needed a turnip," Frank added.

"I didn't. I said my mother always added a turnip."

"I took it to be an order. Whenever my mother said that's how she did something, it was understood by all that it was an order to shape up."

They were trying so hard, Barbara thought then. All of them, trying so hard to make waiting bearable. Wally took a deck of cards from his pocket and laid it on the coffee table. "You're kidding!" Barbara exclaimed. "Do you think for a second that anyone in this house would play cards with you?"

"Not my intention," Wally said. "I promised to teach Shelley a few tricks, let her amaze and confound her pals."

Shelley arrived a minute or two later.

"Have a seat," Barbara said. "Wally's going to show you something."

"Later," Wally said. "Later. But for now, I'll warm up a little."

He took the cards from the pack and shuffled them exactly the way Barbara had seen it done countless times. He shuffled them with one hand then the other, and when he used both hands the cards flew back and forth so fast they became a blur. For the next few minutes he manipulated the cards in ways that Barbara would have thought impossible.

"I wonder that anyone plays cards with you," Frank said, when Wally returned them to the table.

"Well, I don't warm up like that in front of players," Wally said, showing every tooth. "Felt out of practice. Haven't played around for a long time. And, remember, Frank, I never cheat. No need to cheat at cards. Just pay attention, and learn to count. That's what it takes."

He laughed. "Tell you a story," he said. "You learn a

thing or two playing cards and you can spot a cheater pretty fast. I came across one once and watched for a while. He was fair to middling, but taking the fellows right and left. So I sat in on the game." He laughed again. "After he was cleaned out, he stomped off to another table and kept an eye on me, probably wanted to learn a new trick or two. And I began losing as regular as clockwork. What he must have thought was that Lady Luck had been riding my shoulder earlier. It happens now and then. She picks out a poor sap and gives him a night to remember. Not often, mind you, but when it happens the guy can't do anything wrong. Bet on an inside straight, you got it. Hit a sixteen, here's the five, pal. Like that. So that fellow must have been relieved. He'd learned that when the Lady decides to pick a winner it's best to fold your tent and head out. You can't beat her at her own game. He was sort of looking self-satisfied again, a little smug. When the Lady gets bored, she takes off, and you can crash like a meteorite, and I was crashing. Anyway, when I was back to where I started, I got up and left. Winked at him on my way out and thought he'd have a heart attack on the spot. A fun night."

Frank laughed and shook his head, and the conversation became desultory and disjointed.

Finally, it was time to return to court. Judge Wells asked the jury if they had reached a verdict, they said no, and he recessed until five-thirty. Or until the bailiff called to summon them back, whichever came first. The longest day.

Lunch was soup and cornbread, and God alone knew when Frank had found time to make it. No one ate more than a bite or two of either.

Late that afternoon when Barbara passed the breakfast room Wally was teaching Shelley a card trick. "You have a third hand," she said indignantly. "An invisible hand."

"Nope. Watch now."

Barbara moved on. Standing by the fireplace a few minutes later, she heard Frank scolding one of the cats. He came to her and put his arm around her shoulders and drew her closer for a moment, but said nothing. Both cats were at his feet.

The call came at five minutes before five.

In court the formalities were interminable. The parade of the jurors returning to the box, the judge's entrance. "All rise, all rise…" Finally the question, "Have you reached a verdict? and the written verdict handed to the bailiff, then delivered to the judge. He read it, then asked again, "Have you reached a verdict?"

"Yes, Your Honor. We find the defendant not guilty."

Judge Wells polled the jurors, thanked them, then said, "Mr. Lederer, you are free to go."

It was over.

Everything that followed seemed to Barbara both to be in slow motion and from a great distance. Wally grabbed her and bear-hugged her until she gasped; he embraced Shelley; Meg had run around the rail and he took her in his arms and held her close. The jurors were coming forward, some of them with notebooks open, pieces of paper, even a scrapbook. They wanted his autograph. Dodgson came to congratulate Barbara, then turned to Wally and said, "Congratulations…" He hesitated, then added, "Wally. Good luck." And the reporter was asking questions, another man trying to get to Wally with a business card extended.

"Mr. Lederer, would you mind signing it with one hand and then the other?" asked the juror with the scrapbook, a middle-aged woman. The twenty-two-year-old didn't want to go away.

Barbara was aware of Frank's hand on her shoulder and was grateful for it. Gradually the courtroom cleared and only the reporter and the small group at the defense table remained.

"If you could give us a call," the reporter was saying. "You know, about the video."

"Next week sometime," Wally said.

The reporter turned to Barbara. "My editor would like to send someone out for an interview."

She nodded. "Later."

Wally looked at Barbara, then embraced her again, gently this time. "I guess some kind of celebration is in order," he said. "Drinks or something."

She drew back and shook her head. "It will keep. Take Meg home, Wally."

He couldn't hide his relief. "Let's go home," he said to Meg. "We have things to talk about. A chicken house, a worm box, things like that. Ready?"

"Yes," she whispered. "My God, yes!"

"I'll take off, too," Shelley said when Wally and Meg walked away hand in hand. "See you Monday." She laughed. "I don't think I even need my car. I could fly home under my own power." Leaving, she looked as if she were floating.

Slowly Frank and Barbara followed. In his car a few minutes later, he started to speak, glanced at her and held it back. Her eyes were closed, her head against the headrest.

When she got out of the car in his driveway, she said, "I won't come in. I'm crashing. Maybe for all weekend. I'll surface long enough to keep the blood circulating and get something to eat. Don't count on me for Sunday."

"Fine. If you change your mind, come on over. We'll postmortem next week."

He watched her drive away, then went inside, humming softly. "My God," he thought. "My God, she did it!"

FORTY-TWO

On Sunday evening at dusk, with a light rain falling, Barbara entered the little getaway apartment and stood by the door gazing at the table, the living room furnishings. She did not take off her jacket, but put her key down and walked into the bedroom, where she stood for a longer time just looking, then she returned to the kitchen and sat at the table. When she heard steps on the outside stairs later, she stood up.

"Barbara! Why didn't you give me a call? I would have come home sooner." Darren reached for her and she took a step backward.

"I came to tell you something," she said. "I started to write a letter, but that would have been too cowardly. So I came."

He stopped moving. "What do you mean?"

"I won't be seeing you for a while.. I need time to sort things out, to think some things through."

"You're tired. You need a few days rest."

"I am tired, but… The question of whether my mother was happy keeps coming back to me. I said no at first, then I said yes. It's a qualified yes. Considering the circumstances, they were both as happy as they could have been, but that's because they didn't ask any questions. I've been asking questions, and what I'm finding out is that once asked, they can't go unanswered. I don't have any answers."

"We have to talk about it. Tell me what's bothering you." His voice was low, musical, almost hypnotic.

"What's bothering me," she said shaking her head. "This," she motioned around at the apartment. "You. Me. Us. Things in general, I guess. I need some time."

"Barbara, you aren't giving us a chance. You aren't giving me a chance. I love you."

"I know," she said almost absently. "Darren, I'm sorry."

"For God's sake! At least, let's talk about it! We can find the answers together." His face was twisted, contorted, and now his voice broke. "You can't make a decision like this without even talking about it!"

In a low voice, she said, "When I come here, I leave part of myself outside. I've even thought of it that way, now I can stop thinking. But that's the bigger part of me that I don't bring in. That part is who I am. Coming here is like stepping into a dream, but who's the dreamer? A stranger? See, I've been asking questions. They're my questions, Darren. I have to find my answers. You have to find your own questions and answers. You know the old conundrum about the torturer and the victim? Which one in the end pays a higher price? The victim is destroyed physically, perhaps, and the torturer is destroyed psychologically, almost certainly. That's the extreme example, but it applies on many levels. Giver and taker. Each comes with a price tag."

She picked up her purse and cast one more glance around the apartment. Darren didn't move again. She walked out.

Frank was deep in thought that Monday morning. He had made an astounding discovery, he thought of it that way, astounding. He saw Barbara's car in his driveway, and a broad grin spread across his face. He walked faster.

Inside, he went straight through to the kitchen door. She was standing by the back door. "Be with you in a minute," he said. "I have to change my shoes. Wet." He continued down the hall toward his bedroom.

It wasn't really raining, she thought, gazing out, but damp enough to get feet wet, apparently. It looked more as if a big piece of the sky had become tired and decided to settle down and rest a while, an endless piece of tired sky, settling, settling. She felt a great deal of sympathy for it.

"That's better," Frank said, entering the kitchen.

He had changed his suit jacket for a sweater and had taken off his tie. All those years, she wondered, had he hated having to wear a silly necktie as much as she hated panty hose? She never had thought of that before.

He went to the refrigerator and started to rummage around in it. "I had a revelation at the office," he said. "For years I thought I had two books in me, and suddenly realized that's wrong. It's three. I'll wrap up the case law book, and move on. I'm going to write another one after that. Closing statements. Sum up the case, do an annotated closing statement. I'll start with yours, of course. Brilliant beginning—"

"No, Dad. You can't use it."

"What? Why not?" He closed the refrigerator door.

She shook her head. "Just no. I came over to tell you something."

"Bobby, stop kicking yourself over that business with the boat. Wally and Meg gave you an impossible choice and you made it and you saved them both without lying. Wilkins did take it and it doesn't make any difference who put it back. One way or another that damn boat was going to sink and take them down with it. And it would have been both of them. Wally knows that, so do I, and you know it, too. Wally thought it was a lost cause from the start, and I did, too. Right up until your closing statement." He drew in a breath. "You had no choice. You did what you had to do."

"You don't know what I've done," she said in a low voice.

"What else? Something you didn't trust me with?"

"No, Dad. I just wanted you to have a clear conscience if questions came up and you had to deny any knowledge."

He looked at her sharply. "You're coming down with something. You need to get some rest. Didn't you get any sleep over the weekend? I know what you did, and it's all right, Bobby. It wasn't your job to accuse Jay Wilkins of killing his wife. You did your job."

"You don't know," she repeated.

He went to the table and sat down. "Maybe you'd better tell me," he said quietly.

She turned away and, facing his sodden garden, she told him all of it. She reminded him of what Dr. Minnick had said about Eve's attacks, her infantilism at those times. She told him everything Adele had said about Eve, everything Eric had said. And finally she told him about her talk with Stephanie.

"Stephanie knew they would demand access to Eve, demand their own evaluation in the state hospital. And she was right, they would have killed her, or sent her so far back no one could have saved her." Dr. Minnick's words ran through her head. *Sometimes we could save them, sometimes we couldn't.*

"Case number whatever, routine examination. Between episodes she's competent to help in her own defense, except she has amnesia for the whole thing. Right, the convenient amnesia defense. She could not have coped with aggressive questioning, and she would have had it. Or, helpless, an infant with a beautiful twenty-three-year-old body, a lovely face, how long would she have lasted in their hospital before she was raped? You know the stories about that. Stephanie knows them, too. She would have put her daughter back in the private hospital, turned herself in and confessed to murder. And they still would have gotten to Eve."

"Christ on a mountain!" Frank said almost inaudibly. "That's not just an impossible choice. It's inhuman."

"I couldn't sign that girl's death warrant, so I concealed evidence," she said almost tonelessly. "I manipulated other evidence and testimony. I implied things I knew were not true. I told outright lies. I shielded two killers and put my own client at risk. I gambled, knowing Wally's life was at stake, and Meg's, too. I did that knowing what the odds were for his conviction. I did it thinking they've had a good life and that girl has to have a chance at life. I knew exactly what was at stake, and I did it, anyway."

"You gambled, but, Bobby, you won! You didn't save just two people. You saved all four innocent people. That's what counts."

She turned around, but she was no more than a silhouette against the glass door. "Is that what we all come to, finally?" she murmured. "Any means to an end? I used to think I knew what the law meant. But I don't. I don't know what the law means, the rule of law, men's laws."

"Goddamn it, Bobby! They're fallible, those who write the laws. They make the rules, and their rules are hellish! One rule doesn't fit all, not in the real world. Not with real people."

She walked past him. She wasn't listening. She picked up her jacket and put it on. "I've been to the office this morning. Shelley and Maria can wrap up the details of Wally's case, settle accounts. I told Shelley to waive my fee on this one. I wanted to ask you to look things over and make sure she does that. Maria has the key to my apartment. She'll check my mail, pay things that come along." She pulled an envelope from her pocket and put it on the table. "Wally's safe deposit box keys," she said. "Will you get them back to him?"

"What the devil are you talking about?"

She looked startled, puzzled, then said, "Isn't that strange? That's what I came to tell you. I'm going away for a while. Shelley and Maria can manage without me."

"Going where? For how long?"

"I don't know. Nowhere in particular. I have my laptop. I'll be checking my e-mail. You know, if anything comes up. I need time out, Dad. I need to think, and I don't know how long it will take." She was walking toward the front door.

"Bobby!" Frank felt panic rising. She had walked out before, railing at the system, and it had been several years before she returned. He put his hand on her shoulder. She patted it and kept moving.

At the door, she paused and kissed his cheek. "Don't worry about me. Okay?"

Helplessly, he stood on the front stoop and watched her back out of the driveway, watched until her car was out of sight. The door was standing open, and both cats had followed him out.

"Get back inside, you devils," he said in a rough, rasping voice. They strolled back in. He went in and closed the door. "She'll be back," he said in the same harsh voice. The cats moved a few feet away, then began eyeing each other like two hostile alley cats, backs humped, tails fluffed like clubs, circling each other.

He remembered the day she had brought them, two tiny golden dust balls. They had destroyed his Christmas tree that year, ornament after ornament fair game. She named them Thing One and Thing Two, a two-kitten destruction team. He closed his eyes, shaking the memory away.

"She'll be back," he whispered.

* * * * *

*Attorney Barbara Holloway walked away from
everything. Is there anything that can lure her back to
face the people she abandoned—her father, her
colleagues and her lover?*

Turn the page to read an exciting excerpt from

A WRONGFUL DEATH

*the compelling new Barbara Holloway novel by
Kate Wilhelm, available in hardcover in September 2007
from MIRA Books.*

1

The New York branch of the Farrell Publishing Group had six offices, a small reception room and enough books and manuscripts to fill a space triple the size it occupied. Much of the overflow was in Elizabeth Kurtz's tiny office. Boxes were stacked on boxes and the filing cabinets were so packed that they were seldom opened since it was almost impossible to remove a folder to examine its contents. On shelves and on the floor were stacks of dictionaries, science reference books and pamphlets. A bulletin board held so many overlapping notes and memos that some of them had yellowed and curled at the edges. The small sign on her door read: Elizabeth Kurtz Assistant Editor. That door had not been closed all the way in the three years that she had used the office on Mondays and Thursdays. The door would start to close, then stick, leaving a three or four inch gap. It had bothered her in the beginning, but she never thought of it any longer, and paid little attention to any activity in the hall beyond it.

That October day she was frowning at a sentence she was trying to unravel, something to do with paleontology, she assumed, since that was the subject of the manuscript.

The door was pushed open and Terry Kurtz entered and tried to close the door behind him. When it stuck, he gave it a vicious push, to no avail.

"What are you doing in here? Get out! Whatever you're selling, I'm not buying," Elizabeth snapped, half rising from her chair.

"I have a proposition for you," he said, and tried again to close the door. He cursed and kicked it when it stuck.

"I'm calling security," she said, reaching for the phone. He rushed around the desk and grabbed her wrist, wrenching her hand back.

"Just shut up and listen," he said in a low voice, keeping an eye on the door, holding her wrist in a numbing grip. "I just came from the hospital. They're going to operate on Dad in the morning, emergency open-heart surgery, and they don't think he'll make it. He told me something. Mom left us alone for a couple of minutes and he told me. Taunted me with it."

Elizabeth felt no more sense of loss or grief than Terry was showing. She tried to pull away from his grasp, and he tightened his hold and leaned in closer, whispering now. "When he found out you were pregnant, he assigned a share of the company to us, in both our names. He was going to hand it over when Jason was a year old and I was thirty-five, a present to celebrate my birthday, our marriage and a grandchild, but you spoiled it when you got on your high horse and kicked me out. He put the assignment away somewhere. It's still valid, except Mom will get her hands on whatever that document is and she'll shred it faster than she'll order his cremation. I've got his keys, and I intend to find it first. You have to help me."

"I don't have to do anything," she cried. "Get out of here and leave me alone!"

Voices in the hall outside her door rose as the speakers drew nearer. Terry released her wrist and straightened up, and she jumped from her chair and stepped behind it. Neither spoke until the voices faded, then were gone.

"If you touch me again, I'll have you arrested for assault!" she said.

"That assignment means a hefty income for the rest of your life and Jason's if you sell it back tomorrow. And when the company sale goes through that amount will triple, quadruple! No more dingy office where the door won't even close. You have to think what it will mean for our son."

"Our son!" she said furiously. "As if you care a damn about my son. How many times have you even seen him? Three! Goddamn you, three times in five years!"

But it still hurt, like a phantom pain from an amputated limb, she sometimes thought. A year of magic, the princess and her incredibly handsome prince, playing, making love, seeing the world like two wide-eyed children with fairy dust in their eyes. Then her pregnancy. He had walked out when she was just under five months pregnant, and he had not returned until Jason was six months old. She had met his return with divorce papers.

He was still the incredibly handsome prince, with curly dark hair, eyes so dark blue they appeared black until the light hit his face in a particular way and they gleamed with an electric blue light. Muscular and lean, athletic, with the perfect features of a male model, he had won his princess without a struggle, but while he still lived in fairyland, she had put illusions behind her and regarded him now with loathing.

"You can sell your share tomorrow, easily a million dollars. Hold it for six months, and that figure rises astronomically. Two million, three, God knows how high it'll go."

He was whispering again. "I have his keys to the office files, and to his home files. Mom will stay at the hospital for now, but if she finds out that I lifted his keys, she'll head for wherever that document is. The office, or the condo. And we have to get that paper before she gets to it. She knows where it is, and she'll get it, believe me. You can take the condo, and I'll hit the office files. We'll find it first."

She knew he was right about his mother. Sarah Kurtz felt about Elizabeth the same way Elizabeth felt about Terry. She shook her head. "I can't get inside the condo or the office, so forget it. Go search by yourself."

"I'll take you to the condo. I can get in, and I can take you in with me and leave you there while I go over to the corporate office. But, goddamn it, we have to do it now! Before she realizes I took the keys."

In a cab minutes later, sitting as far from him as the seat allowed, Elizabeth asked, "What sale are you talking about?"

"I don't know," he said, almost sullenly. "They don't tell me anything. I just know it's in the works, a Swiss conglomerate. They're doing the preliminary investigation, whatever that means."

She did know they told him nothing about the business. The playboy son had never wanted a thing to do with the business of prosthetics that had made his family wealthy. Then his hasty marriage to a half-breed Spanish dancer, was how Sarah Kurtz had put it when she found out. He had deserted Elizabeth, but Sarah had her own spin on that as well. Elizabeth had snared him, enticed a rich, innocent American boy, got herself pregnant and kicked him out to bring in her real lover, another woman. Elizabeth's lawyer, a savvy, hard-faced woman, had hired a detective to track Terry down on the Riviera, then photograph him frolicking on a nude beach with a movie starlet. The divorce had been a piece of cake, she had told Elizabeth. There was a very good settlement, and Sarah Kurtz would never forgive Elizabeth for threatening to besmirch the family's spotless reputation. Attorneys had handled the whole affair and, as far as Elizabeth knew, not a word had ever been printed about the matter.

In the cab, Elizabeth, gazing out the side window, seeing little of the passing scene, knew she was going along with this as much to strike back at Sarah as for the money itself. Not for how they had treated her, but for the way they treated Jason. No one in the family had ever seen Jason except Terry, who had visited his son twice after the divorce and wouldn't recognize him unless he was wearing a nametag.

Elizabeth had been in the condo several times before, the last visit had been for dinner, when she had told the family that she was pregnant. Joe Kurtz had been delighted.

She remembered that scene, as she looked about the luxurious suite, decorator perfect and lifeless, like an illustration from a glitzy magazine. "Now, he'll settle down," Joe had said that day. "You've turned our boy into a man, a family man, by God!"

Fat chance, she said under her breath, following Terry to Joe's home office. There was a kidney-shaped desk with a black mirror-smooth surface, two file cabinets, black-leather-covered chairs and a tub with a palm tree. She left her briefcase by the door and took off her sweater.

"Here's the key," Terry said, handing it to her. "It will open them both. If you find it, call my cell. I'll give you a call if I find it." He handed her a card with his number, and she told him her own. He hurried out, and she opened the first file cabinet.

At three-thirty she had finished one cabinet, and was midway through a drawer in the second one, when she pulled out a file labeled: Knowlton. After a glance, she replaced it and reached for the next file, then paused as a faint memory stirred. Knowlton. Something. She took it out again and looked more closely at the contents. She saw drawings of prosthetics, joints, arms, legs, things she didn't recognize. Slowly she walked to the big desk and sat down, gazing at the drawings. She caught her breath as the memory took shape. Knowlton had sued the company, accused them of stealing or something. The file was thick, and her fingers fumbled as she picked up and put down papers after scanning them hastily.

"Oh, my God!" she said.

Moving fast, she closed the file folder and ran back to the cabinet to close the drawer, then hurried across the office to where she had put down her briefcase with the manuscript she was to edit. She stuffed the file folder inside, put on her sweater, snatched up her purse and left the beautiful apartment.

Her cell phone rang as she stood on the street and hailed a cab. She ignored her phone. Outside her bank minutes later, she made a call of her own.

"Leonora, something urgent has come up. You have to collect Jason and take him home, then pack a suitcase for him, and one for me. We have to go somewhere. I'll explain when I get there." Leonora wanted to know what was wrong, and impatiently Elizabeth cut her off and said, "Just do it. I'll tell you when I get there. Do it now."

At the bank she made out a withdrawal slip for ten thousand dollars from her savings account. When the teller looked puzzled, she said, as lightly as she could manage, "A friend is selling her car, but she has to have cash. It's a sweet deal." No hassle, she thought. Just don't give me a hassle. The teller asked her to wait a few minutes, and while she waited, she made plans.

She would need a computer, a laptop. Pay for it with a credit card, but no more credit card purchases after that; they could find her through them. No cell phone, possibly they could trace her through it. But she needed the computer and, later, possibly a printer. She had a lot of research to do. She'd sell her car, buy something less noticeable and use cash for everything…

Leonora had done exactly as Elizabeth had told her. She had collected Jason from kindergarten and packed a suitcase for him, and was still packing for Elizabeth when

she arrived home. It was a spacious apartment, shared by
Elizabeth and Terry for several months, until his departure,
and then retained by Elizabeth. Her attorney had insisted
that she should be awarded enough not to have to make any
drastic reductions in her living arrangements. Leonora, her
friend from childhood, had moved in to help out during the
pregnancy and stayed on afterward.

Leonora's mother had left her abusive husband when her
daughter was twelve and Elizabeth's mother had taken the
child into her own household and the two girls had become
sisters in most ways. Elizabeth's father, a State Department
employee at the UN for years, had died in a boating
accident when she was eleven. Her mother had remained
in the States to see her daughter safely enrolled at Johns
Hopkins, where she had been an honors student, and then
had gone back home to her native Spain. The two girls had
shared a bedroom, worn each other's clothes, then had
drawn apart when Leonora married early and Elizabeth had
gone to university. They had drawn together again when
Leonora had come to realize she had married a man very
like her own father. After two stillbirths and several
beatings, she had left him, and had maintained a close
friendship with Elizabeth ever since.

That day her face was drawn with worry as Elizabeth
said, "I have to get Jason out of here and have a little time
to think about something I came across. I'll call you in a
few days and tell you what it's all about, but not now. I want
you to go get my car. I'll finish packing up. A pillow case,
that's what I need, for some toys." She rushed through the
apartment, looked in on Jason watching television. He
waved and said, "Hi, Mama Two." There was a mischie-

vous gleam in his eyes those days when he called whichever one was with him first Mama One, and the other Mama Two. Until recently they both had simply been Mama. Elizabeth ran to the bedroom, with Leonora at her heels, and began tossing things into her own suitcase, rushing back and forth from her closet or dresser to the bed and the open case. "After we're out of here, you'd better go somewhere and stay a few days, maybe even a week. They'll want to ask you questions, and it's best if they can't find you. I'll call your cell phone."

"For heaven's sake, Elizabeth! What's going on? Are you in trouble? Who will ask questions?"

"Just go get the car!" Her voice was shrill. She swallowed hard. "I can't stop to talk about it now. Just get the car. Please! Terry and his mother. They can't find me here!"

Leonora's face hardened, and she nodded. "On my way."

At six-thirty Sarah Kurtz entered her condo where Terry was sprawled on a white sofa with a tall drink in his hand. He raised the glass as a greeting. "How's he doing?"

"He's sedated. They said he'll sleep all night and for me to come on home. The surgery is scheduled for seven in the morning." She looked tired. Every year for the past ten or fifteen, she had put on a few of pounds, never much at a time but never lost again either, and the accumulation had become close to obesity. Her hair was as blond as ever, and would continue to be that color no matter how many more years she had to enjoy. Normally her complexion was good, her cheeks a nice pink, but that day her face looked splotched with red patches.

"What are you doing here?" she asked, taking off her jacket.

"Waiting for you. Miss Dad's keys yet?"

"What are you talking about? What keys?"

"To his filing cabinets here and those at the office. I took them today. And you didn't even notice. I'm surprised."

She had been moving toward the bar across the room, but stopped to look at him. "What are you up to?"

"I found the share assignment," he said lazily. "Thought it would save you a little trouble if I did it myself. Elizabeth helped me look. Thought you'd like to know that we can still cooperate if necessary."

"You let that woman look at his files?"

"Not at the office. While she looked here, I found it at the office. See, cooperation."

Sarah Kurtz's face became noticeably more mottled as she stared at her son. Wordlessly she turned and hurried to the home office. Terry got up and followed her. The key was still in the lock. Sarah yanked open the file drawer and riffled through the folders.

"I told you, I found it, down at the office. She didn't find anything."

Abruptly Sarah swung around, and her hand flashed out in a sharp slap across his face. "You bloody, blithering idiot! Go get her and bring her back here! Now!"

"She won't come. I told her I had the assignment. No reason for her to come back." He rubbed his cheek and stepped out of his mother's reach.

"Bring Jason! She'll come! Go get her now!"

The chilling tale of a parent's worst nightmare, by acclaimed author

CHRIS JORDAN
taken

No parent believes it can happen to them—their child taken from a suburban schoolyard in the gentle hours of dusk. But, as widowed mother Kate Bickford discovers, everything can change in the blink of an eye.

Opening the door to her Connecticut home, hoping to find her son, Kate comes face-to-face with her son's abductor. He wants money. All she has. And if she doesn't follow something he calls The Method, the consequences will be gruesome....

**A new novel of suspense by the author
of _Dead Silence_ and _Dead Giveaway_**

BRENDA NOVAK

**The people of Stillwater, Mississippi,
are asking questions about murder. Again.**

Twenty years ago, Madeline Barker's father disappeared. Despite what
everyone else thinks, Madeline's convinced her stepfamily had nothing
to do with it. But the recent discovery of his car finally proves he didn't
just drive away. Worse, the police find something in the trunk that says
there's more to this case than murder....

DEAD

RIGHT

MIRA®

MBN2439

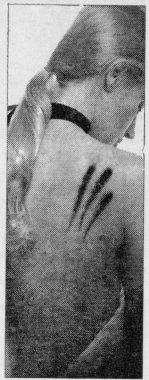

REQUEST YOUR FREE BOOKS!

2 FREE NOVELS
FROM THE ROMANCE/SUSPENSE
COLLECTION PLUS 2 FREE GIFTS!

YES! Please send me 2 FREE novels from the Romance/Suspense Collection and my 2 FREE gifts. After receiving them, if I don't wish to receive any more books, I can return the shipping statement marked "cancel." If I don't cancel, I will receive 4 brand-new novels every month and be billed just $5.49 per book in the U.S., or $5.99 per book in Canada, plus 25¢ shipping and handling per book plus applicable taxes, if any*. That's a savings of at least 20% off the cover price! I understand that accepting the 2 free books and gifts places me under no obligation to buy anything. I can always return a shipment and cancel at any time. Even if I never buy another book from the Reader Service, the two free books and gifts are mine to keep forever.

185 MDN EF5Y 385 MDN EF6C

Name _____ (PLEASE PRINT) _____

Address _____ Apt. # _____

City _____ State/Prov. _____ Zip/Postal Code _____

Signature (if under 18, a parent or guardian must sign)

Mail to **The Reader Service:**
IN U.S.A.: P.O. Box 1867, Buffalo, NY 14240-1867
IN CANADA: P.O. Box 609, Fort Erie, Ontario L2A 5X3

Not valid to current subscribers to the Romance Collection,
the Suspense Collection or the Romance/Suspense Collection.

Want to try two free books from another line?
Call 1-800-873-8635 or visit www.morefreebooks.com.

* Terms and prices subject to change without notice. NY residents add applicable sales tax. Canadian residents will be charged applicable provincial taxes and GST. This offer is limited to one order per household. All orders subject to approval. Credit or debit balances in a customer's account(s) may be offset by any other outstanding balance owed by or to the customer. Please allow 4 to 6 weeks for delivery.

Your Privacy: Harlequin is committed to protecting your privacy. Our Privacy Policy is available online at www.eHarlequin.com or upon request from the Reader Service. From time to time we make our lists of customers available to reputable firms who may have a product or service of interest to you. If you would prefer we not share your name and address, please check here. ☐

BOB07